P9-CDA-667

THE
DANTE
CHAMBER

ALSO BY MATTHEW PEARL

The Last Bookaneer

The Technologists

The Last Dickens

The Poe Shadow

The Dante Club

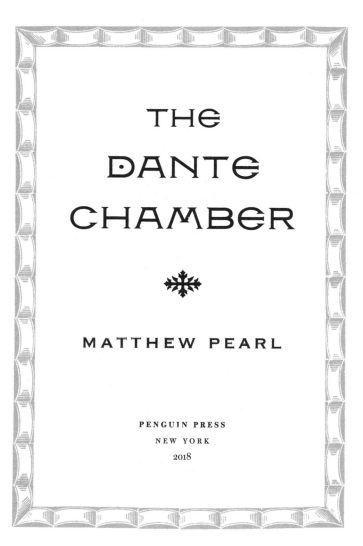

THE

DANTE

CHAMBER

❄

MATTHEW PEARL

PENGUIN PRESS

NEW YORK

2018

PENGUIN PRESS
An imprint of Penguin Random House LLC
375 Hudson Street
New York, New York 10014
penguin.com

ISBN 9781594204937 (hardcover)
ISBN 9780525558958 (e-book)

Printed in the United States of America
1   3   5   7   9   10   8   6   4   2

Designed by Gretchen Achilles

For Tobey, page 65

THE
DANTE
CHAMBER

DOCUMENT #1:
LETTER FROM OLIVER WENDELL HOLMES
TO H. W. LONGFELLOW

The steamship Cephalonia,
November 28, 1869

My dear Longfellow,

I have been assured that I should be kindly received in Europe, and I suppose I'd prefer anywhere on earth to this ocean liner, where a man annoys and is annoyed by the same two dozen fellow beings all day. Growing old, I realize there are few living persons left I wish to meet and few achievements to which I aspire. Instead, I have a certain longing for another sight of places I remember from travels in my youth, or places of which I read but never saw.

As for the intellectual condition of the other passengers who are not named Holmes, I should say their faces are prevailingly vacuous, their owners half hypnotized, it seems, by the monotonous throb and tremor of the great sea monster on whose back we ride. I empathize. I seem to have fewer ideas and emotions than usual.

Besides a short vacation, I have no thought of doing anything more important than brushing a little rust off and enjoying myself, while at the same time I can make my precious companion's visit somewhat pleasanter than it would be if she went without me.

Please give Lowell, Fields, and company my warm greetings and say something witty as if I had written it. Even composing a simple letter taxes me in the rocking and swaying of my stateroom.

What book do you think I saw in the hands of one of the passengers, as I put down this letter to get fresh air above deck? Your Dante. It serves a great purpose, quite independently of its value with reference to the Florentine's poetry. It shows our young Americans that they need not be provincial in their way of thought because of where they were born. We Boston people are so bright and wide-awake, and have been really so much in advance of our fellow barbarians, that we sometimes forget that 212 Fahrenheit is but 100 centigrade.

There is something else tugging at my brain, my dear Longfellow. I am a series of surprises to myself in the changes that years, and a specific period of darkness that I need not name, have brought about. The movement onward is like changing place in a picture gallery—the light fades from this picture and falls on that, so that you wonder where the first has gone to and see all at once the meaning of the other. What a strange thing life is! I may have believed a voyage would remove me from certain memories of—I leave that sentence unfinished. But those memories follow me with a more persistent character than before. I suppose it is terribly American to journey thousands of miles and mentally stay in America, for better or . . .

I reach the bottom of my page. Don't think I expect an answer, or require consolation. I am afraid that my words as well as my handwriting betray the strain through which my nervous system is passing—but I am certain the picturesque hills of Switzerland will vanquish these thoughts, and this page will serve the world best crackling inside the hearth of your study.

In the meantime, my mood makes me wonder: what is faith? It must be a quiet belief in the existence of something not proven. Faith that is genuine enough, religionists say, may accomplish much. Might we humans possess another thing that is the opposite of faith, that is just as important or more so? Knowledge that some things seemingly immaterial—memories, fears, the fog of nightmares—are figments. When I try to leave behind my own, they take on the form of some greedy beast who, abandoned in the wild wood, transforms from tame to rabid, to hunt me down, wherever I roam. Pray as I traverse the Old World it finds some new scent to pursue!

Always faithfully yours,
Oliver Wendell Holmes

CANTICLE
ONE

He would not be long for this world.

Hunched forward almost forty-five degrees, his body braced against the cold January wind, his big, tattered coat billowing behind. His legs trembled with each plodding step.

The coming dawn did not remove much of the gloominess these public gardens boasted at night. Strips of colored paper and beads that welcomed the New Year two weeks before were still scattered over the ground, giving the appearance of colorful strands of hair and lost teeth. Here was one of the garden squares around London that better classes shunned and appreciated. Shunned, because it was a place of blackguards and outcasts; appreciated, because these blackguards and outcasts collected on the Wapping side of the Thames kept out of the way of respectable society. When respectable persons did have a need best served in North Woolwich, they believed themselves invisible here.

Even in midwinter cold, ladies in elaborate, multicolored dresses walked along the elm-lined paths in pairs, objects of desire and subjects of contempt and fear for causing desire. Most of the girls who passed in sight of the plodder felt pity for him, though few pitied these girls. They did not know him; he was no frequenter of these gardens. One thing stood out: despite his terrible condition and his ratty clothing, the rest of him—his face plump and round, crystal blue eyes, silvering hair, smooth skin—all

7

reeked of easier living somewhere else. *Somewhere else* must have been lovely.

He was like Atlas, stooped, about to lose his grip on the world.

The girls kept away, because whatever else the hunchbacked plodder might be he was in trouble that they could not afford. That explains why none came close enough to hear him utter, "God, have mercy upon me!" before his head drooped farther down. A loud crack like a whip followed.

Then he was a heap on the ground.

Another man approached at a stately pace. This man appeared somewhat rotund in his long dark coat and had a beard that extended some six inches below his chin, where it slightly cleaved in two. He lowered one knee into the rain-matted grass next to the body. Full red lips quivered from under the black bristles of his mustache. He pressed his strong fingers to his own eyes as he wept.

A crowd of the bolder girls and other onlookers began to gather. Some men hastily buttoned up vests and straightened hats. The weeping man felt their unwelcome presence. His hazel-gray eyes darted from one face to the next. He threw his hood over his head and down upon his broad brow, and began to walk away.

Another onlooker in the crowd, a shorter man with a wide, crisp mustache, trailed behind him. "*Dante?* Dante, where have you—isn't that you?" he called after him.

Simultaneous cries of distress, meanwhile, multiplied over the crumpled-up man.

"Is the bloke dead? Look at that!"

"It's too dark. What?"

"Don't you see, over there? Writing: on that thing!"

A candle was secured as the sightseers closed in on the spectacle. They pointed in horror. The dead man was no hunchback, as he'd appeared from a distance. There was a massive stone that encircled his neck and back. It had put so much pressure on him that it had snapped his neck like a carrot. Someone feeling very bold—nobody remembered who, as recorded later in the reports of police interviews—reached out and touched the side of the man's head, which wobbled on his limp neck like jelly. The crunch made by the bones as his head rolled would not be forgotten by any who heard it.

Etched into the stone that had crushed his neck were words.

Some people scrambled away from death, and others fled the police whistles that broke through the chill morning air. Those who remained tried to make out the words carved in the stone. One girl with long hair to her elbows whispered in a husky voice:

"Latin."

"Can you read it, sweetheart, indeed?" scoffed a man. "Fancy that. A scholar, out here, in petticoats and torn hose."

"'Tis true!" another girl chimed in, with a touch of awe toward her friend, pointing out that the first girl was half Italian, half Flemish, or something similar, and knew many tongues.

The others cleared space for her.

She hesitated, inhaling a breath of courage before translating the three carved Latin words into English: "Behold, the handmaiden of the Lord."

Witnesses to a horror split up into those who will never talk about it, and those who never stop. By the time the police descended on North Woolwich, the men and women who had surrounded the dead man's body began to sort themselves into these factions.

The anxiety of the park-goers who were already skittish around police was hardly eased by the news that Inspector Adolphus Williamson himself was in the caravan of Scotland Yarders. When Dolly Williamson was assigned a case, people who knew anything knew to get out of the way.

Dolly wore a hat half a size too large, so that he was always shifting his head to keep it from falling over his eyes, which had an unsatisfied look to them.

He was correcting the tilt of this hat as he stepped down from his carriage and asked: "Who is he?"

One of the constables replied they had not yet confirmed it. They had notions, said another. They weren't *certain*, cautioned the first.

"Don't hold your tongues with me," Dolly reprimanded them, removing a sprig of holly he was chewing. "Is his name Jasper Morton?"

(The following reaction was common when it came to Dolly's pronouncements.)

"How . . . ," one constable began in astonishment. "Inspector, it's not possible you could have . . . before you've even . . ."

Dolly rolled his eyes.

Jasper Morton was a seasoned member of Parliament who represented Bristol. Not a particularly popular or effective legislator, but he held his seat in the House of Commons long enough that political longevity alone ensured his continued election.

"Close your jaw, Constable; you look like you're going to bite me," Dolly said. "A dead bloke in this district would not produce ringing at my door any more than the carcass of a cat floating among the rushes of the Thames—unless the corpse made the Home Office nervous. Rest easy that I have my own reasons, beyond those, to think of Morton."

Dolly's reasons had to do with a report he came across at Scotland Yard weeks earlier. Approximately a month before that, the legislator's wife, Eleanor Morton, had mentioned to a police sergeant that Morton had seemed nervous and anxious when he was in public, and though the politician himself insisted nothing was amiss, she worried that some angry constituent was pestering him. Morton did not like to complain about such things, she said with pride in her husband's stoicism.

None of that was particularly noteworthy. What struck Dolly most in his memory of the report was that when a constable eventually attempted to interview the Honorable Mr. Morton about Mrs. Morton's concerns, he could not find him.

"Injuries?" Dolly asked as they approached the body.

The hideous sight had remained in the same state as when first illuminated by the onlookers, though now expert eyes were trained on it. The massive stone fit around the neck and shoulders almost perfectly. The dead man's head hung down loosely.

Another constable answered him. "Broken neck, Inspector. This is some kind of stone contraption—like a yoke made for a man instead of an ox—and it's been *attached* to the poor fellow. No other violence done to the body. Real mystery, isn't it?"

There were words etched on the stone—*Ecce ancilla Dei*—and they were scrambling to fetch a professor of Latin to consult with Dolly.

"Don't bother. I can read it myself," Dolly said, gnashing the sprig again between two side molars. "Now cover that up with your coat. I want no one else to see those words who hasn't."

To himself, he repeated over and over, trying to will it into making some sense: *Behold, the handmaiden of the Lord.*

He thought about the inscription and thought about the word the frightened constable chose: *mystery.* A mystery, by strict definition, was an event that could not be understood. Mysteries were for religions; miracles, things tucked away in holy scrolls. The peculiarities of this killing were neither haphazard nor the mark of the insane. If they were understood by someone, anyone—and certainly they were understood by whoever did it—Dolly would not be far behind. Besides, there were other elements to consider. The public place. The prominent man as the victim. A human yoke made of stone. That inscription. The timing, at the break of day. Nothing hidden about this, no secret scrolls here—this was a page all London was meant to see.

Dolly knew there was one person who would not have missed watching it for all the world: the culprit.

II

Like the sun, her routine could be counted on day in and day out. Fixing breakfast for herself and her mother. Sitting at the sagging but well-organized desk in the drawing room of their small home on Euston Square and replying to, perhaps, a magazine asking if she wished to publish new verses (*Thank you, but no*, was her usual answer), inquiries after her mother's health (*Hale and strong, thank you*), bills for the latest repair at their home (*Thank you, enclosed*), notes from Gabriel beseeching her to call on Tudor House to see a sketch or read a new poem. She would keep copies of any letter she wrote in case the original was lost, and then after a few days she would burn the copy in the fireplace on the other side of the room. If she felt the call to do so, she would write poetry into one of her small notebooks. When she finally left their house, there was church to attend, the market to get to, Saint Mary's to visit, her aunts to take on errands (*We three old ladies*, she would say only half joking; she was not yet forty), her father's grave from which to clear away leaves and pine needles. No wonder Christina would say she only wore clothes fit for ten miles of plowing.

On this day, in the great hall of Saint Mary's home for fallen women, she paused at the threshold, a figure elegant and slender. In her muslin cap with lace edges and dark veil, she blended in with the Anglican nuns in charge. Christina was not part of their sisterhood, though by now the nuns spoke to their "associate sister" as though she were, taking the liberty of referring to her as Sister Christina. For ten years, she had been coming to Saint Mary's penitentiary—no prison, as the word was sometimes used, but an institution of reform—to help the nuns take care of women like the new arrival at the front of the line shyly holding out her wooden bowl for her first filling meal in weeks.

Christina found peace here, a relief to know that her labors while at this charity home were worthy—assisting these women, many having come from foreign countries, most terribly young, though some her own age. It gave her a refuge different from what it gave the desperate women. Those women suffered because of what they had done, while Christina often suffered over what she had not.

But this Sunday, by all appearances similar to most other days, felt incomplete. She'd had an uneasy feeling when bidding her mother farewell after church, and the feeling had not left. Her lithe fingers, emerging from long black sleeves, trembled as she ladled food. Behind that veil, her hazel-gray, oval eyes conveyed a general fearfulness. Even Ethel looked over with concern at the thirty-nine-year-old helper who always held her head high and greeted her and her fellow inhabitants without judgment.

Ethel had been at Saint Mary's nearly half of the two-year limit for residents. Like many of the girls, she was being trained to enter domestic service in a respectable home, and often helped the nuns in the kitchen. She looked younger than her years, which were twenty, her round face splashed with brown freckles and her eyes thoughtful and also brown. She was one of Christina's favorites. The residents were forbidden to speak directly of their pasts to the nuns, but Christina was not quite as strict and would listen with open mind and heart. Ethel had told her how when her wages were lowered at a sewing factory, she turned to accepting men's money in order to prevent her mother from being put into a workhouse.

"Need a hand, miss?" Ethel now asked with gentle concern. "By the by, I found one of your volumes of poems in the library, and don't go telling the sisters I said so, but how it beat those dusty editions of sermons in there something terrific!"

Christina felt her olive cheeks color.

"I remember some of my favorite lines. Shall I say them?"

"Certainly not, Ethel."

Ethel had already begun:

> *I wish I were a little bird,*
> *That out of sight doth soar . . .*
> *Or memory of a hope deferred*
> *That springs again no more.*

"We ought to finish serving, Ethel. Chapel begins soon."

The charity home had a rotating list of ministers who would come and preach, so that there was at least one a day. Christina brought food to the chapel, where the guest on this day was readying himself at the pulpit by looking over some handwritten pages.

"Suffering . . . is . . . not . . . sin," the preacher practiced, speaking slowly to himself as much to prepare his voice as to rehearse the language. This was Reverend Fallow, a stately man who paused to salute Christina as she silently left a plate for him to eat before his sermon.

As Christina continued her duties, she reviewed to herself all the reasons to ignore her ominous foreboding, the reasons circumstances did not justify her apprehension and that her own flawed imagination alone caused her worry. Sound reasons, every one. But she could fight her feelings for only so long. Her father had always urged her to trust her instincts the way her mother urged her to trust the Bible.

"Sister Christina," came a whisper so natural it had to belong to a nun. "Miss Rossetti," the voice tried again.

Christina had frozen in midmotion while carrying another large pot from the kitchen. She blinked herself back from her trance.

I wish I were a little bird.

"Are you feeling ill, dear?"

Christina assured her she was fine. "I'm only feeling as though . . ." She paused to think what it was.

As though he needs me now. When she composed poetry, the voice in her heart was hers and not hers. This was how she felt at this moment. She could doubt herself but she could not ignore the voice. *He needs me now.*

The pot slipped from her grasp and splattered her a deep red and brown. Her apron looked like it was covered in blood.

The nun suggested she go home to rest.

"Not until the women are fed, Sister."

"We have made some progress with you, at least. Yours is the only apron that always remains white and pristine after helping serve fifty-five famished women. You've finally joined the rest of us mortals: not always as steady as we'd like to be. Care to talk about what's weighing on you?"

Christina offered a hint of a grateful smile. Hers was a face so stoic and serious that an artist friend of her brother's had once asked her to pose as Jesus Christ for a painting. She thought of speaking about her worries but didn't. It wasn't just that she didn't want to seem egotistical speaking of her own problems, though it was true she didn't. Christina would not trust even a nun with her feelings.

"Sister Christina," said the woman in the dark habit. "Happy and unhappy Sister Christina. Come, we'll bring the chowder in together." The nun gripped one handle on the pot while Christina held on to the other. She had a mission to finish here, then one to begin.

By three o'clock on club days, the windowless room two flights up in the grand building in Cornhill filled with the greatest literary and artistic geniuses of England. It was said that by the time enough members of the Cosmopolitan drifted in between, say, four and six o'clock, a visitor could not think of a question too obscure that it could not be answered by one of the men in this room, putting aside whether the answer was correct.

One of many poets who belonged to the club, Robert Browning, at first bounded up the stairs on his way to the gathering but abruptly slowed down. Just moments before, he was eager to be going in. Then his brain betrayed him with the following train of thought, which began harmlessly enough:

This would be the first club meeting of January.

With January had come 1870.

With the New Year came another year without Her.

Another year without Her was another to wonder whether he could endure it.

He glanced down the dim stairwell. If anybody were coming behind him, he'd look lively—lock eyes, smile, shake hands. Empty, for now. He pulled off his lemon-colored gloves by the tips and caught his breath. Then he brightened with a better thought. Whenever the Cosmopolitan Club announced a gathering, members would come from across London and beyond—you never knew when the next meeting would come, and as a result, once one was scheduled, nobody wanted to miss it. This being the case, Browning expected he might encounter the one man in the club who truly understood his loss, whatever other differences existed between them. This comforting idea reanimated Browning, sending him the rest of the way up the steps into the smoke-filled chamber that vibrated with laughter and talk.

Cheers and toasts greeted him on all sides—the Irreplaceable Robert! the Glorious Browning!—along with New Year's wishes and quotations from "Childe Roland to the Dark Tower Came" or his recent epic, *The Ring and the Book.* The first people he asked had not seen the man he looked for. On a sofa in the corner of the room, with his feet up on a chair, he spied one of his fellow stars in London's literary constellation. England's poet laureate.

Alfred Tennyson peered over the top of his newspaper, as though just remembering he was at the club meeting.

After they exchanged greetings, Browning asked, "Has Rossetti come yet, by chance?" He asked as offhandedly as he could, though Browning never did succeed in offhandedness.

"You know better, Browning. I can't see someone until they crash against me. Remember, I'm the second most shortsighted man in England."

Tennyson would stay on the sofa so other members had to come to him. Which they did. Everyone paid tribute to the wordsmith with the long pointed beard, and for that reason Browning had hoped Tennyson, eyesight aside, would have already met the man he sought.

"Odd," replied Browning, pulling a chair closer.

"Gabriel could forget about his own birthday, you know, Browning," Tennyson said. "Today's date slipped his mind, I'd wager."

"I don't mean just not coming to the club is odd," Browning said. "I was just thinking of Rossetti on the way here because—well, something made me think of him, and I realized it's been a while since the last time I've seen him at all."

"How long?" Tennyson asked, suddenly interested.

Browning recalled running across Gabriel in Bond Street and talking about a mutual friend who had moved away from London after a mental collapse. *Ah, how I still hope to be an outcast from humanity one of these days*, Gabriel had said, one of the painter's signature comments that could have been in jest or the beginning of a manifesto.

"A month, maybe, since we crossed paths," Browning said with a quick calculation. "Five weeks?"

The timeline might spark an insight in Tennyson. In general, Browning trusted the poet laureate to be practical and well-informed. When Browning wrote his will, he brought it to Tennyson to be witnessed. *It will be a wonder if this is legal*, Browning joked at the time, *written out by one poet, witnessed by another.*

"Look at this!" The laureate returned to a column in the newspaper reviewing the latest crimes and trials in London. "We are tender to criminals, Browning. We are more tender to savage criminals than to ourselves, and that's why more and more exist today than ever. You heard the terrible story about the Honorable Mr. Morton, I suppose?"

"The politician," Browning replied. "Yes. Found somewhere in North Woolwich, wasn't it?"

"That's right, in the pleasure gardens, which are beset by all the sins of man. Have you been following the details?"

Though it dominated the papers, he had avoided reading most of it. Browning had been at a few social affairs at the same time as Morton over the years. Morton, from what he recalled, had been a haughty type, using his seat in the House of Commons to prove himself important.

"The newspapermen relish any story that proves that London is sinking into the ocean under the weight of its vices, and maybe it is," Browning said. "Morton was bludgeoned in the head with a rock, wasn't he? To be honest, my dear Tennyson, I try to stay away from the morbidity that always excited you and Dickens."

"You don't always stay away from darkness, now do you, Browning? No, the poor soul wasn't hit on the head with a rock, nothing so ordinary. The stone was actually *fastened* . . . ," Tennyson said, stopping himself and making a halfhearted gesture of apology before puffing the pipe that perched between his lips. "I suppose Dickens turns loose what you call morbidity in his books, while for me the darker side of humanity seems to better reveal the light. Example: Why do mosquitoes exist, Browning? I will tell you. They exist to remind us that they should not. After God made his world, the devil began adding his touches."

Browning had no patience for Tennyson's philosophies, and Tennyson noticed, circling back. "Careful not to feel too tender about the remarkable Gabriel Rossetti. He doesn't keep skeletons in his cupboard; his skeletons drink whiskey and dance along the road while out for long walks. Why so fixated on him, Browning?"

Browning wanted to say: *He lost an Elizabeth. I lost an Elizabeth.* This came out instead: "He's a friend."

Tennyson gave a skeptical *ugh* and Browning suddenly found the poet's expressive, judgmental face irritating—made to be sculpted rather than spoken to. At the same time, Tennyson always had an uncanny ability to read other people, frequently compared by friends to a Scotland Yard detective, and Browning could not help but be curious what he thought.

Tennyson explained: "That word. 'Friend.' Rossetti talks rather critically of his friends, including the two of us, I daresay, when we're not present. Sometimes even when we are present," he growled out a chuckle.

Browning thought back fifteen years earlier, when he and Elizabeth lived in Italy and made a visit to London, inviting over Tennyson, Rossetti, and other poets and artists. They read from works in progress. Browning read "Fra Lippo Lippi," before Tennyson, first objecting to the idea of reciting at all ("No, I shan't. No, I shan't read it . . . It can be appreciated only by knowing the difficulties overcome!"), went on to read "Maud." "What a beautiful touch!" "How tender!" Tennyson would pause to exclaim *of his own verses*, tears rolling down his cheeks, his fingers rippling in the air. Sitting right beside Tennyson, Ba—as Browning called Elizabeth—swept her curls from her eyes.

Now he *is a virtuoso*, was what Browning imagined his wife thinking. Before she met Browning, Ba kept a portrait of Browning and one of Tennyson on her wall. When Browning was coming to call on her for the first time, she grabbed Browning's portrait off its nail and then, in a fit of justice, took down Tennyson.

During the same evening they heard "Maud," Browning noticed Dante Gabriel Rossetti sketching Tennyson, bestowing his version of the poet with a lordly self-importance. Tennyson never saw the saucy though affectionate caricature. Gabriel, as if sensing Browning's own mixed emotions about Tennyson, later sent the original to the Brownings, and Browning had been tempted to show it to Tennyson on more than one occasion. *See, not everyone takes you as seriously as you do.*

"Pray understand, I would willingly know so fine spirits as the Rossettis more intimately, Browning," Tennyson concluded, "but as he and his sister keep themselves so shut up—even more than I do—it is all but impossible. What is it that Oliver Wendell Holmes wrote? 'We have a special mask we wear for each friend.' That might not be Dr. Holmes's exact quote, but if not, I've improved it. If Gabriel Rossetti decides to hide himself, leave it at that."

Browning replied flatly: "I stick to my friends no matter what."

He was more resolved than when he'd first entered the meeting to discover the whereabouts of Dante Gabriel Rossetti. It was as though the ominous concerns trembling through Christina Rossetti in the penitentiary for fallen women in Highgate had silently traveled up the rafters, floated over Parliament Hill, skimmed over the ponds, jostled themselves against hungry-eyed pedestrians, darted under carriages and omnibuses, and poured themselves directly into the heart of Browning. Half of London society was right here in this room. Someone was bound to have seen Gabriel recently.

Browning shook hands on his way through the crowd and inquired, futilely, as it turned out, for news of his friend. At one point he heard the literary editor John Forster approach Tennyson's sofa and comment on Browning's perturbed mood. "Seems like Browning's still running away from ghosts."

Browning rather liked the response Tennyson barked out: "No. A poet never sees ghosts."

III

Christina's fears for the well-being of her eldest brother deepened the closer she came to 16 Cheyne Walk. She had only the afternoon prior walked this route to Tudor House—that was what everyone called Dante Gabriel Rossetti's residence in Chelsea, up the river from London proper—after completing her session at Saint Mary's alongside the nuns. But she had found nobody inside and the house locked up. She didn't know her brother's doors had locks.

Afterward, she'd hunted up Lord Cadogan to secure a spare key, having to promise nothing was wrong, that her brother was on a holiday and she had to retrieve some documents inside. Christina hated lying, hated all the more telling a convincing lie. She even hated lying to a landlord.

The rambling old-world houses of Chelsea that backed onto the Thames wore their usual draperies of thick fog, mixed with a drizzling rain and the noxious fumes floating in from the city's smokestacks. She paused under her umbrella several times to wait for a clearing. At one point, she thought a horse and rider behind her slowed to mimic the speed of her walking. When she turned to look, the rider dashed out of sight.

She frowned at the vague and foolish suspicions. Worse than suspicions, superstitions. Was she beginning to imagine people sneaking around to trace her movements? *Just like the professore had, and just like Gabriel*, she thought. Christina rarely felt lonely, but suddenly she felt alone. She was glad she had thought to send a message to William, her other brother, asking him to meet there.

The same unwelcome sensation returned as Tudor House came into sight; this time she had no doubt. Someone was following her. On this sleepy lane, a span of horses came to a stop across from her. She squinted into the opaque air. It wouldn't be William. He was probably coming from his house, which would mean he would drive from the other direction. She was torn between the impulse to rush through the big iron gates to the house, and the desire to march up to the rider in the carriage and demand an explanation for shadowing her. She surprised herself by deciding on the bolder course, hurrying across the street.

She pulled herself up to the passenger window. There was nobody riding inside. She turned her attention to the coachman, his face disguised by the fog. He gave a throaty cry and the horses yanked the vehicle away, sending Christina tumbling backward to avoid the wheels and the mud that spun into the air. Perplexed, her concentration broke when someone called out.

"Miss Rossetti."

She had not seen that a man had stepped down from the other side of the carriage. Under the cover of the fog, the figure stood opposite her on the sidewalk, the silhouette of a large head over strong shoulders and a barrel chest.

"Mr. Browning," Christina said.

Breaking through the mist, he brought his hat down to his chest in his gallant way. He had clear gray eyes and a neatly trimmed beard, with light streaks through his dark hair at the temples. Browning murmured an explanation for being there: something about noticing Gabriel's absence at the Cosmopolitan Club the day before, and that it had been far too long since seeing him.

Christina simply said that she was there to pay a call on Tudor House. She did not explain why she was holding a key—pressed so hard against the palm of her hand that its teeth left an indentation in her flesh.

Christina had neither seen nor heard from her oldest brother in a month, putting a hole in her usually reliable routines. No notes pleading for her to come view a painting or critique a verse, or examine the latest piece of medieval furniture bought from a junk peddler. Disappearing was not unusual for Dante Gabriel Rossetti. Gabriel and his artist friends lived on the outskirts of society, fugitives of a certain kind—usually from normal ways of life, sometimes from law and order. They shunned daytime, thrived in the darkness. They ignored responsibilities and sought out experiments in pleasure from the classes of men and women of London who were chased into the shadows by the police; they collected books and pamphlets declared illegal by legislators and immoral by preachers.

Years before, Gabriel rented rooms from a dancing instructor. After the instructor was evicted, the landlord tried to collect money directly from Gabriel—money that he did not have. He went into hiding. During that period, even Christina didn't have Gabriel's address. He'd send the family mysterious notes. One of them asked Christina to sneak back into the rented rooms to retrieve his books, the only possessions Gabriel refused to abandon.

While poverty, debt, and wanderlust drove Gabriel to vanish in the past and caused waves of worry, ever since the death of Lizzie nearly eight years earlier, Christina experienced apprehension of a different sort about Gabriel. The sort that had taken hold of her at Saint Mary's charity home—a certainty that another disappearance would be his last, that Gabriel would end up like their uncle John.

William Rossetti waited for Christina by the front door, warming himself by stamping his feet. He remarked to Browning that he didn't realize "Christina was also dragging you into this wild-goose chase." She showed no reaction but recoiled at the implications about her concern for Gabriel.

"We met on the street and I confess I insisted," Browning assured him. "Whenever I visit here, it occurs to me that rowing out in a shell would be easier passage than the crush of hackney cabs and wagons."

"Because of its proximity to the river, the house was actually used for smuggling two hundred years ago—more or less—first of political fugitives, later for supplies and even pirated and forbidden books, kept in vaults that had direct access to the water. I suppose she told you our wayward brother has been inconsiderately absent of late." William had the same olive-colored skin and wide-apart eyes as their brother, inherited from their Italian father, and in his youth William edited and even wrote and translated poetry like his siblings. By this stage of his life his fussy expressions and dress presented the look of a respectable clerk. ("Respectable!" Gabriel would cry if the word were used in his presence as though an accusation of a heinous crime.)

Christina silently prayed her thanks for Browning's being there. He lent the occasion a feeling of a friendly gathering rather than what it was— a kind of breaking and entering.

Gabriel tended to alienate everyone who dared to praise or support him, but not Browning. He had always been unusually patient with Gabriel. Much of their camaraderie came from shared grief. When Browning returned from Florence in the shadow of Elizabeth Barrett Browning's death, Gabriel was the first of their acquaintances to visit him. When Gabriel lost Lizzie months later, Browning never asked about the rumors. Rumors about the marriage, and her behavior, his drinking. He'd simply said to Christina, upon hearing of it and of Gabriel's sorrow, *Poor, dear man!*

"No servants," Browning mused, when the echo of the big, ancient dragon-shaped knocker on Tudor House's front door went unanswered.

"Not for the last year or so," replied William.

"Gabriel used to say he had become a martyr to unsatisfactory servants," Christina added.

After struggling to fit the landlord's key in a few locks, they found a door around the side of the house that admitted them into the impressive brick structure. The massive house with its sweeping stairs and array of doors unfolding into more rooms still felt a little like the palace it was when Queen Catherine, the luckiest of Henry VIII's unlucky wives, lived there following the murderous king's death. The floors creaked under the weight of the visitors, and every wall and post they touched produced bursts of dust, reminiscent of the fog outside. The place was great and strange, like Gabriel.

"I suppose Gabriel isn't still keeping his absurd—" Browning started, but his question was interrupted with a shriek. A dark shape climbed over a table and leapt over their heads.

"His zoo," Christina said. "Yes. Pray watch for the armadillos; they're rather sly about taking you by surprise."

"There is more than one armadillo?"

The animal that had jumped over them—a monkey about the size of a small greyhound—now perched low on the gilt frame of a mirror and stared with outrage.

"Truth is, Mr. Browning, it is hard to ever know at a given time which creatures Gabriel has. I know the poor bull was taken away," said Christina.

"Yes, after trying to gore Gabriel," William added grimly. "Gabriel only procured the beast in the first place because its eyes looked like those of a woman he once loved. You might imagine, Mr. Browning, how old Lord Cadogan reacted when he heard rumors about a bull roaming one of his tenants' gardens. Then there was the kangaroo found murdered in the studio—"

"Murdered!" Browning exclaimed.

"By its own joey," William continued. "Then, some time later, that patricidal creature himself was found bloodied and clawed to death, which Gabriel attributed to his raccoon—as an act of revenge."

Christina remembered Gabriel reporting to her, with his air of outrage and confusion, how neighbors would complain when a gazelle showed up in their gardens or a raccoon in their chimneys. She could also recall his earlier homes, where neighbors found different grounds for complaints— Gabriel's loud, drawn-out screaming volleys with Lizzie.

Tudor House, where Gabriel had moved not long after Lizzie's death, had at first seemed to be a place where he could do anything. He could fill it with useless collections of objects. With exotic and winsome animals. He hosted raucous gatherings, with artists cavorting naked and sliding down the banisters. The house was a wonderland. An escape from a life without Lizzie.

Christina looked back at the monkey on the mirror, then at the armadillos creeping into the doorway. They were waiting.

Hungry.

The house was stuffed with mismatched furniture from all over the globe, which Gabriel collected from junk shops, with every shelf not holding books lined with plates, china (mostly blue and white), and jewelry. Christina knew what happened when a notion took hold of her brother. It was the pursuit of the objects that gave him pleasure rather than the objects themselves. After he'd decided to collect blue and white china because one of his friends was doing it, she had been present at a dinner party with him. When Gabriel noticed a blue and white bowl at the center of the host's table, he remarked on its exquisite beauty, grabbing it and turning it upside down to examine its mark—spilling soup all over himself, the table, and other guests.

Christina's eyes landed on a self-portrait Gabriel had sketched to mark his twentieth birthday. With the long, flowing dark hair, the searching eyes, the full lips, he was born to attract attention.

Many kinds and sizes of mirrors reflected and expanded the chaos of artifacts and animals. The searchers next wandered around his library of more than a thousand volumes, where they found an eclectic selection of novels and histories in half a dozen languages, with an especially large selection of Italian books. The vast majority of the latter were editions of Dante Alighieri's *Divine Comedy*—divided into *Inferno*, *Purgatory*, and *Paradise*, the segments of the afterlife Dante claimed to traverse—or volumes of the Florentine bard's shorter works, or books of commentary about Dante, or books of commentary about the commentary on Dante.

They inspected the central room of the house, Gabriel's large studio that had once been a great dining hall, for signs of sketches or paintings, but of the many they found none could be identified as fresh enough to give them hope he had been there recently. Many of these pieces of art also incorporated scenes and figures from Dante Alighieri's work. In one corner stood a giant canvas Christina had seen before, which Gabriel called *Dante's Dream*. Some parts had been rubbed out; others had multiple layers of paint. There was no progress on it that Christina could detect, though in itself that wasn't surprising. Gabriel had been working on it for fifteen years.

The painting showed an awestruck Dante Alighieri, the medieval poet, being led by a heavenly figure through Florence to Beatrice, the girl who captured him heart and soul and whose spirit eventually led him to his celebrated journey into the afterlife. The scene took place moments before Beatrice's death. The room where Beatrice prepares to die did not seem to be any earthly setting in Gabriel's version. The floor is covered in poppies, symbols of sleep. It seemed the Florentine poet's chamber of imagination, a dreamy place between his disappointing reality and the better world beyond. Gabriel would often work on this canvas—if sitting and pacing in front of it and staring into it counted as work. He would speak about how he would not be able to finish until he managed to imagine himself in the place of Dante Alighieri.

"It is impossible to do. Impossible! To sufficiently *become* Dante . . . Maria was the only true Dante in our family," Gabriel would say, unintentionally hurting Christina. He would talk about how much he missed their older sister as though Maria were dead rather than in a convent. "You, my darling Christina, are a born apostle. You can learn and can teach, but cannot lead the way as Maria did. None of us can."

Christina did not say so at the risk of sounding conceited, but Gabriel was mistaken—about the painting, at least. It was Beatrice he would have to come to understand before the painting would allow itself to be finished.

As she searched, she found some other chalk sketches hanging above the fireplace related to Dante, including one depicting the Florentine poet's point of view of the sixth terrace of Purgatory, containing the souls besieged with gluttony. At the bottom Gabriel had scribbled a note to solicit Christina's opinion: *CR—need your help.* In the drawing, a penitent soul with face hidden in the shadows slumps on the ground, unable to nourish himself from fruit high upon a nearby tree.

With more to inspect, the searchers split up. William took on one part of the house, collecting fragments of Gabriel's poems left scattered like autumn leaves, and Christina and Browning another. Meanwhile, hoarse cries, which seemed to mock their tiptoeing, were identified by Browning, by peering out the window, as two peacocks debating each other in the weed-infested garden, which led down to the banks of the Thames.

"You must find someone to tend to this menagerie," Browning said to Christina, adding quickly, "until Gabriel returns."

"He likes to look out every time he passes a window," she said wistfully, "and if a lovely woman passes, he rushes out and says, 'I'm a painter and I want to paint you.'"

Browning asked if they assented.

"Sometimes. Usually they scream, and he runs back inside, slams the front door, and hides."

With candle in hand, Christina entered her brother's bedroom, kept dark by thick wall hangings and velvet window curtains. She slowly parted the heavy curtain around his bed and paused at her brother's bedside table. There a small black vial and a small measuring glass sat among other odds and ends.

Browning, coming up behind her, asked what it was.

She smelled the vial. "The skeleton in his cupboard, so to speak. Chloral hydrate." The room's heavy décor made their voices sound muffled and weak. She glanced around. The bed was in a disarray that could have been from a day—weeks, months?—earlier. She let out a tiny sigh ending with a choked-back sob.

Browning rushed closer to her with arms out.

"I am well enough," she insisted, putting out a hand. "Never expect me to faint, Mr. Browning. I will not."

"Something ailed you just now, Miss Rossetti."

"There is nothing the matter, only I am tired and have a headache. There is nothing at all the matter."

Browning swallowed down his protests and turned away.

He deserved better for helping her. "I am overcome not by what is here, but by what is *not* here, Mr. Browning. To be honest, I feared we might discover my brother here—his body."

Christina paused before adding, "Please, do not tell anyone."

He was confused. "Tell them—you mean that Gabriel—?"

Eeeiu! came the peacocks' hollers. *Eeeiu eeeiu!*

She wished she didn't have to say it. "Please don't tell anyone I almost wept."

They reconvened downstairs in the cluttered drawing room, where Browning lit a fire and William brewed tea.

"What about the rest of your family?" Browning asked. "Not one of them has spoken with him?"

"From the time we were children, our family never understood our brother," said Christina, taking a chair to one side of the hearth while Browning settled in at the other. Perhaps their late father, the professore, understood him, Christina thought to herself, though he would never have admitted it. The fact was, their family gave up concerning themselves with Gabriel's endeavors or whereabouts.

"Just as Gabriel avoided his landlord knowing money would be demanded of him, I'm sorry to say we often found ourselves having to avoid Gabriel because of his demands for 'tin'—that's what he calls money—from us." William finished serving tea and sat on the velvet sofa, first flicking off a few layers of fur. "As I'm sure you've felt yourself, Mr. Browning, with those closest to him Gabriel wavers between indifference, neediness, and abuse. It's not all his fault, mind you. He hasn't been able to conjure a good night's sleep for years. Not without the compound my sister found at his bedside, or similar concoctions, anyway, of opiates and other narcotics. He said it also helped his eyes, which often cause him pain, and the dizzy spells that plagued him since he was young. When he cannot sleep, he wanders the streets half the night—finding trouble that way, often, and sometimes thinking he was being watched or followed. It has all grown worse."

"You mean since Eliz—Lizzie died," Browning said, his voice trailing off.

"No, Mr. Browning," Christina said, followed by a solemn pause. She felt as though she were breaking a vow of silence. "Since Lizzie committed suicide."

William hung his head.

Browning's hand froze as he lifted the steaming drink. "Suicide?"

"It was after her pregnancy—" Christina stopped herself and started again. "He came home from one of his walks to find her sprawled out, an empty bottle of laudanum nearby."

"Now the poor man fills his bloodstream with similar classes of poison."

"We wanted to protect our family and protect our brother, Mr. Browning," said William. "He blamed himself for Lizzie. We try not to repeat that she took her own life."

"Did she give him any kind of warning? An explanation?"

Christina looked at William. Her brother did not indicate approval for what she was going to do, but did not object. Christina crossed the room to a painting of Lizzie Siddal posed as a medieval damsel, her thick curls rolling down her back. Being so close to the painting made Christina feel as though Lizzie watched them.

He nicknamed her the Sid and Guggum. Or Guggums. Or just Gug. If she was not home, Gabriel would sometimes mutter "Guggums, Guggums," over and over, to console himself as he painted.

She had luxuriant red hair and bright green eyes. Whether her skin was translucent or pale, her lips full or bloated, her expressions noble or crass, were impossible questions to settle. Lizzie appeared very different to different people, as though she transformed depending on which pair of eyes beheld her. Whichever details stayed with a particular person who met her, she was, in Gabriel's vocabulary, a "stunner." It all made her, in short, the ideal model to paint.

She became Guinevere, the Virgin Mary, and especially Beatrice. She became Lizzie Siddal instead of Lizzie Siddall. She became Rossetti. She became Guggums.

Christina reached behind the frame and removed a folded paper she passed to Browning. "He keeps this close at hand still."

She appreciated how gingerly Browning held it as he read to himself, and then recited the second stanza of the long poem aloud:

> *Hollow hearts are ever near me,*
> *Soulless eyes have ceased to cheer me:*
> *Lord, may I come to Thee?*

Suicide announced by verse.

Browning cleared his throat of Lizzie Siddal's words, nearly in tears, before he asked Christina what they should do.

"We find Gabriel, Mr. Browning," she answered, "before he also does himself harm."

The reporter frowned to the left and then the right, then squeezed himself through the indifferent forest of busy men, many of whom he knew and wished he didn't. They greeted and grunted at him. The

Three Tun's dining room was separated into private boxes by miniature walls that, in fact, discouraged any privacy at all, since you had to peer over each compartment to find the party you were looking for. "Excuse me, pardon the bother," Steven Walker was now saying as he did just this. Inside one of the boxes was the man who had sent him his card. A big book—*The Decameron* by Boccaccio—covered the bottom half of his face.

Walker would have thought he was shaking hands with just another early-middle-aged man in London who read too many books, if he hadn't known Dolly Williamson was the finest and most formidable detective at Scotland Yard.

"Do you know why I've asked you here, Mr. Walker?" Dolly asked. "I'd like to invite you in the queen's name to assist me."

"Inspector, I didn't even know you knew my name," said Walker, who was a short man with saggy cheeks that made him appear to pout even the rare times he wasn't. "Boccaccio. Leisure reading for a police detective?"

Dolly grinned. "I enjoy reading, true enough, though whatever leisure I get while the sun is up I try to give to my gardening or watching the rowers on the Thames."

"I'm surprised to find you here. I've always heard you don't even stop to sit down when you have an open mystery."

"Hyperbole! Sometimes I—even I—put my feet up. I want to give you something, Mr. Walker. Something of considerable value in your field."

Dolly pushed a folded piece of paper across the table, steering it through a maze of wet circles left by bumpers of beer.

Walker picked up the paper and unfolded it. "What is this?"

"Read it."

A little reluctantly, Walker did. He read aloud some of the words: "'Inscription . . . stone . . . Behold . . . handmaiden . . . Lord.'"

While Walker studied the note, Dolly waved his hand over his head, and a Scotch appeared as though dropped from the sky.

"Why pass this to me, Inspector Williamson? I don't even much enjoy penning the police columns. There's plenty of men—why, there's a dozen in this room I could point out to you—who would salivate for something like this, or for a whisper about one of your Fenian cases. I'm just helping out with the police columns while my editor is shorthanded, but between us, I rather fancy—"

"Illustration." Dolly completed his sentence.

"You know?"

"I've seen the drawings you've done in *Punch*. Quite entertaining, the lot of them!"

"Well, won't yet pay my landlord, will they? So if you know my head isn't in mysteries and police stories, why would you . . ." He stopped himself as Dolly sipped his drink through a smile. "You don't *want* me to be too interested in this. Is that it, Inspector?"

Dolly lifted his drink in consent. "You're better at this game than you think. Reporters who are *too* interested in a story want more, alas, than I can ever give them, and eventually turn on me. You are a tourist in the police columns, and that's exactly why you are right for what I need. You wield an able pen but not an insatiable one."

Walker gazed back at the words on the piece of paper. "May I ask one thing. Is this crime so different, to go out of your way like this?"

"Mr. Walker, at any given time I would estimate almost six thousand criminals in London, two hundred who are first-rate thieves, six hundred swindlers and dog stealers, forty burglars and garretteers. The rest, well, common pickpockets, pilferers, children who sneak and steal, and then of course there are the political criminals, the Fenians who want to hurt or embarrass England to change things in Ireland. This? This is different. You'll remember what I wrote down, won't you?"

Walker shrugged. "Yes, Inspector, though I'm sorry to say I still don't really understand the point of it."

Dolly plucked the paper out of his hand and ripped it in half. "It's not *you* I'm counting on to understand it."

IV

Christina and Browning called on every art studio in London and beyond where Gabriel had leased space in the past—sometimes, during those periods, he'd painted with such fury that he would sleep on floors not to lose time, content as a seal on a sandbank—and at the residences of half a dozen of his old friends. Some friends, they learned, had turned into ex-friends because of Gabriel's erratic behavior. The questioners heard about his being warm, generous, and inspiring from some; from others, that he was selfish, spoiled, and a broken-down devil who was mad as a March hare.

Some people they spoke to were almost as anxious as they were to know where they could find Gabriel. One of these was a man who had bought paintings by Gabriel, A. R. Gibson.

On their way to the art exhibit where they were told they could find Gibson, Browning asked Christina if she knew much about the art lover.

"His actual initials were R. A. Gibson," Christina explained to Browning with the slightest hint of disdain that, coming from her, landed with the thud of a raging insult. "But he did not like that the letters of his name spelled something as common and dirty as 'rag,' so he changed it. He is rather infamous for his bossiness toward the painters he commissions."

Browning seemed to find the idea of Gibson's changed name wildly amusing until Christina pointed out Gabriel had done something similar. "Dante was actually one of my brother's middle names."

"Was it?"

"He was born Gabriel Charles Dante Rossetti, but around age twenty shortened it by removing the Charles and changed the order to Dante Gabriel to honor Dante Alighieri. That is why only his artist friends call him Dante—he instructs them to do so, but we wouldn't. To us, he is always Gabriel."

They found the original subject of their conversation smoking a long, thin cigarette and directing the ashes away from his orange-brown velvet collar. Smoking was not allowed in the gallery, but Gibson was too important to be reprimanded. "Your brother owes me two paintings, but you might say I am patient to a fault," Gibson reported to them. "Oh, you know him. When Dante thinks he is unappreciated, he demands attention, but when he knows something is wanted of him, he—what's the word a versifier, like one of you, might use?—*recoils*."

Browning asked Gibson why he still did business with Gabriel, if he had been so difficult.

"Mr. Browning, you must know Dante Gabriel Rossetti is"—he sent out a cloud of smoke as he searched for another word—"irresistible. We have had our battles over the price of my commissions from him. Still, it is rare to find one who is as excellent a poet as a painter, and such a capable imagination improves his craft in both. He always says you could have been a great artist yourself, my dear."

"Me?" Christina replied, aghast at the idea.

"Dante says you have the artistic imagination of a hundred men, but that you can hide more easily in your poetry. He adores you, you know. I always picture you, Miss Rossetti, as something of a caged bird, waiting to be freed. Do you ever feel that way?"

The stare Christina returned at Gibson could have made a murderer confess at Old Bailey.

When after many similar interviews they failed to make progress tracing where Gabriel could have gone, Browning suggested they consult the police, but Christina refused. She didn't give a reason. In part, she was thinking of Gabriel, who would fume at the idea of a bobby looking for him.

More than that, asking for help from the police would confirm there was a problem, and, in spite of herself, she was not ready to admit that to more people. She continued to go to Tudor House, sometimes on her own and sometimes with Browning or William, organizing and examining her brother's letters and notebooks and sketches, hoping a clue would appear. William brought her letters from Gabriel that he could find for her to review.

She found old neglected documents, including some writing and sketches from around the time he'd met Lizzie. The sketches, usually preparations for paintings that would never be completed, often experimented with transforming the visage of Lizzie into the image of Beatrice.

Beatrice Portinari—the real Beatrice, many scholars believed—was one of many girls known for her beauty around Florence of the late thirteenth century, but for whatever reason she, not one of the others, captured the young poet's heart and imagination. When Beatrice's father died, Dante observed her tenderly grieving. This, in turn, filled Dante with grief and with a startling idea that invaded his every waking thought: *There will come a day when beautiful, tender Beatrice, too, must die.* If he had dared look right into her eyes, he would have dropped dead right there, drowned in sorrow. Perhaps the most peculiar part of Beatrice's destiny was that she probably never knew about her poetic admirer's extraordinary preoccupation. Her life was, by all accounts, perfectly ordinary, marrying at twenty and dying of illness a few years later.

Dante and Beatrice had met when she was so young. At that age, men imagine girls as paragons of purity and perfection. No wonder she became an angelic figure in Dante Alighieri's mind, a figure whose only purpose was to rescue Dante from darkness and despair. If they never had to age, all women would be mistaken for angels by men. Dante, however, was a brilliant enough poet not to leave it so simple. When Beatrice finally reappears to Dante atop the mountain of Purgatory on Holy Wednesday, 1300—as he describes in the second canticle of his *Divine Comedy*—she is armed with far more than she had appeared in the vision of a heartsick young poet; she roars with intelligence, anger, determination, righteousness. What Beatrice gains in power at the top of the mountain she loses in compassion, no longer speaking *to* Dante but *at* him.

Strangely, several times when Christina returned to Tudor House to continue journeying through Gabriel's memories and thoughts, it seemed as if some of the books or papers had been moved just slightly—as if by one of the ghostly apparitions so popular with the professional mediums Gabriel sometimes patronized. Every time she opened the door to the house, she held her breath, hoping against hope he would be standing in the hall beyond the threshold. Or, more likely, sprawled on a sofa, head low and feet propped up, staring at the vast ceiling—dreaming of his next painting.

Once, she heard footsteps on the stairs and looked over, thinking of Gabriel, only to see his raccoon scampering down. *Tap tap tap.* When the raccoon, with its shining eyes, would trot by, she could only envision the kangaroo's joey torn apart by its long claws in retaliation. She shooed the animal away. She formed a better relationship with Bobby, an owl with a large face and eggshell green beak. He was her favorite among the wonderland of animals.

Another time, as she read at the table looking for clues, she heard a shout: "You should be in church!" A search turned up Gabriel's parrot, repeating the advice.

"I will not disagree, Parrot," Christina had said with a frown, returning to memories of Gabriel she had tried so desperately to forget.

Gabriel first encountered the woman who would change his life when she was as still as a stone. She was sitting as Viola from Shakespeare's *Twelfth Night* for a painting by one of Gabriel's artistic conspirators and studio mates, Arthur Hughes. But she could not help but follow Gabriel with her eyes as he lumbered around the studio staring at her. "Do not move your eyes so much," shouted Hughes. "Keep your damned eyes over here!" She began to sit for Gabriel's paintings and they remained entranced by each other. As with everything that affected Gabriel, her charm and beauty pleased him not just in themselves but as symbols of something he'd searched for his whole life. He convinced her to change the spelling of her surname from Siddall to Siddal, which he said improved it. More elegant.

Christina balked at the idea of his prodding his lover to alter the spelling of her own name. Gabriel's giant eyes narrowed.

"But, dear Christina," Gabriel pointed out to her, "I could have asked her to change it altogether."

Sometimes, after Lizzie Siddal's tragic end, Gabriel would ponder whether Lizzie's fate had been inevitable all along. "Guggums was ready to die daily," he'd insist to Christina, then added, almost whimsically, "sometimes more than once a day." Other times, he despaired that he caused her decline or at least did not prevent it.

She was buried in the Rossetti family plot in a grave adjacent to that of the professore. During the burial, someone placed a Bible into Lizzie's coffin. In the blur of the funeral, nobody remembered who, maybe one of Lizzie's weeping relatives from the countryside. Gabriel insisted the holy book was the last thing he would have ever included to bring her peace.

Gabriel left something of his own. He dropped in the only manuscript of his latest poems with her body, resting them between her cheek and her flowing hair. "I wrote these when I might have been attending to her," Gabriel later confessed to Christina, "and they will go with her."

Gabriel hated the churchyard that took his wife. As they left the burial, he took Christina by the arm. "Let *me* not on any account be buried at Highgate. When I die, burn my remains where I lay."

It was odd to think of the professore buried so close to Lizzie, so close to those abandoned poems. How the old man's spirit would have hungered for poetry about Dante Alighieri! The man who'd given his son the middle name Dante in the first place.

Christina could still hear the professore talking of Dante to her and her siblings, describing the secrets he found in the medieval poetry, sometimes with a pupil, such as the odd but brilliant young man Charles Cayley, stationed nearby on a hard stool. From his big chair close to the fire, illuminated by a semicircle of candles like an ancient prophet, the professore would lean over his writing desk, on top of which was the biggest snuffbox ever seen and his thick manuscript, the paper of which reflected the light back onto his face. He would make such pronouncements as:

"How many masked sphinxes I have come upon, so many, my bantlings—it is a true marvel!"

The professore, gesticulating with bony hands, would explain that the middle section or canticle of Dante's poem *Purgatory* represented the bold Florentine poet at his boldest. This "second kingdom" of the afterlife between Hell and Paradise—where (as Dante put it) "the human spirit is purged"—had only ever been described in vague terms. In the Florentine's vision, its physical reality came through—beginning with the rocky shores where some "shades," or disembodied souls, dwelled in "Ante-Purgatory," and moving up the mountain where each sin would be repented for on a distinct terrace, starting with Pride, where shades heard the voice of the Virgin Mary cry out humbly—*Behold, the handmaiden of the Lord*—as a counter to their own excessive and destructive pride.

"Dante's words are not *merely* that," declared the professore.

Each mystery about Dante that the professore solved—so he said—led him closer to the glorious revelations of the past and future of religion, literature, and the world. He had sent some of his tedious, grandiose work to Samuel Taylor Coleridge, who ended any budding friendship when he commented in return, "Some of your views of Dante's meaning are just, but you have pushed it beyond all bounds. How could a poet such as Dante have written a secret political and doctrinal tract as you conjecture?"

Now, Gabriel had left his own poetic visions of Dante so tantalizingly close to the professore's coffin, one could imagine the old man's spirit reaching out for them.

Not long after Lizzie's funeral, a poem Christina worked on for more than ten years, "Goblin Market," was published in a collection with some shorter verse. Through unique and witty verses, "Goblin Market" told of a girl who must save her sister from the ravages of temptation held out by a crew of pleasure-obsessed beast-men.

Eat me, drink me, love me, cries the girl, who has consumed the goblin's fruit in order to share the restorative juices with her sister. *Laura, make much of me.*

Gabriel showed the manuscript to a critic he knew. *No publisher, I am deeply grieved to say*, the critic replied in a letter, *will take these, they are so full of quaintness and strangeness. Your sister should learn the strictest employment of meter and then,* perhaps, *can write something the public will like.*

Christina's curious poem *was* published and exploded in popularity. Of course, questions followed: did the troubled sibling who required saving represent Lizzie? Gabriel?

Christina would often be sent for in the middle of the night to help placate or chase down her brother. Every night after Lizzie's funeral, Gabriel saw her ghost. He could not say whether she appeared in anger or sympathy. He'd escape into the midnight streets until Christina or William retrieved him. Like Dante Alighieri after Beatrice died, Gabriel appeared as a savage creature, gaunt, beard thick and uneven, hair greasy. Soon after this period he moved to Tudor House. He took more chloral hydrate to be able to sleep, increased his laudanum to ease his anxiety. He painted and wrote and read. Christina told him to read anything, anything at all except Lizzie's suicide poem. She advised it was also best to stay away from reading Dante Alighieri, with his tales of a quest after death—a quest, at its heart, to reunite with his lost love.

Gabriel would proceed to read either Lizzie's suicide poem or more Dante.

Christina would report back to her mother about Gabriel, and then placid, sensible Frances Rossetti—who most people thought looked exactly like Christina thirty years on, except for those who declared the two looked nothing alike—would shake her head. "I always had a passion for intellect and wanted to instill it in my children," she'd say. "I had my wish. And I now wish that there were a little less intellect in the family, and a little more common sense. You will watch out for him, won't you, Christina, and keep him from . . . ?"

Her mother didn't finish the request and didn't have to. If there would be less and less time for Christina's writing and career, so be it.

"Do you hear that?" Gabriel would sometimes ask Christina in that period when she found herself running to his side at Tudor House on a regular basis.

"What? I don't hear anything, dear Gabriel. What do you hear?"

"Her voice," he would say, and explain it was calling a single word out at him, over and over. "Murderer," it would ring in his ears. *Murderer. Murderer.*

Christina experienced a feeling of relief as she watched the gray streets of London from the dirty little window of the omnibus bringing her to Scotland Yard. Her refusal to involve the authorities proved brief; the deeper she traveled back into Gabriel's darkest years from the confines of Tudor House, the deeper her alarm. As soon as she managed to bear it, she sent word to Browning, consenting to go to the police offices. Browning, always waiting to be a man of action, flew to her side.

William declined to accompany them. He worried. Worried about the reputation of the family, worried about his job at the excise office. He didn't say outright that he didn't want to be seen walking into the police offices, but Christina knew.

No matter. What mattered was that Gabriel would be found. That was what Christina thought about and prayed about on the ride while sitting alongside Browning. *Fear no more*, she imagined a dashing detective reassuring her with a lingering, firm handshake.

But the young constable who met them at Scotland Yard was reticent as a clam as he took down their information. He was only intermittently attentive. Meanwhile, a wide-shouldered, tall man, whom the other officers called Inspector Williamson, burst into and out of the room a few times, chewing on the stem of a flower and complaining to his inferiors about a newspaper that published new details, before permission had been given, about the shocking murder of Jasper Morton.

The constable slowly printed in careful hand in his notebook: *Dante Gabriel Rossetti.*

"Listen to us, young man," Browning said, his irritation pushing out as he seemed on the verge of exploding across at the indifferent official. "We are talking about a missing man here. Aren't you going to initiate an inquiry? Are you going to do something, *anything*?"

"Mr. Rossetti is a grown man," the constable said in a soft, frictionless voice with a hint of an Irish upbringing, as Christina's voice preserved a trace of Italy. "He is fully competent. I believe they are rather prone to wandering. Painters, artists, and men of letters, I mean. I appreciate that you're both concerned. However, without evidence that he is in some kind of jeopardy . . . I suppose you can see for yourselves how busy our men are these days."

In the background, Dolly Williamson was now calling out to some unseen companion: "I want that reporter in irons! That's right! His name is Walker!"

"I didn't want to unduly emphasize this, but do you know who we are, Constable?" Browning asked, leaning over the desk so that his face was almost against the constable's.

"Mr. Browning, please," said Christina, mortified to her core.

Constable Branagan nodded. "I do, Mr. Browning. You're the poet of many popular volumes, *The Ring and the Book*, of course, but 'My Last Duchess' being my favorite. And Miss Rossetti, poetess of the remarkable 'Goblin Market.' Practically everyone I knew took a fancy to that when it was printed. A new volume coming soon, Miss Rossetti?"

"No," she said quietly.

"I wasn't much of a reader before serving as one of Mr. Dickens's porters at Gad's Hill," explained Branagan, "but I've tried to keep up with books since leaving that position."

"I daresay nothing could impress a man after lugging around Dickens's valise," Browning muttered.

Christina already blushed deeply at Browning's attempt to use their renown, then felt another wave of stomach-twisting embarrassment at the constable's mention of her most lauded poem.

"Miss Rossetti, has your brother ever before left his home without telling anyone where he went?" asked the constable.

He had.

"In those previous occasions, has he stayed away for days? Weeks, sometimes?"

At that moment she knew all their other arguments were lost.

"Gabriel is not all gloom and eccentricity, Constable," she said. "He does things that are at once beautiful and absurd, and his tender heart feels stabs from all sides. When he chooses to, he becomes the sunshine of the family."

The young man nodded with sincere reflection, but closed his notebook and the case.

Speechless, helpless, she exited the building in a hurry. Her legs felt weak, as if they had been detached, as the cold wind whipped around her. The relentless noises of London rumbled around them, an obnoxious taunt, it seemed, emphasizing the indifference that met their pleas. The walls of nearby buildings were covered in advertisements, something her father always hated, saying London had written all over itself like a badly abused book. Flowers, milk, hot pies, all offered for sale from one direction or another, over the cries from bootblacks and street sweeps.

Browning broke their silence. "If I ever cross that constable's path, I shall probably be silly enough to soil my shoe by kicking him. I suppose there is nothing better to do at this point except wait until—"

Christina held up a single finger, silencing him. "Did you hear it?" she whispered, so as not to drown out the noises.

It started again. It was a faint cry.

A phrase.

Repeating itself.

Christina walked as though in a dream state down the street, turning the corner until she traced the cry to a newsboy, who was shouting to the point of hoarseness.

The boy called again: "'Behold the handmaiden of the Lord'! Extrey *Ledger*! Cheap as dirt. Full account by crack reporter Steven Walker— what was found written upon the dead MP in Wapping. 'Behold the handmaiden of the Lord'!"

She was gripped by a double realization: that a terrible danger had come to London, and that she knew what had happened to her brother.

DOCUMENT #2:
LETTER FROM DANTE GABRIEL ROSSETTI
TO WILLIAM ROSSETTI,
OCTOBER 5, 1869

READ THIS ALONE.

My dear brother,

I want to tell you something lest you hear it from anyone else first. It is that I am going to recover my old book of poems. Only lately I made up my mind to it. I hope you will think none the worse of my feeling for one I held the dearest.

The truth is, William, no one so much as herself would approve of my doing this. Art was the only thing for which Lizzie felt very seriously. Were it possible for her to do, I believe Guggums would open her grave, and before you knew it I would find the manuscript on my pillow at night.

The matter is of a less dreadful nature than might seem possible, dear brother. I have received medical assurance that all in the coffin will be perfect, otherwise I would not have the courage to make the attempt. As I write, I wonder if it is hardly worth all this, but the conflicting states of mind one passes through about life are among the things which most call for making allowances.

I am very anxious to know your view of this, and to remind you beforehand that no mistrust or unbrotherly feeling could possibly have caused my silence till now regarding this undertaking. Difficulties continue to be raised by the cemetery's authorities as to whether we are attempting theft—theft of my wife's body, and my own verses!

I have begged those helping me with this to hold their tongues, but I suppose this will all ooze out to a wider circle in time. What would Christina think? She seemed to know my burying the thing was a mistake, but her religious strictures and unnaturally pure morals would surely forbid this attempt at recovery. With Christina, once a mistake is made, there is no undoing it. It is very desirable, as you will think with me, that Christina and the rest of our family should not know of this.

Yours in affection,
Gabriel

Browning did not disrupt Christina's concentration on the ride back to Tudor House. While she sat, he studied her strong profile, the slightly curved tip of her nose, her firmly set lips, her shoulders in a forward shrug, her mystical eyes directed straight ahead.

The only thing she said to him on the way was: "Mr. Browning, I am truly sorry for my ebullition of temper toward you at the police office."

"What? Your . . . ebullition of temper?" Browning searched his memory before realizing she referred to her almost imperceptible change of tone after he alluded to her poetry to the constable.

He didn't mind the quiet the rest of the drive, as he was busy pinning down his own thoughts after reading the late edition of the newspaper Christina had hunted down from the newsboy. The article, by the reporter named Walker whom they had overheard Inspector Williamson excoriating, unleashed a chain of unanswered and disturbing questions.

When they arrived back in Dante Gabriel Rossetti's disorderly drawing room, Christina smoothed her glossy brown hair and then, in a breathless flow of words, began sharing her thoughts from the armchair in front of the fireplace. She sat, perfectly composed and collected as usual, suggesting the slight but strong figure of the queen dowager who was said to have once dwelled there. "Mr. Morton, the representative of Bristol in the House of Commons, was discovered in the gardens with a backbreaking stone fastened to his neck. I suppose you have heard all about his horrifying murder, Mr. Browning."

Ever since the day he watched Elizabeth die in Florence, when her ravaging illnesses had made her look more like a young girl than his fifty-five-year-old wife, Browning could not brood on death—peaceful or painful, premature or expected, by illness or hanging, it didn't matter—without his soul aching. It's true that there were exceptions, as Tennyson made sure to remind him. *You don't always stay away from darkness, now do you, Browning?* Eventually, Browning chose to write a long poem about crime and death—*The Ring and the Book*—but that came out of much hand-wringing and singular circumstances. He certainly had no desire to read about death or violence to pass the time over breakfast. He wanted to explain all this to Christina. Instead, he offered a version of the excuse he made on the same topic at the Cosmopolitan Club when Tennyson was devouring his newspaper. "I do my best to stay away from morbid excitement of the masses, Miss Rossetti. What does this have to do with Gabriel?"

"If I am right? Enough to place my brother in far graver danger than I believed. That is my fear, unless we can disprove it. Follow me, Mr. Browning. I avoid newspapers, too, but this story was impossible to escape. My aunts talked of nothing else. The backbreaking stone, as I say, was latched around Mr. Morton, and there were rumors a phrase had been etched into the horrid device. But until now the inscription was merely that—rumor—and the supposed Latin phrase not known to the public. Now the inscription on the stone has been exposed by this newspaperman, to the chagrin of police, as we witnessed in Inspector Williamson."

Ecce ancilla Dei.

Behold, the handmaiden of the Lord. The call of the newsboy *and* the words Mary speaks about herself after she is informed she will carry the son of God, announcing her compliance. Dante Alighieri, as he enters into the first terrace of the mountain of Purgatory, hears Mary's words emanating from a stone carving as an example of humility to instruct the prideful souls consigned there.

Each terrace of Purgatory introduces a different sin that traveling souls must exorcise in order to progress upward, and in passing through that region devoted to excessive pride, the repentant souls carry crushingly heavy rocks on their backs—sometimes for hundreds of years. The murderer of Mr. Morton intended for the world to discover Dante in his scene of death. Not only did the mechanism of Morton's death mimic Dante's description, but the stone carried the very words of Mary heard by Dante.

"Why? Why Morton? Why the Prideful?" Browning asked. Questions felt much safer to him than any attempts at answers.

"From the newspaper eulogies of the man that I've seen, there are numerous ways Morton's life exemplifies excess pride. He strongly pushed to expand the number of foreign lands over which to impose British rule. He helped pass measures to punish the Irish people at large for the violence of the few who call themselves Fenians. He refused to allow another seat to be added to the House of Commons, alongside his own, to represent Bristol—according to his adversaries, a way of maintaining complete power over constituents. He even supported the horrid Contagious Disease Acts."

"His primary sin is being in Parliament, then. When does the paper say Morton was last seen, before he was found dead?"

"Approximately two weeks before Gabriel went missing from our sight." She gave a single, firm nod to emphasize the implications. "Mr. Browning, this all suggests the same thing—there is some kind of Dante-obsessed maniac in London. He must have overpowered and kidnapped Morton, then waited weeks before carrying out this grotesque killing. I believe he might have taken my brother also, and if the police do not want to listen to us that Gabriel could be in jeopardy, so be it. But if I'm correct, we may have days to act before this villain decides to do evil to him, too."

Browning found it remarkable that she remained composed while speculating about violence against her brother. He ducked all thoughts that anything so awful could happen to a friend, and now summoned his courage even to consider it. "Gabriel wanders."

"Mr. Browning?"

He had barely whispered the words. "He wanders the streets in the middle of the night when he cannot sleep, right?" Almost against his will, Browning gave voice to the fearful images taking life in his mind. "Reciting poetry, or with an open book in his hand . . ."

"A book of Dante Alighieri's verses, often enough," she said, finishing his thought. "He is renowned for painting scenes inspired by Dante and Beatrice on canvas and murals." Christina held up Gabriel's drawing she had come across in their first searches of the house, showing a scene from the punishment of the Gluttons in Dante's Purgatory, with the scrawled note.

Browning read: "'CR—need your help.'"

"Maybe he wasn't reminding himself to ask my opinion. Maybe he was beginning to sense that his work on Dante had brought him into an atmosphere of danger. Maybe it wasn't just the mental effects of chloral and morphia; this time he really *was* being followed. The drift of all this is that if there were some lunatic with a vendetta against Dante, or acting upon some kind of perverted monomania, my brother would be a tantalizing prize. He is even named for Dante."

Browning studied the sketch—it showed vividly the suffering of a shade in a state of starvation. Many of their literary circle studied the Florentine bard—including Browning himself, who had taken an episode from Dante's *Purgatory* and turned it into a long (too long, according to Browning's critics) poem called *Sordello*, named for one of the shades who helped show Dante and Virgil the way up the mountain. When Ba died, it was a quote from Dante that Browning copied out to memorialize her, in which the Florentine expressed his faith that one day he would be reunited with Beatrice.

Thus I believe, thus I affirm, thus I am certain it is, that from this life I shall pass to another better, there, where that lady lives of whom my soul was enamored.

Dante meant Beatrice; with the same words Browning meant Elizabeth. At the time, he could not help but think of Percival Shelley, who had read *Purgatory* aloud to Mary Godwin (later, Mary Shelley) after their baby died. Some thought Shelley's choice of *Purgatory* was meant to distract her with its sublime lyrics, while others assumed it was meant to console in a more direct way, to show that in death all are reunited.

Ba's father had cut her off from the family starting the day of their marriage. When her father was told she died, it got back to Browning that Mr. Barrett unemotionally replied, "I never had much objection to that dandy poet, but my daughter should have been thinking of another world." Browning buried Elizabeth Barrett Browning in Dante Alighieri's city in a summer heat like a razor wrapped up in the flannel of sunshine. In many ways, Florence had provided a glorious setting for the Brownings' fifteen years of marriage. He and Ba were out of reach of the control of her father. Mr. Barrett had turned her life in London into a prison, and just getting through the obstacles to reach their secret wedding before her father could enact his plan to take her away, Ba looked like death, but transcendently beautiful. *How necessity makes heroes*, she mused when they'd recount the elopement, *or heroines*.

Once they were abroad they could raise their son, also a Robert (Pen, for short), in the congenial Italian climate and culture. Browning had brought their boy with him on marvelous excursions, including to visit the ancient castle near Sarzana that had belonged to the Marquis Malaspina, one of the sanctuaries where Dante stayed after being exiled by political enemies from Florence. The place was in a state of decay when the Rossettis came to see it, but Dante's cramped little chamber had been preserved and, with proper credentials, could be entered.

Prior to his exile, Dante already had begun composing his *Comedy*, named such to distinguish it from the form of tragedy since he'd planned to end with the poet's ascension to Heaven. The poet, his life turned upside down by his enemies, had to find beds to sleep in, food to put on his plate. In the meantime, the pages he had already composed about his journey into Hell were lost. They gathered dust and mold in a trunk. The trunk was hidden from Dante's adversaries and transported under the cover of night to a patron of the poet's, who then carried it to Malaspina. The marquis hurried to Dante with the pages—probably into that very chamber of Dante's where Browning stood—and begged the Florentine bard to continue it.

Dante contemplated the peculiar second realm that would follow that first section—the kingdom of Purgatory. As a subject for poetry, it was without a doubt intimidating. It was this canticle that would reveal the penance that every one of them—not just the purely wicked—would have to pay one day. "Since fortune unexpectedly has restored my work to me," Dante answered the marquis, "I will proceed however grace shall determine for me." Dante dedicated *Purgatory* to Malaspina.

The room where the exchange took place was a simple stone enclosure. It exuded the loneliness and bitterness of exile. Yet there was a window, and outside the brilliant outline of the Alps.

"Nothing to see, Father," noted Browning's son, peering out.

"Not so, my boy," Browning whispered to Pen of the window, where there came in a rush of mountain air. "There is where Dante saw the heavens."

Dante Alighieri's legacy in Italy remained complicated by continued debates over his politics, variations of the kind that had left Dante without a home hundreds of years before. All the more reason English-speaking writers prized their own commitments to Dante. In addition to the Brownings and Christina, other British writers, including John Ruskin and Tennyson, turned to Dante for inspiration.

The translation of Dante's *Divine Comedy* into English a few years earlier out of America, by Henry Wadsworth Longfellow with the help of James Russell Lowell, Oliver Wendell Holmes, and other members of Boston's land of letters, spread the gospel of Dante further through Great Britain, as did a translation by the Rossettis' friend and former pupil of Professore Rossetti, Charles Cayley. But in England, no single writer had been immersed as completely and *personally* in the Florentine's life and *Comedy* as Dante Gabriel Rossetti.

Since the beginning of this quest to find Gabriel, somewhere tucked into Browning's mind was the idea that it had all begun with Gabriel's loss of Lizzie, that whatever path of descent he was on now, it might just as easily have been Browning.

Browning grappled and battled with the possibilities Christina proposed—that Gabriel's disappearance was the responsibility of a Dante-doused fiend. "Nonsense!" he cried at one point, and then exclaimed at another, "I refuse to believe it! Worse than nonsense!" Into his mind came the image of the ancient warrior Cato, the guardian of the mountain of Purgatory, glaring in disbelief at Dante, the new arrival—*a living man*, a man still casting a shadow! How was this poet breaking all the rules to enter the sacred kingdom? Virgil, Dante's guide, eloquent almost to a fault, must convince the doubting sentry that the journey was authorized from higher powers.

Browning's head filled with images of the grim reality of London—both its shadowy districts of hidden sin and its corrupt pockets of luxury—stirred together with Dante's array of purgatorial designs meant to cleanse the souls of the afterlife before being transported to Paradise. Wise Virgil teaches Dante the structure of the mountain as arranged by the sins it removed. The first group of terraces—Pride, Envy, and Wrath— comprise "ill love" or love that has been warped. The second category contains the terraces of "lax" or insufficient love, namely the Slothful, Avaricious, and Prodigal, while the final terrace of the mountain purges "profligate" or excessive love. Then a heavy thought struck Browning, and he no longer held back his obstinate doubts.

"It's not the first time."

Now it was Christina who was startled. "Gabriel disappearing?"

"No. Dante inspiring crimes and horrors in real life. It's happened before. Some believe that the torturers of the Inquisition with their intricate, vicious punishments found motivation in Dante's classifications of sins. There were even tales that something happened in America just a few years ago, around the time of the six-hundredth anniversary of Dante's birth. Do you recall?"

"I heard rumors, passed to me by William from the usual literary gossips. But never for a moment did I think to believe them."

"There was some kind of booklet printed later that purported to tell of what happened in Boston, and it proved a bit of a nine days' wonder in some circles. I remember seeing it a few times even in rarefied homes of London." Browning rose to his feet and gathered his hat and coat.

"What are you going to do?" Christina asked.

"That booklet about the Boston events. If there is a connection between those incidents and what is happening now—what may be happening to your brother—we must find it." Browning knew it would not be in any university library. There were some resourceful booksellers with whom he was acquainted who might be able to secure a copy, though he was impatient just thinking how long that might take. He began to list the bookstalls and reading rooms they'd visit.

Then a smile of gratification formed on Browning's lips. He began removing the gloves, coat, and hat in reverse order of how he'd just put them on, and stacking them.

"Tell me," Browning said. "If you were looking for an obscure publication with anything to do with Dante, where would you start, Miss Rossetti?"

Christina knitted her brow, then realized.

Gabriel had collected every book and scrap of paper on Dante he could ever find. It began with the volumes inherited from their father, including one fourteenth-century edition. The professore circled the world to hunt down a rare Dante edition or a piece of ephemera. There was even what was supposed to be Dante's death mask, sent from Italy by the eccentric Seymour Kirkup.

They were standing among the most comprehensive assortment of Dante writings, high and low, in all of England—as close to everything written about Dante as could ever exist.

Together they entered Gabriel's library. With the eyes of a wombat and parrot looking on, they picked and pulled books from the shelves until Christina gingerly removed a thin pamphlet poorly printed on yellow paper.

Thrilling Mysteries of
THE DANTE MURDERS
in the City of Boston,
Never Before Brought to Light

by One Who Knew

They promptly used up their writing paper taking notes. As Christina crossed through the labyrinth of rooms in the house, gathering up loose sheets, she paused at the doorway to a small chamber, where one object stood out. It was a wooden cradle turned upside down to be used for a drafting table. She remembered a time when she entered the house Gabriel had lived in before Tudor House, when Lizzie was alive, calling out in her shy way to see who was there.

"Gabriel? Lizzie?"

As Christina wandered the hall, she peered into a room where Lizzie sat. Startled by Christina's footsteps, Lizzie snapped her head and shushed her sister-in-law. Thick, wet hair covered her brow. "You'll wake the baby with all that noise, Christina," she whispered. Lizzie rocked the empty cradle in a gentle, hypnotic rhythm.

Christina expected to find a blank expression staring back from Lizzie's eyes. What amazed her was that in the grieving woman's eyes she observed only love—the purest form of it. It was maternal love for a child—and in this case, a child no longer of this earth—that Christina secretly doubted she herself could possess. Perhaps, deep inside, that had always led her to swerve and duck attention from men who had been interested in her, to swat down the possibility of new family by using existing family as her excuses. *My mother needs me . . . My aunts . . . My brother . . .*

And yet, Christina had in the years since gradually composed poems she thought of as new nursery rhymes. As the playful lines came to her, she thought of the adventures she'd shared with Gabriel as children, when people used to say the two of them could see and read each other's private thoughts. They tumbled, wrestled. They raced each other. They both read stories by Edgar Poe when others feared to. They competed to write verses quickly and argued over the greatness of nature. When Christina would stop to examine an interesting insect or patch of moss, Gabriel would stand in an impatient pose and shrug, not seeing what was at all interesting about it. Sometimes when writing her children's lyrics she thought of Gabriel and Lizzie's son, had he lived, and what he might have grown into.

People admired her poetry, but she knew there were plenty of readers who questioned it. How could she write brokenhearted verse if she never loved? Why did she compose so much about death if she knew little of life? Her emotions and insights must be affectation. Maybe they were right. Years earlier, she received a letter from a family friend complaining that her poems were sad and despondent. *If my verses are sad*, Christina replied, *I suggest few people reach even the age of twenty without sadness, and if despondent, I take shame and blame to myself, as they show I have been ungrateful for the daily love and mercy lavished upon me.* She added: *(Please remember to see to it this letter is burned.)*

The same people would think an unmarried, childless woman ineligible to understand and inspire children. She kept the nursery rhymes locked away in a drawer.

As she continued harvesting sheets of paper on her return to the other side of the house where Browning feverishly worked, Christina paused again at one of Gabriel's mirrors, brushing off a film of dust. Both the mirror and her own reflection seemed to come from another place and era. There were so many mirrors in the room that you were never looking at yourself; you were looking at yourself looking at yourself.

Christina knew she had been a prettier girl than a woman, in part because of the preoccupied and remote expression usually fixed on her face, which convinced people she was in pain. Her skin looked olive from her Italian blood and yet also somehow colorless. But she knew that when deep enthusiasm and interest came to her, her sleepy oval eyes would beam, her pale skin would glow with warmth, and she became beautiful, and then ashamed because of it.

She knew how others saw her—even Robert Browning. Now that she was almost forty, her choices meant she had all but given up any chance for marriage; if there was still time left where it could happen, it was almost gone. She had given up one suitor in her youth because he did not share her strict religious views. She lived with her mother. She was, in short, an old maid. That is what people saw. They saw what she turned away— being a wife, being a mother.

One of Gabriel's compatriots, Algernon Swinburne, had written a novel with the main character based on Christina, but unlike Christina, the character engaged in rather shocking and wild behavior; Christina pasted strips of paper over those startling sections but liked much of the rest of the story of her literary double. She would never say it to a living soul, but she enjoyed imagining *what might have been.*

Her place in society was small, fixed. Family, home, church, charity. Sitting at her writing table and sitting at her tea. There was her poetry, for which she was acclaimed. But she had produced only one volume of poetry in the eight years since "Goblin Market."

There had been a time, of course, as an unknown poet when she had to introduce herself to the magazines if she wished to publish something. She could hardly bear it. To one editor, she wrote: *I hope that I shall not be misunderstood as guilty of egotism or foolish vanity when I say that my love for what is good in the works of others teaches me that there is something above the despicable in mine.* She woke up in the middle of that night, her head hot, her heart throbbing, realizing that "what is good in the works of others" could be construed as implying there was some that was not good, and that Christina's was better. The next morning marked the first day she began to burn all of her letters she could find and to instruct correspondents to do the same.

There was nothing quite like the heat produced by those burning letters—or from the discarded poems and the particular short story she once wrote that was morally deficient—a heat that prodded her to try harder, to do better, to prevent future shame.

She had never been like other writers. She did not read voraciously, instead choosing the same stalwart books (the Bible, *The Arabian Nights*) to read again and again, and did not really seek inspiration from reading.

She never sought advice from publishers or friends, and when advice was proffered, from Gabriel or others, and she listened, her writing suffered for it. She hardly revised her work. She refused to publish a portrait of herself, however flattering and *unlike* her, in the frontispieces of her books. She did not chase fame or money like those other female poets who far surpassed her in popularity, such as Jean Ingelow. Poetry for Christina was not a mechanism but an impulse and a reality, and her aims in writing were directed to that which is true and right. If events of the last weeks and days proved anything, it was that her calling had increasingly become to serve her family, and at the moment that meant finding Gabriel.

CR—need your help. Gabriel's message rang like a bell in her thoughts.

The way Christina and Browning pored over the ratty *Dante Murders* pamphlet for the next four hours, elbow to elbow, a bystander would have been forgiven for mistaking it for a sacred document.

The pamphlet was written in sloppy but enthusiastic prose. It recounted a scourge in Boston after the end of the American War of Rebellion. Prominent citizens had been discovered murdered in the style of the punishments Dante memorialized in the *Inferno*, the first part of Dante's *Comedy*: a minister in the crypts beneath a church near Harvard College buried upside down, his feet set aflame, like the venal religious figures Dante encounters in one of the circles of Hell; a judge in Beacon Hill eaten alive by a rare breed of maggots, imitating the eternal state of what Dante named in another infernal circle the "neutrals"; and deaths even more shocking to the senses and less intelligible to the police.

The anonymous pamphleteer told how, in absence of wider knowledge about Dante, several preeminent men of letters, poets and a publisher among them, were left to decipher the true inspiration behind the horrors and became entangled in unraveling them as they prepared what became America's first translation of Dante. Just as the pamphlet's cover page withheld the name of the booklet's author, the names of the literary participants in the narrative were concealed by aliases.

Christina sent for William to come to Tudor House to help examine the booklet for any insights into the eerie occurrence in London, so she and Browning could pursue finding more information that might lead them to Gabriel. Twice they called for a family friend, Charles Cayley, to look over a passage of *Purgatory*; the agreeable translator was so studious and eager to please, he never asked about the peculiar assortment of labors in progress at Tudor House.

"Any excuse to read Dante, Miss Rossetti," Cayley said, flashing his awkward smile, "counts as a good one."

"Just what my father would say, Mr. Cayley."

Christina and Browning traveled by steamer to the North Woolwich Gardens, a simple recreation space with a small lake at the center. The newspaper articles they collected, with all their shouting declarations about the unacceptable and hideous crime against a member of Parliament, were sparing in reliable details about the exact location. Christina wanted to see it for herself.

Browning lamented that the gardens seemed completely deserted. It was frigid and foggy. There were few people whom they could even try to question.

"I suppose such an event frightens some people away, at least until a new spectacle makes them forget," Christina mused, looking up at the gray sky through a canopy of tree branches.

Thinking of the recent overturning of her tightly controlled routines, Christina had a revelation.

"The time," she said to Browning.

Routines: every person of every class had them—even if most were not as devoted to them as Christina. She proposed that they return closer to the time of day the body was found. Browning protested the gardens would not be safe in the darkness or at dawn, but Christina was undeterred. They would be more likely to encounter individuals whose routines had taken them there at the same time as the awful discovery. After passing time on their own, they reunited at the gardens.

Christina's conjecture seemed correct. Despite the cold, the gardens came alive under the cover of darkness. Young women—their painted cheeks and bright-colored garments enhanced by the moonlight, putting on a display for passing men—shied away from the obtrusive light of the lantern Browning held up. Soon enough, several recognized Christina and waved her over.

After a few minutes, she returned to Browning and explained that she knew several of the girls from her work with Saint Mary's penitentiary for fallen women—they had stayed there in the past, but left by their own will, or had been asked to leave the charity home for intoxication or other misbehaviors.

"They worry you are one of the men who come here to inspect them," Christina reported to Browning.

The Contagious Disease Acts authorized the government to order physical inspections of prostitutes and lock them up if they were found to have signs of venereal diseases, with the stated purpose of protecting soldiers.

"Is that what I look like?" Browning protested.

"I've convinced them, Mr. Browning, that regardless of appearance, you are not."

Browning came back with her to the circle of girls, and Christina asked each one if she had been present in the gardens when the politician collapsed dead. Christina also brought one of the many thick sketchbooks from Tudor House filled with Gabriel's self-portraits as well as other drawings, to determine whether any of the girls happened to have spotted her brother around London. Some of the sketches were in pen and ink, others in pencil or in red chalk. None of the girls whom Christina interviewed remembered seeing Gabriel at all recently, and none owned up to being in the gardens at the fateful moment in question, but one of the girls quietly slipped away and returned with another on her arm.

"Pamela's my sister; she was there," said the first girl. "Now don't be shy, Pam! Miss Rossetti is as true as the sun, strike me blind and dead."

"I won't be *reclaimed*, miss," protested her sister, as she flailed her arms around as though ready to fight Christina, "if that's what you're after, to reclaim my soul at Saint Mary's!"

"My name is Christina, and I've come for my own purposes. I'm trying to find my brother, I believe he is in danger, and we're here only for information. Could you possibly show us what happened to Mr. Morton?"

This girl, whose messy, thick orange hair surrounded her head like a crown, reluctantly led them to a clearing. She pointed out where she first saw the doomed man walking, hunched over, and then again after he fell to the ground and she and other onlookers rushed to see what happened. She recalled his wobbly steps, and how they thought he was a hunchback at first.

"I know him!"

The declaration, interrupting their interview with the witness, came from another girl in the group, one of the youngest. She was a waif of sixteen wearing golden garments and a bonnet decorated with flowers. She and two other girls had taken hold of the sketchbook, mostly as a novelty, and were thumbing through the drawings by the light of Browning's lantern.

"Gabriel? You've seen Gabriel?" Christina asked with breathless anticipation. She hurried over.

The waif wasn't looking at one of Gabriel's self-portraits. She had come across a different sketch pasted into the book, one Gabriel had made of painter Arthur Hughes, a member of the generation of artists who considered themselves avid followers of Gabriel's.

Christina pressed, asking how she knew the man. Her defiant shrug answered the question.

"When was the last time you had a meeting with that man?" Christina asked, continuing the gentle tone.

"It was right here. Nearly two weeks ago. The same night, matter of fact, as . . . ," she began, her gaze falling, her long arms wrapping around her narrow middle. "When that poor fellow was found, his neck broken under that stone, we heard the hubbub and came to see, like everyone else who was near."

Christina itched to go right to Hughes's studio when they left the gardens, but she suspected that he'd be asleep for hours more. Like Gabriel, most of the London artists tended to paint until late at night and then sleep through the afternoon. Browning accompanied her back to Tudor House, where they were surprised to find William asleep at the library table, his head buried in the crook of his arm. Around him, in addition to the now-well-worn booklet on the Dante murders of Boston, and Bobby the inquisitive owl, were various editions of the *Divine Comedy*, as well as an assortment of American poetry volumes and novels. He stirred, and cleared his throat when they entered.

"William, didn't you ever go home to sleep?" Christina asked.

"I suppose I lost sense of time," William replied, waving around an edition of *Paradise* until the owl fluttered off. He returned to the Dante murders pamphlet he'd been examining. "This little booklet is rather atrocious in its content, Christina, but I must confess it's difficult to put away. The crimes examined within it, the murders that supposedly came to pass in Boston, were re-creations of Dante's vision of Hell in the modern world. The culprit there, we can rest assured, is no longer capable of doing harm."

"But if the perversion behind those events has now spread, if someone has decided to carry them forward from *Inferno* to *Purgatory* and from Boston to London, then we must understand how this started," Browning replied. "You are performing a great service, Mr. Rossetti."

"Kind encouragement for a tired man," William said, his voice charged with skepticism. "I'm afraid it is almost impossible to divide the fantasy from the truth in a scribbler's tract such as this. However, I have made progress, I like to believe, in identifying the aliases of some of the individu-als dramatized here. The literary men, in particular. I believe one, called Kensington here, a translator secluded in a mansion described as yellow as the sun, is the famous Mr. Longfellow himself, and another, a short man called Gabbert described as possessing special medical training as well as poetical skills, I've determined is meant to represent Boston's celebrated Dr. Holmes. Now, there is also a noble investigator, hired, according to the story, by Universe College—that's Harvard, naturally—to shadow the schol-ars. I am trying to match this investigator with a real name. If we could find out who his model is, and write to him, he may know—"

"Hold on there," Browning interrupted. "Did you say Holmes? Oliver Wendell, *The Autocrat of the Breakfast Table*?"

"That makes sense, doesn't it?" Christina replied, looking back over her brother's shoulder at the material. "I remember it was said he was one of the writers in Longfellow's little translation circle. Do you think there's a reason to doubt it, Mr. Browning?"

"You confuse my excitement for doubt—I believe I recently came across the name of Dr. Holmes."

Christina and William followed as Browning hurried to the drawing room, where he reached for the stacks of newspapers they had combed through for mentions and details about Morton before his death—when he had been reelected, for the twenty-third time, to the House of Commons—and in its aftermath. Christina had carefully organized the newspapers based on their publication date and their quality of information.

"It was here . . . ," Browning said with frustration, tearing them open and perusing the columns. "Somewhere!" As he tossed papers aside after unsuccessful searches, Christina picked them back up and sorted them again. "An announcement about a speech or a lecture . . . I know I saw it . . . Ah!"

Christina felt her impatience about to burst. "Mr. Browning?"

Browning held up the newspaper. "We'll get the story from Dr. Holmes himself!"

OLIVER WENDELL HOLMES ON TOUR

Having come with his daughter from Boston and after visiting other stops in Europe, Dr. Oliver Wendell Holmes, the American medical professor at Harvard, author of the Breakfast Table satires and many memorable poems, has received the academic tribute of an honorary degree at Oxford. He will visit Cambridge after that. It has been nearly thirty-five years since the celebrated New Englander last sailed to Europe, and his return is most welcome.

VI

Wearing the academic gown with the square-topped cap and dangling tassel transmitted a thrilling sensation to a man. Dr. Oliver Wendell Holmes stood in front of a sea of young faces watching as he was presented with his doctor of letters degree, an honor insisted upon by the university authorities who'd heard Holmes would be sightseeing in town. A chorus of voices grew. Some called for him to recite the John Howard Payne lyrics "home, sweet home!" in tribute to his name; others wished more generally that the American poet would deliver a "speech! speech!" Gregarious, garrulous Dr. Holmes on this morning instead stepped away from the platform with just a fleeting smile and wave.

Holmes's tour through Europe, starting with Switzerland and Holland, then Scotland and England, had brought him pleasures, including honorary degrees from Edinburgh, Oxford, and now Cambridge. He especially liked Cambridge, even in the wet weather. He delighted in walking through the quadrangles, along the riverbanks, beneath the giant trees which bordered it. The other Cambridge—that is, New England's Cambridge—was his mother town, and since she was the daughter of Old England's Cambridge, by his calculations that made the town he visited his grandmother town.

Being in Europe for the first time in decades, though, brought with it a kind of unexpected dread. Holmes tried not to reflect on the events four years prior that he and his friends labored to keep secret. Back home in Boston and Cambridge, the safe familiarity of Holmes's carefully maintained routines mostly kept the dark memories at bay. When possible, he would avoid walking or riding by the places that would remind him of the occurrences. But now, so far from home and unmoored from routines, his brain found a way of sauntering right where he didn't want it to—through the unassuming byways and crevices of Boston where the gates of Dante's Hell opened before his eyes.

Those visions invaded Holmes's waking hours and his dreams alike. It had come to this: even the admiration of enthusiastic English students seemed to be a demand for him not just to speak but *remember*. After all, one of those young men suddenly, momentarily transformed into an eerie double of one of the victims of that violent spree in the *other* Cambridge, the one whose demise brought Holmes more pain than any other, while another began to resemble the perpetrator, and more members of the audience took on the forms of the other people who had become mixed up in those blood-drenched days.

Holmes's daughter, Amelia, who had arranged their European journey together, knew something was amiss. She had asked after his health often during their voyage, and ran into his staterooms and hotel rooms when he shouted during nightmares. It was a passing nervousness always brought on by long trips, nothing more, he reassured her.

The perpetual round of social engagements—breakfasts, luncheons, dinners, teas, receptions with spread tables, two, three, and four deep each evening—usually came as welcome distractions. Holmes was his entertaining self, reciting poems, leaving guests awestruck with his much-loved anecdotes—one favorite was the time he climbed a mountain in the Berkshires with Hawthorne and Melville, when Hawthorne couldn't stop talking about his new *Scarlet Letter* and Melville argued vehemently against Holmes's proposition that the English would always be superior to Americans.

He slept better while in Cambridge than he had on most of their previous stops. Their rooms in Nevile's Court at Trinity College were decorated with the imposing family ensigns of those who had lived there. Taking a stroll in the evening through the hoary library of Trinity College, he studied the marble busts. Holmes paused to look at the stern likeness of Alfred Tennyson, dated thirteen years earlier, showing a fresh-faced but already imposing poet.

The morning after Holmes received his doctor of letters, he found himself in a sufficiently tranquil mood to write—first a few verses, then a valedictory address on what a young physician should aspire to do. *The best a physician can give is never too good for the patient.* These exercises helped him. In younger years, he'd wonder whether he was more doctor or writer. Since the dark period back home, he questioned if he was really either—witnessing death all around him had robbed him of both.

He wanted to advise his imagined listeners . . .

I warn you against all ambitious aspirations outside of your profession. Medicine is the most difficult of sciences and the most laborious of arts. It will ask all your powers of body and mind. Do not dabble in the muddy sewer of politics, nor linger by the enchanted streams of literature. The great practitioners are generally those who concentrate all their powers on their business.

. . . if only it didn't seem hypocritical. Here he was, supposed master of so many arts, not just doctor but—as the titles of his three Breakfast Table books identified him—autocrat, professor, poet.

He was still in his dressing gown when the door shook with knocking.

Expecting Amelia or the college porter leaving his breakfast, Holmes bounded over. Nobody was there. He found a telegram that had been laid at his doorstep. It was from Robert Browning in London, and at first Holmes assumed it was another invitation to a literary gathering in the city—feeling a tickle of pride that the famous Browning, a poet who was even more respected than read, would be anxious to see him. Instead, the telegram contained a verse in Italian—

Maestro mio, che via faremo?

—which he swiftly translated as:

My master, what way shall we take?

Holmes, who was famous for his rapid step, never moved faster than he did to feed that telegram into the fire.

I t was six days earlier, moments after the forlorn pair of Christina Rossetti and Robert Browning had exited Scotland Yard into the unwelcoming fog, that Inspector Dolly Williamson, who so studiously ignored the frustrated literary callers, paused with a thoughtful expression at the desk of the constable first class, Tom Branagan. He put a hand on the brawny shoulder of the younger policeman, who'd conducted the interview, and waved him into his office.

Dolly's private office was not very different than the others at Scotland Yard. Except for two things. First, there was the number and varied selection of books on the shelves. Second were the plaster casts of heads along the wall, with ropes hanging alongside some of them.

Even in the midst of a crisis, other police affairs would find a way to invade Dolly's time. There were the silk curtains stolen from Windsor Castle that showed up at an auction house. There was the latest band of conspirators fighting for Irish freedom—over the years the diverse revolutionaries had come to be known as Fenians—arrested in a trap sprung by two of Dolly's detectives, Thornton and Clarke. Even though the Fenians' threats produced far less actual violence than garden-variety blackguards, the public feared them out of all proportion. But at the moment, Dolly couldn't take his eye off the case that he felt growing more perilous—and peculiar—every day.

"Well, Branagan," Dolly said, "there go our poets. What did you think of them?"

"They certainly seem to know Mr. Rossetti is in some kind of trouble and to have no better idea than we do of where he is."

"I said they would come here sooner rather than later, didn't I?" Dolly boasted with a grin that landed heavily on one side, like his hat. He had a fondness for being correct, a trait that suited this career. "Notice the younger Rossetti brother, William, wasn't with them."

"Inspector Williamson, why not tell Miss Rossetti what we know so far about her brother?"

"Branagan, a person will always be inclined to reveal more by *asking* questions than they will answering them."

"I am sure you are right, Inspector. However, now we've heard what they have to say about Mr. Rossetti. What harm could it do to share some of our information, to tell them, at least, about the sighting of Mr. Rossetti at the scene of the crime?"

Dolly thought about the suggestion before exiling it with a sigh. "Branagan, did you look into the eyes of that lady? Miss Rossetti has the eyes of faith. If she knew our suspicions . . . well, she'd tell us nothing."

"But what will she tell us now that we've dismissed her? It's doubtful she'll ever come back here at all."

"Now that she will presume we are uninterested in the issue of Mr. Rossetti, she and Mr. Browning will be more determined to do something about all this themselves. Especially when they read the *Ledger* and come across the information I gave Walker to write about. Mark what I say. Miss Rossetti and Mr. Browning could provide us revelations that, if they knew we are paying attention, they would not. For the moment, we continue to watch."

Dolly had already searched Tudor House and ordered Branagan to continue to shadow the movements of Christina, her brother William, and Browning. The detective was not intimidated by the celebrity of the visitors, nor the literary and artistic reputation of the missing Dante Gabriel Rossetti. Ever since he had handled a case that required him to trace the author and publisher of an anonymous book advocating the assassination of the French king, the commissioner selected Dolly for any matters related to books, authors, and artists. Even written and painted forgeries came to Dolly's desk. Dolly considered it an advantage that he did not look as though he read the enormous number of books that he did. He seemed wonderfully average.

It was the burden of the literary man or woman of a city such as London to feel themselves superior to the herds of common people. But Dolly felt confident that, if necessary, he'd outwit any ordinary genius. This case, in all events, had little room for error. With the murder of a member of Parliament, and the widow Morton assembling more public memorials than received by the ancient pharaohs, the Home Office roasted on hot coals.

A week and a half later, Dolly was searching through another box of materials Branagan brought to him. The constable had urged Dolly not to take more than an hour, when he would have to bring them back before they would be missed. It was fortunate, Branagan said, that none of the sinister animals of Tudor House had attacked him yet.

"Branagan." Dolly called him back to him after examining the spoils. "You've done decent work. Get your things together. We have a scenic ride ahead of us. We are on to our best witness yet."

"Truly? Who is it, Inspector?"

"Dante Alighieri."

VII

Robert Browning lagged behind Christina as they made their way up two long flights of stairs leading to Arthur Hughes's studio. The poet was impressed by how swiftly his companion, so much sturdier than she appeared, scaled the creaking treads in her restrictive skirts and heavy boots—or maybe he chose to believe she was quick moving rather than think his own fifty-seven years were finally slowing him down. Though he was average height, Browning prided himself on his physical strength, particularly in his shoulders and legs. Despite Christina's reputation for reclusiveness, she exhibited none of the hesitation Browning himself felt in entering these chambers, which emitted obscene shouts and the strong odors of cheap perfumes and cheaper tobacco.

How odd it had been at the Wapping gardens seeing her surrounded by society's discarded outcasts, while Christina herself was such a—well, what *was* Christina? She wore colors that were too dark and skirts that did not extend to her boots as was standard. She had been a beautiful if pale girl who avoided marriage. She was an astoundingly original poet who swatted away fame. Browning couldn't help but think of first meeting his Elizabeth when she was held in seclusion by her father. But Ba could not wait to be part of life, of politics, of movements. Christina cultivated her seclusion. With her complexion and the vaguely foreign rhythms of her speech, she really seemed to be taken out of one world and put into theirs.

Generally speaking, Browning wasn't shy about being out in society. He had appreciated hearing secondhand one acquaintance's comment: "I like Browning—he isn't at all like a damned literary man." He frequented dinners and concerts and plays. One magazine writer had even named him the poet most accessible to the common public in the history of England except for Chaucer. Browning, unlike Tennyson, hadn't gone to Oxford or Cambridge, cut off from such opportunity because his family had been dissenters from the Anglican Church; he started then abandoned London University, finding it useless. Still, the fact was that over the last years he felt himself become more accustomed, even reliant, on being around the wealthiest classes of London society. Especially as his poetry's popularity expanded.

Ba would have challenged it all. *Of course you seek company in white tie, Robert*—she might have reprimanded him—*because it will always be easier to make people like you in the dappled lights of chandeliers than through your poetry, which you would consider a failure if it didn't push away as many people as it invites in.*

"Aren't you coming, Mr. Browning?" Christina asked.

As Christina's gaze fixed on him, he realized she was the age Ba had been when he'd first met her. At least, he believed so. Ba, sensitive about being older than her husband, had been coy about revealing her exact age.

His legs had stopped and he was standing lost in his thoughts. "Apologies, Miss Rossetti."

At the top of the stairs, they entered into a labyrinth of easels, half-complete sculptures, and stacks of papers and canvases, along with an assortment of artists and their models. Hughes, a beardless man with a meticulously combed mustache and luminescent skin, seemed to be about to attack his canvas with his brush, though he withdrew his hand before committing paint to it. A young woman in a long, silky green dress stretched herself over a sofa in front of him.

"If you stay perfectly still and look at me as if I were Hercules," the painter was saying to the model, "I will cosmeticize you to appear the age you claim to be, but every time you move your chin I will add a wrinkle."

The model's eyes widened with fear—she did not move a muscle.

"If you leeches come here for rent," Hughes now declared with contempt to the approaching footsteps, continuing his pantomime with the brush and never taking his eyes off the woman, "then let me finish this commission so it shall come into your filthy paws all the sooner!"

"We do not come for money, Mr. Hughes."

Hughes put down his brush and slowly turned toward the woman's voice.

"Everyone!" he managed to say after a few sputtering attempts. "An honor, an honor. Everyone, at attention, please! What an honor, the queen, here in my studio!"

The other artists barely raised their eyes from their canvases or, in the case of one, from a pile of sketches on the floor used as a pillow. Hughes had become one of Dante Gabriel Rossetti's better-known disciples, but Browning did not recognize most of the artists, each of whom were Hughes's junior by at least half a dozen years. Hughes had been around in the days of the so-called Pre-Raphaelite Brotherhood, a league of men with ambitions—mystical and artistic—to change the world. Christina had been the only woman among them, and was loved in different ways by all the men there, known as Queen of the PRB. Glancing around the cavernous and decaying paint-splattered studio, Browning noticed relics from the lost days of their bygone Brotherhood, including a page on display called "Creed," with this somewhat sacrilegious heading:

We, the undersigned, declare that the following list of Immortals constitutes the whole of our Creed, and that there exists no other Immortality than what is centred in their names . . .

The names that followed included Shakespeare, Cervantes, the author of the book of Job, and, one that Browning underlined with his finger, Dante Alighieri. Each one had written of suffering and had suffered. The manifesto was in Gabriel's handwriting.

The Brotherhood exhibited their paintings around London and printed their poetry in select publications. They gradually received acclaim for revolutionizing art by overturning conventions—not by seeking out what was new but by salvaging the old and forgotten.

"Christina Rossetti, such an honor," Hughes reiterated. "And a pleasure to see you, Mr. Browning."

Hughes broke into a quote Browning heard regularly during encounters with his readers on London streets:

> *In a sheet of flame*
> *I saw them and I knew them all. And yet*
> *Dauntless the slug-horn to my lips I set,*
> *And blew. "Childe Roland to the Dark Tower came."*

"Oh, I have painted a few canvases inspired by your jaunty 'Roland,' which I admire so much, certainly far more than your *Sordello*. After reading it I still didn't know if Sordello was a man or a city or a wine. What is it the magazines always call you—'the greatest diner-out and second greatest poet in England'? They mean next to Tennyson, of course."

"Indeed," Browning said, wanting to wring his neck.

Hughes waved away his confused model and offered the sofa to Christina and Browning.

"Excuse the crudeness of my current canvas. Is there no girl in London who can inhabit the exact form of Guinevere I seek? Dante—I mean your brother, not the medieval bard—always tried to coax the rest of us into painting more scenes of Beatrice and visions from the *Divine Comedy*, but my mind's eye inevitably returns to our native legends. It is an honor to have two such esteemed poets in our studio, and always an honor to be in the presence of a Rossetti, or any friends of Dante's."

Browning and Christina exchanged a brief glance at the mention of the *Comedy*, then Christina returned the artist's compliments with a smile of benediction worthy of her nickname of queen. "Mr. Hughes, we do apologize for our making a visit without sending word first. But it is rather a pressing matter. We are curious about the day that Mr. Morton was found in such a horrifying state in North Woolwich."

The painter raised his brows in surprise. "Yes?"

"It is our understanding you were passing through the same area where it happened," she continued diplomatically, omitting that they were told this by a young prostitute. "We have personal reasons for wishing to better comprehend what might have been witnessed there by you or others."

"No," Hughes said, dropping into an irritated whisper. "I daresay you have me confused with someone else."

"I beg your pardon, but I don't believe we do," Christina started. "The fourteenth of January, early in the morning."

"Come, we don't care a straw about what you were doing there," Browning said, forfeiting Christina's patience and tact. When Hughes continued to profess ignorance, Browning added: "Perhaps your wife *would* wonder what you were doing out there under the cover of night!"

The painter deflected further questions and insisted on resuming his work before he lost the train of his vision altogether.

After they were back on the street, Christina did not say a word of reprimand. She would just as soon overturn a room of furniture as openly criticize anyone. But Browning knew she was silently condemning him for his temper. She had an inhuman way of withholding judgment so genuinely and completely, that whoever was with her presumed she must be judging as harshly as possible. He began defending himself against these imagined accusations, point by point. The more implacable her expression, the more he argued how the fault was Arthur Hughes's and not his.

"Mr. Browning! Miss Rossetti! Frigid as the North Pole out here."

Hughes came out of the building, walking toward them. Wearing a big smile, he shook their hands once again, and then apologized profusely for not answering their questions candidly. "You see, I did not want the others to hear that I had been at those gardens. Not because of the park whores, as you seem to believe, Mr. Browning. I have been doing a study of Londoners in gaslight and moonlight, from the highest to lowest members of society. Sometimes the whores are the best subjects, even if they tend to be shy about being painted, as they've lived such tragic lives. That's why I was there. You see? I did these that night in the gardens."

He held out a pile of sketches. Browning took them and placed them where Christina could see—rapidly drawn faces of men and women surrounded by chalky outlines of the night sky.

"Gentle with them, if you please, Mr. Browning! Those gardens are where I have been recruiting my best female models as of late, and I do not want any of those sneaks inside my studio to steal my territory. There is no honor as there used to be in the days of Dante's Brotherhood, before our round table of art and life was dissolved by illnesses, marriages, financial disappointments. I am already short on passable Guineveres, as I mentioned, and do not want them poached from me by lesser or, worse still, better artists. Why, I suppose the word must have already spread, if that is what Dante was doing there."

"Do you mean my brother?" Christina asked with a gasp. "You *saw* him? At the gardens in North Woolwich?"

Hughes's face twisted into a state of confusion. "Isn't that how you knew I was there that night? I just assumed Dante told you."

"You're saying you saw Gabriel there? The same time Jasper Morton was killed?" asked Browning.

"That's right," Hughes answered very slowly, suspecting their sanity. "He was in a funk, too, Mr. Browning. I tried to speak to him. 'Dante, where have you been? Dante, is that you?' I cried out. But he did not answer. He kept on walking before I could reach him. I believe Dante happened upon that poor politician, Morton, before anyone else who was there. He seemed to be standing right near the body before the rest of us noticed what had occurred. All right, my queen of us all?"

Christina stumbled back. "My head is spinning, Mr. Hughes."

"I think she might faint, Mr. Browning!"

"She does not faint," said Browning.

Browning steadied her anyway, and was glad she allowed him to help. He thought back to how upset Christina was when she believed Browning noticed that she *almost* cried as she held Gabriel's vial of choral hydrate—meanwhile, Browning could drop a tear just by finding Pen at his front door for tea! It was at that moment back in that dark bedroom of Gabriel's Tudor House that Browning knew he would stay at her side until the matter of her brother's disappearance was resolved.

It was at that moment, too, he knew he was doing this for her as much as for her brother.

He asked Hughes whether he had seen Gabriel since that day, which he swore he had not. Browning rattled off more questions for which Hughes had no helpful answers.

"One last thing, Mr. Hughes," Browning said before they parted from the painter. "Did you tell the police? That you saw Gabriel there?"

"They buried me in questions. As if I hadn't anything else with which to occupy myself. One of the 'shadow police'—the detectives—a Scottish fellow with shrewd eyes and a beard worthy of Moses, seemed extremely interested in the fact I'd seen Dante there. His name was Williams or—no, that's not it—Williamson. I believe he introduced himself as Inspector Williamson."

Dr. Holmes boarded the train to Liverpool, feeling his spirits lift. Having completed his tour of universities and libraries, entertained at dinners given by scientists and physicians and editors, he could move on to planning the next portion of their journey, on to Paris. Originally, father and daughter had expected a week or two in London before sailing. But since receiving the cryptic telegram from Robert Browning, Holmes made excuses to Amelia about the unhealthiness of smoky London, the Fenian threat, and the general degree of the city's chaos, until she crossed London off the itinerary.

When the train halted for more passengers on the way, Holmes recited a poem to a few delighted admirers while taking tea at the station before he and Amelia noticed the time and rushed back onto the train. As they reached their compartment in the first-class carriage, Holmes was beckoned. "Why, the famous Dr. Holmes!" Turning with a broad smile to greet another admirer, he found two somber men instead.

"The famous Dr. Holmes. Now, you know there are many pickpockets in the trains these days. Take care with that, it's quite handsome."

Holmes tucked the gold watch back in his vest pocket. "Do I know you, sir?"

"I'm Inspector Adolphus Williamson, superintendent of the Metropolitan Detective force," said this man, who was very tall and had a flowing beard. "Would the lovely Miss Holmes mind if we spoke privately?"

Amelia took her leave to return to their seats. Holmes followed the officers to an empty compartment, which, by the newspaper on the floor and the smell of sweat, had just been cleared of other passengers. Across from Holmes, Dolly Williamson and the younger man, Constable Tom Branagan, settled in.

Dolly gestured toward Branagan, who took this as a signal for him to hand Holmes a *Morning Post*. "Dr. Holmes," Dolly began, "a man has been killed some two weeks back in my jurisdiction in the style of Dante."

Holmes was thankful to be sitting. The whole scene came out of the distant corner of a nightmare. Somehow he found his voice to reply to the detective.

"How do you know about Dante?" Holmes asked.

"I'm not a fool, Dr. Holmes," Dolly replied. He gestured again at the constable, who this time reached into his satchel for a large volume he dropped on the seat next to Holmes. "Thank you, Branagan." Back to Holmes, Dolly said: "I know the same way everyone does these days."

Holmes recognized the book's green covers on sight. Henry Wadsworth Longfellow's ubiquitous translation of Dante.

"*Inferno?*" Holmes asked.

Dolly spun around the book so the gold-lettered spine faced Holmes. "*Purgatory*," the detective read aloud. "The man I'm speaking of had been crushed by a heavy stone, just as Dante reports witnessing on the—what is it he calls the different levels of the divine mountain?—the *terrace* of the Prideful. There was an inscription on the stone, and it even matched some of the language in the scene from Dante."

"Why tell me? It was a few years ago and I merely served as an occasional assistant, a kind of aide-de-camp, in Mr. Longfellow's translation. You might say I was heard more in the dining room than in the study."

"Nevertheless. You know more than most about Dante. So I thought you could help me understand something, Dr. Holmes. Dante tells us he travels through Hell before being transported up the mountain of Purgatory, then is brought to Paradise. As Dante meets the shades trapped in Purgatory, he doesn't feel the contempt he does for the residents of Hell. Does he?"

"No, he doesn't," Holmes said, nodding thoughtfully. "Dante actually tries to embrace the shades he meets early on the mountain, only to find his arms go right through them. Looking down, he notices that he is the only one who casts a shadow in the sunlight. He doesn't belong there. He is an outcast."

"Boccaccio offers a convincing explanation of how the terrors of Hell might be hard to look away from. What is it about *Purgatory* that commands a reader's attention?"

Holmes could have made any number of points. *Purgatory*, in some ways, was the most fascinating of Dante's three-part narrative about crossing through the afterlife. The middle canticle was replete with human drama and humanity. And surprises. *Inferno* implies that all suicides are assigned to suffer in one of Hell's circles, but guarding the entrance to Mount Purgatory is none other than Cato, the ancient warrior who stabbed himself with his sword instead of subjecting himself to the tyranny of Julius Caesar. *Purgatory* at first seems to chronicle Virgil's authority over Dante, but in fact turns on the need to separate from Virgil, the need to accept the partial wisdom of many temporary leaders in order to complete that portion of the pilgrim's quest. Even Virgil confesses he can only teach Dante so much, ultimately admitting: *It's for Beatrice only you must wait.* Then, another surprise. Dante's journey seems to be about reuniting with his beloved Beatrice all along, but upon reaching Beatrice, she behaves differently than anyone expects.

All of our guides, all of our leaders, must inevitably disappoint, must fail, must leave us to ourselves. *I crown you a lord and bishop over yourself,* Virgil declares to Dante with hints of pride and sadness.

There was another way *Purgatory* consumed its readers. Most people could feel that whatever flaws and mistakes they'd made in life, they in no way qualified to be placed among the ultimate evil of *Inferno.* Hell was for other people. But with the exceptions of some saintly types, Purgatory, with its excruciating torments, its long-enduring anguish, was for every single one of us.

It was an idea more terrifying than Hell.

"As I said," Holmes replied after thinking about all this, "I merely lent Longfellow a hand."

"We brought another book with us, Dr. Holmes," said Dolly, who again signaled the constable. This time a pamphlet was removed: *The Dante Murders.* "More booklet than book. I had a friend with a bookstall near Scotland Yard procure this particular copy for us, but from the interpretations I saw scribbled out by Mr. Browning and Miss Rossetti, we gather that one of the poets portrayed as being involved is meant to be you. Speaking of Miss Rossetti, her brother—the painter Dante Gabriel—was seen near the murdered man, and now cannot be found anywhere. Then there's his preoccupations with Dante. Please."

Holmes waved away the invitation to look at the booklet. "I suppose there comes a time when every lowly book in the library is wanted by someone."

Dolly scrutinized Holmes's face. "You're familiar with it. Very familiar."

"That booklet is pure fiction," Holmes answered, with the most conviction of anything he had yet said to the detective. "It was written by a disgraced Pinkerton detective who was mixed up somehow in the technology catastrophes a few years ago in Boston, and wrote something about that, as well. I believe he served time in prison. Name was Simon Camp. Why, he just tries to squeeze a profit from speculating in the fertile horrors of the public imagination."

"Like Dante himself," Dolly said.

"Dante never profited from the *Comedy*, Inspector, not in that way. It stole what was left of his youth. That poem became his life and death."

"No poet is ever really young," Dolly said quietly.

Holmes glared at him.

"Their delicate ears always hear the far-off whisper of death, which coarser souls must travel towards for years before their duller senses touch. It's a quote from you, isn't it, doctor?"

"A paraphrase," Holmes managed to admit.

The detective directed a long stare at Holmes, the kind of stare that went through a man's soul, and Holmes imagined, for a moment, he could trace the line of a kind of sly, lopsided smile beneath the detective's dense bushel of a mustache.

Dolly, the smile now fully exposed, removed a gold pocket watch from his coat—Holmes's. Holmes patted his vest in disbelief.

They all laughed. "I see your point about pickpockets," Holmes said as he accepted his watch.

"Well," Dolly said, "I suppose we're finished, Dr. Holmes."

"What?" Holmes was startled that, in the end, the detective relented so easily. "Why?"

"Do you wish to speak further, doctor?"

"For heaven's sake! No! What I mean is, after all that, well, why end our interview there?"

"Because just by looking at you, I can see well enough that you couldn't help hunt a murderer, like the pamphlet claims. What I mean to say: I believe you. You can stop worrying. I will find out who killed our Mr. Morton, don't doubt it, and with a little luck it will all stop there."

Holmes agreed, feeling relieved and, after another moment to mull it over, insulted.

VIII

Few stretches of London streets had this many dancing saloons, gambling houses, and grogshops. When night fell and lamps sputtered on over St. James's Street, the crowds grew. Some of the people hadn't woken up until shortly before. Others came here to forget the unpleasant or dangerous labors they carried out over the course of a long day among machines that kept up the industrial underpinnings of London and expelled their fumes. There were many sights that were commonplace around these streets but unacceptable almost anywhere else. Drunkards reeling, emptying the contents of their stomachs in the alleys while men and women in stupors, arms and lips linked, stepped over them.

Here, another example: A woman walked by in a dark blue cloak. She did not appear quite young enough to be one of the country runaways that fathers railroaded into London searching for. But she still had that bloom on her pretty cheeks that made her look as though she were freshly kissed. Her auburn hair fell loosely in waves as she staggered from one side of the sidewalk to the other. She waved her hands to catch herself and appeared as though she might lose her balance at any moment. In a more civilized quarter of the city, some Good Samaritan or at least Halfway Decent Samaritan or at the *very* least a pickpocket would have taken hold of her arm. The police might be notified—a fellow human was in trouble. Not here. Nobody here liked sending for police. A few people did notice her; a man laughed at her, a woman in the early stage of inebriation shook her head in sisterly disapproval.

Besides, this passerby was not the first young woman to be staggering and swaying over these sidewalks. In fact, she was not even the only one who met that description at this moment in time. There was a distinct air about her, though. A profound urgency.

A man followed a few feet behind her, watching her with an expression blending concern and fascination. His coat was buttoned up to the throat. His body was muscular but not athletic. His very round face exhibited the interest that, in spite of our better natures, each of us takes in a scene of distress. Something more sparkled in his hypnotic, deep-set dark eyes, which in narrowing emphasized the penciled ridge over his nose. Dante Gabriel Rossetti was studying every move, committing them to memory.

She stumbled again, this time off the sidewalk. She wandered into traffic and found herself spun around. There was a loud thump as her body collided with an oncoming omnibus and was thrown high into the air, landing clear on the other side of the street.

She came down on the iron railings in front of a house. The railing impaled her in four places.

Blood poured from the wounds, first slowly, then with a gush. Onlookers rushed over—now that she was mortally wounded, interest in her increased at a fast clip. The force of the impact was so great that, as the bystanders attempted to lift her off, one of the spikes of the railing broke off into her chest, causing her to howl in anguish. She remained sensible for a few more moments. She even spoke, though it was a struggle to eject her peculiar words, which sounded like, "There is no more wine."

Gabriel Rossetti joined the onlookers briefly, but when he felt eyes on him, he turned on his heel and walked away, as he had at the North Woolwich Gardens.

Meanwhile, those who had moved closest to the dying woman—a tavern keeper, a barmaid, the intoxicated workman who had laughed at the victim minutes before—could see her face clearly now under the glow of the gaslight. What they saw horrified them. What they saw was more terrible, if possible, than the spikes tearing apart her flesh. It was not drunkenness that had made her stagger and stumble into death.

I t was true what everyone said. Dolly Williamson hated to ever rest during a case in progress. This was not a product of impatience, to which Dolly hardly could be accused of succumbing. When he first moved from his family's home in the Scottish hills to London, he earned a name for himself as a very methodical clerk in the War Office. Then he resigned from civil service to apply to the police. "You're joking, Dolly. Turn yourself into a common policeman?" his friends protested. "I want an open-air life," he retorted, "and I won't be long in uniform."

No, as a rule he did not hurry life along. But he also hated missing any opportunities due to inaction.

As the superintendent of the detective division, Dolly was forever pushed and pulled at by the other detectives. Inspector Thornton needed him to authorize a bargain he was cooking up for his investigation into the latest Fenian activity. Thornton sent for Dolly from the back of a beer shop, up a flight of dilapidated stairs, and through a corridor stinking of stale liquor and burnt narcotics. After passing through two more doors, Dolly and Branagan came to a small chamber where Thornton waited for him. He wore an oilskin cloak and had a twitchy mouth that looked determined to yawn.

"I believe the Fenian bastards are planning something big," Thornton told Dolly.

"You always believe that, Thornton," Dolly said. "We just put four of them in Clerkenwell, and for two of them we still don't have enough evidence to take them to Old Bailey."

"Well, I believe that big, dark devil over there can help me nab some even choicer blackguards."

At the far end of the room was a large man wearing a turban and with skin the tint of brown parchment. He was kneeling on the floor toward the wall and emitted a chant in his resonant voice.

"What did you do to him, Inspector Thornton?" asked an alarmed Branagan.

"He's not hurt, Constable. He's praying, that's all," Thornton answered.

"Morning and evening," Dolly said, nodding. "Twice a day he prays toward the sun in Zend, an ancient tongue that few people on earth still know, Constable Branagan. That's Ironhead Herman."

Thornton gave a meaningful nod of agreement.

Confusion lingered over Branagan's face as he watched the scene.

"Opium is no longer the province of druggists and doctors alone," Dolly explained to the constable. "People have discovered an escape from the crush of the modern world around them, in forms and amounts never before consumed in England. Unavowed shipments come from India and other ports, away from official channels, never passing through tariffs or inspection for adulteration. Herman over there, Branagan, is one of our city's leading suppliers for hole-and-corner opium dens and the like, and I suspect that's where Inspector Thornton sees a move to make—isn't that so, Ironhead Herman?"

Dolly projected his question in a loud voice, and Herman turned toward them. The dark dots of his eyes danced with what seemed—for a moment, at least—amusement.

"You know I don't like waiting, Dolly," Herman said. "I *hate* waiting."

"I've come across evidence that can link our friend over there with some shady transactions," Thornton said.

"Bring him in, then," Dolly said. "Herman's been to the Yard enough; he can lead the way."

"See, that's where I have a better idea this time, Inspector," Thornton said excitedly. "I have reason to believe one of the Fenian leaders, Mc-Cord, has been trying to buy some of Herman's surplus phosphorus and other material for arms and explosives. If Herman keeps us informed, we can foil whatever scheme McCord and his Irish rats are hatching."

McCord—who boasted a dozen other aliases—was one of the generals of the Fenian movement.

"McCord is back in London?"

Thornton nodded. "He's boarding for now at Sixteen Lombard, Chief, but I haven't enough to pick him up yet."

"Very well, Thornton," Dolly replied after thinking for a minute. "I'll sign off with the Home Office if you wish, but don't underestimate Herman. He is as dangerous in his own way as the Fenians."

Thornton turned and glanced skeptically at Herman, who was now lying facedown on the floor, as though taking a very uncomfortable nap.

"Didn't you notice, Inspector Williamson," Branagan commented to Dolly as they exited, "even that big fellow sleeps."

Branagan would practically push Dolly out of Scotland Yard at intervals during their inquiries to force him to go home. Instead of going to bed as he promised he would, Dolly gardened. Or he walked around London. He could remember the feeling of freedom when he left the War Office as a young man and put on his blue "bobby" uniform to patrol the streets and direct traffic. His former colleagues in their fine suits would stop and gawk with pity. At night, instead of imitating other policemen of his rank by taking on private security assignments to supplement his reduced income, he took lessons in French and German, having observed the rapid growth of London's foreign neighborhoods.

He had been right about not remaining in uniform for long, and wasn't directing traffic for very long, either. He happened to run across a man near a mansion where a daring robbery had occurred. When the man gave Dolly an innocuous reason for being there, Dolly replied: "That's a lie." He had noticed the residue of lime on the man's boots and knew the substance came from the scene of the recent crime. The commissioner, hearing how the suspect came into custody, ordered that Dolly be transferred to the recently established detective division. Criminals came to fear being pursued by Dolly, who was assigned many a daunting mystery—that word Dolly himself came to hate as an excuse to leave a case unfinished—and he became so well-known that a number of English novelists based characters on him. Once, when it was reported that Dolly was given an infamous case of poisoning, the poisoner turned himself over to Scotland Yard instead of waiting for Dolly to hunt him.

The murder of the Honorable Mr. Morton was different, though. Dolly could sense that nobody was out there cowering in fear that he was on the trail. It was not the criminal but the public—and Dolly himself—who seemed to fear what might come. Every moment was of importance, he told Branagan. Yet here he was, wandering the streets at dusk, bracing himself against the cold, thinking about Dante Alighieri. Dolly had been a reader of all kinds and categories of books, but he began to believe there was something different about Dante, different from any other author he had read or learned about. Not only the subject matter of the afterlife, which most writers were too wise to approach. Dante had done what so many writers could only imagine—turned poetry into a living power, and a living power was something no one could cage inside the covers of a book.

The character Dolly liked was not Dante, the fervent and nervous poet journeyer, but his guide, Virgil. However out of place Virgil was on the mountain of Purgatory, he kept his composure and maintained control. Virgil played the part of a kind of detective—having been sitting quietly keeping his own counsel, when a troubled visitor, Beatrice, arrived to send him on his assignment. To save Dante's life.

Dolly heaved a big sigh as he kept on walking, and his eyes met those of a dirty child in ragged clothes. The boy's glance was shifty, uneasy, and the detective recognized the signs of desperation that led to petty crimes and, later, far worse.

Dolly stuffed a little money into the boy's pocket. "Good gracious, use it for food," he warned in German, recognizing the way the trousers lay on the boy's boot as being typical among that community. The boy nodded.

Crossing a footbridge over the Thames, Dolly gazed around at the dark, silent river lapping away at docked boats and at old wooden posts. He thought of the secrets—bags of stolen money, at least a dozen bodies—that the black water had given up to him over the years.

Nearing Smith Square, Dolly knew the quiet and solitude waiting in his parlor would only throw his mind back into the case. The time would hopefully come for a wife, maybe children, to join him there—but that was another realm of life in which he remained patient.

As Dolly got to his gate, a bobby waited on his front steps.

Dolly exclaimed, "Take me there!" before the policeman could say anything.

The visitor climbed onto the driver's seat of the carriage and raced Dolly through the night to the scene.

It had begun to drizzle. Branagan was searching for Dolly at the scene, with a host of other police and city officials.

"Inspector Williamson . . . ," Branagan began, seeming to brace himself for what he had to say.

"The eyes are sewn shut," Dolly said.

Everyone in earshot turned and stared at Dolly in amazement. Branagan raised his eyebrows, then nodded.

The crowd of blue coats stepped aside for Dolly. He moved closer to the body.

Dolly snapped his fingers. "Constable, the cyclops!"

Branagan opened his greatcoat wider. At the center of his belt was a lamp or "flaming eye," nicknamed by police as the cyclops, which Branagan shone over the scene.

"Name," Dolly ordered, frustrated not to recognize her.

"Miss Lillian Brenner, the prima donna of one of the opera companies, Inspector," someone answered—Dolly didn't bother turning around to see who was telling him.

"Lillian Brenner," Dolly repeated to himself. He cursed himself for knowing little about opera.

He ordered lanterns and candles be placed around the body for his examination. Blood continued to stream from where she had been impaled on the railings. Her face gave the appearance of being thoughtful. Her mouth hung open, her teeth white and regular. Just as Dolly predicted, her eyelids were sewn closed with wire. That had caused her blind stumbling into the street.

"Iron wire, looks like," Dolly said, wiping his brow from the hot lamps. "'The sin of envy is scourged within this terrace,'" he said under his breath, continuing: "'No man walks the earth that he would not be pierced with compassion for what I saw.'"

"Inspector?" Branagan replied.

"We've reached the next terrace, Branagan."

There was no blood around the iron wires—someone had taken care to clean it off, so as not to detract from the effect. Dolly gently pushed up one of the sewn eyelids with the tip of his finger. Tears, which had been caught inside, rolled down her cheek.

IX

Oliver Wendell Holmes steadied himself as he boarded the Paris-bound steamship at the Liverpool harbor. In what had become a kind of catechism the last few days, his daughter asked yet again if he felt himself coming down with something. Holmes swore he was healthy—as a lion. But once on deck, he immediately dropped himself into a chair and requested his medical valise. He extracted the breathing trumpet he used when he felt the signs of his asthma.

Everybody remained on deck as long as possible before they'd have to go below, even in this gusty, murky weather, which at least was a little warmer than previous weeks. Glancing around through the fog at the passengers, all wrapped up in blankets and rugs on the chairs, the deck looked as if it had a row of mummies on exhibition. Holmes didn't often experience the asthma that plagued his youth, but as Dolly Williamson's words circled his brain, he felt his chest constrict. He inhaled air through the long, hollow neck of the trumpet device.

Just by looking at you, I can see well enough that you couldn't help hunt a murderer.

The unwelcome feelings seemed—he convinced himself—attributable simply to preparing for a voyage on the ocean. He could never help but picture the ocean floor white with the bones of humans swallowed up by the waves over the ages. An old sea captain once told him the only way to get rid of those thoughts was to keep oneself under opiates until reaching the destined port—then again, opiates were the solution to every problem of mankind these days, as if the lotus-eaters of Tennyson's poem were in charge. Holmes did not mind the sounds of the rushing winds that would soon greet them at sea, nor the sight of the billows, nor even the impression of unending depths brought by looking over the side. But the sight of the boats hanging along the sides of the deck, which most people found reassuring, suggested doom to him.

He thought of the legendary figure of Ulysses telling Dante in a low circle of Hell how he piloted his ship toward the sight of Mount Purgatory, trying to skip right to salvation, when the waves began to overtake him.

There he was again! Dante, back in his thoughts!

Along with the usual baggage and mail being shuttled on and off the ship before departure, Holmes noticed something less typical, which disrupted the Dantean images in his mind. Constables. They strolled through with a highly artificial and unconvincing casualness. Holmes walked to the rails and looked across to another docked ship: more constables. Looking out from the port side, there was a ship that had just arrived that had not attracted the presence of the blue-coated officers. *They don't care who's coming in, no, they're looking for someone who might be trying to leave*, Holmes thought to himself.

He returned to his chair to close his eyes, but when he did he saw the scenes of *Inferno*-inspired death he tried so hard for the last four years to forget. These memories mixed with a vision of Christina Rossetti he'd been seeing ever since Dolly Williamson implied she was searching for her brother Dante Gabriel (and probably for Holmes, as he now suspected she had been a party to the telegram from Browning): the lovely and soft-spoken Miss Rossetti in fear for her brother, with the dashing Browning assisting her. All this swirled with the fragments of sentences he could hear from two constables conversing with each other as they walked by: *impaled . . . bloody . . . eyes wired shut.*

Holmes envisioned Dante Alighieri, pressing closer to the shades who suffered together on the second terrace up Mount Purgatory. "No man walks the earth," Dante cautions his readers, "that he would not be pierced with compassion for what I saw." The Envious lean on each other for support and guidance. Dante examines their eyes, sewn shut, and compares it to the hawks who undergo the same treatment to be trained not to fly away from their masters.

Was Holmes really hearing the constables correctly? Or was his treacherous brain tricking him, inserting Dante where he didn't belong? His eyes widened like a man trying to wake from a bad dream.

After Amelia settled the arrangements for the passage, she took the sea chair adjacent to Holmes. "Father, I refuse to even ask you again if something is wrong, because I know something *is* dreadfully wrong, even if you won't admit it to me. It has to do with that detective from Scotland Yard you met on the train, doesn't it? Terrible Inspector What's-his-name?"

He smiled wanly. Like him, she was short and youthful enough to be dismissed by many, and so persistent as to make the doubter sorry. *How do I explain a thing I cannot really explain? How can I explain that it is beginning again, or never stopped?*

She folded his right hand in both of hers, warming it between her leather gloves. "Heavens, you're trembling. I suspect, too, that this business has to do with the telegram from Mr. Browning while we were at Cambridge."

Holmes wore the face of a man about to object to an injustice.

"Come, Father," Amelia said with a sharply creased brow before he could speak. "I did not spy on you, if that's what you're going to carp about. I was taking a walk early that morning at the university, and the messenger gave me a telegram from London for you. *I* left it at your door."

Holmes protested that he couldn't breathe well in the cold air and needed to go below. She pointed out that Holmes always said he couldn't breathe belowdecks, either. He insisted.

"You never said anything at the university," Holmes began once they were inside the ship's small library, inhaling and exhaling in a deliberate rhythm. "About having read the telegram."

"I suppose I hoped you would tell me yourself when you were ready. When you didn't, I began to consider that whatever that telegram from Mr. Browning meant must have been upsetting. It meant little enough to me. It appeared to me to be Italian. What did it say?"

"It was a quote from Dante," Holmes said quietly, switching from one foot to the other as he scanned the ship's paltry selection of books on the shelves. "Dante has just entered the shores of the mountain of Purgatory, and asks his guide—the shade of Virgil who has escorted him all the way through the dangers of Hell—which path to choose in order to climb higher. The telegram translated as: 'My master, what way shall we take?' It's Dante's question to Virgil, showing his humility and his reliance on a guide. He has not yet fully become his own man, you see—though before he reaches the mountaintop, he must."

I crown you a lord and bishop over yourself.

Amelia nodded with interest. "Mr. Browning was communicating with you through Dante. He was requesting your advice, your counsel. I remember you constantly reading Dante some years ago when—well, at a time Mother was so worried about you she confided in me that she wanted to take you away from Boston to Providence or to Manchester-by-the-Sea, or anywhere away from whatever was going on closer to home. Now you again read Dante late into the night."

Holmes nodded. After Inspector Williamson and his assistant had announced the completion of their interview on the train, the detective had left behind the copy of Dante's *Purgatory* on the seat. No purpose on earth could compel Holmes to renew the conversation with the detective by trying to return the book to him. But he also could not just abandon the volume there among the debris of newspapers and cigar stubs. Dante had become part of him, whether he liked it or not. He took the book with him.

If there was one trait of Dante's that Holmes noticed every time he dared read him, it was bravery. Dante did not shy away from writing about bloodshed and violence; he converted it into beauty and poetry. He found meaning in the seeming cruelty and indifference of God's ways. Holmes could never find meaning in violence and disease.

His years as a medical professor had pushed him even further away, it seemed, from life and from death. He could recall sitting in the courtroom when his friend and fellow Harvard professor Dr. John Webster was being tried for murder. *Such an extravagant proposition*, the defense counsel told the jury, *why, we might as well suppose Dr. Holmes committed a murder!*

Holmes didn't know whether to laugh along with the rest of the courtroom or object (as if he had standing to do so).

I can see well enough that you couldn't help hunt a murderer.

"Whenever Dante's name came up," Amelia continued, "you always told me that Dante managed the improbable, to be a poet and a man in equal parts of his soul. I may not be a scholar of Dante, but I know there must be something you could do, Father, to banish whatever eats at you."

"The great thing in this world, my dear 'Melia, is not so much where we stand, but the direction we are moving. Thank you."

Holmes embraced her, giving her instructions and letters of introduction for the remainder of the European tour. Upon returning above, he found a porter and filled the palm of one of his hands with coins to bring Holmes and his trunks to the first train to London straightaway—and arrange a cab to meet him at the other end ready to drive to the home of Robert Browning.

Browning peered down from the large casement window as he soothed himself with a taste from his glass. He looked out at the tangle of chimneys and spires, the brickwork and woodwork of the other houses, attempts to keep the world out and the warmth in. He hoped he'd catch sight of Christina. He was more than anxious to hear what she'd say they should do now. Though he'd been the one to try to calm her in their initial meeting at Tudor House, as they had descended into the mysteries of her brother she proved to be the comforting force between the two of them.

The latest edition of one of the London newspapers was nearby, and he caught a glimpse of the society column. *Oliver Wendell Holmes, expected as a guest to literary and medical luminaries in London, has regretfully called off his visit to the city due to conflicts of schedule* . . . Browning tossed the paper away in frustration before he'd feel compelled to curse the selfish Holmes—who never replied to his telegram—or to read the latest crime columns again.

He steeled himself—their inquires would intensify with the news of another murder. He withdrew from as many of his social obligations as he could. There was one dinner in his honor he could not avoid, which he had attended the prior evening. Since the publication of Browning's four-volume murder poem *The Ring and the Book*, the degree of "Browningolatry," as his son called it, had increased manifold. People still criticized him for the poem's length and complexity, but they celebrated the narrative and the travails of the characters—to him, the least interesting and important parts.

What readers enjoyed most was what he was unmoved by; and what his ambitions thrived upon, a bold and metaphysical intricacy, left readers cold. "Childe Roland" came to him in a dream, with hardly any thought, and readers adored it. One thing he knew he couldn't do was alter himself. It turned out success wasn't something to achieve for Browning, it was something to conquer.

"Why not make it *easy* to read your verse?" a young man once asked him.

It wasn't that he tried to make his writing obscure. But he never pretended to offer literature as a substitute for a cigar, or a game of dominoes, to an idle man. He wasn't about to be Walt Whitman.

He had not planned on staying at the dinner long, and while the other men gossiped and traded amusing stories, Browning's mind wandered to Christina, to Dante Alighieri, to Gabriel. That literary gadfly John Forster was present, and seemed to sense Browning's distraction. He was the last person on earth Browning wanted to be near. Forster thrived on rudeness and felt he earned the right to say anything to Browning by publishing a laudatory review of his poems some thirty-odd years earlier. For the most part, Forster's close friendship with Dickens protected him from any repercussions for his behavior. The Dickens camp detested Gabriel Rossetti, too, the great novelist having declared the unorthodox art produced by Gabriel's Pre-Raphaelite Brotherhood at turns *mean*, *odious*, *repulsive*, and *revolting*.

It didn't take long at the dinner for Forster to target Browning. Forster mentioned that he had heard Browning had been seen often lately with Christina Rossetti. "I am glad to hear it, Browning," Forster continued, his jowls shaking with delight. "She was never as homely as her clothing. Perhaps Saint Christina has realized, albeit later than the rest of women her age in London, that she can do better than a barren life sputtering out verses as a vestal virgin—oh, but is she *still*?"

Browning felt the rage rush to his face.

"Dare to say another word in disparagement of that lady," he roared, "and I will pitch this into your head!" Browning lifted a heavy glass decanter over his shoulder.

It was almost comical how the whole table of diners encircled Browning—as though it would take six men to stop the poet from throwing the decanter of claret—while the pale and trembling Forster retreated to the next room under guard of a magazine critic and a playwright, planning out his complaints about it to Dickens.

Browning would never tell Christina what Forster had said. Not because he thought her overly sensitive, but because he knew how strong she was, and she did not deserve to hear insults from one who didn't understand her and never would. What many saw as her aloof languidness, he knew was serious observation of the world. What people believed was inflexible religiosity, he'd sensed contained a potent and unusual spirituality. What others thought her stilted cultivation in conversation, he knew held gentle wryness ready to be sprung on any unsuspecting pretentiousness. In the throes of what she felt passionate about—her family, for one— she became animated and alive, and Browning saw beauty where others didn't, as he had with Ba.

Now Browning scanned the street below his window. He removed his watch from his vest pocket. On the watch chain was also Ba's ring. It looked so *small*. Rather than reminding him of her, it made her seem unreal, as if no individual such as Elizabeth Barrett Browning ever existed. Nine years after her death, he was no longer unhappy, exactly, when thinking about Ba. He was resigned. An even worse feeling.

Browning set down his glass on the table and resumed pacing the room. He had only taken up port after living in Italy. Having so much wine in Italy had soured him on drinking it. Around him, all across the study, were books inherited from his father, who spent his life trying to make up for the fact that he worked in a bank, as well as remnants of the Brownings' life in Florence, including a portrait of Dante Alighieri. That portrait! That portrait in which Dante was missing one eye. That portrait, tainted with so many strange meanings.

During the fourteen years they lived in Florence, the Brownings' careers as English poets paradoxically flourished—the power of exile, it seemed. When Wordsworth died, both Brownings were said to be considered for the poet laureate position before it was awarded to Tennyson. Ba had laughed at the prospect for herself, but Browning wanted it for her more than he'd ever admit. He would have renounced all his ambition and would have destroyed every line he wrote, if by doing so she received the fame and honor she deserved.

It was in Italy where Ba got caught up in the craze of spiritualism. "My poor husband will make no profession of faith till he has the testimony of his own senses," she would say with a ringing laugh to her new friends before Browning had a chance to voice his skepticism about raising ghosts for the purpose of conversing with them.

How different it was than just a generation before. There were so many styles of worship in so many different churches now, so many sets and sects and subsets and subsects of religions, so many foreigners from other lands with other, peculiar beliefs; there were atheists and new secularists. Nobody knew what they were supposed to believe or what neighbors and relatives believed. Ghosts suddenly became as legitimate an option as anyone's god.

The gravest offender among Ba's spiritual advisors in Italy had to be old Seymour Kirkup, who moved to Italy thirty years earlier. The narrow angles of his face suggested aristocratic heritage, but the Englishman's eyes were wild and raw. In an Italian church, he had discovered a lost portrait of Dante in profile, a fragment of a fresco by Giotto that had been painted over. Kirkup, who fancied himself an artist, traced the portrait. (Dante's eye had been obliterated by a nail.) The discovery of the portrait, and the distribution of Kirkup's own copies, brought him acclaim from the artistic and literary worlds. But Kirkup was not content with resurrecting Dante's noble, war-wearied profile. He claimed to carry out regular and friendly communications with Dante's ghost.

Kirkup married the daughter of his maid, and proudly announced to the visiting Brownings that when his bride happened to be "in tune," she possessed great spiritual abilities.

The girl, who looked younger than the seventeen years of age Kirkup claimed, sank into a kind of trance during which, in a high-pitched Italian, she spoke as Dante. First, she—or Ghost Dante—said that Alighieri should henceforth be spelled with two *l*'s: Allighieri. With that settled after hundreds of years, Kirkup quizzed the ghost about Beatrice. He asked whether Beatrice was a real Florentine lady. *No*, said Ghost Dante in the grating voice of the maid's daughter. Who was she, then? *Era un'idea della mia testa*, came the reply. *An idea of my mind.*

It made Browning burn to see the delight on Ba's face at the charade of supposed ghostly séances. What was it that made this brilliant woman and poet he loved so wholly believe fabrications and utter frauds? Their disagreements on this topic became arguments. Somehow his refusal to think ghosts were anxiously waiting to speak to them or to rap on tables became coupled with his distaste for cigars. "It would do you good to smoke occasionally, too," she snapped, before citing Tennyson and his ever-present pipe. "Well, if the great Tennyson does it . . . ," Browning would retort. *Tennyson knows all, Tennyson sees all, every woman would rather marry the all-knowing, all-seeing, queen-beloved Tennyson!* Those arguments—arguments over nothing—haunted him after her death, genuine haunting of a sort he was sure none of those spiritual mediums could recognize.

His blood would cool; he would tearfully apologize. "I love you, Ba, because I love you." He'd celebrate their wedding on the twelfth of every month, which would always catch her by complete surprise. She never knew the date.

After her death, Browning tried remaining in Casa Guidi, their home in Florence. He appeared solid enough, keeping in one place like a worm-eaten piece of old furniture. But when he tried to move, to do anything, he went to pieces. He remembered, around that time, being in a plaza and catching sight of Tennyson, who was traveling in Italy with his wife and boys; Browning ducked out of sight—he could not tolerate having to greet the perfect family and the perfectly rich and successful poet. Browning pulled his hat down to hide his face, though it was not necessary since Tennyson couldn't see an inch away from his nose.

Kirkup kept calling on Browning and bothering him about taking a copy of the rediscovered Dante portrait. Since Browning never wanted to see Kirkup again as long as he lived, he agreed to purchase one, in hopes the old ghost-wrangler would have one less reason to harangue him.

When Browning returned to London, his friends dutifully called on him. Gabriel was the first at his doorstep and the only one who didn't try to cheer him. He just sat with him. Talk turned to religious balms for grief. "I have a knowledge of a God within me," Browning said, pointing to his heart and pausing. "I know him, he is here, and it matters little to me what tales anyone tells me about him; I smile, because I know him." Gabriel chewed on his lower lip, then in his deep, velvety voice said, "I lack only a confessor to give me absolution for all my sins." It was the first time Browning had laughed since Ba died. He laughed until he felt sore, then cried.

He didn't have to put on a performance with Gabriel, but Browning did his best to reassure most visitors. Days, weeks, years could go by. He could continue on, he could grow old. But he could not feel he'd ever take root in life again any more than, at his age, he could think of learning a new dance step. In a few short years, Pen would be a full-fledged adult, and Browning couldn't think what he would do with his own idleness then.

There were bleak times. Christmas. New Year's. Birthdays (his, Hers, Pen's). Those times he wasn't so sure he wanted to grow old without Her. He'd try to pray, but he, too, had been raised with an ineffective jumble of spiritual influences. He had no particular church allegiance. He tried out atheism and vegetarianism, though neither suited him; he enjoyed the family lore that he had a Jewish ancestor. He always came back to the belief that creeds, religious and otherwise, were for those who did not have sufficient internal moral guidance.

The magazine writers, when faced with a blank column and nothing to write about, sometimes took to criticizing Browning's new life in London. He spent his time in gilded salons, they would sniff, of the great and wealthy, snobbish like his poetry. He was fond of expensive Scotch. (He hated it, but the writers had mistaken his port for it.) He liked to be among refined people who appreciated him. Very well. But what did any of it have to do with poetry? Besides, mixing with society and the friction of ideas were necessary things to a writer. These were the arguments Browning would make to himself or to sympathetic companions. He would never say—hardly ever let himself *think*, really—how he needed society for a more pressing reason, to avoid the emptiness that existed without Her.

After the death of Lizzie Siddal, Browning made himself available to Gabriel. It was not only to repay Gabriel for being there when he returned to London after his own Elizabeth died. He knew what Gabriel was experiencing and, selfishly, having a companion whose wife was torn away would mean Browning was not quite so alone.

But Tudor House had been the oddest of odd places for two widowers' grieving. It once came out in conversation, somehow or another, that Browning had never seen a raccoon. Gabriel couldn't have been more excited. He rushed Browning to a large packing case with a slab of marble on top of it. He induced Browning to help him move the slab. Gabriel then dipped his hand inside, pulling out his latest creature by the scruff and holding it up as it bared its teeth and tried to claw at anything close enough.

"Does it not look like a devil?" Gabriel asked with an open-mouthed smile.

Gabriel had worshipped Lizzie, as Browning had Ba. At times, Browning felt alienated by Gabriel's version of grief. Séances, for example. Browning would call on Tudor House and there would be yet another medium discovered by Gabriel or one of his bons vivants who swore Lizzie's spirit was impatient for contact.

All the frustrations Browning had felt from Ba's interest in spiritualism returned with Gabriel's enthusiasm. The medium, while searching the afterlife for Lizzie, announced contact with Gabriel's uncle John who, through knocking on the table, indicated he hadn't committed suicide, as was believed, but had been murdered after the publication of *The Vampyre*. When Gabriel promised to reach out to Ba's spirit, Browning excused himself. If it had been anyone but Gabriel, he would have shouted and screamed about the cruelty of charlatans. But he could never bring himself to try to take away Gabriel's faith that, one way or another, Lizzie might return.

Each had to pay tribute in his own way. For Browning, it had been *The Ring and the Book*. He first found the story at a bookstall in Florence in an old yellow scrapbook of personal accounts and newspaper clippings of a seventeenth-century murder of a young woman and her family. Browning was enthralled and repulsed. Ba was certain: *You must turn it into poetry, my love. Tell her story.* It was the last idea for a book he ever discussed with her. Browning tried to rid himself of it. He wrote to Tennyson to beg *him* to write it. (*This is not mine,* Tennyson wrote back in a moment of gentle sensitivity, before adding, *and it is doubtful it can ever be popular.*) Browning knew that however bloodcurdling the story, it was his great venture.

He had come to basically live upon milk and fruit, usually did a good morning's work, went to bed early, and got up earlyish. But as Browning continued to wait for Christina, he realized they had all slipped in the wrong direction. Not away from the past sorrows, but heading inexorably toward more, more sorrow, more death.

When there was a pull at the doorbell, instead of finding Christina, Browning opened it on a man in a cabdriver's hat arranging a pile of trunks.

"What is this about? Whose are these?" Browning demanded, before he looked past the driver.

At the curb was a carriage; Oliver Wendell Holmes stepped down and sprinted toward the house, out of breath as though he had run the whole way from Liverpool.

Shrews! No I won't!"

Even Saint Mary's, so cloistered behind its high walls, seemed to fall under the spell of disorder that had spread across London. While Christina was instructing a group of girls whom she'd classified as illiterate or nearly illiterate, there was a commotion from the hall. Two nuns were trying to calm one of the newer girls, who was shouting.

"I won't! No, I won't *just quiet myself down!*"

The two guest preachers that day, Reverends Anderson and Fallow, offered assistance. Anderson tried to perform a blessing on the girl. "Sibbie, please take these," Fallow said, giving his handwritten sermon to a quiet, dark-haired woman who had come along to assist him.

"Steady there, my young friend," Reverend Fallow was saying, in a skillfully reassuring tone. "What is her name, Sister?"

"Ruthie," answered a nun.

"Steady there, Ruth," Fallow purred.

The unruly girl continued. "No, nothing steady about it, preacher! No friends here, you're our jailers!"

Ethel had also been trying to intervene and sprang to Christina's side.

"What happened to Ruthie, Ethel?" asked Christina.

Some residents were suspicious or hostile to the greener girls who were in the position they had been as little as a few months before, but not Ethel. She was always a sympathetic advocate.

"In prayer circle, she wished to talk about how she came to be here, about a man who punched her for sport, and her baby who was ripped out of her arms."

Christina nodded with compassion. Ruthie flouted Saint Mary's strict rule that the residents not speak of their pasts, and certainly not taint the purity of the nuns' ears.

"She'll be sent to the workhouse, won't she, Sister Christina?" asked Ethel, her eyes filling with tears. "Or turned over to be inspected by the government physicians. I know it. Oh, how awful it is, poor lass will run right back to the streets for sure, and be as likely to end up with a slit throat as anything else."

"I'm certain it will be all right," Christina said, not certain at all as she watched with sadness the nuns and Saint Mary's wardens escorting the offender out of sight.

Christina always walked with a martial gait, but when she exited Saint Mary's, she moved at a clip even more decisive than usual. Since the evening she and Browning had visited Arthur Hughes's studio, she continued searching for details about what Gabriel could have been doing on the Wapping side of the Thames when Mr. Morton was discovered. She had begun to have flashes of unwelcome memories—memories of stories she had been told long ago by her mother and aunts about searching for *their* brother—Christina's uncle.

A kind of British version of Oliver Wendell Holmes, John Polidori was a physician also known for his writing. Polidori, spurred by a challenge posed in the presence of Mary and Percival Shelley and Lord Byron, had written a tale about a monster inspired by foreign folktales largely unknown to the English-speaking world. *The Vampyre* ended up being published without Polidori's knowledge, and readers became obsessed with the book's subject and with guessing its author. Many thought the author was Polidori's friend Lord Byron. Some said this odd circumstance of Polidori's art taking on its own separate life drove him mad. He disappeared, sending his family into a scramble until his body was finally discovered. Uncle John poisoned himself with cyanide.

I knew, her mother had reluctantly told her, *as soon as my brother disappeared, I knew I would never meet him again in this world.*

Christina's thoughts had turned to her uncle as she headed to wait for the omnibus, until she was hailed—and for a moment her heart skipped. The voice was Gabriel's.

Until it wasn't. "There you are. Finally. That silly charity home of yours is the one place where I knew I could find you," William Rossetti said.

"You found me, William," she said flatly.

"Have you discovered anything new?"

She wanted to boast of progress, but her demeanor crumbled. She knew he would pounce.

"Christina, you are risking your health with this useless exercise. I do not want that and Gabriel—wherever he is right now—would never want that."

"If you are no longer assisting the cause, I thank you not to interfere with it and certainly not to tell me what Gabriel would want, as if he is not as much my brother as yours."

William's practiced sigh came from a life surrounded by artists. "Do not say such unfair things, Christina. The 'cause,' is that what it is? Didn't I probe line by line of that grotesque pamphlet on the Boston murders at your request? But there must be limits. There are natural limits to everything, and we ought to respect them. This is a matter for the police to finish—*the police* alone."

"Do you think they can ever be as versed in Dante as we are? It is in our blood. Do you ever wonder what would have happened if Father had not gotten out of Italy when he did, William?"

William groaned. "I heard the story as much as you."

The professore would stare out the window, recalling it all with a bitter smile. *Closer, my bantlings, hear of my time as a hunted fugitive.* Ferdinand I had declared the professore a criminal for his poems critical of the ruler. The professore went on the run in Sicily. It was an admirer of his poetry, the Englishwoman Lady Moore, who saved him. She was in Italy with her husband the admiral, who sent a squad of naval men to drill in front of the house where he was hiding. Meanwhile, the professore was given a blue jacket and slipped out into the drill, marching with the Englishmen right onto Moore's ship. *You, my bantlings, are in your own country but I have always been an exile.*

"You heard it but you never really listened. Everyone thought he was as good as dead," Christina continued. "His life, the lives of his future family, all saved because one person, one woman, a heroine to all Rossettis, believed in him."

Christina stopped and smoothed out her dark dress. Since childhood, she had developed her methods for suppressing any outbursts of temper or anger—for remaining steady no matter the chaos ensuing around her. Making adjustments to her clothing was one of these tricks that carried into adulthood. "We know that Arthur Hughes told the detectives he saw

Gabriel at the North Woolwich Gardens. The police already knew that when I called at Scotland Yard with Mr. Browning, and yet indicated nothing of the kind."

"Maybe you spoke with the wrong person at the Yard," suggested William.

"Inspector Williamson—the head detective for the case of Mr. Morton—was standing there as we spoke to the constable. He was *listening*. He wanted it to seem he was not paying us attention, but he was."

"Why would he do such a thing?"

"Think of it. Gabriel is seen at the place of Morton's death before anyone else knows what happened. At the same time, Gabriel disappears from public view—even from his family. He is a known fanatic of Dante's poetry and ideas. It is not much of a leap to read the story Inspector Williamson must have in this."

"Sounds reasonable to me."

She began walking down the sidewalk again. He followed at her side. The omnibus was coming on at a roaring gallop.

"Please, listen to reason, Christina. When we were children, you stopped playing chess even though it was one of your favorite games."

She slowed down her steps, curious in spite of herself at the point he wanted to make.

"You stopped playing chess because you said it made you too eager to win. That it was an unworthy emotion for a Christian woman. Perhaps this puzzle with Gabriel is merely making you too eager to win, to be the first to resolve it before anyone else, whether you are equipped to do so, and whatever darkness it will force into your life."

The conductor on the platform shouted for passengers.

"Mr. Browning is waiting. There has been another death in the style of Dante, and we must decide our next course of action."

"It is as the professore used to say: you and Gabriel are the storms, Maria and I were the calms. Only while you grew to master your passion, Gabriel gave in to his, and Maria gave hers up in exchange for God. Our brother may have the voice of Jacob but he has the hands of Esau. Do you not imagine I would have liked to live every day without duty or worry, Gabriel-like? I am left as the head of the family, Christina, and as such I forbid you from boarding that omnibus to Mr. Browning's. I cannot stand by as Gabriel's irresponsibility leads you to become as lost as he was!"

"*Was!?*" she responded, her heart breaking.

The conductor gave her a hand to the ladder. She willed herself not to look out the window at her brother as the vehicle pulled away.

Nineteen Warwick Crescent, Browning's residence, was as lonely and quiet as Christina knew her own home would be one day, whenever her mother was gone. Amid all the Florentine bric-a-brac of Browning's study, the marble bust of Elizabeth Barrett Browning stood out. Browning's late wife seemed to give a questioning glare at Christina's presence, and Christina knew that by now the gossips of the London literary world would do the same. Elizabeth's black haircloth chair supported a stack of books—a way of stopping anyone, Christina thought, from trying to take her sacred place. She put a hand carefully on the back of the chair, then lifted it off as though the furniture was burning.

Just an old maid.

Christina learned from Browning's butler of the surprise arrival of Dr. Holmes; Browning had stepped out to take Holmes to a nearby telegraph office, where the doctor was to send some wires about his changed plans and to secure certain arrangements for his daughter as she continued her travels.

Meanwhile, William's exhortations blotted out what might have been elation at the news about Holmes. Standing on Browning's terrace, the cold air washing over her, she shut her eyes tightly, suppressing her tears and memories until it became painful.

After boarding Admiral Moore's vessel, the professore eventually fled to London, which he thought sounded ideal for an entirely new life, akin to Dante's *La Vita Nuova*. His pockets were picked twice the week he arrived. He would teach Italian and he would labor over his masterpiece, his great commentary on Dante. He had found in the *Divine Comedy* secrets that, he claimed, were earning him dangerous enemies who wanted to destroy him.

Concealed in Dante's text, he insisted further, were the mysterious mechanisms to overthrow all the corruption and degeneracy in the world. He also insisted that his work would elucidate the mysterious and previously misunderstood role of Beatrice. Those who thought she was merely the object of Dante's love were terribly mistaken. She was a spiritual representation of truth, and should be embraced—like the Virgin Mary—as a kind of guide to the moral life for all mankind. The professore was certain a vast fortune could come to him and to his family from completing his text on Dante.

The professore, on a typical day, would come through the door after teaching whatever students he could recruit, and sleep on the rug in front of their fireplace on Charlotte Street. When he had restored his strength, he would go to his desk where his books on Dante were open. Their father was a little man with a broad face and forehead and strong open nostrils. The children, hearing him grumble and shout about Dante, began to stay away from their father's desk, afraid they might meet Mr. Dante himself in the shadows. Once, Gabriel tried to sneak into that dark corner and capture the hated Mr. Dante for himself. When the professore found out Gabriel had trespassed into his private territory, he glared at his son and told him, in a tone that suggested neither condemnation nor compliment, that Gabriel was a born rapscallion. ("He takes after the Polidori side," Christina once heard their father say to their mother. "Your *pazzo* brother John, murdered by a book.")

She remembered Gabriel strangely unmoved that he had been caught in the transgression. Had it been her, she would have dropped dead of humiliation. Then again, Gabriel always experimented with his effect on people's emotions. When he was young, he developed an alarming habit along these lines. He would make himself appear to be lame and, when a bystander would try to help, he'd run off in a fit of laughter.

The fact is, she'd come to hate Dante Alighieri.

He had been like a banshee, his screech always audible but not examined. For years, she read Shakespeare, Milton, anything but Dante. But living in the Rossetti household made her an unwitting expert and, over time, a reluctant appreciator. Dante had formulated the most perfect romance, a love so pure for a woman that it guided his entire life, even after Beatrice's death. *Especially* after her death.

Dante, ensnared by politics and hatred on earth, could only be disentangled from his past and renewed for the future by exploring the world of desperate ruin (Hell, or Inferno), the world of pain and hope (Purgatory), and the world never seen by mortal eye (Paradise). For Dante, simply put, Beatrice connected our world with God, the essential role of an angel whose form we know but whose mind and heart transcend our understanding. Centuries could not exhaust the wonder, sympathy, awe, and admiration that Dante left behind by responding to all that was lovely and terrible.

Christina never stopped being wary of the horrors of the Florentine's punishments. Gazing down a precipice fascinates the gazer enough to think of what a shattering fall must be like. So it was with sin and retribution. She had to put aside those reservations. She had to inhabit Dante's vision so completely that she could pull Gabriel out from inside it.

Christina saw herself, as though in a dream, as a girl around six years old. Such a louder, wilder being than she'd become.

There. *There she is.*

They are at her grandparents' home in Holmer Green, surrounded by fields. She finds her father under a reading lamp, though the day is sunny and beautiful and everyone is outside. She is caked in mud and tells her father of a dead mouse she found that she buried in a mossy bed. The professore laughs and laughs, compliments her rosy cheeks and sparkling eyes, her face like a little moon risen, tells her to return to playing "like a butterfly among the flowers, and when I see you next, my impertinent darling, vivace

Christina, you shall be prettier still." He sneaks her a fig, which he keeps hidden from Frances, who doesn't approve of sweets for the children.

She returns to the spot she marked where she buried the mouse earlier that day. She slowly moves the moss coverlet, and a black insect squeezes out. She flees in horror.

She scurries inside, but they are no longer at Holmer Green. They are in their little house on Charlotte Street in the city. By her eye level entering the room, she is ten years old, eleven maybe, as she runs to the grand desk over which her father is slumped, long locks of white hair spilling down his shoulders. She begs him to look at a drawing she had made of a wombat at the zoo, when turning around the professore scolds her for interrupting his train of thought—something about discovering a pattern inside Dante's medieval stanzas that would spell the final doom for the modern papacy. "What do you think, young lady, could be more important than that? Pull those curtains back, the sun stings me. Do you know not the rules to follow, after the many times I've announced them? If you are ever to be wanted as a worthy man's wife, you must learn obedience, deference!"

The girl scrambles upstairs, weeping so hard she can't breathe. She grabs a pair of scissors and rips up her own arm, watching the blood rise up in large drops and collect into a unified stream, dulling the sting of her father's rebuke. The tears dry up as the blood flows.

Gabriel's footsteps follow, and he pulls his sister—now in the dream-vision five or six years older, slipping from a girl into a young woman, even as he metamorphoses into a strapping buck—pulls her into one of his strong shoulders. Forget Dante, forget their father. Father's an exile from his home country, says the older brother. He shuns daylight, and makes a goblin of the sun. He has lost his people, and so have we; we must protect each other to survive.

"Miss Rossetti," Browning called out from inside. "I have Dr. Holmes with me. My dear, are you unwell?"

Christina stood in the wintry sunset on the terrace, gripping her arm as though the skin around the old wounds had ripped wide open.

———

The flat center of his bare foot digging into the tip of the ladder, his other foot balancing in the air, his large body wobbled in rhythm with the motions of his hands. He assailed the wall with paint, thrusting his brush back and forth, shouting in frustration from time to time, and throwing the brush into the air. He would then reach for another one, certain that *this* brush would meet the unrelenting, intoxicating demands of his vision. Few of the techniques he used would be sanctioned by the art masters of London, but it was hard to quarrel with the beauty and power of the results so far.

As the painting progressed, the massive chamber began to transform from an empty, useless place, an echo of soulless monotony, into a space made for this fresco, rather than a fresco made for the space. Dante Gabriel Rossetti struck and swiped, had tantrums lying down, naps sitting up, overturned his easels, then resumed creation.

I still hope to be an outcast from humanity one of these days, he recalled saying to someone—perhaps it was Robert Browning. Browning's solicitations and attention toward him sometimes turned into spying. He wondered if Browning could understand what all this was about. An announcement. A declaration. Browning—of all men, he who held Elizabeth Browning in his arms as she breathed her last breath—must have understood finally that death and art were inseparable.

Verses he had composed floated through his mind, giving him a rhythm to paint by.

> *Could I have seen the thing I am today!*
> *The same (how strange) the same as I was then!*

Gabriel went to work again. The image, as it came to fruition, showed a variety of tableaux, a panorama of living nightmares—one depicted a man crushed by the weight of stone on his shoulders, another revealed a woman suffering with eyes sewn closed. The solitary painter paced and stomped, raged at the sunlight streaming in to blind him, punched the wall here and then there, filling the place with clouds of dust. Then he'd return to his labors.

There was an incomplete portion in Gabriel's panorama in progress, a painting of a cloud of smoke, dark as night. This, the next step, the next revelation, the next ledge to reveal that made the depths of Hell timid by comparison: the terrace of the Wrathful.

CANTICLE
TWO

A few piers down the harbor from where Oliver Wendell Holmes disembarked—only half an hour later going by the nearby clock tower at Salisbury Dock—another American stood tall on the deck of an ocean liner. The three-masted *Daniel Webster* had just made its arrival. The visitor in question brought to England one sole-leather trunk, two gun cases, and the mission of a lifetime; a mission combining literature, life and death, and a great fortune.

Simon Camp, a scowler from birth, scowled over the railing at the dirty masses of people along the docks. The Pinkerton detective agency had cut ties with him before, when he was convicted for extortion and assorted peccadilloes, though Camp got a laugh by regaining his original position through *more* extortion after his release—extorting old Allan Pinkerton himself. But now the Pinkerton detective agency had struck him from the payroll once and for all after discovering he was the author of four anonymously published twenty-cent pamphlets about cases he'd investigated. Camp decided not to fight this latest dismissal. The job hadn't been worth the bosh that he dealt with most of the time, and he preferred relying on his own judgment than another man's any day of the week.

He wanted to write a new crime pamphlet, and, with the extra time on his hands after his latest schism with the rotten, double-dealing, beastly

Pinkerton, he had found his perfect opportunity. When he read in the foreign news columns of the *Boston Herald* about the dead politician discovered in a London public garden, he recognized similarities—possibly a direct connection—to the gruesome Dante murders in Boston he'd gained a pretty penny writing about (losing those pennies subsequently, which was an entirely different story). That's when he booked his passage across the Atlantic. Now, upon arrival, practically as soon as he stepped down to the harbor, there was a ready-made scene for his pamphlet-in-progress!

Camp studied the police constables flitting back and forth along the piers, some of whom were the same ones Holmes glimpsed earlier that day. Bloodhounds yapped and howled as they ran up and down lines of passengers waiting to board. This wasn't just the usual customs operation looking for pirated books to confiscate and restricted goods upon which to heap extra fees.

Liverpool, the dirty and ugly gateway to England, in the lazy late winter of 1870, amid the decidedly English stench of mutton pie and horse dung, witnessed a horde of police "bobbies" and their dog detectives scouring the seaport, all looking, hunting, searching: but for whom? A ghastly and heartless murderer still nameless to all but the fiend himself!

He scribbled these words into a pocket-size notebook and punctuated his creative burst with a chortle of joy. When he later reached the train depot, he would find an even more promising development, for his purposes, than the sight of the constables. The papers hawked by the newsboys would inform him that a woman died in yet another method taken from Dante. Dante had a natural imagination for inventing torments. In fact, the surly Italian poet never seemed to run out of them.

This mission would be even easier than Camp thought.

And Camp's own narrative would be able to feature a different champion this time. Not gawky students as in the story of the so-called technology disasters of '68 (a pamphlet he'd entitled *Science Run Amok*), not stately poets as appeared in his original *Dante Murders* booklet, but *him*, Simon Thomas Camp (S. T. Camp, he thought of styling himself). This time, he would resolve the mystery by himself, unveil the identity of the murderer, and chronicle it every step of the way. He would be the alpha and omega. He would be the teller and the hero of the tale. *Like that Dante fellow*, he thought to himself, proud of how he'd educated himself since the first time he heard that name from the lips of a Harvard swell: Dante, a name that had already changed the course of his life, and was about to again.

Dante, abbreviated from the Italian's given name, Durante, or at least that's what Camp remembered reading in some dull-as-lead book.

Dante, a name about to carry him back to wealth and glory.

The opera proved a rousing success. Spontaneous cheers interrupted the performance several times, nearly one-third of the audience stood for an ovation at intermission, encores drew the lead female soloist back to the stage at the conclusion, and only twenty-four audience members were counted sleeping.

Perhaps just as satisfying was the number of distinguished members of the audience, including politicians, businessmen, philanthropists, and literary lights such as the poet Robert Browning.

Browning's natural element—society. His brilliant white tie and waistcoat, his spotless dark frock coat. *Mr. Browning, the greatest diner-out and second greatest* . . . Browning tried to drown out the words still ringing in his ears from his visit to the Hughes art studio. When he had reached the box in the upper tier he'd reserved for the performance, champagne and a plate of galantine awaited him. Browning took a bow at the round of applause given by the audience members who noticed him enter—as though he were one of the tenors for the evening's show. His shoulders were practically as broad as theirs, at any rate.

The opera told the story of a woman rescuing her husband from imprisonment. Not that Browning concentrated much on the drama of the opera, not with so much on his mind, ranging from the plans made that very morning to events that took place five hundred and fifty years before (approximately speaking).

The thoughts that dwelled in those centuries long past belonged to the world of Dante Alighieri. It occurred to Browning that he was now about the age Dante was when he died. Unlike the sociable Browning, the great Florentine had been a severe man, by most accounts, though the earlier poet supposedly was courteous enough unless provoked. As Dante walked the lonely lanes of out-of-the-way Tuscan villages, the peak of his red cap drooping to one side of his head, he faced one of the many crossroads in his life.

His wife and children pined for him since his exile. The hidden victim of his adoration for the memory of Beatrice was Gemma, Dante's wife, whose thankless lot it was to be compared with angelic perfection. Now the poet had to choose between devoting himself to his poem—one that would probably take the rest of his life to complete—and initiating all-consuming plans to transport his family to be by his side. It was a decision all poets and artists make at one time or another, whether to stymie their art on behalf of the people they loved.

There was the anecdote from around that same time recounting when Dante, as he strolled along in contemplation, heard one of his sonnets being sung—but with phrases added that didn't belong. Dante followed the song until he came upon a blacksmith striking his anvil. He entered the workshop, took the blacksmith's hammer, and threw it across the street, and did the same to more of the man's tools.

The livid blacksmith, nearly pulling out his own hair, accosted Dante. "Are you mad? What the devil are you about?"

"What are you about?"

"My trade, and you spoil my tools by throwing them into the street!"

"If you do not wish me to spoil your things, do not spoil mine," Dante replied. "You sing songs from my pen, but not as I wrote them. I have no other trade and you spoil it for me."

The blacksmith from then on would sing of Tristram, Lancelot, Grendel, anything but Dante.

There were some writers who wanted all the world to read them. Then there were writers like Dante, who wanted as few readers as understood him.

It was that kind of commitment that must have brought Dante to his final decision. He would leave behind his family, never to see them again. Perhaps not only because of the complexities of his creative needs and the hardships of his political exile but also because his masterwork hinged on love for a woman who was not his wife. His love for a dead woman—Beatrice—had become holier to him than his relationship with his family.

Browning was increasingly convinced Dante spent much of his life searching for reasons *why* Beatrice had to die. Browning felt confident in this because he had done the same when it came to his Ba, though both women—Beatrice in 1290, Elizabeth in 1861—died of natural illness. He always thought about what might have been different had Ba been chosen as the laureate instead of Alfred Tennyson. Would the Brownings have returned from Italy to England? Could her health have improved, could she have grown stronger, *could she have survived*?

Ba used to reminisce to her husband about her childhood, when as a girl she went to sleep each night with a nurse by her side because her father insisted she was too frail to be alone. *I shall not like to be grown up*, she remembered thinking to herself, *because then I shall have nobody to take care of me—nobody to trust to take care of me.*

Browning was often asked about the seventeenth-century figure of Pompilia, the young wife murdered by her husband in *The Ring and the Book*. She was the center of his poem that had brought him a boost of wealth and respect. But so was Ba. It was why he'd dreaded to write it and why he knew he had to.

Could she have survived?

At the close of the opera, Browning accepted an invitation to attend the banquet with the performers and the supporters of the opera company, including many beautiful ladies sparkling with diamonds.

This night of opera and celebration was unusual. All the proceeds would go to the family of Lillian Brenner, the company's recently deceased prima donna. (*Deceased* sounded peaceful. Recently *destroyed*.) The proceeds left over, that is, after the expenses of the elaborate performance and banquet.

In the banquet room, through the glittering crowd, Browning's eyes fell on a young woman in the corner, covering her face with her hands. Typical Robert Browning—to be interested in the one woman who was hidden.

He began to make his way over to her when he was interrupted by the proprietor of the opera company, who insisted on presenting him to other distinguished guests invited to the banquet.

"Some people of your tribe are here," whispered the proprietor, taking him by the arm and pulling him in a different direction. "I mean the literary sort. Come." Then, louder, "Perhaps you already know one another? Mr. Browning, may I present an esteemed visitor from Boston, the famed 'Autocrat' Dr. Oliver Wendell Holmes—poet, essayist, medical professor, is there nothing he doesn't do?—and over at this table, the dear, one and only, Miss Christina Rossetti, who, believe it or not, had been in the stalls among ordinary people."

"What a happy surprise," Browning said with a fulsome smile.

Poets investigate. Don't we? Isn't that what we do every day?" Browning had philosophized back at Tudor House.

This was four days before the opera.

Browning sounded as if he wanted to reassure himself, though ostensibly he made the comment to convince Christina and Holmes as they plotted how to expand their search for clues after Lillian Brenner became the second victim.

Tudor House had completed its metamorphosis from being the home of Dante Gabriel Rossetti to being their own version of Scotland Yard. William refused to play any further part in what he called their mad quest since Christina last met him outside the omnibus, though he still came to Chelsea to help organize Gabriel's outstanding correspondence and bills and tend to the animals and property; the arrival of Dr. Holmes compensated for the loss of William's help, as did consultations with the translator Cayley on obscure portions of the Dante text.

Holmes's medical and scientific expertise was a particularly welcome addition to their examinations. As he reviewed the vast amount of information they'd harvested, Holmes came to the conclusion that the perpetrator had to have been a master in anatomy to have designed the device attached to Morton and to have employed such a precise method of sewing Brenner's eyes.

Holmes, not belonging to this side of the Atlantic, had not known the Rossettis very well and knew Browning only slightly better, though all the celebrated American and British writers kept up with each other through regular letter writing and sent each other copies of new books and articles. To be asked personally for help—as Christina and Browning had asked Holmes, first through the cryptic telegram and then in person as they explained all that happened—was a matter of camaraderie between literary nations. That tradition could be traced back, at least in a symbolic sense, to the long-ago handshake of James Fenimore Cooper and Sir Walter Scott, when the two gods of the page crossed paths inside a Paris stairwell.

Holmes could not in good conscience let anyone—litterateur or not—be left with the haunting feelings that he carried around.

To his new comrades Holmes spoke about what he had taken pains to hide from both Amelias (wife and daughter), from his two sons, from Inspector Williamson and Constable Branagan on the train—from everyone in the world, really, outside the circle of intimate friends who experienced the events with him and Longfellow. Holmes's introductory speech, as it were, was given shortly after his arrival at Browning's house.

"It was four years and a smattering of months ago when it began—when Dante's *Inferno* came alive before our eyes in Boston. What followed changed us. That sensation pamphlet by the scoundrel Simon Camp eventually made it a topic of morbid fascination, but I watched the horrors too closely to feel anything a reasonable man would call fascination. If one had proposed that I would find myself in London in Robert Browning's drawing room with Browning himself and Christina Rossetti, how many matters I would have wanted to speak about instead of . . . Well, my friends, we'll postpone leisurely conversations. We have too much work to do, and we must do it with much caution, with the police watching you closely."

Christina dropped an edition of *Purgatory*, the pages fluttering from her place. Browning leapt to his feet. She and Browning in unison asked Holmes what he meant—or rather, Browning demanded:

"What on earth did you just say, Holmes?"

While Christina's unflappable politeness came out as:

"Dr. Holmes, please elaborate your point regarding the police."

Holmes told them every detail of his encounter on the train with Inspector Williamson. Dolly not only brought along his own copy of *The Dante Murders*—the detective made it very clear he had seen Dante Gabriel Rossetti's copy of the same with notes written upon it by Browning and Christina. Holmes came to the conclusion that Gabriel's copy of the booklet must have been studied by the police inside Tudor House, or taken from the house for that purpose and then placed back inside.

Christina nodded her head vigorously. She was especially tidy and careful handling her brother's belongings, in part out of a vague superstition that keeping his belongings in good order would make him more likely to return. She recalled the times over the last month that objects in Tudor House seemed to migrate an inch or two from where she remembered putting them. The culprit had not been her brother's monkey, nor one of the poltergeists Gabriel sometimes searched for; it had been the wily operatives from Scotland Yard.

After Holmes's revelation, whenever the trio was at Christina's house at Euston Square, which they avoided so as to not disturb her mother or worry her about Gabriel, or at Browning's house on Warwick Crescent or Tudor House—their base of operations—they made certain to keep an eye out for any signs that they were followed or observed. They took pains to arrive separately and to conceal papers and books that contained their more important notations.

It no longer helped Christina to will herself not to fall into the trap that had plagued her father and Gabriel—that anxiety about being watched and followed by some outside menace. This time those anxieties were justified.

They planned expeditions to try to learn everything else they could about the deaths of Jasper Morton and Lillian Brenner. There were discreet visits to the deadhouse to see the bodies. It was customary for victims to be displayed for the public in case people remembered anything of value to the police by looking at the faces of the dead or their articles of clothing (which were hung on hooks next to the bodies, while the bodies were washed with a stream of water to keep them fresh). Browning dutifully went but could hardly remain in the observation area for two minutes without sobbing; Holmes studied the bodies with an expert's eye, and Christina seemed to take in the gruesome sights with an unflinching glare, taking a special interest in Miss Brenner's clothing before rushing out with her head down, nearly crashing into several other bystanders.

Browning was far more comfortable attending a London memorial for Morton, though there wasn't much of interest to observe there (other than the conspicuous, slouching figure of their friend-rival-paragon Tennyson among those attending). There was a memorial prayer service for Miss Brenner at a small church that Christina had attended in the past, so she went there to hear more details about the opera singer: her dreams as a small child of singing for the public, her rigorous training by her father, her quick rise to prominence because of the immense compass of her voice, even if it lacked the flexibility of the best soloists. They secured seats for the benefit opera performance of *Fidelio*. Christina insisted on purchasing a seat in the stalls for herself, not in one of the frightfully expensive six-guinea private boxes where Holmes and Browning would be. They would not sit together, but of course that was part of their plan.

Browning's plan. He thought that by attending the opera separately they increased the probability of overhearing information from other audience members who knew Miss Brenner. Christina had been less than pleased with the entire visit to the opera house, but agreed it was a necessity. Although she enjoyed operas and plays in her youth, she long ago swore never to attend them because their dramatized stories were so often vulgar, if not utterly impious and unchristian. Christina followed the same practice with reading books, as a result almost entirely swearing off modern novels and, until the recent events, most newspapers. *Look elsewhere for news*, she would tell family members, *but not to me*. When it came to operas, the actresses and singers and musicians all had reputations for what Christina would kindly call moral agnosticism.

Charles Cayley, during the years when studying under the professore brought him to the Rossetti home, had once laughed to Christina about her managing not to notice the existence of anything improper in a place like London. "How I wish," the translator said in a state of sudden reflection, "I could see through such innocent eyes."

Part of the purpose of their expeditions to memorials and to the Haymarket Opera House was to identify any person Morton and Brenner might have known in common with Gabriel—someone who might have been involved in their disappearances who was also in a position to have known and taken Gabriel.

They continued to prepare and study their notes. For hours at a time Holmes—as though delivering one of the famous medical lectures Christina had heard about over the years—narrated more details about the murders that shocked Boston. Christina and her accomplices faced a dis-advantage in trying to trace the influence of Dante around London com-pared to that surmounted by Holmes and his Dantean friends. Boston in 1865 had been a time and place when almost nobody had knowledge about Dante or the *Divine Comedy*. Now that Longfellow's translation of Dante had been widely published on both sides of the Atlantic, competing translations multiplied. With Dante so fashionable, they could not limit their suspicions to those who were so-called true Danteans. Holmes, in telling his tales, pointed out some of the key lessons they'd observed in Boston. One of these was the special appeal to the eye and mind of a sol-dier in the way Dante organized the world in pursuit of rightness and jus-tice. Dante also had been a soldier in his youth, and since the beginning of human history the soldier and the poet had shared great (or terrible) imag-inations that remade their surroundings.

The words poured forth from the doctor's mouth whenever he worked up steam on a story, but in talking about the Dantesque occurrences in Boston, there was something more than his ever-present energy and mo-mentum of narrative; there was relief. He had liberated a part of his his-tory that had festered by being locked inside him. There was also a degree of pride in what he and his friends accomplished.

"After all," Holmes tried to explain, realizing this pridefulness had been revealed by his tone, "Dante could have been blemished for ages if not for our clandestine intervention."

"With due respect, Dr. Holmes, what I care about, *all* I care about, is the safety of my brother," said Christina. "I wish to make it very plain that the integrity of Dante Alighieri does not concern me."

Holmes hung his head a little and apologized with a nod.

She did not mean to dismiss the importance of protecting literature from being perverted through violence. Dante, after all, buoyed her father to his dying day, and had inspired her siblings and herself—but this was the problem. She had to employ her expertise without getting sucked into the Dantesque vortex.

When the Rossetti family's fortunes crumbled, it seemed to happen in a single moment, though it had been coming for a long time. As children, they were often surrounded by Italian refugees and exiles who came to their home for conversation with the professore (mostly in Italian, though sometimes slipping into French) and to share the little food the family had. The professore said most of these callers were either *cercatori* or *seccatori*, the begging or the boring. But sometimes they were revolutionaries, conspirators, even assassins. Young Gabriel would stop his sketching or his dominoes to listen carefully to these stories of overthrowing corrupt rulers in the name of liberty. The boundary between being an exile and being mad seemed to be a fine one, convincing Christina that losing one's rightful place in the world could mean losing one's mind.

There was a man named Fiorenzo Galli, to take one example, who sat in their house giving a very careful speech to prove he was Jesus Christ. Then there was Signor Galanti, who offered predictions of disasters to come, claiming first would start the Age of Roses and Thorns, then the Age of All Thorns, then the Age of Death. When the professore dismissed Galanti as a bird of ill omen, the visitor rose, crying, "You will see one day, Rossetti, whether I speak the truth, and you will confess it, but I will not await the direful time that is coming upon us!"

Galanti then went to his house and slit his own throat.

The professore quietly carried around his own superstitions. In the Abruzzo region of Italy where he came from, stepping over a child was said to stop the child from growing. There were always children on the floor of the small Rossetti home—playing, drawing, writing verses and novels, and even compiling their own family magazine printed by their grandfather. There would sit the professore, in such a fury of work at his desk, but when he needed to retrieve a book, he would begin a slow, delicate dance across the combined study and drawing room to reach the shelf, ensuring that his shadow did not touch any of them.

Fewer refugees came over time—few visitors at all—as the professore began to conclude that a cabal of bloodsuckers around the world, including the novelist Victor Hugo, sabotaged his labors. He feared his own reflection in the mirrors, so Mrs. Rossetti took almost all of them out of the house. As Christina prepared *maccheroni asciutti* with Parmesan cheese and butter for the family, she overheard the professore confiding to her mother: "Whether Neptune or Vulcan devour my vigils, I shall not see it, I shall not suffer." Meaning, in his dramatic language, his work would end up at the bottom of the sea or in ashes. And another outburst another time: "My own shadow terrifies me, Francesca! I have become like one of those people of exaggerated piety who think that in their most insignificant action they have committed a mortal sin."

Maybe they had entered Signor Galanti's Age of All Thorns.

As the professore continued to spend more time working on Dante in solitude, his eyes and health worsened. He had nightmares if he could sleep at all. He was forced to resign from the university, where there were fewer students who wished to study. (When Queen Victoria married a German, studying German became all the fashion, leaving Italian further behind.) In his best year the professore made no more than ten pounds, which they kept in a box in the house, never having enough to open a bank account. A few loyal pupils like Cayley continued to engage him as a private tutor of Dante and Italian, mostly as an excuse to help the struggling Rossettis. The family was left with little money and no expectations of future income. What the professore did next amazed everyone: he kept working on his Dante. He would spend the rest of his life, if necessary, but swore he'd finish his Dantean labors.

Maria and Christina, who put her poetry aside for neither the first nor last time, both sought work as governesses to keep them from starvation; Christina also helped copy out the New Testament for a new edition until her fingertips bled from calluses, their mother worked as a teacher, and William picked up extra income outside his clerical job when he could. Gabriel, meanwhile, would wander around museums and galleries for inspiration, remarking that he was in too lively a poetry phase to waste himself on menial work. He was his father's son.

In the professore's final years, when he was an invalid, he was hardly able to move from that desk where as children they believed he conjured his friend Dante. He wore a visor to prevent light from hitting his face and insisted the curtains remain closed. "I am so tired of life that I shall bless my death when it comes. I wish to die, but God will not yet concede me the great benefit." His shrunken, bent form was wrapped in a dressing gown in the bed where he died.

The Age of Death.

Dante's power over her family destroyed the professore and—if her supposition that this had been the reason Gabriel was taken proved correct—Dante was destroying his namesake. This time, though, she had been blessed with a chance to stop it.

At the banquet in the opera house following the performance, Christina could tolerate no more. It was some form of punishment to be forced to observe moral decay disguised as amusement. She took another look at the young women nearby, some throwing their arms around men, others leaning on shoulders or holding court with two or three admirers at once. That was it—the performance and its gaudy costumes had already shaken her; she could not stay a moment longer.

Over the last weeks, she'd become accustomed to justifying her deceit toward others for the sake of finding Gabriel. For example, to pretend that she had not known Holmes and Browning were present when the zealous man from the opera company brought them to each other. But to descend into this elegant debauchery! She thought of her sister, Maria, in her convent while Christina stood here. *Here!*

As a young girl, Christina admired the liberated, eccentric set she encountered at her parents' dinners more than she cared for the handsome, well-dressed people. She most envied those who roamed London freely at night. When she discovered the ways of God through her mother's strict

Anglican Church, however, she knew her path, however far out of fashion it fell. Many people blossomed as they moved into adulthood, but not Christina. She retreated to safety. In this way, she felt herself join with the poet she had tried to run away from her whole childhood: Dante Alighieri. According to Boccaccio, Dante had been a noisy and social boy, then somber and lonely as a man and as a poet. He had found a higher calling that had to be preserved and protected. He became impregnable.

That was a word to which Christina aspired.

She fled outside to the front of the opera house, into the cold night air of busy Haymarket. Every rattling coach and strolling couple invoked judgment against her.

She could almost hear William chide her with what he had been thinking during this whole affair of Gabriel's disappearance: *Where did you expect to end up, when you decided to follow Gabriel down his path of darkness and selfishness? Where else, but where you utterly despise?*

She pulled her scarf tightly around her neck. Slender Christina felt chilled with the slightest breeze. She would not acknowledge it to anyone, but it was one of the reasons she almost never left her house after dark.

Standing out in the cold night brought memories of one of the last times she had seen Gabriel before he disappeared. He had turned up without warning during the night at Euston Square and called to Christina's window. She ran down the stairs before his shouts could wake their mother.

"I saw her today," Gabriel confided to Christina in the garden. The expression on his face was an odd mix of euphoria and fear.

At first she thought he meant he had met someone, maybe a woman who could take his mind off his torments. She was about to ask her name. Then she worried he meant Lizzie herself. A mirage, a ghost, a phantom, as had plagued him in the dismal days he'd heard *murderer* echo through empty rooms.

"It was at Highgate."

"The cemetery? You visited her grave?" Christina asked, deeply concerned. That was the worst place for Gabriel to go to preserve his mental state.

"William took me," Gabriel had said, so hastily that it did not sound entirely truthful. Then he smiled. "Her hair is like the sun, Christina, and runs down her back like a cape. Oh, dear sister." He took both of Christina's hands in his. "What would it mean to be blessed with a new light? 'So that all ended with her eyes, Inferno, Purgatory, Paradise.'"

Christina recognized the verse from one of Gabriel's sonnets on Dante that he had buried with Lizzie. She had half expected him to forget the poems that he had put under the ground. "Remember, Gabriel, remember Father thought everything was to be found in Dante, and he ended with nothing."

"Don't you see, Christina? We Rossettis will always be prisoners trapped between Dante and Beatrice."

She tried a different tack: "You ought to stay away from Highgate, Gabriel."

"You know how I am, Christina," he said, suddenly pensive. "What I ought to do is what I can't do."

The memory broke down as Christina heard her name called out from the doorway of the opera hall. She expected Browning or Holmes had followed her out to reproach her for leaving. Preparing to stand her ground, she turned to see Charles Cayley.

"Miss Rossetti," he said shyly in his nasal voice, unconsciously frowning at his attempt at a formal outfit as though seeing it only now through someone else's eyes. He wore a rumpled shirt with no collar and a shabby tailcoat. "I thought I wouldn't find anyone to speak to here. I grew rather tired standing in the corner alone."

"What brings you to an affair such as this, Mr. Cayley?" She regretted her accusatory tone, absurd considering she was there, too.

Cayley paused for a long time, as he tended to do when asked even the simplest question, then explained that the opera company had engaged him to translate some of the more obscure German lines of the production so the singers could understand their scenes.

"It is a little pocket change to help finance my latest translations of Dante and Homer," he added, turning red at his own mention of money. "Excuse me if I seem unable to put one foot in front of another here, Miss Rossetti. It is not my usual environment, nor the clothes."

"Count me in that same category." In fact, Christina had worn her usual dark, plain dress, refusing to make a show of herself.

"Has Gabriel been back home?" he asked with a smile. Cayley was always on the verge of smiling, as though appreciating a joke only he was hearing. "I would imagine he is the only one alive who could persuade you to come."

Christina started to speak, then simply shook her head.

"Well, I suppose he will be armed with some good stories whenever he returns to London from . . . wherever it is. Miss Rossetti . . ." He was about to ask a question before he stopped himself. "I remember Gabriel's hearty greetings when I first knew your family, when I would come to study at your father's feet. The professore adored you all; I fancy you helped him forget his exile. And I remember first seeing you."

"Do you, Mr. Cayley?" The idea shocked Christina more than she could have explained.

After another of his pauses, he exclaimed: "Certainly! A slight, murky-eyed, lovely little girl standing at a narrow desk, with a profile made dark by the winter light coming in, composing industriously, never looking over at me, not even once, as though I were a figment. Then, another evening, your father invited me to come back for dinner, and I looked forward to being able to speak to you. You were reading in your room, and never came in. I always wondered if you even knew there was a visitor."

She had. She had trembled down to her feet at the presence of the brilliant, nervous pupil of her father's. Though she was not going to tell him that, not then, not now, never. "Were you going to ask something a moment ago, Mr. Cayley?"

"This is terribly presumptuous of me, but if you are half as miserable going back to that noisy, crowded banquet as I am . . . well, do you fancy taking a walk?" He offered his arm.

Christina looked back at the windows of the opera house, blazing yellow and red.

She offered her arm and gave a slight nod, proud of herself that she managed to hide the slightest hint of a smile.

Browning took in the scene before him. Some of the women wore masks over the upper part of their faces, and many members of both genders wore dominoes, or long, satin robes of all black or all white.

Browning knew—even from across the room—how uncomfortable Christina was. Her eyes, made mysterious by their unusual tint of blue-gray that at times appeared hazel, projected a fearful glare at her surroundings. The traditions of the opera balls were associated with times of decadence and celebration that brushed against Christina's every fiber. Browning knew this and hated making her come along. Still, Christina was their best hope for recognizing associates of Gabriel's, which made it all the more alarming when a few minutes later he could no longer spot her. As for Holmes, Browning was impressed with his superhuman conversational powers as the doctor fluttered through the room like a hummingbird, progressing gab by gab.

For a while, Browning also lost sight of the woman he'd been curious to try to interview—the one, though not masked, who concealed her face in her hands.

When he found the same young woman again, he could see the reason for her posture. She was periodically sobbing.

"For just such occasions," Browning said, holding out his silk handkerchief emblazoned with his initials.

She smiled a little and introduced herself as Jane Cary. She had wide-set green eyes, which she now dried with his handkerchief, and pinned-up hair the color of wet sand. He recognized her from her small part in the opera.

"It was a terrific success, wasn't it?" she said.

"But . . . ," Browning replied, gesturing at her tears.

"Oh, don't mind what a sight I am, sir. This all—well, not to burden a stranger, but it just makes me miss Lilly even more."

Browning nodded sympathetically, trying to hide his desire for more. "You were a close friend of Miss Brenner's?"

"Inseparable," the young woman corrected him. "A day didn't pass when we weren't together. Hardly ever, at least. I was in the countryside with my sister's family for a few weeks when she vanished. I curse myself that I wasn't with her! What kind of villain, what kind of devil would do such a thing? To think of the terror she must have felt, to die like that, alone in the streets, and her eyes . . ."

From the emotion she showed as her lips trembled, Browning's mind turned back to the unimaginable moment Brenner would have experienced when realizing her situation. With her eyes sewn, she would be lost in a whirlpool of unhelpful voices and noises. *When I approached close enough to see their condition*, Dante Alighieri recounts in *Purgatory*'s Canto Thirteen, *the heavy grief pushed tears from my eyes.*

The young woman continued, telling stories of Lillian's career and family. "Lilly's father was a great singing teacher, and kept her in a military regimen of lessons before he abandoned the family. That changed her."

"Did it?"

"Indeed. I think she always wondered had she been a different singer, a better one in the upper registers, for instance, which her father reprimanded her about—had she practiced more, might he never have left?" The weeping young lady turned fierce with anger. "There! That's who took it all away from her!"

Browning wheeled around ready to confront a monster. Her accusation was directed toward the lovely prima donna of the evening's performance, who sang the part of the heroic wife.

"What do you mean? *She* did it?"

Jane explained that this new prima donna, Miss Spalding, had been eyeing the position held by Lillian for the better part of a year.

"Lilly worried about it all the time," explained Jane.

"Did she?"

"She worried Miss Spalding was younger, prettier, with a better range of voice."

The sin of envy is scourged within this terrace, Browning heard Virgil's lesson (and warning) to Dante. He tried casually asking, in a quieter voice, "Tell me something, Jane. Did Miss Brenner speak about her feelings toward Miss Spalding—this envy that plagued her—with anyone other than you?"

"Oh, yes," Jane said, leaning in closer with a confidential tone. "Lilly spoke about it with almost everyone she met."

Browning frowned.

"I remember once," Jane went on, "being at a grand banquet like this with Lilly—oh, wasn't she feted by everyone there! Every man wanted to dance with her! Real aristocrats, too. Then when we left she immediately burst into tears."

"But why?"

"Lilly said all the attention made her realize she was a mere opera singer."

Jane reached for champagne from a passing tray, and when dancing recommenced, Browning was divided from her by a sea of revelers.

Later on he noticed that the spirits Jane drank seemed to free her from her melancholy over Lillian Brenner, at least temporarily, and he overheard her ask Holmes, in a giddy, intoxicated treble, "Is it true you're a doctor?"

After exchanges with a few other people, Browning pulled Holmes aside. "Have you seen Miss Rossetti?"

"I leaned out the window for some air, and saw her walking with someone," Holmes answered.

"In this cold? Whom?"

"A man."

"Are you certain?" Browning replied, swallowing down an unwelcome sensation of amazement and resentment.

"I couldn't see the fellow clearly," Holmes added.

"Miss Rossetti can take very good care of herself. And if she is walking on the arm of a man, he must be some kind of saint. Holmes, there was one of the lesser singers here, Jane, who spoke with you . . ."

"Strange girl."

"How so?"

Holmes explained that Jane had apparently overheard him speaking to someone else about his medical lectures. That's why she approached him and asked him if he really was a doctor. Though she was not familiar with Holmes's poetry (a fact Holmes found extremely hard to believe), she was quite interested in his profession.

"I wonder why," Browning said.

Holmes's reply was unexpected. "Opium."

"What do you mean?"

Jane had insisted to Holmes she used it only occasionally, but that both the apothecaries and the shady street dens had been insisting that supplies were running short, depriving even some injured soldiers and others who depended on long-term use of the medicines. She thought Holmes, as a doctor, might have advice.

"What's bothering you now, Browning?"

"It's about the opium," Browning replied, struck as though by a thunderbolt. "It reminds me of something you said shortly after your arrival. Let's find Miss Rossetti—right now."

A long the way on their walk, Cayley spoke about the histories of the buildings and squares and monuments they passed in the halos of the street lamps, recalled the old structures that had been swallowed by long-ago fires, chronicled the riots and scandals that had occurred at various spots. Christina for the most part listened, not minding at all Cayley's arbitrary pauses and the hurried tone of speech that many mistook for madness. To be out around the city at night brought a thrill and fright like a sailor's discovery of a new world. As rain began again, Cayley held up an umbrella, trying to place it over her head more than his own, accomplishing neither.

"You surprise me so," Cayley said to her.

"Finding me out for a nighttime walk is rather a surprise to myself."

Cayley gave a snort followed by his unwieldy laugh. They had turned back toward the massive structure of the opera house. He finally explained: "I don't mean that. Thank heavens I found you here, or I should have dug a hole in the banquet hall and hidden inside. I refer to the *Divine Comedy*."

"Oh?" Christina said, concerned about what he could mean.

"How I've enjoyed stopping by Tudor House the last couple of weeks when receiving your requests to help interpret arduous passages. I've always found *Purgatory* invigorating! Full of secrets. Just when you think it shall mimic *Inferno*, when you believe it will turn down the one corridor you've been searching for, Dante opens two more you never expected. Still, it always seemed to me your father's obsession passed to Gabriel more than to you."

"I suppose there is a time when we all must enter our fathers' tombs so to speak, and find what was left behind."

"And your own writing, your poems? I always anxiously await the latest, and have felt it has been too long a wait."

Christina paused to relish the comment, then cursed herself for it. Her main feeling related to her writing rushed upon her: embarrassment. "Jean Ingelow has a fine new volume, I understand."

"That's so?" he responded with confusion. "Your company, of course, exceeds even the pleasure of your verse. Miss Rossetti, there is something more I wanted to ask about your father's work on Dante. I believe I have found new information pertinent to your father's theories on Beatrice and his conviction that she was not a real woman. I wonder if you would allow me to search through and organize the professore's materials held in Tudor House as I continue my research?"

"I suppose that would be fine."

"Truly? Well, I am as pleased as a cat eating a mouse. May I tell you my strategy for my investigation into Beatrice?"

"Mr. Cayley, could you excuse me for a moment?"

"If I've spoken out of turn . . ."

In a way she could do even to a stranger, Christina silenced Cayley simply by raising a hand. Her eyes were fixed ahead of them, at one of the entrances to the opera house, where a slouched figure waited. Waited, she somehow knew, for her.

Christina walked toward this figure, and at the same moment Browning and Holmes emerged from inside the building.

"Miss Rossetti, it's urgent!" Browning called out. Whatever he was about to say was lost as he and then Holmes saw the same distinctive silhouette that transfixed Christina.

Moving toward her, drops of water traveling down the uneven brim of his hat onto the same tattered, food-stained frock coat he'd worn for thirty years, Alfred Tennyson nodded a greeting.

"Miss Rossetti," growled out the poet laureate, his neck craning toward Browning and Holmes before his stern gaze returned to Christina. "I've come about Dante."

That same morning, Alfred Tennyson had taken his breakfast in bed. He usually smoked and breakfasted in the bedroom before climbing to his sanctum on the top floor of the house to contemplate his poetry in progress and smoke another pipe. When he first came to the remote country estate of Farringford—isolated within its vast grounds and, if that weren't enough, located on an island—two of their servants burst into tears. They said they would not live somewhere so removed. Tennyson just smiled. People often said the man never smiled, but this was not so—his smile was hidden under uncombed whiskers that concealed a mouth made jagged by dental procedures, like many other things about the poet that were secreted away.

On his regular walk through the rolling meadows of his estate, Tennyson brought along his dogs and a thick stack of letters handed to him by his butler. Among the day's letters was a message from his publisher expressing increasing irritation at not reaching Dante Gabriel Rossetti. Reading this slowed down Tennyson's brisk shuffle. He thought back to Robert Browning at the Cosmopolitan Club inquiring whether he'd seen Gabriel Rossetti lately. *I stick to my friends*, Browning had bragged of his persistence on the topic about which he seemed haunted.

Browning made a spectacle of himself, but that wasn't new. Tennyson's thoughts reeled back in time to his elder son Hallam's christening, eighteen years earlier, where Browning proceeded to show Tennyson how to hold the baby—to tell a father how to hold his own child! Then Browning tossed Hallam into the air. Even Thackeray, who never paid much attention to anyone, seemed to look askew at Browning's antics that morning. Browning's happiness for the Tennyson family's new addition was quite genuine, though; whatever complaints you could have about him and his discursive poetry, Browning was genuine down to his boots.

While Browning pestered him at the Cosmopolitan Club about Gabriel Rossetti, Tennyson had been distracted by the crime columns he was reading in the newspaper—the gruesome discovery of the body of Mr. Morton. Even the vague details of those early reports struck Tennyson as Dantesque (confirmed in a very literal way by the later revelations). Browning had not seemed the least interested in the crime, so Tennyson dropped the topic. But Tennyson's brain quickly began to associate the two seemingly disparate things—news of the murder, and the mystery of their Dante-obsessed, Dante-named mutual friend, Gabriel.

Browning would probably die in white tie, but Tennyson attended the clubs and the dinners around London only grudgingly. Though England's poet laureate owned a small residence in London, the city usually only dulled and interrupted him. He required quiet, and to keep himself to himself, more than any writer he'd known. He was a shy beast who loved his burrow.

More to the point, he carried the strain of black blood that had always been in his family, and it worsened when trampled by the outside world. *That* feeling. The feeling that every stranger harbored ill will and machinations. The same feeling that—along with drinking—fueled Tennyson's father, the village rector, sending him stomping through the house, hurling insults and objects at young Tennyson and his ten siblings.

Still, at times Tennyson had little choice given his laureate duties but to show himself in public, such as the memorial gathering he had attended in London for that fallen member of Parliament, Jasper Morton. Before that had already been the proper funeral in Bristol, with this second ceremony for the purposes of London folks showing off their grief and their importance in public. Tennyson hated writing epitaphs, but they'd bother him out of his wits if he refused. Doing it was the best way to peace. His first and last draft read:

> *Stand here, among our noblest and our best,*
> *J. Morton, MP, thy long day's work hast ceased.*

The distraught widow Morton at first seemed honored by Tennyson's presence. But as he took her hand she held it too long and trembled, staring at him in fright.

"What is it, Mrs. Morton?" Tennyson asked, a little too brusquely for speaking to a freshly christened widow, he was sure Emily, his own wife, would later chastise him.

"Your hair, sir!" she said with a gasp, and nothing else for a moment or two. His hair was one of his finest features, along with his almost Spanish complexion and iron cheekbones, and among the reasons Hartley Coleridge once told him he was far too handsome to be a poet—so he was rather offended at the widow's agitated allusion to it. There was not a single gray or silver strand in it even at sixty. Eventually, the widow found her voice to apologize. She explained that Tennyson's hair—the long, disheveled strands of raven black—reminded her of something that recently had frightened her. Before her husband died, she had found a wig of dark black hair, which felt as though it were made of silk, in one of his trunks. She had never seen it before. She recounted to Tennyson that she asked Mr. Morton why he seemed to be sneaking around at night, and he'd said he was an "easy target." "You see, my husband had been scared, scared enough to disguise himself with wild hair like yours—he was trying to avoid detection by someone! Money went missing, too. He had been acting peculiar; at first I had thought it was only due to some strange tidings about his family that he had discovered."

Wild hair?! Tennyson thought, aghast.

That was his whole exchange with the widow Morton and it was, if peculiar, at least less monotonous than the rest of the memorial. Tennyson also saw Browning from a distance at the memorial but did not get close enough to speak with him. At one point, as the flock of people moved from the church to the outdoors, the flow came to a halt, and in fact seemed to move in the wrong direction; Tennyson felt trapped.

"What is going on? We're hemmed in, why won't they move?!" Tennyson growled.

A nearby man gave him a gentle, embarrassed smile. He whispered to the poet: "I don't think they will go, sir, as long as you are standing there."

Tennyson realized with a sinking heart—he was the reason for the crowd. They were all trying to see him, to get close to him. He felt trapped because, well, he was trapped, by humanity. The kind man next to him helped him fight his way out of the crowd and out a rear door, then requested that Tennyson send him a photograph and autograph. The poet emitted a sound of disgust: ugh.

Even the Isle of Wight, the setting not only of Farringford but also one of the queen's rural retreats, was not free from encroachment, as freshly proven on this day that started in such typical fashion with breakfast, walking, and reading the mail. When cold rain began to fall, he whistled for his dogs, who stopped abruptly and doubled back for him. The letter he'd read from his publisher, and another letter concerning literary matters from his stack were on his mind. As he neared Farringford again, he could see something ahead. He squinted, which he had to do to make out anything not right in front of his face. There was a group of people loitering, one of them holding a map. The poet turned on his heels and took a longer way around. But then while he and his wife had their luncheon inside there was a commotion in the gardens. They peered outside the large window that opened on a hill to see the gardener pointing a rifle up a tree, where a man was perched to try to steal a glimpse of Tennyson.

"Look at that hill, Emily," Tennyson said. "It's four hundred million years old. Think of that. Now look at what is happening in this nineteenth century, and in the rain!"

He threw down his silverware and, thinking again of the day's mail, announced he'd stay in London for a few nights and attend to some business. He gathered a few things. On the stairs, he passed the print of the portrait of Dante, discovered hidden under whitewash in an Italian church, with the nail obliterating one eye, given to him by old Seymour Kirkup in Italy. He thought about what Kirkup had said to him during his trip to Italy. *Something in you*, the strange little exile said to Tennyson, staring up at him, *yes, something in your face, Mr. Tennyson, suggests the lofty brow and aquiline nose of Dante.*

Of course, now there were those across England railing against Dante's vicious imagination, as if the great Florentine himself had come to London to choose victims. Murders aside, Tennyson did not think Dante an unflattering face for his own to be compared. Dante was not only a brilliant poet but a serious one, something in short supply since the beginning of time. He did not suffer nonsense. Tennyson enjoyed the story of Dante meditating on his life and art in the church of Santa Maria Novella. A local bore, who did not respect the poet's need for solitude, came up to Dante and began chattering and asking trivial questions.

Before I answer, Dante replied, *you must solve a question for me. What is the greatest beast in the world?* Thinking about it, the man replied that the philosopher Pliny supposed it to be the elephant. *Well*, Dante replied, *Elephant, do not annoy me.* The man, dumbstruck, slipped out of the church.

After promising Emily he would not overexert himself, Tennyson rode a ferry and train to London, where he met with his publisher and, after a slew of other errands and appointments, then a late supper, hired a driver to go to Tudor House in Chelsea.

When he had met Gabriel in the past, it was usually out in society.

Tennyson couldn't remember the last time he'd called at Tudor House—perhaps after the death of Gabriel's wife? Tennyson had dragged his feet as usual when it came to the awkward routines of paying condolences. When he had finally made it there a month after Lizzie's funeral, Gabriel, in his painting coat, was beginning a portrait of a bride-to-be who was straining to keep smiling. She was the sister of a friend's friend, and no doubt the session had been arranged as a gentle distraction for Gabriel. The pretty bride heard a strange noise behind her.

"You've moved your head," Gabriel admonished her.

"I do believe that a wombat has got my hat and is eating it!"

Tennyson and Gabriel rushed to the corner of the room, where Gabriel pulled the masticated hat from the wombat's teeth.

"Oh, poor Top!" Gabriel exclaimed.

"I should have thought you might have pitied me, Mr. Rossetti. I shall have to go home without a hat!"

"But it is so indigestible."

The evening rain began to fall harder as Tennyson approached Tudor House once again. He sheltered himself on the portico and knocked. The door opened on William Rossetti.

"Mr. Rossetti," Tennyson said. "How d'ye do? Forgive me if I appear surprised. I am looking for your brother, and I suppose I didn't actually expect anyone to be home."

"Mr. Tennyson. Gabriel isn't—what brings you out here from the Isle of Wight, on a night like this?"

"Your brother was given a commission to do a drawing for a new illustrated edition of my poems—perhaps you know. He was meant to illustrate a few of my verses, starting with my 'Ulysses.' In all events, I'm afraid he was paid but never submitted the artwork. The publisher wishes to pester him for holding up our publication but cannot find him, so they pester me. Your talented but evasive brother, meanwhile, has not replied to any of my letters so, since I am staying in London for the night—"

He paused.

"What's wrong, Mr. Tennyson?" William asked.

"I'm being followed," he muttered back, peering over his shoulder.

"The police?"

Tennyson stared back with an air of confusion. "A carriage full of tourists who have been after me half the day. Did you hear that? I think that's the sound of the rascals coming again now. I hate publishing. Why could I not have the money from my books without notoriety? Let me inside." He stepped into the house. "This is better, Rossetti. It's been too cold and wet outside to keep a pipe lit. You don't mind my smoking."

He threw his hat on a table and started up his clay pipe. Most of the curtains were closed. There were papers spread over the table.

"Gabriel, he's been—well, he's away, and I'm afraid I'm detained here a few hours a day because I must collect all the demands from creditors and such so I can try to plead for time," William explained, stepping over his own words. "Christina also has been . . . helping clean here."

"Pack of lies," Tennyson said under his breath, with a grunt.

"What?"

Tennyson's eyes lingered on the motley assortment of hats and coats hanging on the rack. He then flew right past William to the far wall, where there was a curtain—but not a window. He drew aside the curtain to reveal illustrations pinned to the wall depicting scenes of Dante's *Purgatory*, side by side with cuttings from London newspapers about the two violent deaths that had mesmerized and terrified the nation. All of these were scrawled over with annotations and circled words and phrases.

Tennyson closed his eyes and thought about one of his first walks with Gabriel through the London streets, many years before. Tennyson had been, as always, fused to his pipe, but Gabriel never smoked. Smoking was the one vice Gabriel said his constitution could not tolerate.

"Oh, you make a great mistake," Tennyson had said that night, puffing with relish. "What were you saying before?"

"That I grudge Wordsworth any vote he gets!" Gabriel continued the usual literary parlor game of picking the great geniuses of the past. "Utter muffishness. The three greatest English imaginations are Shakespeare, Coleridge, and Shelley."

"The one I count greater than them all—Wordsworth, Coleridge, Shelley, even Byron—is Keats—thousands of faults! But he's wonderful. Any new paintings of yours to admire around town?"

"Oh, certainly, Tennyson, I hate showing my pictures to the public, but I've been agreeing to put more in galleries. I've been hanging myself daily, you might say."

"Something else, Rossetti. Too many of my family members have been stuffed with it by druggists and doctors."

"What do you mean?" Gabriel asked.

"Laudanum, chloral, whatever it is you are ingesting to help you sleep, or to help stay awake, whatever it is making you rub your eyes red as fire. To quote an essay I read of late by Dr. Holmes, no families take so little medicine as those of doctors. Opium is a millstone, and will drown you. It will make you who you are not."

"Aren't we all doomed to be who we're not, sooner or later?"

Tennyson made no further comment, and after a few minutes the subject had faded away. They passed a building one could hardly see because there were so many hackney cabs around it. Tennyson asked what it was, and Gabriel said it was one of the most infamous dance halls in London, filled with rogues and prostitutes. Tennyson wondered aloud what it was like inside, and Gabriel took his arm to lead him—Tennyson, who had had tea with the queen weeks before!

"You wouldn't really like to take me inside there, Rossetti!"

"Tennyson, I never do anything that I don't like."

There was a twinkle in Gabriel's eye, looking over at that nefarious den. Tennyson had not meant he actually would ever go in, but there was no hesitation in Gabriel before Tennyson stopped in his tracks. None at all. His face at that moment, the strong brow creased, the big nostrils flaring, ready to flip the world on its head, remained imprinted in Tennyson's mind.

Tennyson noted the contrast to the well-groomed and overwhelmed countenance of William Rossetti who was wishing with every fiber of his being that Tennyson might leave.

"Mr. Rossetti," Tennyson said to William, "where can I find your sister, Browning, and Holmes right now?"

William appeared completely befuddled, gawking with a combination of fascination and fright as though witness to black magic.

"The handwriting," Tennyson explained, gesturing at the annotations. "The more nearsighted a man is, the better he becomes at recognizing life on a small scale. Same goes for my hearing. Why, sometimes at night in Farringford I hear the shriek of bats from the stables. I have corresponded with Holmes over the years and I certainly know how to spot Browning's hand. Please, where is Miss Rossetti?"

After finding Christina, Browning, and Holmes outside the opera house, where William had directed him, Tennyson returned with them to Tudor House, where they could speak in privacy.

William left as soon as they got back, as though scared of the conversation about to occur. Tennyson contemplated for a while as he smoked, then put his feet up on a table with a thud. "When there is trouble, I'm afraid I've come to assume Gabriel Rossetti might be mixed up in it. So I cannot say it is a surprise to me to realize that you believe there is some connection between his apparent disappearance and these horrible crimes. But what if Gabriel is the fiend as the police suspect?"

"Heavens!" Browning boomed. "How would you know the police suspect Gabriel?"

"Because if they didn't, William would not have worried I was being followed by the police. Because if they didn't, I presume you would be sitting in Scotland Yard sharing these ideas you've scribbled over these clippings and cuttings, and these lists of Gabriel's past locations, instead of doing all of that in here behind drawn curtains. Don't you agree?" Noticing the simultaneously chagrined and impressed looks on the others' faces, he added: "And the new generation of critics say I have no imagination!"

Tennyson rose to his feet and returned to the wall covered with the products of their inquiries, eyes narrowing behind his thick double glasses to make out details. "So Mr. Morton, MP, disappears until he is found crushed in the pleasure gardens—his death represents the first terrace of the mountain of Purgatory that Dante travels up. On that terrace the great Florentine encounters the Prideful, shades who are weighed down by unimaginably heavy stones. Dante stoops down to speak to them, as if he, too, is being *crushed*—because Dante, in a sense, must take part in every punishment he witnesses. Shortly after the time of Morton's disappearance, the singer Brenner fails to appear in an opera where she is expected to sing. Later, she stumbles back into the picture among the grog halls of St. James's Street, impaling herself not from being inebriated, as it initially appeared to witnesses, but from her eyes being *sewn shut*—reenacting the second terrace of Purgatory, where the Envious suffer that awful form of purgation as retribution for disdaining the happiness and success they saw in other people.

"Now, I presume you fear the third terrace will feature your own Gabriel as one of the Wrathful, subsumed in the afterlife by noxious, dark smoke. But I ask again what all three of you surely have already thought to yourselves, one time or another, for as long as you've been engaged in this quest: What if Gabriel is not missing because he is a victim-in-waiting of these Dante Massacres? What if Dante Gabriel Rossetti cannot be found because somehow he perpetrated these crimes? Put it another way: how do you know he did not?"

Holmes and Browning jumped right into the fray, arguing against Gabriel's being responsible. Holmes used examples from his experience during the Boston horrors. Browning pointed out how the detective seemed to have made up his mind without hearing their information, and soon Browning and Holmes, each trying to outtalk the other, somehow ended up debating Gabriel's philosophy of poetry and art. When there was a pause in the exchange, Christina stepped forward.

"He is my brother," Christina said evenly. "That is how I know, Mr. Tennyson."

Tennyson squinted again, studying her.

In a window across from Tennyson, where the curtains had not been pulled closed all the way, a woman flattened her face against the rain-soaked window before shouting to unseen friends, "You can see the laureate well from here!"

Tennyson hurried over to yank the curtains together. He turned back to the others, speaking at the same time as he took a puff of courage from his pipe.

"That, Miss Rossetti," he said, "is good enough for me. Though there is one brother of *mine* who, I am certain, might have been a murderer, had he even a tithe of ambition."

S imon Camp reached the bottom of the stairs beneath the bowling alley, where a man in a turban was emerging from one of the rooms, glaring at Camp as he passed him to go upstairs.

Camp turned into the same door from which the turbaned man had emerged but was blocked by a gorilla of a man in a dark sackcloth coat.

"Who was the sheik?" Camp asked.

"Ask him, why don't you, if you want your neck separated from your head," the man said. "Lost your way." It wasn't a question.

"Not yet," Camp said. "Tell Mr. Matt Kadnar, won't you, I bring presents from Boston."

The gorilla disappeared behind the door, which was next opened by a shorter man with prominent ears, a crooked nose, and sore-looking, red eyes. He was missing his left arm.

"What can I do for you?"

"Greetings. May I?" Camp asked, waving himself into the room.

The smoke-filled room was populated with men and women playing cards, with large stacks of money piled up all around. The man followed right behind Camp.

"This is for members of our club only," he warned Camp. He stroked his beard, which he wore long.

"Oh, I haven't time to play whist today," Camp said. He reached into his coat and yanked at a bundle of envelopes, showing just their corners. "You are Matt Kadnar, aren't you? Or at least, Kadnar when you are in Austria and Germany. Porter in Paris. McCord in Ireland. I've brought some letters to deliver from Boston, with some important information from your colleagues there in freedom and revolution. New trade routes for your arms shipments that aren't currently being monitored, some instructions for building weapons, that sort of thing."

McCord put out his hand.

"Not so fast," Camp said, letting the letters slip back into his pocket. "Your friends in Boston assured me that in return for safe delivery of these you could give a stranger some advice."

McCord formed a small grin. "Look around. I can simply have those letters removed from your possession if I want."

"And I've given instructions to my associates in London that if they don't hear from me in an hour, they deliver copies of these same documents right to Superintendent Williamson at Scotland Yard."

Some of the gamblers finished a game and rose to their feet. McCord nodded to the now-empty table, and Camp sat across from him.

"What is it exactly that you want, stranger?"

Camp glanced at the stump of an arm under McCord's black suit. "I suppose you're no longer one of the soldiers in your organization."

"You could call me one of its generals."

"I understand that you Fenian gentlemen keep a close eye on every criminal going-on in London."

"We know enough, aye. Enough that other activities won't get in the way."

"Fine, fine, Mr. McCord-Kadnar-Porter," Camp said, taking the letters out and slapping them onto the table. "I want to know all you've heard about these Dante killings."

McCord gave a shrug. "It's a mess out there. Bobbies everywhere. They even got their bloodhounds running around causing a ruckus."

"With all the ears you have listening, no gossip has reached you about who might have done it or why?"

"Not much to hear. MP Morton, he was some bastard, voting down any hint of rights for our people. The opera singer wasn't one of the girls who were, well, available at a price, if that interests you. Not to say any actress or singer could be called 'chaste,' but she wasn't mixed up with that sort."

McCord put his hand down on the pile of letters, and Camp slammed his hand down on McCord's, causing four and then five men to appear behind the Fenian leader.

"Who killed them?" Camp demanded.

"If I knew that, I'd take a knife to the bastard myself," said McCord. "Get rid of our friends in blue staring everyone up and down. We can keep our ears open, and keep you in mind for anything we hear."

Camp nodded, satisfied, then slowly lifted his hand away. "We have our bargain."

"What makes you so interested?"

Camp, rising and ostentatiously brushing off his suit, paused and thought about it. "You could say I'm something of a Dante aficionado and want to know the story before anyone else."

"Don't know much of the fellow myself."

"Dante? Oh, he's something. Breaks all the rules of God and the afterlife, all for love of country and glory."

"What is it you're doing now?" McCord asked, irritated.

Camp was scribbling in his notebook. "I liked how that sounded, didn't you? Love of . . . country . . . and glory."

"Leave your name and address so we can find you. But I'm afraid you're never going to be the first to know what happened, not with Dolly Williamson on the chase."

"Why is that?"

"Inspector Dolly has gotten in our way more than once. We have a number of comrades essential to our cause rotting behind bars because of him and his detectives. Nobody gets the jump on him."

From the time he was ushered to the body of Lillian Brenner, everything began to change for the police investigation into what quickly came to be known as the Dante Massacres or the Great Purgations (depending on which clever newspaper writers you read). Dolly felt the change in his bones before it happened, the way sailors knew a storm was coming. He sat up in his bed the night Brenner was discovered, writing notes on the case, but also waiting for the changes to come.

In the morning, Dolly was called over to the deadhouse to restore order. There was a throng of people, doubling back on itself into the street, to view the bodies of Jasper Morton and Lillian Brenner. The public clamor was not to help—or not chiefly so—but to share in the spectacle.

Two days later—as certain as daylight—a message arrived at Scotland Yard from the Home Secretary requesting Dolly visit Buckingham Palace. The constables and other detectives glared upon him with jealousy and pity on his way out. He didn't fear what was coming from the visit to the royal palace—Dolly didn't fear much, other than not finding his quarry in a case. But he didn't like the interruption to his plans for the day or the distraction this would provide to the policemen who worked under him. He remembered, at the last moment before entering the palace, to discard the sprig of grass he had between his teeth.

He was escorted by an attendant through chandelier-lit halls and up

broad flights of stairs. His colleagues back at Scotland Yard probably envisioned him playing whist with Her Highness. But he only saw the queen
for a moment through a row of open doors—Victoria was chubby and pink
and sat with some ladies over tea. The rest of the visit he was seated in a
non-palatial office with the queen's private secretary, Charles Grey. Grey
was an ex-military man and ex-member of the House of Commons and, as
a result, carried himself with an air of competence and urgency. Grey
liked speaking more than listening, and he diplomatically prodded Dolly
for information on his investigation and in return passed on mostly
irrelevant advice.

Grey had known Jasper Morton in Parliament, and although he admitted to never actually liking the man, he became impassioned when speaking about his murder, and insinuated the queen was similarly impassioned
(which, at the moment, was hard for Dolly to imagine, having just seen her
tear a dainty bite of chocolate sponge cake). "Her Highness has come from
Windsor to deal with a multitude of pressing matters, this included. She
wishes me to convey that the police ought to take some *very* stringent measures." The secretary also railed against the notion of a young woman
murdered, as though Miss Brenner's was the first such death in England.
Dogs? asked the royal secretary.

"We've taken the bloodhounds out, yes sir, to the harbor and to some
of the neighborhoods known to shelter criminals on the run," Dolly assured him, with little confidence in his voice. The dogs were trained to
take in scents—from the scenes of the two deaths—and try to match them
elsewhere, but the method was little more than an experiment, and had
not yielded clues.

Grey promised all kinds of resources from the palace, though with the
exception of one or two, most were distractions.

There was a larger, unspoken message of the unusual visit, and of making sure Dolly had that glimpse of the queen: Dolly was to bring this case
to a conclusion quickly, and put a stop to further public ripples. Grey
commented that many inside the palace favored a theory that the culprit

had to be a foreigner. Maybe even an Irish Fenian to distract the police from the scoundrels' real plans.

"Theories, theories, theories," Dolly said. "We are nearly lost in them."

The Home Office the next morning announced they were providing Dolly with more men, no doubt a modification insisted upon by Grey. By order of the commissioner, extra policemen, armed to the teeth with revolvers and cutlasses, were to observe the city from the roofs of buildings and down in the sewers looking for the Dante-inspired killer, but reports came back to the police offices as "all correct" (though one police sergeant got lost for four hours in the sewer system and, after it was feared he might have gotten stuck and drowned, turned up safe on the other side of London). The Home Office also ordered that two detectives and two men of lower ranks be sent abroad, one to Italy and one to France, to investigate whether the menace in London might have had some faraway source.

Some of the extra operatives were useful as Dolly scoured London looking for connections between Morton and Brenner, and between either murder victim and the literature of Dante Alighieri. The fact was, members of Parliament sometimes attended an opera, opera singers sometimes voted in elections for Parliament, but beyond that, the two unfortunate people might as well have lived on separate planets.

There was an assortment of new items of greater interest that floated across Dolly's desk—for example, that Morton had been seen wearing a disguise as he hurried through the London streets one night, and that Brenner visited several opium dens.

Now Dolly had Constable Branagan driving him all over London through a seemingly random set of destinations. The detective interviewed some of the individuals identified by the new men as having additional information. As they went along in the more troubled quarters of the city, Dolly would inevitably be noticed by bulging eyes and, in a peculiar way, welcomed. Pickpockets would flip their pockets inside out to show their lack of booty. Miscreants offered vulgar toasts to Dolly's health with pots of ale. A woman raced across a street to shake his hand, and other women smiled gently at him.

Some of the locations Dolly wanted to visit were perplexing.

There was the modest box of a house at Charlotte Street. Dolly walked back and forth in front of it. He wasn't quite pacing. He seemed to be counting his steps.

"No garden," he mused. "They must have stayed inside—reading, no doubt, writing."

"Who?" Constable Branagan asked—who could say why he asked, as he knew the detective would not give him an answer. Not yet.

"Twenty-five, thirty years ago this street was filled with poverty and struggle."

Dolly announced his credentials to the residents and scurried around the house. He called out from inside one of the rooms: "House looks bigger from the outside, Branagan, then it is inside, doesn't it?"

True. But the observation didn't render the visit to the little abode particularly relevant to the constable at a time when all of London was in an uproar and bills were being posted not to go out alone after dark. Nor did their next stop, which was a cemetery, seem pressing. Dolly went in but told Branagan to wait at the gates and watch.

"Inspector?" Branagan replied. "There's no one around. What exactly am I watching for?"

"We are looking for information on people, Branagan, and that means there may be people looking at us."

On his way inside, Dolly tore off a bill posted on the gates. It read: *Jew and Gentile, Tory and Radical, patrician and plebeian, can agree the police detectives are failing to protect us!*

After spending a half hour in the cemetery, Dolly's figure emerged from a cloud of gray fog to declare to Branagan their next destination: the British Museum. Once they arrived, Branagan idled outside, assuming he should keep guard again.

"No, Branagan," Dolly said, popping his head back out of the building, "come inside with me. It's as quiet as a stopped clock in here. If someone enters with an eye on us, we'll know."

There was a line of hopefuls trying to get tickets of admission. As Dolly and Branagan went past several attendants in the entrance hall, Dolly took pity on the constable and explained a little more.

"To understand someone's soul, you must understand where they come from."

"So that house on Charlotte Street," Branagan replied. "I take it that was where Gabriel Rossetti grew up?"

Dolly nodded. "And it seems a home where the world would open to a young man primarily through his bookshelves and his parents."

"And the cemetery. His wife is buried there, I suppose?"

"You see more than you reveal, Branagan. His wife and his father. But it wasn't her burial that interests me as much as her *exhumation*. That grave I saw back there had been opened."

"Opened? Why?"

Dolly waved away the question as he and Branagan entered the museum's reading room under the great dome. With several witnesses near Lillian Brenner's murder recognizing Dante Gabriel Rossetti there, earlier suspicions became certainties. Coincidence could not be entertained; Rossetti was the man they needed to find.

Inside the reading room, men and women studied books and newspapers in the soft glow of lamps. A trustee of the museum, with whom Dolly had exchanged messages in advance, greeted them with a stack of papers and a smattering of memories.

"He would sit right there, as I recall," the trustee commented, speaking in a whisper. In the chair he pointed at was a bald man with a straggly white beard who was roused awake by the attention. He was surrounded by the pages of a manuscript. The trustee handed Dolly some papers. "Yes, Gabriel Rossetti would sit and translate these medieval love poems of . . ."

"Dante Alighieri," Dolly said.

"Indeed."

"But why," Branagan broke in, "do you possess them? If he labored on them so, wouldn't he have kept them?"

"Well, Constable," said the trustee excitedly, "that is just it. This was eight, nine years ago, mind you, so I cannot bring back every detail. But I can still see him as clear as I see you, Constable, and you, Inspector—yes, I see forty or fifty examples of man and womankind a day, but I could still see what a—well, never mind my memory of him. You could not look at him too much, in any event, because he was constantly looking over his shoulder, as though worried that someone would be spying on him. Back to what you ask. He would leave the papers here, like a trail of carrion abandoned by a predator pursued by hunters."

"Remarkable metaphor," Dolly commented drily.

"Why, thank you, Inspector. Yes, Mr. Rossetti would be consumed by his labor here—but he had no *interest* in what he was producing. These papers, so dazzling to me, were worthless to him. It was the act of entering Dante Alighieri's mind he wanted. These translations are quite wonderful, so I preserved them instead of throwing them away."

"What does he look like when you see him in your mind's eye?" Dolly asked the trustee before they moved on in their examination of the room. "Dante Gabriel Rossetti, what did you think of him?"

"He looked like a man who could lead armies, if he wished to, Inspector, and destroy worlds. Quite like . . ."

"Who?" Dolly asked when the trustee stopped himself.

"You, Inspector."

The stains of cheap ink on her fingertips stubbornly resisted washing, even when she mixed water with lemon juice. Never in her life had Christina spent so much time with newspapers. When she wrote poetry, she looked for what she thought of as the moral movements of the words and ideas and stories. To share something with the public she equated to a spiritual responsibility, and she felt she had to deserve the honor of publication. Reporters, she realized as she immersed herself in the publications of various political stripes, wrote as though morality did not exist; there was hardly a beginning and never an end to stories they told, and no lessons to draw from them. They were fragments of unrecovered truth.

Shaking her hands dry, she returned to her work at the big dining table at Tudor House, where Browning and Holmes created disarray as quickly as she tried to impose order.

During the opera and at the banquet afterward, Christina had done her best, before her walk with Cayley and Tennyson's appearance, to collect names of those attending before the dancing and the revelry. People sometimes asked her how she could spend so much time among prostitutes at Saint Mary's but become so upset by dancing or other relatively innocent merriment. She always tried to explain that the unfortunate women she helped were hated by society even when they attempted to remove themselves from their field, while the immoral acts of respectable society were utterly ignored. The women, in other words, never had a fair shake.

It had been after meeting Tennyson, once they got back to Tudor House from the opera, when Browning and Holmes shared their story of Lillian Brenner's friend, Jane Cary, and Brenner's all-consuming concern and jealousy of another singer becoming the prima donna. "Envy," Christina replied, closing her eyes tight and picturing the scenes of Brenner fearing she would be replaced. "There is the reason Miss Brenner would be chosen to be punished for it. Whom did Miss Brenner share her feelings with who would have had the idea to associate her with the Envious?"

"That is the bit of bad luck. It seems she spoke about it with anyone who listened," Browning, a bit demoralized, informed her.

There was more: Holmes recounted Miss Cary's discussion of using opium—and while she didn't say if Brenner participated in her dangerous habit, she had told Browning that she and Brenner were inseparable. It would be hard to find an opium fiend inseparable from a friend who abstained. "She revealed something else, too," Holmes added. "She commented that opium has been much more difficult to find around London, even for those who need it, including soldiers—"

"—and that is what made me think of what Holmes had already told us," Browning interrupted, "about the natural appeal of Dante's justice to the mind of a soldier."

Holmes continued, "If one of these soldiers observed Miss Brenner and her friend obtaining opium he required, this might have directed a soldier's attention on Miss Brenner and, possibly, also on . . ."

"Gabriel," Tennyson finished his sentence. "Who also relied on opium, and may have been searching to replenish his own supply."

A soldier trained in stealth and in the execution of violence could have carried out the "punishments" of Morton—who had callously voted to send soldiers around the globe to fight in useless conflicts—and Brenner. Their reasons to examine connections to soldiers strengthened with information added by Tennyson. From him they learned how the widow Morton believed her husband had been disguising himself in order to hide from someone who may have been hunting him. Morton had commented to his wife that he was an "easy target," an expression used by soldiers in the field hunting an enemy. If the madman had in fact skillfully stalked his prey, it was another hint that fit with a soldier's training.

There were other soldierly reflections throughout Dante's poem of the afterlife. Lucifer, around whom Dante's Hell is structured, led a military rebellion against God. Beatrice herself, guiding Dante's journey, is described by Dante as an admiral. Cato, the supervisor and guardian of Purgatory, had been a soldier in war against Julius Caesar.

"Promising ideas, indeed," Tennyson praised them. "We could have a Cato of our own in our midst."

In the Tudor House drawing room's burgeoning museum of the Great Purgations, they had kept track of all those mentioned as witnesses to the crimes. Some of these names they had collected themselves through their interviews, others they found in newspapers. It was a slippery process. Prostitutes, like the ones they spoke to in the public gardens, were nervous about being identified, and it seemed women in general were rather skittish about even admitting seeing such horrors. In fact, a blond woman at Morton's death and a brunette beauty at Brenner's were described in their library of newspapers as being among those closest to the scenes, but both presumably refused to provide their names, making it impossible for the group to pursue valuable information from them.

Within the catalog of witnesses, the group set out to identify all the soldiers or former soldiers they could. As luck would have it, English reporters made a fetish of pointing out a man as having served in war, however briefly, bestowing authority upon whatever it was those witnesses had to say. This was true even if they had very little to say. Example number twenty-four: *The situation of Miss Brenner's death created chaos in the street, according to eyewitness H. M. Everton, a sergeant in the recent affairs in India.* Tacking the names to the wall, however, amounted to little progress for the researchers—none of the names yet matched associates of Gabriel's, and each was identified as being near the Morton death in the North Woolwich Gardens or the Brenner death in St. James's Street, but none at both.

Tennyson pointed to a classified advertisement in one of the papers. "Here is something important."

The advertisement was a letter that read: *Dear Sirs at Cockles' Pills, Like most literary men I am subject to violent constipation, & your pills I find of the greatest possible comfort. Yrs A. Tennyson*

"Did you really write that, Tennyson?" Browning asked.

"Of course not!" Tennyson said with a laugh. "That is my point—only trust what we find in these news rags to a degree."

Tennyson changed the mood of any room he was in. Part of it was purely physical. His face was an interesting combination of strength and suffering. Christina understood women's fascination with and men's anxieties about him. Being with him was something like being with a king, she thought. Then there was his personality. He was decisive and autonomous. For example, he suddenly stood up to leave the house and promised, with a flicker in his dark eyes, that he had a notion of how to find more to test their ideas about a soldier's involvement.

Christina had also invited Cayley to come again, arranging one of Gabriel's studios upstairs for the project he'd proposed to Christina on their walk around Haymarket. He was organizing the late professore's vast unpublished notes and materials on Dante. She could tell that the other parties, Browning, Holmes, and Tennyson—who had to stare two inches from Cayley's face to realize he wasn't Browning or Holmes—thought it a questionable choice to have Cayley in the house at the same time as they were engaged in a confidential endeavor. But little sound traveled in or out of Gabriel's upstairs studio, and Christina had observed Cayley from the time he had been one of her father's pupils. When he was engrossed in his books and papers, the world could crumble around his ears and he wouldn't notice. Cayley also provided a mastery of Dante—whenever they needed another opinion—that even the combined minds of Christina, Browning, Holmes, and Tennyson couldn't match.

Besides, there was a kind of ballast provided by Cayley studiously hunched over Dante material *without* worries of violence and crime. When she stopped in on him to ask if he needed anything, she tried not to feel too flattered by the quick, sloppy smile toward her.

At times, she thought what it would be like to see Cayley more, not just under the pretense of scholarship. Then she would remind herself: any ability to devote herself to family, the essential quality for a wife and mother, had failed miserably in connection to Gabriel, who might already be forever out of reach.

Cayley would tell her about his research. "I believe I've located indisputable evidence, Miss Rossetti, through a series of documents, that the historical Beatrice Portinari was indeed the Beatrice known to Dante."

"Mr. Cayley, Canto Thirteen, when Dante meets the Envious, he remarks that the shades wore cloaks the color of the stones, which in turn are described as '*col livido color de la petraia*'—the livid color of stone."

"Yes, I often wondered about that language, and discussed it with your father, who convinced me the color referred to was a combination of blue and black."

The cloak. Christina thought of the clothes folded near the body of Lillian Brenner in the deadhouse. Which included a dark-colored cloak. *The color of the stones.*

Now, as she continued the labors with Browning and Holmes downstairs, Christina checked the time on one of Gabriel's less unreliable clocks. Tennyson had been away from the house for three hours. Meanwhile, with the documents spread over the table, the other weary scholars searched for more mentions of any of the soldiers in recent newspapers.

When the front door flew back open, Tennyson strutted back in with files on fourteen of the eighteen soldiers whose names they had gathered so far. After Tennyson bowed to cheers and applause, he explained that he had gone to the War Office in Pall Mall just as they were about to lock their doors. *I'm at work on an ode*, he told the official there with a self-importance that was both part of his act to fulfill the day's purpose, and a part of being poet laureate. *An ode, my dear fellow, to the courageous men who keep our empire strong and growing as we sleep and dine comfortably in our homes.*

Holmes cried out, "Bravo, Tennyson! And they opened their whole cabinet to you?"

"Nearly all of it," Tennyson boasted, lighting his pipe to celebrate the victory he recounted. "There are benefits of my post, I admit, though I often feel it crushing me. When I was first asked to be laureate by the queen, I wrote two letters, one accepting and one declining. I sat and stared at both until my eyes, weak to begin with, watered. I settled on accepting when my sister convinced me that as laureate I would surely always be offered the liver wing of a fowl when I dined out."

Christina noticed a flash of emotion on Browning's face as Tennyson spoke of the topic. For her part, she could never imagine using her fame from her poetry to coax a favor—in fact, she never accepted that she possessed fame. "My name is Christina," she would introduce herself even when faced with someone who had already squealed with delight upon recognizing her as the famous poetess.

Ten of the fourteen military files borrowed by Tennyson included photographs. The documents inside listed tedious details about what wars and contests each man served in. The group studied these cold facts. They debated which man's experiences most likely could have left him sufficiently scarred to turn toward Dante for a sense of justice.

Christina could not help remembering Gabriel's own experience being a soldier of sorts, however short and uneventful. It was ten years before, a time when everyone worried Louis-Napoléon was going to invade England. The "Artists' Rifles Corps" was composed mostly of painters. Gabriel and his fellow artistic troops trained with weapons and were reviewed by Queen Victoria in Hyde Park, though Gabriel soon grew bored of the whole thing and dropped out.

The day of research wound down without anything definite enough to satisfy Christina—a morass of grand ideas, theories, hypotheses, notions. The four retired to their own beds with a plan to meet again in the morning. Christina could hardly sleep, though, thinking of the faces in the photographs. They were mostly nondescript men with bold military mustaches meant to make them dashing but, at the moment, they gave Christina a pit in her stomach. One of the men could hold her brother's fate in his hands. Or could she and her companions be chasing shadows, supposing one of these former soldiers guilty based on conjecture, just as that inscrutable Dolly Williamson seemed to be doing about Gabriel?

In her dreams that followed, Gabriel urged her on, first with charm, then shouts. He always possessed a quick temper, and there had been a time the family hoped his marriage to Lizzie would ease it. But Lizzie, for her part, was just as unpredictable, and had lost her temper more easily after the stillbirth of their child.

It was another of Gabriel and Lizzie's arguments on February 10, 1862, that sent him stomping out of the house to seek out drink and distraction. When he returned, he found Lizzie in bed, breathing in a shallow rise and fall, an empty vial by the bed. The strong smell of laudanum pervaded the air. After the first doctor pronounced her dead, Gabriel called for another. Then another. As though all it would take would be to find someone with more imagination to bring her back.

Lord, may I come to Thee?—that poem sat in between the bed and the mortal vial, her poison of choice. As one of the doctors examined her lifeless body, Gabriel read it through tear-blurred eyes.

> *. . . My outward life feels sad and still,*
> *Like lilies in a frozen rill.*
> *I am gazing upwards to the sun,*
> *Lord, Lord remembering my lost one.*
> *O Lord, remember me!*

As Christina drifted in and out of sleep thinking of these verses and scenes, she had other visions. In one, she and Gabriel walked through Regent's Park at sunset, a sunset Gabriel said made him imagine the sun setting fire to the distant trees and roof ridges. Then a yellow light swept from the trees, circling in a mass, and becoming all the canaries in London escaping their cages to be together, before each willingly returned to his or her captivity.

The faces from the photographs flowed through her mind again, this time like images in a magic lantern. She sat up straight in bed, with an exhale that began in sleep and ended with her fully awake. She knew why the faces would not leave her alone.

She had seen one of them before.

"Reuben Loring," she called out once Browning, who was rubbing the sleep from his eyes, appeared at the door at 19 Warwick Crescent.

"Very unconventional hour for a visitor, Mr. Browning, and a woman!" cried the servant who had admitted her.

Browning dismissed his domestic back to his chambers upstairs and brought Christina in. "Pay him no mind. No man is a hero to his valet de chambre. Who are you talking about, Miss Rossetti?" asked Browning, pulling his nightclothes more tightly around himself.

She handed him the file Tennyson had secured for Reuben Loring. He was a thirty-four-year-old man listed as having served most recently in the Ethiopian conflicts. Browning took out the photograph—a deadened stare, curled mustache, a strong brow.

"Do you recognize him?"

"Should I?" Browning asked, shaking his head. "You know this man?"

"No. But do you remember when we called on Arthur Hughes's studio? Hughes ran after us and showed us the sketches he made the night of Morton's killing—the studies of park-goers in the gaslight and moonlight. The man in this photograph was one of them." She added before he could question it: "I am certain."

"I have found your certainty as reliable as steel, Miss Rossetti. But I'm afraid I don't recall the sketches as clearly as you do. Wait a minute. Loring was on our list of witnesses at Miss Brenner's murder. But Hughes sketched him—if it is the same man—at the gardens where Morton was found, which would mean—"

Browning stopped himself, swallowing hard. Christina gave a severe nod to confirm he had landed on the most significant part of the discovery. *Loring was at the scenes of* both *deaths.* They had given a name to their adversary, their Cato-like overseer of a new Purgatory, and it was a name that seemed utterly unlikely to contain evil depths: Reuben Loring.

B rowning sent messages to Hughes's studio and learned from the artist's late-night reply that the sketches he had showed them three and a half weeks earlier had been carried to one of his patrons to decide if he wished to commission a painting from the study. Christina insisted she and Browning call on the patron at once. Though too early to visit any civilized home in London, where calls were made between two and six o'clock, Christina was content to be a nuisance under the circumstance.

They already met this same patron once since Gabriel vanished. Their earlier interview with A. R. Gibson had been to inquire whether he had run across Gabriel, to whom he also served as a patron. "Painters appear to steal patrons from each other as much as they steal models and themes," Browning observed to Christina.

Gibson welcomed them inside his impressive home, not mentioning or seeming to even notice the early hour. He wore his coat over his usual elaborate dressing gown. It was a large and mostly empty mansion. They sat in the airy library and asked about the sketches Hughes had sent over to him for review.

Gibson—also patron to Gabriel compatriots James Whistler and Edward Burne-Jones—was a youthful, angular man, with brilliant blue eyes and the lazy demeanor of one who grew up steeped in wealth. Even the volume of his voice refused to labor, remaining the same whether a listener was beside him or across the expansive room.

"Isn't it something," Gibson said, one hand carelessly caressing his velvet collar, "how this room could be the coolest in the whole house in the summer, and the warmest in the winter? Why, I practically live in the very library my father used to forbid me to enter, lest I muddy the floors with my always-bare feet."

He spread out his toes, and only then did Christina notice he was shoeless.

"Father and Grandfather manufactured clothes—I joined their enterprise for a while, but stepped aside when I was twenty. Had you known that?"

"You're as surprising as usual, Mr. Gibson," said Christina.

"There is so much else in the world other than clothes, don't you think?"

Christina tried gently to remind him of the reason for their visit.

He sighed at being forced on course, tickling the point of his short beard. "Well, Miss Rossetti, I haven't had a chance to look over those sketches by Hughes very closely. I haven't decided whether I wish to commission Hughes on them, truth be told, or whether they are just more of the same Hughesian drivel—people staring into space looking as though they wonder where they went all wrong. If I do commission them, I should want them to myself. What good is having beautiful art over your hearth, if other people have the same beautiful art over *their* hearths? Its magic ceases."

"We will not use the drawings for any purpose," Christina said. "We need to study them for a few minutes, and then will trouble you no more."

Gibson accepted Christina's promise and agreed to retrieve them. He left his visitors in the library while he crossed to another wing of the mansion.

Browning took down a first edition of her *Goblin Market and Other*

Poems. He opened to the woodcuts by Gabriel showing the two sisters of the titular poem in a protective embrace next to an image of the coming goblins. "Look over here, Miss Rossetti."

She gestured for quiet.

"I am sorry, Miss Rossetti," he said. "I blame the loudness of my voice, and the fact that I go too close to people when I speak, on the deafness of my father in his later years."

"It's not that. Seeing one of my books where I don't expect it is like having a stranger leap up from behind a wall and yell 'surprise.' Yet somehow people in both instances expect you to smile. Did you see this?" Christina asked, reaching a variety of Dante volumes.

"What do you know? Dante galore."

"It is a respectable collection," Christina said, whispering as she studied the titles. She drew out a volume sandwiched between Dante translations—a book delicately bound in red and brown calf leather. A book with no title.

"I saw one like that at Tudor House," Browning said. "I don't recognize it."

She ran her finger along the bumpy spine. "My father's final commentary on Dante. Nearly all copies were burned. Gabriel must have given one to Mr. Gibson."

"Yes. Your brother turned me into a lover of Dante," Gibson said when he returned to the room and noticed where their attention landed. "What passion!"

"Dante Alighieri's, or my brother's?" Christina asked.

Gibson smiled and threw his head back in laughter, as though she had told a great joke. Christina never told jokes, and examined him with her serious eyes wide.

"Imagine Dante walking among us, nearly a god on earth! We can't complain about his being exiled, I suppose, for without that happening, he would have never been driven to write his *Comedy*. There is the story that during his exile he came to Oxford to study. Think of Dante, so close to where we are now, breathing the air we breathe. Now, as to Dante," Gibson said, "oh, but now I speak of your brother—Dante Rossetti, he is unlike anybody else, an out-and-outer. A pagan, you might say, a hero for all that is beautiful and great.

"I have a memory—may I indulge by sharing it with the two of you? Thank you. I was walking with Dante—again I mean Rossetti!—late one night. Poor fellow never sleeps, his nervous system, as you know, is all to pieces. A doctor I know says that if Dante were put into a Turkish bath he should sweat chloral at every pore. In any event—as we walked it came out that he was not so certain the earth revolved around the sun. I drew back in surprise at his unscientific declaration. 'Well,' said your sage and nonsensical brother, 'our senses did not tell us so, at any rate, and what does it matter whether the earth does move or not? What Dante Alighieri knew is enough for me.' In our age of sofas and divans, your brother teaches me to ignore comfort, and in an age of material things, he teaches me to test all that is unseen. Just the other day, I told him that he is the world's truest teacher."

"The other day, Mr. Gibson?" Christina asked, for a moment excited.

Gibson stopped and thought about it. "Oh, the other month—well, I hardly ever know the day or date, you know. Take your time with these, my friends."

Breaking into more throes of odd laughter, Gibson left them with the sketches as he shuffled from the room again to attend to another caller.

From the front hall of the house, they could hear a woman's voice, a crying child, and Gibson crying out "Responsibility? Responsibility!" over and over, as though each time the word was more absurd.

Christina flipped through the sketches rapidly until she came, hands trembling, upon the one she sought. Browning held the photograph from Reuben Loring's military file next to the sketch of the man in the gardens.

The men were one and the same.

<hr />

As he sat engrossed by his work, Dolly Williamson was interrupted by Branagan. The constable announced a visitor who wished to see him.

"If he does not need to see me in particular," said the detective, not looking up from the paper where he was copying down a line from a book, "shoo him."

"To quote the gentleman: 'I would like to see any fellow who desires to make solving these Dante killings as easy as lying.'"

Dolly's ink blotted as his hand stopped. "Easy as lying?"

Branagan shrugged. "Some kind of Americanism. I remember hearing it when I traveled through New England."

Following Dolly's instructions, Branagan returned to the inspector's office with the gangly visitor, who sported a checkered waistcoat and bowler hat, which he tossed on a hook.

Dolly asked him his name and business.

"I've come all the way from Boston to help you. You see, I'm a Pinkerton man, of the famous American detective agency"—he omitted the fact he was no longer actually employed by the Pinkertons, and that they despised him—"and, simply put, I want to know what *you* know."

"If that nervous little Boston doctor-poet has engaged you to protect him from my questions, you can reassure him I have no further interest in him."

"Doctor-poet?"

The chief detective saw by the visitor's interested face that he had not, in fact, been sent by Dr. Holmes. The visitor brightened as he examined the plaster heads on the walls.

"And these are . . ."

"Casts of some of England's most notorious criminals," Dolly said.

"Yes! I recognize many of them from my studies of criminal history, Inspector. You brought all these to justice, I take it. There's the lass—Mrs.

Kidder, wasn't it? Drowned her stepdaughter in a stream, if I recall. And that ugly phiz must be Karl Kohl, who cut off his neighbor's head and left it in the mud for the rats to chew on."

"Those ropes are the ones from which they were hanged at the gallows."

"Ah, that one, now that one is Barrett, the Fenian, ain't it, Inspector? Last man England ever hanged in public. Won't the people miss the entertainment?"

"They can pick up a book," answered Dolly.

The visitor's eyes floated along Dolly's desk, landing on a book of poems by Dante Gabriel Rossetti.

"Speaking of that. Interesting reading, for a busy police detective."

"I repeat," Dolly said with less patience, "who are you?"

"I'm Simon Camp, a Pinkerton man—I thought I mentioned it. I've come to Mother England to investigate these horrid occurrences."

"On the Pinkertons' dime? Peculiar assignment."

"My own dime. And I'm not under anyone's wing anymore. Inspector— Dolly, is that the quaint nickname for you?—my proposal is simple and benefits us both. If you share with me what you know so far in this case, I can lend you my ingenuity and, rarer still, *experience* in such matters. Perhaps I can even give you some tips on your Fenian problem."

The way the Pinkerton man lingered on "experience" made Dolly's mind turn to the booklet they had acquired about the Dante incidents in Boston. Dolly had recently received a letter from a former policeman in Boston who had been intimately involved in that case, giving him details that had been withheld from the papers, including about the work of a private detective who had tried to use his knowledge for the purposes of blackmail: Simon Camp.

"I have a counterproposal, Mr. Camp," Dolly said. "Shall I share it?"

"Fire away, Dolly."

Dolly rose from his chair. "My counterproposal is that this second you leave my office, today you leave London, and by the end of the week you leave Mother England, or I shall find you and arrest you in the queen's name."

The visitor, grinning a little, bowed and made his exit at a leisurely pace, glancing once more at the heads of the executed rogues.

"God save the queen," he mumbled.

Holmes slept well. It defied logic, he knew. Here he was, voluntarily embroiled in trying to resolve what seemed unresolvable, but it felt so much better than standing aside without trying. Correction: Holmes slept well *until* a persistent knocking at his hotel room door roused him early in the morning. A messenger waiting on the other side passed him a folded paper, pierced with what Holmes's trained eye identified as a woodchuck's teeth marks, on which was written in Browning's hand a request to come to 16 Cheyne Walk (Holmes had learned Gabriel's street's name was pronounced "Chainie") two hours earlier than planned.

It was a clear day and the streets outside already burst with activity. Finding a cab in London was easier than in Boston, where you had to wish on a star that one would come, but getting anywhere in a hurry in London was an exercise in frustration. A man did not know his place in the universe until he found himself a drop in the ocean of London, and an American in particular did not know his place until he faced the fact that seven dollars was worth one pound. The many flowers sticking out from men's buttonholes and women's hats did not change how dismal and gloomy the city seemed to him. But London was finally, in a sense, his true way home.

The doctor arrived at Dante Gabriel Rossetti's house of strangeness right behind the cab carrying Tennyson, who'd received an identical message. The superbly energetic Christina, hair tucked under a cap in a fashion shared by precisely no women in London outside convents, told them her stunning suspicion that a soldier who had been reported by the newspapers as being present at the second killing was also at the first—recorded by Hughes in a sketch made in the early morning hours on January 14 now held by the moody art collector A. R. Gibson.

The sketch matched the photograph obtained by Tennyson. Reuben Loring.

"Remarkable," Browning said, "that Miss Rossetti could recall the man from the sketch."

"Remarkable, yes, but not unexpected," said Holmes. "You see, Browning, you can very often carry two facts fastened together more easily than one by itself, as a housemaid can carry two pails of water with a hoop more easily than without it. You can remember a man's face better than you can his nose or his mouth or his eyebrow. In this case the sight of the photograph was the second pail."

The documents in Loring's file, which in several places had a line or paragraph sliced or cut out (not unusual in government documents), gave his current domicile as "unknown." That Loring's name appeared nowhere in the London city directory provided them further frustration but was not unexpected. Soldiers who went back and forth to faraway assignments were often left out of the annual publication. Through her charity work, Christina had heard the names over the years of several preachers, ministers, and religious teachers who made a mission of helping soldiers back in London after being in the various campaigns and battles managed by the War Office. The chaplains of these nonsectarian "soldiers' chapels," as they were called, preached temperance and provided reading rooms of religious materials and other comforts. While Browning headed to examine municipal records, she made a list of churches to visit with Holmes and Tennyson.

As they went down the steps of Tudor House, Cayley was coming through the seventeenth-century iron gates. "Won't I have the pleasure of your company this morning, Miss Rossetti? Gentlemen?"

"I'm afraid we are still engaged in a bit of our own research, Mr. Cayley," Christina replied.

Holmes noticed poor Cayley's face dropped like a flower scorched by the sun, and noticed further that Christina was entirely oblivious to it.

The first three religious officials the trio interviewed did not recognize Loring's government photograph—one of the chaplains who was quite ancient couldn't have recognized his own brother, for Holmes was positive he was half blind.

As a friend of Henry Wadsworth Longfellow's, into whose arms children would often throw themselves, Holmes was no stranger to being around literary royalty—not to overlook Holmes's own hard-earned fame from his poems and stories. Still, it was impressive to watch strangers react to the presence of Tennyson (even if some, one out of fifteen, say, thought Tennyson was Charles Dickens, to which the laureate would bark, "Can't two men wear beards and take to the pen without being confused for the other?"). But if Longfellow's gentle manner and otherworldly kindness kept his admirers charmed, Tennyson's personality worked in the opposite manner. Tennyson was as shy as a bat with people he didn't know, and could be aloof to the point of horrifying those who lionized him.

"Modern fame is nothing," he told Holmes and Christina. "I shall go down, and up, and down. I am up now, as is obvious. But I'd rather have an acre of land. To own a ship, a large steam yacht perhaps, and go round the world, that is my notion of true glory."

Holmes recalled Hawthorne years earlier telling him Tennyson shuffled instead of walked, like he was in too-big slippers; it was still true today, though the poet seemed to have grown into the slippers. Despite his shabby coat and his general disdain, Tennyson was a magnificent specimen and a kind of god to people, as if the poet laureate's role was to watch over their good and bad deeds. While Christina (who seemed to will herself not to need to stop to eat or drink) was asking after a preacher in a nearby chapel, Holmes was crossing through a busy square with Tennyson toward a restaurant when they encountered a man Tennyson later said he'd never seen in his life. "Beg pardon, Mr. Tennyson," the man said, with a swift motion pulling off his hat. "I've been drunk for three days and I want to make a solemn promise to *you*, Mr. Tennyson, that I won't do so anymore."

Tennyson seemed to enjoy this more than other interruptions. "That is a good resolve, and I hope you shall keep it."

"I promise you I will, Mr. Tennyson!"

Holmes was surprised, given all this unsolicited adulation, how many times in a short period Tennyson inevitably introduced the topic of some critic or reader who savaged him. At one point, Tennyson quoted verbatim from an angry letter. It went: *Sir, I used to worship you, but now I hate you. I loathe and detest you. You beast! You've taken to imitating Longfellow. Yours in aversion.* Holmes coaxed out of Tennyson that he had received the letter some fifteen years before. Holmes understood, of course, the peril of the author who stood defenseless against negativity, but reminded Tennyson that writers should not mind what anyone said about them.

"Holmes, I mind what *everybody* says."

The laureate provided a stark contrast to Christina Rossetti, who Holmes noticed made herself invisible, in a public sense, despite the universally warm reception of the few volumes she published. Sometimes a passerby in workman's clothes would see Christina and call out, raucously, "Come buy, come buy!"—as the goblin men did trying to tempt the girls of "Goblin Market." Christina would shrink into herself. Holmes had heard her described as "mysterious and precise" by those who had met and esteemed her, and "cold and skittish" by those who met and were confused by her.

She was outwardly calm and stoic, but her inner life—Holmes suspected—must have been a swirl of turmoil and distrust. She blamed herself for every fault in herself and in the world. She was, in short, a sinner who had forgotten to sin. She was so interesting from the first moment meeting her, but she made absolutely no attempt to be interesting. How odd to think of her helping fallen women and Gabriel helping women fall.

The descriptions of Gabriel, whom Holmes had never met, made the brother and sister sound like a study in opposites, but the doctor couldn't help wonder if Christina might be Gabriel turned inside out.

Then there was Browning, who was on a separate errand for their cause in another part of the city. Browning's noble head with its broad forehead and wide mouth reminded Holmes of an ancient warrior's. His eyes were as bright as a child's, and as open as Tennyson's were suspicious. Upon greeting you he clasped your hand with both of his for a long time, looking squarely into your face, but in conversation he was far more interested in what he had to say (loudly).

It took three tries before Tennyson picked a restaurant he deemed inexpensive enough. "But you own a mansion on an island with butlers, and you and Longfellow are the most popular poets in the world!" Holmes objected. Tennyson replied: "Poets are poor, Holmes, no matter how much money they have. There were times I drank bitter drafts out of the cup of life, which tend to make men hate the world. I should have liked to be a country squire quietly living on eight hundred pounds a year, with wife and family. Come, let's take some soup." (The soup was cheapest.)

After they dined, Holmes and Tennyson reunited with Christina, who had not met with success with the latest preacher, and together they traveled to another house of worship on her list, to a gentleman called Reverend Fallow. Christina had met him when he had given sermons at Saint Mary's. He recognized Christina, and confirmed that he ministered to soldiers.

"Yes, as a matter of fact, in addition to places of unfortunate women such as Saint Mary's, I have been attending to these noble men of arms for some years now," he said with an undertone of sadness. "I fear London presents a difficult place for the strongest people, ofttimes, and to go from the experiences of war back to this rather callous city can be especially trying. As long as they are active on the rolls of the War Office, the men are not allowed to marry and start families. No wonder so many of them are wanderers, spiritually and geographically speaking, as perhaps we all are in our own lives, at one time or another."

Christina handed the minister the photograph. "If you please, Reverend Fallow, could you tell us if you recall this man attending any of your services?"

Behind the chaplain trailed a young woman with short hair that was black and glossy. Though nearly as tall as the chaplain, she appeared so timid she blended in with the scenery of the church. The dark-haired woman and the chaplain exchanged a long glance over the photograph.

"Yes. I recognize him," admitted Fallow, unfolding a lime-colored handkerchief from his pocket to wipe his brow and brush aside chestnut curls of hair that were long enough to cover part of his bull-like face. "I know his name is Reuben—not certain if I even recall his surname. If you'll excuse us, friends, I need a hand from Sibbie before we hold some meetings with church officials."

"Just a moment more," said Holmes. "Reverend, we believe this man could be involved in the terrible murders that have struck the city of late. Any information you have that will help us find him would be invaluable."

A visible shudder went through the minister. "Do you mean—I assure you, Dr. Holmes, Reuben would have nothing to do with committing murders!" He composed himself. "I am afraid I'm confused why you're even asking about such things. I would think the police would be the ones inquiring into that kind of matter."

"We have reasons," Tennyson replied, a little too haughtily to placate him.

"I fear it would take a long time to explain, and we would not want to trouble you," Christina added.

"I really am not at liberty to reveal *anything* about the men we watch over. You ought to know the importance of remaining confidential, Miss Rossetti, having worked with those poor girls at Saint Mary's. Besides, I would be rather anxious that amateur investigating, such as the lot of you seem to be engaged in, could bring trouble down on Reuben Loring or others who count on my protection for body and soul. Sibbie, if you please, we are falling behind a very busy schedule before we must leave the city. In addition to tending to whatever these men need in London, and delivering sermons at Saint Mary's and other reform homes, some assistants and I also help operate one of the sanatoria outside of the city for those who feel alienated by the polluted surroundings, this tossing-and-turning metropolis, a place sicker than many of its patients." He put his hand on the young woman's shoulder and she turned away.

"Then you've remembered his surname after all," Holmes said cheerily, causing the minister to pause midstep. "Loring. Progress, for sure! This is vitally important, I assure you."

"As is my service to those who only seek a measure of hope when they are left without any. *Please* excuse us."

When the questioners exited to the grounds outside the church, Holmes asked his companions whether they noticed anything odd about the minister and his assistant.

"His hand rather lingered on the girl's shoulder," Tennyson replied.

"I think she had something more she wanted to tell us about Loring," Holmes said, indignation rising. The young woman tethered to the minister had reminded him of his daughter. "I'd wager he has a hold on that girl."

"I'm afraid I was given a similar impression when Reverend Fallow visited Saint Mary's—the way he looked at the girls as he preached . . ." Christina was too proper to finish her observation. She merely nodded to drive home her implication.

She insisted on looking around the rest of the church to see if there was anyone else to question about Loring.

Holmes felt a chill down his spine, and found himself drawn to look at someone behind them. "Tell me, Tennyson, do you think the police could have followed us here?"

Tennyson, taken aback by the idea, traced Holmes's gaze: on the other side of the church gates, a large stranger, with a tint of dusk in his skin, paced back and forth, his hands resting on a cord tied around a loose-fitting tunic. "I don't believe that man works with Scotland Yard, Holmes."

"Not likely, I suppose. But he seems rather intent on something."

As Christina rejoined them, Sibbie exited the church and walked the grounds carrying some books to a stone outbuilding at the other side of the yard.

"I'm going to try to speak to her," Christina said, darting off.

"I'll go, too," Holmes remarked, still thinking of his daughter—as though Amelia herself, now far from England, could be in danger.

Holmes suggested Tennyson stay where he was. He did not want to make her feel interrogated.

"Excuse me," Christina said, without a reply.

"Sibbie," Holmes called.

"Isobel," the woman said, turning around. She had a fragile, melancholy beauty.

"My apologies. I heard Reverend Fallow call you 'Sibbie.' But I suppose the chaplain's informality may prove rather uncomfortable to you."

"What can I help you with?" Her voice was as muted as her general presence. Her skin was a kind of alabaster, which made her soft blue eyes stand out even more.

"Please, it is crucial we find out more about Reuben Loring," Christina said, "and learn where he is. Immediately."

Holmes noticed through the veneer of Christina's usual politeness a hint of disdain escaped. This young woman had yielded to the whims of a dictatorial man—perhaps the greatest sin to an independent woman like Christina, far more so than falling into the habits of the girls who turned up at Saint Mary's. But giving Sibbie an order, as she was obviously accustomed to receiving from the preacher, was not going to help. If they were going to convince her to speak, it would fall to Holmes to do it.

"We know it's not your doing," Holmes said. "But if you know anything more, it would be helpful."

She gave a hurried glance around her with her sparkling eyes, then, after brushing away a dark lock of hair, offered a very slight nod.

"I do know more. Something happened in the war, with Mr. Loring," she said, then stopped herself.

"My dear," Holmes said, "Reverend Fallow need not hear about *anything* you say, and Mr. Loring, wherever he is, will never find out that you have aided in our search. Do not fear repercussions."

"You cannot understand." She said this, before she hurried away, with a haunting emphasis on each syllable of her rejection—or, maybe no rejection was implied. Maybe it was a caution.

I n an austere government office a mile and a half away, facing more mundane bureaucratic obstacles, Robert Browning prayed this strange prayer to himself:

Let this lead to our Cato.

Did the clerk notice his lips moving? Having copied the last address recorded for Reuben Loring in old tax ledgers, Browning took his leave to rendezvous with Christina, who had gone to the census office while Holmes and Tennyson searched for other congregants of Reverend Fallow's soldiers' chapel to question about Loring. Between the census office and the tax office, they had gathered five addresses the soldier had used at one time or another.

"Are you certain you don't wish to stop for a while before we continue with these?" Browning asked Christina, hearing of her busy afternoon with their compatriots—but her answer was clear when she made no reply.

Following the map of Loring's addresses brought them through streets and byways that formed a different London altogether. One of the addresses had actually disappeared, the building having been demolished. A portly woman who answered the door at another one did not know

Loring, but knew the name belonged to a man who had lived there once, and had last heard he was living in a place called Rat's Castle in Dyott Street, in the notorious Saint Giles. "Number Twelve, I've been told." She warned that region was "only fit for Jews and Irish." Browning could not help replying, "Then we shall enjoy our time there." The woman nodded without seeming to notice his self-righteous reproof.

In truth, Browning was as much a stranger to the lost corners of the city he was entering with Christina as Dr. Holmes still was to England itself. Browning wished he wasn't wearing one of the well-tailored suits in which he took so much pride, and crossed his arms as they walked, as though he could conceal it. He both feared for Christina's safety here and leaned on her guidance. Even Christina, though, had her shoulders up in a way that people did who felt they might have to protect themselves. "Good afternoon, lady! Good afternoon, gentleman!" came sarcastic calls from windows, followed by chortling. Their path to the so-called Rat's Castle was lined with animal bones rejected by scavengers.

The boardinghouse, as large as a luxurious hotel might be, smelled of liquor, human waste, and the drowsy odor of opium. Most of the doors were numbered. Through a series of smoky corridors and a staircase they reached Number 12. The toll of a church bell striking the hour vibrated through the handle of the door. The door squealed open allowing Browning—thinking now he ought to take the lead—to step in first. Inside was darkness.

"Empty," Browning guessed, half relieved.

Christina held out a candle they had bought from an old woman outside. "No, Mr. Browning," she said. "Not quite."

Their steps were short and slow. Browning, without thinking, took Christina's hand. To his surprise, she firmly gripped his. His heart raced in anticipation.

There were papers scattered around the floor. It looked like someone had left in a hurry. Browning collected them as quickly as he could and handed them to Christina.

She examined them under the light. After a while, Browning asked what she found. She replied: "If I'm understanding these, there is an ongoing exchange about some crime . . . Loring was arrested for murdering a man before, some years ago."

"It's him," Browning said.

"It's certainly suggestive evidence . . ."

"No, no, it is *him*, it has to be. Miss Rossetti: look over there. The next terrace."

In the far corner, there sat a solitary piece of furniture. A low table. Lying upon it was a copy of Longfellow's translation of Dante's *Purgatory*—opened to Canto Fifteen, the third terrace, the purgation of the Wrathful.

Constable Branagan stood in the shadows, waiting. The alley was dark and out of the way, made darker still by the overcast sky. It was only a few minutes' walk from Scotland Yard, inconspicuous, and not visible from the street—in short, a perfect meeting place for secret conversations.

An eternity seemed to pass. He still had reports to deliver to the Home Office for Dolly. As these made clear, one of the other cases Dolly was overseeing had fallen apart: Inspector Thornton had received the expected word from Ironhead Herman about the exchange of funds from the Fenians in return for explosive materials, but in the subsequent days had lost track of the location of the Fenian agent, McCord (alias Kadnar).

Branagan had made up his mind to return to Dolly's office when he heard heavy footsteps in puddles of water.

The figure of a man paused at the opening of the alley, as though in contemplation, then moved toward him.

"Tell Inspector Williamson to expect nothing more from me," said Tennyson, handing him a piece of paper.

Branagan unfolded the paper and, by the dim light, could make out a series of names and details scribbled out by the poet.

It was on one of his walks around Farringford—the day one of his over-zealous pursuers climbed a tree to gawk at him—that Tennyson was opening mail handed to him by the butler and, after reading his publisher's note about Gabriel Rossetti's illustrations, found half a yard deep in the heap of correspondence a letter from General Sir Charles Grey, Queen Victoria's private secretary. He thought it might be an invitation to take tea with the queen again, or an expression of royal admiration for his latest lyrics. Instead, Grey explained in the letter that there were some literary individuals with information vital to Scotland Yard's investigation of the recent shocking crimes around London, and that Inspector Williamson needed Tennyson's help. That motivated Tennyson to go to Scotland Yard and meet with Dolly and Branagan that same wet afternoon before ending up at Tudor House and the opera in a night that ended with him joining Christina's search.

"Thank you, sir," Branagan said, pocketing the note.

"Ugh. Thank me by bringing this to a swift conclusion," grumbled Tennyson, turning on his heel and shuffling away.

Interesting how four people could place themselves so differently in their seats on the train.

Christina sat away from the window in their humid compartment, her frame entirely still, her fingers woven together, staring down in concentration and prayer.

Browning peered out the window at the scenery, absorbed in the details of the little towns and villages and people they passed, while from the window behind him Tennyson looked dreamily through the thick lenses of his glasses into the blue sky.

Holmes, for his part, couldn't sit still. He sat on the edge of his seat, then would leap to his feet to walk up and down the corridor of the train.

The train sped on its way toward the man they hoped could point the way to Reuben Loring.

The night before—after Christina and Browning found Loring's lodgings—the same group had sat around the Tudor House dining table.

We must find him now and variations of that sentiment echoed around the circle, "him" standing sometimes for Dante Gabriel Rossetti, other times for Reuben Loring. Christina was staring at the photograph from Loring's military file so long she felt she could see through to the man himself. Her concentration was broken when she heard the question of whether, armed with their latest discoveries, they oughtn't return to the police.

Christina looked over at Tennyson, who'd made the proposition. "If we're right that Mr. Loring is preparing to unleash the punishment of the Wrathful upon Gabriel, by tangling ourselves up with Inspector William-son we would be slowed to the pace of a lag-last snail, practically ensuring my brother's demise. When Gabriel is back, when he is safe, we will shower the detectives with all we know—which, remember, Mr. Tenny-son, they didn't accept in the first place, and may still ignore."

"Do you really suppose we'd be able to stop this man by ourselves, Miss Rossetti?" Tennyson asked, without responding directly to her points, his words entirely devoid of the confidence he had shown since becoming part of the search.

"We may have surpassed the knowledge of Scotland Yard."

Tennyson contemplated the answer with his pipe before leaning back in the armchair, seeming to resign himself to Christina's iron will.

The most interesting and relevant pages from the letters they had found scattered around Loring's room represented communications with lawyers and assorted military officials about an incident that had occurred three years before while Loring was stationed with the British army in Ethiopia. Loring had a disagreement with a fellow soldier, and after the row between the two became vicious, Loring accidentally killed him; but because of issues of jurisdiction, there had never been any prosecution. He was released a few months after his arrest.

"Reverend Fallow all but admitted to us he knew more about Loring than he could share," Holmes said. "The fellow thinks he is following an ethical path. But if we cannot find the soldier himself in London's sea of life, we can at least find Fallow and try again to convince him to lead us toward the man."

Tennyson pointed out that Fallow mentioned helping oversee a sanato-rium that served as a refuge to those alienated by London, and that the minister and his female assistant seemed prepared to return there after their brief interview. They sent a messenger back to the London church where Fallow served as one of the chaplains to soldiers; soon they were in possession of the location in Lancashire of his rural sanctuary, known as the Phillip Sanatorium. They chose the first train out of London on Wednesday morning that could bring them that far north.

Christina, ever practical, at first suggested that one or perhaps two of them should stay behind to research other matters. But Browning argued that Fallow had already resisted their initial pleas, and that perhaps with a united effort they could succeed in recruiting his help.

She mused on the topic: "Evidently I was unpleasing to Reverend Fallow and his associate, and could we exchange personalities, I have no doubt I should then feel the same with their feelings."

The comment was so reasonable and gracious, Browning could never imagine thinking it.

Now, after Holmes paced through the railroad cars, he returned to his seat having gone entirely pale.

"What's wrong, Dr. Holmes?" Browning asked.

"I thought that I saw a ghost," Holmes said, then, trying to lighten his mood, added, "as people always say who don't actually believe in ghosts." He explained that after pacing through the smoking compartment, he thought he came upon a familiar face. Of all people, it was the rascal Pinkerton man Harvard had once hired to investigate their Dante scholarship—him, or a man who looked like he could be his twin. But Holmes rushed back through the car, examining every seat through thick clouds of smoke. The man was gone. He searched other compartments of the train and did not find any sign of the Pinkerton operative.

"A figment!" Holmes concluded the topic.

There were some lighter moments produced in the monotony of the four-hour train passage. They played a hand of cribbage only after they agreed to Christina's terms that no money be wagered. Later on, Browning mentioned he could make a rhyme for any word in the English language. Tennyson immediately intoned, in a low, ominous voice: "rhinoceros."

There wasn't a pause.

Browning wrote furiously, then declaimed:

O, if you should see a rhinoceros.
And a tree be in sight,
Climb quick for his might
Is a match for the Gods, he can toss Eros.

"Toss Eros!" was echoed throughout the compartment. Tennyson made strenuous objections but couldn't help breaking them up with laughing fits, his glasses slipping down the steep bridge of his nose. Browning triumphantly tore up his poem into small pieces and threw them out the window of the moving train, even as Holmes tried to recover it for posterity. Christina covered her whole face in her hat as she shook with laughter.

Simon Camp was certain Oliver Wendell Holmes had lost sight of him, and by this point the poor little doctor probably thought himself mad for believing Camp was on the same train he and his friends were riding. After Dolly Williamson at Scotland Yard inadvertently let it be known that Dr. Pipsqueak had something to do with this affair, Camp had easily traced the fellow American to a London hotel.

I'm afraid you're not going to be the first to know what happened, the Fenian McCord had taunted him. *Nobody gets the jump on Dolly Williamson*. The great Dolly. But hadn't Camp already trumped him by finding out about Holmes?

Camp soon enough discovered Holmes was conspiring with two other men, led as though on leashes by a peculiar-looking, yet somehow not altogether unattractive woman, all of whom Camp eventually identified as poets. Heavens, didn't writers ever tire of each other's company? Was nobody in London *ordinary*?

More interesting still, that peculiar woman who walked around unadorned as a Quakeress, Miss Rossetti, was sister to Dante Gabriel Rossetti—whose book of poems Camp had seen in a prominent place on Dolly Williamson's desk. After visiting Dolly, Camp had begun going to galleries around London with Gabriel Rossetti's overdramatic paintings and studied two or three of the painter's morbid poems he had dug up in a reading room.

> *"A soul that's lost as mine is lost,*
> *Little brother!"*
> *(Oh Mother, Mary Mother,*
> *Lost, lost, all lost between Hell and Heaven!)*

Such bleak poetical nonsense all blurred together in Camp's eyes.

If Holmes and his friends had been sticking their noses into the matter of the new Dante killings for a while, Camp may have stumbled into a shortcut. He would shadow them until he learned what they knew, then leave them behind in his dust. When all four of the fancy poets boarded a train north together, Camp knew it had to be important and followed behind them. That weaselly Holmes, with his quick-darting eye, looked right at him, but he managed to lose the nervous doctor in the train.

Here was how Camp did it. He even wrote it into his notebook to use the scene in his new pamphlet (though he would have to change the harmless poet-doctor to a dagger-wielding rascal of the London underworld, maybe even a dreaded Fenian, to elevate the drama). When Camp spotted Holmes walking by him in the smoking compartment, while the doctor's back was still to him, Camp switched seats. This was the real trick: he moved to a seat *closer* to Holmes's position, knowing the doctor's gaze would overreach in searching for him. Using the ample smoke clouds as cover, Camp switched hats with a sleeping man and picked up an abandoned newspaper. By this point, Holmes had doubled back through the car, then once more in the other direction. As the confused poet looked again, Camp rose from his seat as though going for a stroll and walked right behind the searcher before ducking into another compartment and convincing the occupants he spoke little English and was looking for his seat. Camp's years as a Pinkerton man hadn't been for naught.

Camp had two paths he considered taking next: one, to follow the quartet of scribblers until they led him somewhere useful; and two, if one didn't work, was to demand they tell him what they knew when they all returned to London. He'd brought his pistol along to make sure they complied with the latter.

The day was unusually warm and muggy for early March. The literary passengers disembarked at Walsden, a sleepy market town in Lancashire. From there they took a wagon for half an hour. Gray clouds of smoke hung over factories in the distance that had avoided the ruin much of the neighboring industry experienced during the decline in trade from the American War of Rebellion. The open-air, horse-drawn vehicle came to a stop in sight of iron gates looming above them.

Browning asked the driver to take them through the gates to the sanatorium's offices.

"Not permitted, sir. All this land ahead was once a busy mill and factory, but now it's used to help men and women whose nerves need shelterin', so it's said, from the city and all its machines and commotion. Stuff and nonsense, if you ask me. That commotion includes anything pulled by a horse, they say, so this is where I must leave you."

Inhaling the fresh air, they walked along a winding path past the gates and into the meadows. London receded farther with every step. The grounds were expansive, with a half dozen buildings nestled in a hilly section of the property and arranged around a canal as black as ink, which seemed to reflect nothing on its surface despite sitting calmly. Outside the largest building, they came across a man whose uncovered head was shaped like an onion, draped in a white gown, the garb of the residents at the sanatorium. He was at work on the earth, occupied in what seemed to be weeding or digging. When he noticed visitors, a look of surprise passed over his seemingly implacable expression. Browning asked him if he knew whether Reverend Fallow was present.

"*Here*, no," answered the man, blinking hard as though he had not looked up in many hours. "I'll tell you—I saw him leave for town to fetch some supplies."

Holmes asked: "What about his assistant Sibbie—Isobel?"

The man's surprise deepened with Holmes's use of the nickname, and he had even less to say about her, which he did in a whisper. "He's likely staying close by her, so I'd think."

The visitors decided to pair off to give themselves a better chance of spotting Fallow as soon as he returned so they would not waste more time away from their search for Loring than necessary. Christina and Tennyson took one path through the clover-covered meadows, while Holmes and Browning went along the water's edge.

Tennyson commented that some of the smaller, thatched structures looked as though they might purr to life if you petted them. Stone walls covered in ivy ran in irregular patterns, with doors cut into them from time to time. From a distance, they spied more of the white-robed residents—and a few wearing a light shade of green—on their way from one place to another, sometimes in clusters. Though the residents barely seemed to move at all, their pace was so slow, most appeared to be engaged in one variety of labor or another. One group, for instance, conveyed large sacks on their shoulders.

"This place brings to mind a verse," Tennyson said before he paused and, in his monotonous but smooth delivery, with fingers strumming the air, recited:

> *Gray twilight pour'd*
> *On dewy pastures, dewy trees,*
> *Softer than sleep—all things in order stored,*
> *A haunt of ancient Peace.*

"Isn't that splendid?"

"You quote yourself often, Mr. Tennyson," Christina pointed out.

"Mine are the easiest verses to remember. Besides, I am the only one who can say my lines properly. Don't you feel so about yours?"

"Heavens, Mr. Tennyson," Christina answered. "I should rather be before the firing squad than spontaneously recite my lines. It is the great vice of being a poet."

"What do you mean?"

"When I share my poetry, I am extraordinarily happy to receive praise, and bitter when more praise is given to another, someone such as Jean Ingelow."

"Ingelow?"

Christina, realizing what she had said, seemed to startle herself. "Never mind, Mr. Tennyson."

"But you just said . . ."

"Jean Ingelow. The poet, of Ipswich? Examining the newspaper columns during our inquiries, I inadvertently noticed her latest volume is in its eighth edition. Eighth! Perhaps you noticed as I sat looking at the papers that my complexion became a green tinge."

Tennyson just kept repeating *Jean Ingelow, Jean Ingelow.*

"Yes, you will have to forgive me for confessing it," Christina went on. "How conceited I must sound! The vanity—the pride and jealousy—of writing is a constant threat to consume us."

"Threat," Tennyson repeated, trying out the idea, "no such thing! The vanity is what carries us along. Do you truly believe Miss Ingelow, who I recall as perfectly lovely and harmless in person *and* verse, will be read in a hundred years rather than your 'Goblin Market'? In all events, I suppose we already know the good reverend does not feel particularly blessed to have poets trying to question him. I fear he will not be very happy to see us at all when he returns, no matter any of our literary accomplishments."

"He seemed quite worried our inquiries could bring down trouble on those under his protection."

"What was your opinion of the girl with him?"

"Sibbie?" Christina replied.

"She seemed like a nice woman. 'Nice' sounds objectionable to the ear, but it is useful—a 'nice' person is one that you're satisfied with."

"I think women can persist in all kinds of imprisonment by men, and convince themselves otherwise."

"She ought to leave his service."

"Perhaps she hasn't the choice. Here is a discovery, Mr. Tennyson: women are not men. There," she said with sudden alarm.

"Is it the minister?" Tennyson asked, squinting helplessly through his double-thick glasses in the direction she looked. "You know I'm the second most shortsighted man in England. Where is he?"

"No, not him."

Her next word pierced the air.

"Loring!"

She had studied the photograph for so long that she could have picked out the soldier in a crowd of hundreds. The man was walking on a path toward them, and was conspicuous for his ordinary clothes—a black coat and boots—rather than the robes of the others they had seen. He was tall and powerfully built. Even at a distance, he seemed to sense something amiss. He turned and disappeared back toward the little grouping of buildings.

Around the same time, on the other side of a hill, Holmes and Browning were both looking over a decaying brick building that retained hints of its more functional use in the property's industrial past.

Browning was asking a question about Holmes's searches around London with Tennyson, in a way that suggested Browning worried about how he and Tennyson compared in Holmes's mind.

"True, we do look at the object of art so differently," Browning said of Tennyson (even though Holmes did not ask or even wonder about this divergence). "Holmes, you'll remember there is in Tennyson's *Idylls* a scene of a knight being untrue to his friend and yielding to the temptation of that friend's mistress. I should judge the conflict in the knight's soul the proper subject to describe. Tennyson? He thinks he should describe the castle, and the effect of the moon on its towers, anything *but* the soul."

"I sometimes think that every man has a religious belief peculiar to himself. Tennyson is always a Tennysonite, for example. Some of our peculiar religions are simply incompatible with others. Perhaps the Browningite's truth must always differ from the Tennysonite's."

Holmes hoped to leave it there. Though usually game for debating schools of poetry, he couldn't stop pondering Simon Camp. Even if he had imagined the sight of the private detective on the train—as surely he *must* have—the thought of Camp made Holmes think of all that had gone wrong during the days of hunting for the secrets of Dante back home. Whatever their accomplishments under Longfellow's leadership, Holmes had also witnessed death he had been helpless to stop. Being a poet and a doctor, it turned out, both teased lifesaving powers the roles couldn't always sustain.

He willed their quest to move more quickly. In *Inferno*, time blurred and meant nothing, but in the middle realm, every minute mattered. Holmes could picture the moss-covered sundial in Longfellow's garden back home, its inscription from *Purgatory*, Canto Twelve, line 84, fading a little more every year: *Remember, this day will never dawn again.*

"How thoroughly England is groomed," said Holmes as he looked around. "Our New England out-of-doors landscape often looks as if it had just been born." Holmes lifted his head like a man awakened. "Do you hear that?"

"Hooves. Wheels."

Thinking of how horse-drawn conveyances were forbidden on these grounds, they both realized something had to be wrong. They hurried toward the sound. Across the meadow, horses moved at a brisk trot and tore up rows of clover in clouds of dust. When the vehicle came to a stop, a figure stepped down familiar to the doctor. A towering, dark-skinned man in a wide tunic. Ironhead Herman.

"That man. Tennyson and I saw him in London. We thought he seemed to be watching us."

"Why would he be following us?" Browning asked.

"We asked the same question."

"And who's this, now?"

Stepping toward them from the other side of the hill was a lean figure who made a mocking bow. "Dr. Gabbert!" he called out.

"So help me Phoebus, it was him," Holmes gasped.

Browning looked with concern at Holmes, who gestured that he stay back.

"But Holmes—it was who?"

"I have unfinished business with this man."

There was Simon Camp right before Holmes's eyes. *Dr. Gabbin' Gabbert* was the appellation given to the character representing Holmes in Camp's grotesque pamphlet on the Dante murders because, in Camp's witless formulation, he could not stop gabbing.

Holmes charged toward Camp.

"That was no illusion on the train," Holmes said.

"But I led a genius like yourself to think it was—so you'd bring me along on this quest none the wiser."

"What are you even doing in England?" Holmes hissed.

"Same as you," said Camp. "I find Dante's potency irresistible."

"No, you are nothing more than a literary cannibal. You seek to exploit suffering and make money from it. I'm trying to prevent any harm coming to innocent parties."

Camp rolled his eyes. "We each play in our own game. Tell me exactly what you have discovered so far. I want to know where that lunatic Dante Rossetti fits into this jumble, and I want to know what or *who* is on the grounds of this place of such interest."

"I'll tell you nothing." Holmes crossed his arms in front of his chest. "You may act bold, Camp, but don't think I'll ever forget how you shook in your boots with the barrel of a rifle in your face."

Camp's face darkened. "Let's see this time how you and your fellow bookman react when faced with the same." He slid his hand under his coat.

Christina's shouts began to ring out, followed by Tennyson's. Holmes and Browning left behind the two intruders penning them in on either side—Camp and the mysterious stranger in the tunic—and hurried toward their friends' voices.

When the poets came into sight of each other, Tennyson was yelling the startling news—Reuben Loring was *here*. Christina called out that Loring had to have Gabriel somewhere on the grounds. The fear blazed through her usually steady voice. The four hurried in the direction where Christina and Tennyson had spied Loring. As they approached a squat, gray stone outbuilding once used as a drying shed, they all heard a thud. Its door had slammed shut—followed by a more ominous sound. A man's harrowing scream from inside.

Reaching the stone structure, a tangle of arms tugged and pulled at the door as wailing continued to come from inside. From somewhere nearby, there began the indistinct, incongruous sound of singing.

Reverend Fallow and Sibbie had also arrived and raced toward the same disturbance. Fallow, seeing the uninvited guests, demanded to know their business.

"Reuben Loring is here, and I believe he's locked my brother inside!" Christina cried.

There was thick smoke inside escaping through the space around the frame of the door. Christina could almost hear Dante's timid question to Virgil as he reached the smoke-clogged third terrace, posed in the way a questioner does who does not want to hear the answer: *Tell me, what trespass is purged in the circle where we are?*

Christina also thought of the answer that Dante was to discover: he had entered the purgation of the Wrathful.

Browning, pulling back a muscular leg for more leverage, kicked in the door on the third try, as he cried out, "We're not afraid of you, Loring!" The noxious fumes billowed out, causing the onlookers to break into fits of coughing. There was the figure of a man on the ground. Holmes tied a handkerchief around his mouth and rushed in, grabbing hold of the prostrate man. The victim, however, would not budge. Holmes groped in the darkness, looking for something that might be holding the victim down, until he felt with absolute terror a steel manacle. It was attached to the man's leg. There was no saving Gabriel from this. As more light came through, Holmes gaped with amazement. The trapped man moaned and panted for air. He was still alive, but barely, and only for another moment. And he was not Dante Gabriel Rossetti, but Reuben Loring. Louder singing from outside could be heard, with a chant of *Agnus Dei*. Then, a pronouncement:

"*Beati pacifici*, who are without ill anger!"

The doctor's handkerchief slid from his mouth and he began to cough and retch. "No!" cried Sibbie bravely, jumping in and trying to pull Holmes out. In the darkness and confusion, their legs became knotted, and the others had to carry Holmes out. But Sibbie's arm had become lodged under the deadweight of Loring's body. By the time she was also pulled out, the reverend's assistant had succumbed, motionless, spread out across the grass.

Fallow rushed to her, feeling for signs of life on her limp neck and wrists.

"What have you brought here? What unholy evil?" Fallow screamed at them.

Standing uphill, Dante Gabriel Rossetti's hand stroked his beard thoughtfully. He tottered forward, in a wobbly series of steps, toward his stunned sister and friends.

"Was it you, Gabriel, after all?" Browning said through coughing. "What have you done?"

"Gabriel," Christina said. "No."

Dante Gabriel Rossetti's eyes met his sister's, just before his legs buckled.

DOCUMENT #3:

FROM PHONOGRAPHIC MINUTES OF POLICE

INTERVIEW BETWEEN INSPECTOR ADOLPHUS

WILLIAMSON AND DANTE GABRIEL ROSSETTI

AT SCOTLAND YARD, WHITEHALL,

MARCH 3, 1870

WILLIAMSON: Do you confess to trapping the deceased, Reuben Loring, in that outbuilding, chaining him down, with the malicious intention of poisoning him with smoke?

[Rossetti gives no reply.]

WILLIAMSON: Mr. Rossetti, I have been trying to puzzle out how you knew Mr. Loring would be present there. Had you been surreptitiously watching your sister and your friends, and trailed them to the sanatorium in Walsden? Is that how you found him?

[Rossetti gives no reply.]

WILLIAMSON: Call me Dolly, Mr. Rossetti. My friends call me Dolly. Since this began, and we discovered your having absented yourself from your usual life and being observed at the scenes of these crimes, it occurred to me that an obsession with Dante might lead a creative-minded fellow like you to try to bring his words to life, a kind of "living art." Start, at least, by telling me that you regret what you've done.

ROSSETTI: Vain regret. Vain desire! Vain—[trails off]

WILLIAMSON: Let's start at an earlier date, shall we, Mr. Rossetti? Do you wish to smoke? No, very well. I wonder how you knew Mr. Morton, the member of Parliament who was killed, and Miss Brenner, the opera singer who died after him. You realize, sir, that we know quite well these killings were modeled after Dante's *Purgatory*, your favorite part of your favorite writer's masterwork on the afterlife? I read that Dante Alighieri's own father was also exiled for a time. Strange, how a son's life repeats his father's in so many ways. I had a chance to examine some of the transla- tions of Dante you made from Italian into English at the British Museum.

ROSSETTI: In those early days all around me I partook of the influence of the great Florentine, from my father's devoted work, till from viewing it as a natural element I, growing older, was drawn within the circle.

WILLIAMSON: Excellent. We're getting somewhere together now, aren't we, Mr. Rossetti? We know you trained in the early sixties with the rifle corps for painters and other artistic types, trained a bit for combat and with artillery. Let me speak plainly with you, and I hope you shall do the same in return. I will tell you what some police officers around here think about your connection to Mr. Loring. Some of the other detectives—smart men, they are. They believe that this unfortunate Mr. Loring happened to have the bad luck to spot you at the scene of the two earlier crimes. Loring's had trouble with the law before, mind you, and probably did not like talking to police, but these detectives of mine think Loring was dogging you, even studying Dante to better comprehend your crimes and expose you. And that is why you next turned your attentions on him to silence him once and for all.

ROSSETTI: If an isolated life has any sting, it is felt in the absence of those friends who made for years unheeded avowals of obligation and gratitude. Still, this will come, in time, to pass and be forgotten, not emphasized by momentary visits once or twice a year. Life is a coin that I once shared, but which has now quite passed from my pocket into another's—doubtless rightful enough. Only I desire no half farthing of its small change.

WILLIAMSON: Small change. I don't—I'm not certain I really understand, Mr. Rossetti.

ROSSETTI: So that all ended with her eyes. Inferno, Purgatory, Paradise.

WILLIAMSON: I've been learning about your exhumation of your wife's grave in October of last year, after I noticed the cemetery plot had been disturbed. Now, I have kept quiet about it until I understand what it was all about. The petition filed with the church authorities indicated you looked to retrieve some poems buried with her. Did you do so? Won't you say something about it? I try to be a fair man. I'll tell you what we will do, Mr. Rossetti. I know you're feeling out of sorts, and it may be difficult to answer all my questions in one interview. Is that so? [Rossetti again gives no reply.]

WILLIAMSON: I thought you might be able to express what has happened a different way. We've brought some things from your house.

[On a signal by Inspector Williamson, an easel, canvas, crayons, paintbrushes, paints, etc., are wheeled in by First Constable Thomas Branagan.]

[Mr. Rossetti eagerly picks up paintbrush.]

WILLIAMSON: Good, good, help yourself. That's right! Go on. Whatever you wish to do with it, to your heart's content.

[Mr. Rossetti studies the brush, dips it in paint, slowly runs it back and forth into Inspector Williamson's beard.]

ROSSETTI: Now shall *all* things be made clear.

Prying his eyes open, he took in as much as he could in the deep shadows of the frigid chamber. When he tried to raise his hands, he found his wrists latched down tight. His head feeling light, his thoughts cloudy, he had to try hard to remember the origin of his predicament.

The scribblers: that's where all this bosh and bunkum had started. He'd been on the Yorkshire–Lancashire train with them. He'd gotten off at the same station—what was it called, Walsden—where they did.

Camp had traced the scribblers' movements once off the train, and that's how he ended up at an odd destination. His driver, whom he instructed to stay as far behind the scribblers' conveyance as possible, told him that the property where the poets entered had been a mill in the past, but now was some sort of sanatorium. Rehabilitation from the ills of city life for the weak-minded.

Sneaking around the fields and buildings, Camp watched his quarry, trying to determine exactly what it was this literary squadron was doing there—and most importantly, what connection their expedition had to the recent murders that would comprise his newest sensation booklet. He wasn't planning on showing himself unless he had to, instead pursuing information from them back in London. But as he usually did, he grew impatient, and that's when he confronted Dr. Holmes. That was one of his last clear memories. He was about to make Holmes tell him everything, yes, he could remember that . . . He was reaching for his pistol. Until there was the sound of a woman's scream and Holmes galloped away like a spooked pony.

That's when it happened—as he peered around the corner from behind one of the sheds. A painful blow to the back of his head. That was the last thing he remembered clearly.

Now that he regained consciousness to find himself in the drafty, unlit chamber, Camp couldn't decide what to yell out. He settled on:

"American! I'm an American!"

This would suggest to his captors—Camp hoped—that the United States Navy might be on its way with a warship to rescue him.

A lamp was carried in, the sudden dash of light stinging Camp's eyes. By the time he recovered himself, the light vanished, leaving behind darkness. He shouted again. The glow of the lamplight soon returned, held up by one of the white-robed residents he had seen wandering the grounds, a man with a head roughly the shape of an onion. He was followed by a slightly pug-nosed man in a dark suit who had an expression on his face intense enough to be worthy of the first son of man. Camp took advantage of the light in order to examine the place of his captivity—he could now see that the room, which he had expected to be a kind of old-world dungeon, was actually quite opulent, with book-lined shelves and marble statues of ancients.

"Mr. Camp, I am glad to see you are safe. We are sorry for the chill in here. I'm afraid it's unavoidable in these old structures. We do our best. I believe you were trying to say you lived in America before your pilgrimage. You may disregard that. Here, we are all citizens of one true city."

"Who—I demand that you release me from this blasted dungeon right now! Why, I am an American and—" Camp stopped. "How did you know my name?" He had not given his real name to anyone except Dolly and McCord during his trip to London, not the steamship line, not the lodging houses where he boarded.

"Take those manacles off, if you please," the dark-clothed speaker requested of his companion, who unlocked Camp's restraints.

Camp immediately reached into his coat for his weapon, but it was gone.

The man giving orders handed Camp his bowler hat. "My name is Reverend Fallow," he said. "Shall we stretch our legs?"

Fallow did not wait for an answer before starting up the stairs, and Camp, not able to think of a better alternative at the moment, replaced his hat on his head and followed behind. They had been inside the subterranean chamber of a large, brick structure. Once they were up aboveground, Fallow put his arm through Camp's.

"Old gray London—like New York or Boston back in your United States, Mr. Camp—is one of the most licentious and depraved cities in the world. To be part of it is to be trampled, spit on, disrespected, and disheartened. The city in the modern era is taking a severe toll on the souls of good men and women," Fallow said. "Here, on these grounds, we have begun to change that."

As they stepped into the brisk afternoon air, more men and women cloaked in shining white robes sauntered about. It was another abruptly humid day, as though winter had been given no time for a graceful exit.

"I see what you are. Some kind of utopia, is that it?"

"A utopia, a utopia," the minister mulled over the word. "No, not that, Mr. Camp. Our aspirations here are quite more important than temporary tranquillity."

"I'll ask again, fellow, how do you know who I am?"

"All questions are answered where we dwell, though not always when we wish them to be. This way, please."

They followed a gravel path along the slow-moving canal that ended at another structure. They entered a generously open space in what appeared to be a chapel, and Camp's eyes were drawn to the rounded ceiling. A mesmerizing, if incomplete, painting had begun to fill the white spaces above them.

Camp took in the astonishingly expressive and emotional faces in the fresco—the agony in the eyes and mouth of a man being crushed under impossible stone weight, the confusion and helplessness in the woman whose eyelids were sewn together with wire. At the shore of the mountain was a fearful man with a flowing beard—the beard, not the man, reminded Camp of old Longfellow—and eyes of fury, the image of Purgatory's ancient Roman protector, Cato.

The style of the paintings was singular. It combined medieval splendor and modern taste. It was the style of Dante Gabriel Rossetti, whose art and writings Camp had been examining since marking Dolly Williamson's interest in Rossetti.

The preacher recited: "'These passages are nothing like those to Hell, for here songs usher us in, and down there with savage laments.'"

"Dante," Camp said. "You're behind these grotesque deaths, ain't that the truth? *You're* the lunatic Scotland Yard is hunting for? What is it that happened after I was knocked cold?"

To Camp's surprise, Fallow calmly filled him in about the ex-soldier Loring dying in the old drying shed and Sibbie, who had arrived with Fallow, getting caught in the poisonous smoke.

"What is it you're doing, tricking some of these feebleminded people you have stumbling around here into helping you imprison your victims until you decide when and how to finish them off? And now you're paying the price, with that poor girl getting stuck inside? I suppose a man like you sacrifices your pawns without a second thought?"

The accusations caused no change to the placid, paternal expression on Fallow's wide face.

"I can't picture you snatching people off the street with your own two hands. No, I've been in this line of work long enough to know that's not what's going on. Dante Gabriel Rossetti did these horrifying paintings, didn't he? From what I've read, he seems to be a bear of a man, and he has a monomania for Dante's *Comedy*. Is he the henchman for your crimes?"

"You asked how I know who you are, Mr. Camp," Fallow said, taking one long step toward him. "I have known of you for quite a while, actually. You wrote admirably about the Dante phenomena that took place in Boston. Those were revelations, but faint glimmers of possibility compared to how Dante begins to come to life. The few were punished, but the many were left unprotected, unchanged, except perhaps to be tickled by your pamphleteering. The soul of London and of the modern age is at stake. Do not dwell upon the forms of torment. As Dante tells us as he leads us onto the shores of Purgatory, consider what comes after our life, for mere pain cannot last beyond the final judgment. From now on, it will be your role, Brother, to write the story of how the great serpent is chased out of England before our eyes."

Fallow stretched his arms out.

Camp threw a glance over his shoulder and saw more white-robed ghouls blocking the doors. His years as a private detective trained him to know when to stand his ground and fight, or, at times like this, when to comply with a lunatic—especially a lunatic who, from what Camp could tell, had murdered at least three people.

Two of the berobed denizens of the place carried in a massive stone bowl filled with water.

"Baptism?" Camp chuckled. "I never subscribed to one religion or another."

"Like too many, you have felt God is but a myth, an antique of our forefathers. That, also, is changing." Fallow shook his head. "This is not to baptize, but to cleanse—for your face. To wash away the stains of Hell."

"You must be joking." Camp waited, but there was no hint of a smile. He prepared to duck his face into the bowl. "Well, farewell to Hell's stains."

"Fallow!" a voice bellowed from outside. The minister, irritated at the interruption to the ritual, excused himself. Camp was still being eyed by Fallow's followers, but couldn't stop his instincts to investigate. He moved his position slightly, on the pretense of viewing more of the chapel ceiling's mural, but in actuality to steal a glimpse outside. Fallow stood there with the new visitor—a very large, darker-skinned man in a turban. He thought of the man he glimpsed leaving the Fenian gambling den and wondered if this was the same one. Camp could not hear every word in the conversation, but the visitor was impatient and Fallow, Camp took note, seemed afraid.

From Fallow he heard: "If you . . . tell him . . . simply wait . . ."

The visitor: "How much . . . patience! . . ."

Fallow: "A critical time . . . our . . . mission . . . finally coming to realization . . ."

The beautiful young lady would have died—so wrote the London reporters who gathered to trade notes in the Three Tun tavern, insatiable as ever for stories about beautiful young ladies in danger, and all young ladies, incidentally, were beauties when they were in danger—yes, the beautiful lady would have died if not for the exertions of the famous American Dr. Oliver Wendell Holmes and his highly advanced medical techniques. He consulted with some of the London doctors but they were all specialists, impossible to get to say anything the slightest step away from their own subjects as it would be to get help from a policeman outside of his own beat. *We have dermatologists, gynecologists, oculists, aurists,* the reporters quoted Dr. Holmes as remarking, *and, mark my words, one day in the future I expect to hear of laryngologists, cardiologists, urinologists, syphilogists, and for aught I know rectologists.* Holmes seized control over her case, having her moved to Tudor House, where he converted one of Rossetti's bedrooms into a convalescence chamber. Even with one of the most celebrated doctors of the nineteenth century in charge—even with the Parkman Professor of Anatomy at Harvard University—she remained in grave danger. Nor could she tell them or the police or the press anything more about what happened. She was in a coma.

Holmes felt lost in a blur.

Upon reaching the mountain of Purgatory, Dante believes he has left behind the torments he witnessed in the infernal passages carved into the earth's core; in fact, one the first requirements onshore, after wrapping a smooth rush around his waist, is to wash Hell's stains away from his face. His goal is lofty. Virgil, his trusted guide, announces it to Cato, the suspicious and battle-hardened guardian of the mountain: *He goes to search for liberty*. But Dante soon discovers Purgatory can be harsh, at times harsher than the infernal circles. (He also will learn that fire is actually more prevalent in his journey through Purgatory than it was in Hell.) By the time he enters the terrace of the Wrathful, he witnesses the terrified shades of men and women shrouded in thick black smoke. In their lives, they blinded themselves with anger and rage; on Mount Purgatory they themselves are blinded until that anger is fully released—purged—from the depths of their souls, a process that could take hundreds of years. Dante realizes traversing Hell was only the beginning of the trials he is to undergo to save humanity. *Darkness of Hell*, as Dante warns readers, *had never made so thick a veil over my eyes as the rough smoke with which Purgatory covered us.* The murderer of Reuben Loring meticulously staged this scene by piping in coal smoke and smothering Loring—and then inadvertently felling poor Sibbie as she tried to rescue Holmes from sharing Loring's fate—in a mixture of carbon monoxide with other noxious fumes.

"We looked backward," Browning said in a raspy, uncharacteristically quiet voice, but everyone sitting around the Tudor House library heard him and everyone understood, for they battled similar regrets. When Dante begins his ascent up the purgatorial terraces, the angel at Peter's gate carves the letter *P* into Dante's forehead—representing the sins (or *peccatum*) that must be removed from his soul—then points his sword and gives the voyager a crucial instruction: that he should never look back during his climb, or he will go to the foot of the mountain.

Enter, but hear this warning, he who looks back, returns to the beginning.

"By thinking too much about making this fit what happened in Boston, we looked backward," Browning continued, "instead of forward.

Then we brought danger to the people around Reverend Fallow by going to the sanatorium in search of Loring, exactly as Fallow had warned us we would if we persisted."

Later, Tennyson and Browning were sitting alone by the drawing room fire, still anguished.

They could speak more freely with Christina out of the room. Tennyson, hanging his head over his lap, added to Browning's accounting of mistakes. "You see what it was, Browning? We denied the possibility of Rossetti's involvement for selfish reasons, because of his importance to us as a person, and because he is an artist and a poet like we are. We thought he could not, *must* not be dangerous."

"Do you believe Dante was right?" Browning asked, glassy-eyed. "Not that Dante really made the journey he claimed, but that there is something after this life, something that can make up for what goes wrong in our lives here, or make it worse."

"Absolutely," Tennyson said flatly. "I am certain of it, Browning. There must be some extension of individual consciousness after death. I would rather know I was to be damned eternally if there wasn't; I'd rather sink my head right now in a chloroformed handkerchief and have done with it all than not to know that I was to live eternally. There must be a form of immortality or it is all—*this* is *all*—useless!"

"It is a great desire, certainly. But I see no reason to suppose that it will be fulfilled."

"Listen to me talk of danger. My father, the late, great, drunken Reverend Tennyson, would be proud—but would he? I eat my heart out with silent rage at the man, when I am not wondering if I slowly become him. You know, Browning, my father traveled through Russia a few years before I was born. He used to tell us thrilling stories. He had begun to suspect a group of nobles had been involved in the assassination of the emperor, and slyly investigated the matter of his own volition. Well, he gave a speech at a dinner accusing these men—accusing them in public of murder! As soon as he left the ballroom, he was hunted. He had to flee and hide from his pursuers in the Crimea, where dwell the wild people of the country. He learned that twice a year—never at the same time—a carrier passed blowing a horn, a signal that it was safe to cross the border. He lay waiting through the nights for that sound, waiting to make his escape. Do you know what my dear father told my uncle when he heard I was publishing my first volume of poems? He said, 'I hear that my son has made a book. I wish it had been a wheelbarrow.'"

"What is it, Tennyson?" Browning asked. "What happened?"

Tennyson suddenly appeared stricken.

"My watch has stopped," he said, holding it in his trembling hand. "What am I to do?"

Tennyson was frozen in his distress. Browning rose from the chair, asked for Tennyson's watch key, took the instrument and wound it, then silently returned it.

They heard Christina and Holmes coming back down the stairs. They had been checking on Sibbie. The expressions of Browning and Tennyson grew heavy with anticipation.

"No change in the poor girl," Holmes mumbled to the questions written on the others' faces.

"Her mind," Browning began, stopped, then began again. "Is it still . . . working?"

"The connection between the condition of our brain and our thoughts is so close to each of us, and yet always out of our grasp," replied Holmes. "We have never found Hamlet and Faust, right and wrong, the valor of men and the purity of women, by testing for albumen, or examining fibers in microscopes. I'm afraid the answer is that I don't know the answer."

"There must be something to do," said Tennyson.

"People have shown they will do anything to recover their health, my dear Tennyson. We have submitted to be half drowned in water, half choked with gases, to be buried up to our chins in earth, to be seared with hot irons, to be crimped with knives like codfish, to have needles thrust into our flesh, and bonfires kindled on our skin, to swallow all sorts of abominations, and to pay for all this, as if to be singed and scalded were a costly privilege, as if blisters were a blessing, leeches a luxury. Of the many things uncertain in this world, among them will always be the effect of a large proportion of the remedies prescribed by physicians."

No change in the poor girl. Holmes meant Sibbie but could have been speaking about Christina. She alone had remained unchanged in her position on her brother. Her companions, one by one, resigned themselves to Dante Gabriel Rossetti's culpability. The evidence, after all, seemed insurmountable, especially once Inspector Williamson told them some of what Scotland Yard knew. It came together in a bleak picture.

There was Gabriel's obsession with Dante; his disappearance from home just around the time these events began; his presence (for which Dolly had witnesses) at the scene of the first two deaths; and, of course, front and center at the third as witnessed by Christina, Browning, Tennyson, and Holmes. They had to accept that it was Gabriel who seized Loring, rather than the other way around.

Christina refused to change her stance one whit. Logic may have stacked up against her, but she was not doing math. It was faith, no different from her faith in God. "My faith is faith. It is not evolved out of argumentation." At other times, talking to her friends, she pointed to Dante's *Purgatory* itself as evidence. "Remember, Dante struggles to understand why the penitent souls on the mountain must suffer so. Virgil implores Dante that mankind should accept that our knowledge is finite and limit ourselves to the *quia*—the what—not the why."

Christina visited Gabriel in his cell. After Gabriel collapsed near the scene of Loring's death, they realized on closer inspection that he was teetering on the point of being almost insensible. He had consumed an excessive amount of opium. Dolly and his men were not far behind reaching the sanatorium—in the blur of all that had happened, it seemed they appeared almost out of thin air.

Dolly was courteous and respectful toward her when she called on Scotland Yard.

"There's another element of the case," Dolly Williamson said to her in his office, trying his best to hide his pride in his own analysis and his usual success in the resolution of a knotty mystery. "Your brother's wife hastened her demise by the use of opiates. Then, in the subsequent years, your brother's own habits worsened, you see, distorting his judgment and scruples—and combining with his unhealthy preoccupation with Dante. Literature, like a parasite, can envelop a man's whole soul when weakened."

The detective's manner had softened considerably since the police were called to the sanatorium. He had been victorious. He'd caught Gabriel. Now he could show her compassion and did. But she found the detective's narration of her brother's deterioration as unpersuasive as all the disheartened laments by Browning, Tennyson, and Holmes that shrouded Tudor House. Even William Rossetti could not bring himself to defend his own brother.

"Gabriel has many faults, many of which come from our father," William conceded to Dolly and Constable Branagan, having accompanied Christina on one of these many interviews with the police in the days after Gabriel was found.

"Not this. Whatever faults, whatever weaknesses, their sum does not add up to this," Christina interjected.

"Tell me, Miss Rossetti, Mr. Rossetti, about Thirty-eight Charlotte Street." Seeing their surprised expressions, Dolly added in the tone of an apology, "I visited there, you see, as I learned more about your brother. Is it where he began writing and painting?"

"Yes," said Christina. "We used to play games of *bouts-rimés*—we would give each other rhymes to finish lines with, and we would have to create verses from them. Gabriel was remarkable at it."

"Not as remarkable as our modest sister, Inspector," William said. "It's true Gabriel's imagination is rare, as visual as it is literary. Mr. Longfellow once sent two letters from Boston, one to Mr. Rossetti congratulating him on a volume of poems, and another to Mr. Rossetti about one of the paintings he had seen, thinking Gabriel had to be two different members of our family."

Dolly seemed to take pleasure in the intimate glimpse of their family life. "Do you still remember any of them? Those poems from when you were children."

Christina thought of one she had written about stacking up the casualties of a plague.

> *Then all is over. With a careless chuck*
> *Among his fellows he is cast. How sped*
> *His spirit matters little: many dead*
> *Make men hard-hearted. "Place him in the truck."*

She never could get the worms out of her verse, Gabriel had once told her. She shuddered. "Inspector, it was so long ago."

Outside the police offices, Christina confronted William on his treachery toward Gabriel.

"Call it treachery, if you wish," William said, heaving his usual I'm-done-for sigh, "but this will become public soon enough, and I am here to limit the damage this will do to our family."

"And I am here to protect Gabriel. There is something I've wondered, William."

"Yes?"

"I remember one day, meeting Gabriel, and he was in a terrible state, talking of a vision of a woman. He had said you took him to Highgate to visit Lizzie's grave. Looking back, I must wonder if his state descended from there. Why would you do that, knowing its effects on him?"

William's shoulders dropped and he looked off into the distance. "Gabriel was lying to you. He did go to Highgate, but I did not bring him there and only found out in a letter shortly beforehand. He had Lizzie's coffin exhumed."

"What?"

"So that he could retrieve the set of poems he buried with her. He entreated me not to tell you, knowing what your reaction would be. You must know, I could not stop him."

Christina drew back. "He was right about my reaction. Perhaps you could not have stopped him, William, but you might have tried. I would have tried."

William shook his head. "You blame me still, after all that has come to pass! I truly hoped, Christina, that telling Mr. Cayley to go to Tudor House would provide you with some distraction. Something to take your mind off of Gabriel."

"*You* told Charles Cayley to come?" Christina asked, her heart sinking.

"He is quite fond of you, Christina. Dear sister," William said, taking her hands in his, "imagine what a full life you still might salvage, alongside a decent and brilliant man such as Cayley, a man Father loved with all his heart. He hasn't much money, it's true, but I could assist the two of you in setting up a household."

Christina felt her hands trembling. She pulled them free.

"Christina, where are you going? Christina . . . !"

She was expected at Saint Mary's to test the reading and writing abilities of two new girls. She had considered taking a leave from her post as associate sister there but could not bring herself to tell the warden. How could she hope for God's love and mercy for herself—for Gabriel—in this great ordeal if she did not honor her own commitments to those who needed her?

At Saint Mary's, it was one of the days scheduled for Reverend Fallow to be a guest preacher. She thought he might decide not to show up, but he came right on time. Christina was awash with anxiety to see him, knowing that he blamed them for leading Gabriel to the sanatorium—for leading him to Loring—and for the accident from which his poor assistant might never recover. Fallow paused when he saw Christina and gave her a big nod; it carried no sense of admonishment or anger, and Christina felt grateful.

She stood in the back of the chapel as he preached on the power of penitence and the importance of charity.

"That poor, weary, outwardly hardened, sin-debased creature at your side—a victim to man's brutal requirements—is, in the eyes of Heaven, your sister and mine. *Suffering is not sin.*"

Christina noticed many of Saint Mary's young residents were very taken with the imposing, eloquent speaker. Ethel, her eyes moist, placed her hand over her heart as he spoke of the relationship between repentance and renewal. The man had a certain magnetism on the pulpit one wouldn't guess at seeing him away from it. Even after the sermon ended, the girls flocked around Fallow with praise and questions.

After Saint Mary's, she hastened back toward Dolly's office, where she had an appointment for further review of the evidence in the case, so that she could begin to prepare to engage legal representation for Gabriel.

Christina may have relied on faith, but she was not above presenting her own reasoning to Inspector Williamson and to her collaborators at Tudor House. For instance:

First Point. If true that Gabriel chose to target Loring because Loring was a witness to two of the murders and could have implicated Gabriel in them, how had Gabriel known this about Loring?

Second Point. Where was Gabriel keeping his various victims before their murders, without a shilling to his name, and Tudor House occupied at almost all hours by Christina and her companions?

Third Point. If Dolly was so sure, so certain of Gabriel's guilt and had no doubts, why had he protected Gabriel's reputation by keeping it out of the newspapers; why hadn't he given the full story to one of his ink-slinging stooges like Steven Walker at the *Ledger*? Gabriel's Italian heritage, after all, fit nicely with the Home Office's suspicions of a perpetrator with foreign origins.

Then there were Gabriel's eye problems, his dizzy spells, his insomnia, and added to that his obvious recent indulgences in opiates; with all that in mind, how could he have overpowered all the people the detective believed he'd murdered? Including the hale and hearty soldier Reuben Loring! Quite true, Gabriel had been part of the "Artists' Rifles Corps" years before, but he hardly received training worth mentioning before dropping out to discard his uniform in favor of his painting coat. On a similar note, Dr. Holmes had marveled at the exactness in the mixture of gases released in that fateful drying shed. Gabriel, a proud Luddite, did not have the scientific skills to create those conditions in the death of Loring, nor the required medical and engineering knowledge to bring about the deaths of Morton and Brenner.

The detective shook his head at these objections and spoke of the many mysteries of man he had seen in his line of work that would never be answered.

"You do not strike me as a man who believes in mysteries, Inspector," Christina said.

Gabriel, meanwhile, passed in and out of varying degrees of coherency; as time passed since his last ingestion of narcotics, his body and mind struggled even more. He slept and slept, not very restful and not very restorative. He sweated and trembled, opened and closed his hands over and over. Sometimes he spoke to her, though his words still did not make much sense. "Within my first life . . . ," he'd mutter.

CR—need your help. Christina heard the words again from Gabriel's notation echo as a reprimand for failing to prevent all this. The old scissor slices across both her arms from youth, long faded from sight, seemed to pulsate and sting under her skin.

In her mind she returned to her visit to the observation chamber of the deadhouse that had become a Dantean landscape. Morton, on one display table, with his neck bent and distorted. She leaned far forward toward the glass, trying to comprehend how it must have felt. Nothing transfixed her like Lillian Brenner's eyes. She had tried to distract herself by examining the clothes folded nearby, but kept returning to those eyes. The police had left the iron wires that crisscrossed her eyelids, in case any member of the public recognized something about the material or the technique. But in death the eyelids gradually drew apart, so that a muted coconut brown strip of each of her eyes revealed themselves. Christina squinted to examine and to imagine and to reassure herself. She squinted, also, to hold back tears standing in her eyes before rushing away. *Not Gabriel, never Gabriel.*

"My dear brother," Christina whispered, even though his eyes had shut again, "I know, whatever mistakes you have made, whatever you found yourself mixed up in, the evil we have witnessed had to be wielded by someone else. I vow to you, I will find out who, and prove it."

Gabriel's eyes snapped open. "I seem to see it—yes, every detail of it— as though in a dream."

DOCUMENT #4:
FROM THE SURVIVING MANUSCRIPT FRAGMENT
OF *IN DANTE'S SHADOW*, BY S. T. CAMP

To achieve a deeper understanding of the role of Reverend Orin Fallow in the honor and glory now under way before the eyes of Great Britain and the world, it is necessary to divert the course of this narrative, momentarily, to introduce some early history of this fine gentleman's career. As a young man, Mr. Fallow succeeded in various private commercial endeavors before giving himself over to preaching. Growing up the son of an Anglican minister, he had witnessed how people's faith in God could be dislodged, and sought ways in and out of the pulpit to present a higher meaning of life to congregations caught in the commotion of dissipated

London. Fallow earned the nickname "Fellow" for his ability to speak to men and women of any station and class, and was called by some the Prophet of the People. As for doctrinal arguments he mostly thought them worthless, and this led to his switching denominations several times, including at one time training as a Baptist, before deciding to leave behind formal denominations.

Graver challenges awaited. Fallow, even at twenty-four years old, was an inspiring preacher—while many men of the British pulpit of the era lulled their audiences, he stirred them awake. As the popularity of the young preacher increased, rivals leveled criticism. He did not sufficiently concentrate on teaching the Bible. He was not educating, he was badgering his flock, daring them to shirk the vices of the modern age. The more strident he became, the more criticisms and crowds he attracted, until he had to hold his sermons in theaters and music halls. There was talk of traveling to America to preach, though this did not come to pass.

Tragedy struck; it struck his burgeoning career and his congregation. During one of the reverend's giant sermons near London, in which four thousand five hundred people had come, intent to hear his every word, Fallow became increasingly impassioned—more than usual—about the urgency to save weak souls from the creeping decay of secret sins. "The Lord's curse is upon the house of the wicked. Flee for refuge," Fallow cried out, "flee!" One man, somewhere in the middle of the audience, became so distressed and worried for his own moral state, or simply confused by the direction, that he stood up, screaming and shouting, running through the aisles.

There were disputing accounts in the press about exactly what this man shouted. Some heard it as "We're falling!" or "I'm burning!" In all events, fear began to spread through the audience that there was a fire in the theater. Panic reached all sides of the building. People were trampled, others tumbled over balustrades and fell to the floor below. Men pushed over women and children. Seven people died.

Fallow watched it all from the stage—the roles reversed as he became the audience. He thought if he tried to continue preaching he might stop the madness. But he failed. "There is a terrible day coming . . . ," he announced, then fainted dead away.

Fallow disappeared from public after that day. He dreamed of manifestations of death all around him. He was fearful of being in crowds, and certainly could no longer think of preaching to large audiences.

When he finally felt ready to shed his seclusion and begin preaching again, it was by necessity to far smaller groups. His name no longer reverberated with the public, and he had no desire to stand before a sea of people. He found a specialty in serving those citizens in and near London who moved from place to place, never fixed long enough to become part of a particular church. God can find all men, but man cannot always find God: this was an axiom for this chapter of the preacher's career. In addition to churches that required assistance with transient persons, such as traveling merchants, fallen women, and soldiers, Fallow volunteered visits to poorhouses and sanatoriums. Because of these experiences, the preacher was offered a place among a party sailing to the Continent to observe similar institutions and report back on their latest advancements to the English civil and religious authorities.

Reverend Fallow, it ought to be added, had in those years become casually fascinated by the literature of Dante Alighieri, like many others, through the recent translation into English by the famous American poet Longfellow and the much more modestly published volumes by the British scholar Cayley.

While traveling around the Continent on his observation tour, staying on an island off the coast of Italy, Fallow, accompanied by his assistant, happened to be introduced by their guide, Signor

J. Giuseppe Alviani, to an enigmatic man known as the Dante Master, from whom the preacher learned more. A man does not take hold of Dante, so it is said, Dante takes hold of a man and never lets go. Though Dante was not a priest, the "divine" poet, more than almost any other individual since the Son of God himself, made ordinary people believe in damnation and salvation—the rewards and, a more trying and remarkable subject, the necessary penalties to reach Paradise.

"I can tell right away," said the Dante Master, "when someone comes to me by walking in the footsteps of Dante."

The Dante Master kept an extensive library of books on Dante, including many considered heretical or dangerous. One of these was a rare complete set of the fifteen-volume commentary by the late Professore Rossetti, of which most copies had been burned by the professore's wife, not realizing that the rarer she made the text, the more potent it became. "The Vatican knows," said the Dante Master, "how dangerous Dante remains to established religion even hundreds of years later. The pope has recently banned the word 'Divine' from the title of the *Comedy*."

Fallow felt dizzy as his knowledge of Dante grew. "What is to be done now?" he asked his tutor.

The Dante Master made a temple of his long fingers as he contemplated. "By asking the question, you will be led to the answer, sooner than you know."

Returning to England, the preacher also relished the very different material contained in a small booklet (by the current author) entitled *The Dante Murders*, furthering Fallow's interest in studying the power of Dante over our minds—a power that reached beyond any mere transitory literature. Around this time, the preacher had been engaged to serve the religious needs of the residents of a Lancashire-area sanatorium that was to open on the property of a former textile mill, which itself had been forced to close after being found to employ children under the age of thirteen without the required school certificates. The place had been built along a canal in a rural county, ideally suited to provide solace from the city. However, the proprietors of the planned sanatorium fell into financial distress, and Reverend Fallow, as well as a superior in his endeavor, were given control over the property. The new Phillip Sanatorium was established. But if it was once to be a place to simply assuage anxieties, it had a different goal at hand now, one handed down by Dante: deliverance.

XVII

The first few days after the disastrous turn of events at the Phillip Sanatorium, the weather grew colder and the routine of the poets at Tudor House churned on; when the streets came alive in the mornings, Browning and Tennyson would arrive cradling the latest newspapers to review with Christina, who was often preparing to visit Gabriel or returning from a visit to him, or on her way to meetings with more barristers at unusual locations to keep them secret from the public. One morning the routine cracked. Tennyson never appeared. The others dispatched word to his London address, and after two messages went unanswered, they learned from a cousin of Tennyson's in the city that the poet laureate had returned to the Isle of Wight.

Holmes gave up his hotel lodgings and moved into Tudor House in order to maintain his vigil over Sibbie. Though Christina had made up a room for Holmes near Sibbie's on the second floor, he often slept in the hard chair next to her bed so he would be present to monitor developments. In that same chair he would sit watching her as he whistled and tapped his foot. Other than a few flutters of her eyelashes and occasional twitching in her body, there were no signs of life. He didn't want to tell the others that prolonged comas most often ended in death within the first weeks. The great secret of success of every form of quackery was hope kept alive, but the fatal gift of science was a prognosis of despair. Holmes's own medical studies at Harvard had demonstrated to his satisfaction that during sleep there was a diminution of blood flow to the brain, a deadly aspect of such an unnatural condition of unconsciousness as experienced by Sibbie.

The patient was also losing weight at a rapid rate. He cleaned her lips and carefully tipped water into her mouth. At least their era was removed—only by a few short decades—from the time when patients in such "marvelous stupors," the females sometimes called "sleeping beauties," were toured around for people to gawk at.

Everything about an era of history could be told by its medical barbarities.

Holmes was relieved to have a good reason to be away from the discussions of Dante while holed up in Sibbie's quarters. His mind had turned strongly against the Florentine. He could not help but feel that Dante somehow harbored some of the blame for unleashing his "justice." He wondered whether Dante himself, toward the end of his life, had feared giving the world a poem so untamable.

There was a story about Dante during his exile, not long before his death. Dante, the story went, had wandered into a monastery. A prior came up to him and asked him if he wanted something. Dante just stared. Finally the exiled poet, who had been away from his family and friends so long they would not have recognized him, removed a volume of his freshly printed *Comedy* (*Divine* would be added to the title later by an Italian writer of the next generation, Boccaccio) from his frock and handed it to the prior. The prior was taken aback when he noticed it was written in Italian instead of Latin, with the exception of a few phrases sprinkled throughout (such as the voice of the Virgin Mary appearing as elevated Latin, *Ecce ancilla Dei*). Dante explained he chose Italian (the "vulgar" tongue) because he wanted the poem to be read by every class of readers, since its contents were about to change the world. The prior, by this point very curious about the visitor, pleaded again that the exile explain to him what he sought. Dante wheeled around as he took his leave and finally replied: *"Peace!"*

In addition to serving as a medical steward for their resident sleeping beauty, Holmes unexpectedly found himself playing the part of society host. Sibbie's mother came, having read in the newspapers about what happened. A widow as quiet and retiring as her daughter, with the same bright blue eyes, Mrs. Worthington still lived in the countryside in a small village near where she raised "dear Isobel." She spoke on and on about Sibbie's natural gifts, about how she was so nurturing as a girl and always solicitous of the ill even as a child. She wept over not seeing her for the last few years, since Sibbie had begun helping Reverend Fallow, whom she guessed had some kind of supernatural sway over her daughter. Holmes did not intend to be rude, but he found himself rushing her visit to a conclusion. Normally, he would be the first to encourage a grieving relative to reminisce. But there was a stack of medical books and articles on comas he still wanted to review in a desperate attempt to reverse Sibbie's course before time ran out.

Reverend Fallow called on Tudor House, too. Holmes felt he ought to apologize to any man of religion for the décor: heavy and black, gloomy with strange objects from Gabriel's collections such as grinning gargoyles and Chinese Buddhas.

Holmes regretted having distrusted Fallow, and regretted even more the part they played in what happened. Fallow seemed genuinely stricken by his assistant's ordeal. Holmes tried to apologize for leading Dante Gabriel Rossetti to the sanatorium and to Loring, but the minister did not want to talk about it. He sat with the hand of the unresponsive girl in his, and wept with a slow, dignified grief. *You will be back where you belong*, Holmes heard the minister whisper to her. When Fallow left her room, the preacher was so disoriented that he got lost in the endless corridors and rooms of the house, and Browning had to find him and guide him back to the front door.

Despite his sympathy and feelings of guilt, even now Holmes harbored some discomfort at the familiarity the minister exhibited toward the assistant. Like the girl's mother, Holmes fretted about the man's hold over her. Of course, now there were bigger matters at hand—to start with, her survival. Even Fallow seemed to acknowledge, reluctantly, that Holmes represented her best chance. When Christina asked the minister as he exited the house if he planned to move her to one of the churches where he was involved, or to Phillip Sanatorium, the pious visitor stiffened, muttering, "It wouldn't be safe."

Perhaps out of habit, the police still seemed to keep a watch on Tudor House, for one particular boat would periodically row up the Thames and lurk behind the house. Whenever they tried to come out to see who was rowing, the vessel would be whipped into a high speed. They knew it was the same craft because it had a green streamer tied to one end. The group had also discussed on several occasions who the turbaned man seen first at the church and then at the sanatorium could have been, and why he would have been following them. Perhaps it was coincidence. Christina—looking for any last sign of Gabriel's innocence—felt the enigmatic man must have had something to do with the actual murderer.

Despite all that had happened, Holmes still felt hope, not just for Sibbie but also for himself. He had thought helping the Rossettis could finally banish the memories that hounded him. They had been magnified instead. But here was one last opportunity not just to grasp in the dark for confidence but to prove himself, to save the life of the woman right in front of him.

At one point during the long days Holmes watched over Sibbie, he realized he had fallen asleep only when he was woken up by the sounds of a conversation from outside the house. He looked down out the window and saw Tennyson at the front door. His heart jumped—the return of their prodigal partner, the first hint of good luck in a long time. After Holmes rubbed the sleep from his eyes, he headed down the stairs. He slowed to a stop when he heard a debate in progress. Tennyson had stepped inside but had not even removed his hat.

"Holmes, I was just remarking," Tennyson said by way of greeting, "how our labors here have dried up, despite our greatest efforts. There is no longer any chance of helping Gabriel. Leave Castle Crazy to the beasts and birds and return to your lives, as I have."

Holmes looked to Christina, wishing to shield her.

Christina, of course, would not want to be shielded, nor did she need to be. She replied first: "There remains much more to do, Mr. Tennyson."

"What else? Think of the success in all this. You wished to find Gabriel before harm came to him, and we did."

"Now we must show he is innocent—to Inspector Williamson and to the public, if necessary."

"Innocent," Tennyson repeated, then made one of his frequent guttural *ugh*s. "Forgive me if I am now obliged to make reference to facts, Miss Rossetti. Let the police conduct their investigation, and then Gabriel will be fairly judged."

"None of this has been *fair* to Gabriel at all," Christina said.

"There's that police boat again," Browning said as he looked out the bay window over the overgrown gardens. "I want to get a better look—the roof!"

Browning mounted the long flights of stairs to the perfectly flat roof and leaned over the edge. Tennyson, who had followed behind, seemed particularly interested as he looked out at the vessel with the green streamer among the rubbish and frozen animal carcasses floating on the river. "You're certain it's the police?"

"We haven't been able to see who is in it, but it's constantly rowing back," Browning said. "I'm tempted to swim out there and capsize it."

One by one, the others joined them out in the frigid air, hair and clothes tossed around by the wind. Christina pulled them back to the topic at hand. "Mr. Tennyson, perhaps you could petition for intervention from Queen Victoria before this goes further."

Tennyson threw his head back. "The queen!"

"You are the laureate, Tennyson," said Browning, each word emerging at a slow, deliberate pace. To Holmes, the words conveyed admiration, envy, and bitterness at once.

"To honor the English language, not to rope the royal family into lost causes of law and justice. As poets, our lives and our work are one and the same thing. We don't have the right to ask for more. Let the police do what they do. Let the police finish their investigation!"

Christina continued her polite but intractable defense, while Tennyson thundered out his objections.

"It will not work, Miss Rossetti!" Tennyson finally blurted out with such force that the exchange came to a halt. "I wonder that all of you don't see the impossibility of what you really seek."

"What do you mean?"

Tennyson's inhibitions vanished with his frustration. "You won't find love from your father by trying to save Gabriel, Miss Rossetti. Believe me, that phantom can never be captured."

"We each have the same goals here, haven't we?" Browning asked.

"And you, Browning!" Tennyson continued. "Don't you think it's obvious what you're doing? Following Miss Rossetti snakelike down these paths you can't really believe in won't rid you of guilt over wherever it was you never followed Elizabeth. Look at Miss Rossetti. Look at her! She is not Elizabeth, and deserves better than being her substitute. You cannot rescue Elizabeth, not by rescuing Miss Rossetti, not by writing *The Ring and the Book*, not even by bringing Gabriel back from his abyss where Lizzie sent him. As for our kinsman from over the water, good Dr. Holmes—"

"No!" Holmes interjected, his voice cracking and his heart spilling out. "No, Tennyson, not yet. You mustn't do what you've come to do. I've given up on a cause too soon in my past—well, more than one, in all honesty—and, I'll tell you, it's a heavy burden to bear, heavier than whatever you think you'll free yourself from by fleeing. I'll do it no more. This group—the four of us, I mean—together managed to shine light in darkness. The evidence is rather bad for Gabriel: yes. No one will deny it. But Sibbie still has a chance to recover." He hated how that sounded, and tried again. "She will recover, at any rate, for in my experience in the medical field, women are the stronger sex—and she may have seen something important before Loring was killed, something that could help Gabriel."

"No one saw anything else," Tennyson retorted, his face crimson from his consternation. "What miracle could we expect from her, or you, or from some strange man in a turban Miss Rossetti hopes might show up and confess he did it all? Why would that young woman know some secret nobody else does?"

"The task of the physician is to generalize the disease and individualize the patient, Tennyson. There lurks more in her, I know it. If I can just make her well, I will throw out my poetry notebooks and become only a doctor again."

Debate ensued on all points. Holmes was not listening to the arguments, not exactly; he was watching Tennyson's face instead, watching the frightened black eyes swell behind the thick ovals of glass. In the laureate he saw a man who had already given up before he came through the gates, a man who had determined in advance nothing would convince him to stay. Holmes knew what would happen if they lost Tennyson for good. The doubts they each possessed privately would expand and multiply until the whole thing fell to pieces. Somehow it seemed to him that would spell Sibbie's death, too, an outcome he could not allow.

"'Death closes all . . . but something ere the end,'" Holmes began, waiting for the group's attention. When he had it, he continued:

> *Some work of noble note, may yet be done,*
> *Not unbecoming men that strove with gods.*

Christina and Browning stared with wonder. The verses were from Tennyson's poem "Ulysses," based on Dante's version of the aging Greek hero sailing toward Mount Purgatory. Tennyson kept his eyes fixed on the river below, puffing his pipe in a furious motion, then, grudgingly, looked up at Holmes with an expression of interest, rubbing his mustache with his free hand. Taking one step forward, and raising his volume over the wind, Holmes went on.

His chest inflated, he felt twelve feet tall, and his thoughts raced with possibility:

> *The lights begin to twinkle from the rocks;*
> *The long day wanes; the slow moon climbs; the deep*
> *Moans round with many voices. Come, my friends,*
> *'Tis not too late to seek a newer world—*

Holmes held out his hand to the laureate.

"Enough!" Tennyson roared, slapping Holmes's hand away. He glowered around the roof. "Enough. You know as well as I do how that tale turns out. Let me remind you that according to Dante's rendition, old Ulysses and his crew drown just in sight of Purgatory. One need not wonder why I left that out of a poem otherwise inspired by Dante, and meant to inspire others. No, Dr. Holmes, indeed it is too late for us. Too late."

After Tennyson marched down into the house and out the street door, silence overtook those left there. From out front of the house, they could hear Tennyson cursing at some of the members of his adoring public who had found him, branding them with the epithet of "a many-headed beast." Back inside, Browning later complimented Holmes for a good attempt to persuade Tennyson. "The harder you try with a man like Tennyson," Browning advised him, "the farther he retreats."

Then Sibbie really is lost, and Dante is lost, Holmes thought, not sure himself whether he meant the medieval one or Gabriel Rossetti.

Browning tried to comfort and encourage Christina, but she quickly excused herself into the gardens, where she formed a lonely tableau looking out over the river with Bobby, the owl.

This time Holmes advised Browning.

"Sometimes, my dear Browning, it seems every person's feelings have a front door and a side door by which they may be entered. Some keep their front doors open. Others will latch and bolt and even nail it up. The side door, though, opens at once into the sacred chambers. I believe Miss Rossetti misplaced the keys to the side door a long time ago."

"No, Holmes," replied Browning, his eyes still on her. "She holds all her keys tightly in her hand, and waits to loosen her grip."

DOCUMENT #5:
PREFATORY NOTE OF THE AUTHOR, INCLUDED
IN PROFESSORE G. P. G. ROSSETTI'S
DISQUISITIONS ON DANTE

I saw this all by myself, without the help of man. Now that it will come to us, now that Truth will live in the market square, I will never look backward. No one shall. No one shall have to. No one shall be able to.

If we learn how to see it, Dante's *Divine Comedy* provides us the one primitive and universal religion, which, destroying all the difference of men, is truly the religion of love, and the death of human oppression. The keys I provide will unlock all of Dante's hidden treasures and unmask enemies.

I do not approve of all the furies of the Florentine poet revealed through knowledge of his secrets. But who knows whether I am about to put into the hands of you, my good and attentive reader, a thread that will untie the knot of all civilization.

Gabriele Pasquale Giuseppe Rossetti,
professore nel Collegio del re d' Inghilterra—
a Londra 1854

T he Tudor House group complied with Holmes's silent prophecies of demise. Tennyson stayed away, as he vowed. Holmes, for his part, was too occupied with Sibbie to help much in other areas. Browning did his best to remain chipper for Christina's sake. *She deserves that*, he thought, remembering how such thoughts sustained his brave face worn for Ba during her final illnesses. But with all the intractable suspicions surrounding Gabriel, Browning's facade began to crumble, too. Not that Christina appeared to notice. She labored as usual, methodically and carefully, blaming only herself for any misstep, and nothing slowed her down.

Her retort to those who said there was nothing left to try was simple. If Dante Gabriel Rossetti was innocent, as Christina believed, then whoever was the true culprit would commit another atrocity soon—would not be able to resist continuing to re-create the seven terraces of Purgatory, starting with the next: the fourth. All a good Dantean had to do was anticipate how and where, and then come face-to-face with the real perpetrator.

"'All a good Dantean has to do!' How in God's name . . . Forgive my being profane, Miss Rossetti. But what makes you think such a thing is even possible?" Browning demanded, his composure peeling away at every turn.

"Mr. Browning, I'll be happy to explain."

Using Dante's text, the illustrations they had gathered together, and her handwritten notes, Christina demonstrated that each murder had been accompanied with some other element from Dante's *Purgatory* besides the punishment itself. In the Prideful terrace that took the life of Morton, there was the engraving in stone of the Latin quote. In the death inspired by the Envious, where Miss Brenner died, she had been put into a blue-black cloak of the kind described by Dante as worn by the souls on that terrace (the color of stone signifying the bruised hearts of the Envious). As for the poisoning of Reuben Loring in the style of the Wrathful, *Agnus Dei* was chanted by someone unseen (everyone but Christina believed Gabriel sang it), just as it was on the corresponding terrace in Dante's poem.

The next terrace would contain the Slothful, who are consigned to run without pause for hundreds of years. After considering all the possible details within Dante's verses about the punishment, Christina was certain she had identified the more likely elements for the perpetrator to reproduce, and how these could lead her to the location of the next murder before it happened.

"The odds against you would be astronomical, Miss Rossetti! To anticipate the next move of a maniac, assuming one really is still out there, you'd have to be . . ."

"A sibyl. Perhaps Manto," Christina suggested almost cheerfully.

"Yes, Manto!" he said, as though he'd thought of it.

Manto was a Greek oracle and an even greater prophet than her famous father, the soothsayer Tiresias, who was both man and woman. Manto and Tiresias are found together by Dante in *Inferno* for their attempts to tell the future.

"Maybe so. But, Mr. Browning," Christina continued, "the maniac you speak of is entranced by every word of Dante's. Because of that, he cannot hide. We do not need to see into the future. We merely need to follow the verses just as closely. You were right, in Purgatory you cannot look back or you are sent to the beginning. But that is not the only lesson we are taught. To ever leave Purgatory safely, you must go through it—through it *entirely*. We have not yet done so. The way out of Purgatory is up."

"Forgive me, but this makes me think of your—"

"Yes?"

"It seems to me, my dear Miss Rossetti, perhaps you have come to believe that the more you sacrifice of yourself, the closer you come to doing your duty."

"Isn't it so, Mr. Browning?"

He did not finish his aborted thought, could not bring himself to say, *This makes me think of your father*. Browning had heard how Professore

Rossetti gradually sank into Dante, into uncovering a secret society devoted to undermining the orthodoxy in religion and politics. Patrons and friends begged the professore to condemn his writing to the fire. But the old man refused. He even began to have books of his writings printed.

The more Christina walled herself in with stacks of books and notebooks in her latest phase of the undertaking, the more Browning fretted.

He would go out saying he was on some errand related to their labors, but in fact he would walk through London, even in the unseasonable cold, just to clear his thoughts. Had there ever been a woman so hardheaded? He could almost see Ba's grin before him and hear her reply, *How about the woman who enraged her father, abandoned her family and country, taking only her little dog, just to be with a poet named Robert whom she happened to love?*

Inspired by Ba's genius and her love, he'd set out to be England's great poet. Yet, the more the years went on, the more he wondered. Was he just another Sordello, laboring so hard on his poetry but most of it falling far short, while his contemporary, Dante, sullen and unsociable, changes the Italian language and, subsequently, the history of literature?

If he only had had more time to learn from Ba, from her strength. To the very last she spoke of plans for the next summer, the next year. She slept that night in a broken fashion. When Browning offered to bathe her feet, she said, "Well, you *are* determined to make an exaggerated case of it!" "How do you feel?" he asked her. "Beautiful," came her smiling reply. Within a few minutes she died with her head on his cheek.

Browning's mind was still so cluttered that he hardly noticed the commotion in front of one of the oldest surviving Roman Catholic churches on the outskirts of London. Then he looked up to find his weakened senses assaulted. There was a barrel bonfire, with books being fed into the flames. He stepped closer and saw: volumes of Dante. Or about Dante. Many were copies of Longfellow's translations. He saw one or two of Charles Cayley's translations, some volumes featuring Tennyson's "Ulysses"—and even a copy of Browning's own much-derided Dante-inspired *Sordello*!

The mob of people pouring the books into the fiery mouth of the barrel represented a mix—from their style of dress, anyway—of laborers, bankers, lawyers, even one man whom Browning recognized as a librarian. Behind them, an effigy of Dante—unmistakable by the flat-nosed profile—was feasted on by fire.

The cries flew from all sides.

"Find the monster!"

"Hang 'em from London Tower!"

Most creatively:

"This vampire Dante takes hold of some man, and turns him into a murderous devil!"

Browning rushed to his house, heart in his throat. He was startled to find his publisher, George Smith, waiting in his drawing room. He was holding *Sordello*. Browning felt his hands trembling. Smith was there to break the news gently.

"I already know, Smith," Browning cried. "Couldn't I have even a moment's peace?"

"You know?" Smith asked with curiosity. His usually dull eyes seemed to dance. "We've been having a hard time finding you. Isn't it wonderful?"

"Wonderful? Aren't you going to tell me *Sordello* is to be removed from circulation for its association with Dante?"

"*Sordello* removed!" the balding, bearded publisher replied, then gave a gravelly laugh. "Why, it's flying off the shelves, Browning. People's fascination with Dante has no bounds."

"I just saw my poem, as well as a hodgepodge of Dantean books, being burned in a bonfire by a band of fools."

"How many books inspire that kind of passion? Only books that provoke hate and disgust also have the power to provoke adoration. Besides, people have to buy the books before they burn them. Now, we'll need your signature on some new contracts with all the printings we're having to do . . ."

"It's like something down the rabbit hole of Dodgson's Wonderland,"

Browning roared, turning around and fleeing over his publisher's protests.

Back at Tudor House, Browning was in the overgrown garden putting out food for the animals when he could hear a caller come to the door. He recognized Cayley's voice at the front door. Browning slipped back inside, listening the best he could to the conversation between Cayley and Christina in the next room. He could not make out the entire exchange, but he heard the visitor say he was going to the country to the Cayley family estate for several months. Cayley invited Christina to come stay with them. Browning pressed his ear closer.

"Mr. Cayley, I did not want to address this," Christina said, "but I know why you've been coming here."

"I don't understand, Miss Rossetti. Why, I've told you in quite thorough detail, I need to dig through your father's . . ."

"I *know* William sent you as some kind of tactic to distract me, to disrupt me, to pretend to . . . to woo me."

"That's not true," Cayley cried.

"Isn't it true that William told you to be here at Tudor House?"

"Well, yes he did, Miss Rossetti, but—"

Browning worried that Christina would hear him sneaking around, and returned to the garden before the finale of the conversation. When he reentered the drawing room, Cayley, in a dejected state, was leaving, and Christina was hovering again over her books and documents. Browning felt something unexpected mixed with sympathy for Cayley. Pleasure that the translator would no longer be vying for Christina's attention.

When Christina was ready, she began chasing her ideas in and around London. Browning came along by coach and omnibus and ferry, to various destinations that she inspected. Some he could see no relation to Dante's text at all, or perhaps he had stopped trying. One was a pathway through a village outside of the city.

"Do you see how it is nearly a perfect circle? Ideal to run around in perpetual futility."

Perpetual futility echoed in his mind, epitomizing their wild-goose chase.

"I'm afraid, Miss Rossetti," he replied, realizing as he spoke that he was short of breath from their surveillance of various sites, "this will not do any longer."

"If you doubt the cause or methods, I perfectly understand if you step away from it."

Her lost faith in him, the lack of anxiety from her that he might cease helping her, broke his heart. "Miss Rossetti, you will become so polite one of these days that you will be impossible to speak with. At what point will you put this behind you?"

She blinked at him, seeming to reflect on it. Her enormous eyes answered for her, as though to say: *Never. I will never stop.*

XVIII

It would almost have been fair to say that Simon Camp's wish upon ar-
riving in London came true—up to a point, at least. He was writing the
new booklet he'd set out to write about the Dante deaths, the one he
thought could make such a splash. The problem was he was doing it with
one leg chained to an immovable block.

He was also made to wear a long robe, tied at the waist by a crude
rope made of plant stems twisted around each other. He wrote with a
goose quill at a standing desk, at the insistence of Reverend Fallow.
While engaged in his composing, he was confined inside the well-
appointed library dungeon, the only such library dungeon in the world,
to Camp's knowledge. In the times he was not chained up, when he was
being moved from one place to another in the so-called sanatorium, he
had studied the books on the shelves and realized that each and every
volume, many of them cracked and ancient, had something to do with
Dante or medieval Italy.

Fallow would march himself on his thick legs into the chamber, lectur-
ing and sermonizing to Camp about how the recent deaths witnessed by
London had begun to purge the metropolis of its many sins, to transform
it. Camp was supposed to transcribe Fallow's ramblings and select what

to include in the booklet. The preacher had also left stacks of newspaper clippings about his earlier, short-lived career preaching to crowds of thousands and other relevant topics. Instead of making himself the hero of the narrative, the fearless private detective Simon Camp, as Camp had planned, he was compelled to turn this rabid minister into some kind of avenging angel.

"Brother," said Fallow, as the shades in Dante's *Purgatory* called each other, "we will soon all be citizens of one true city, and you are among the most important witnesses to the why and how."

People rarely used their given names on the sanatorium grounds; they were "brother" or "sister."

Sisters: indeed. Fallow kept a collection of comely young women wrapped up loosely in their white robes close at hand.

Camp bided his time. He smacked his lips with his tongue and bobbed his head while in Fallow's presence, as though he were a puppy eager for scraps of the preacher's genius. He was waiting for the perfect opportunity to escape his strange imprisonment and, if possible, avenge himself for this ordeal with a good beating on the good minister.

Though most of the time when Camp saw Fallow, the preacher was surrounded by his adoring sirens and the rest of the flock, the prisoner happened to witness two more unpleasant meetings between Camp and the dark-eyed stranger with the tunic and woolen cord around his waist. The stranger's voice was a powerful baritone that could make a man jump, and he carried a walking stick that was topped with an ugly gold beast that Camp fancied was a symbol of the man's soul. Whoever he was, he was not among the sanatorium's herd of followers. Camp caught that Fallow referred to him as Brother Herman and, at a different point, in an agitated state, the preacher called the visitor by the peculiar sobriquet "Ironhead." Camp noticed that Ironhead Herman did not wait for Fallow to be notified of his visits by one of his handmaidens; this caller commanded his own kind of attention and authority.

It soon became clear that Herman was not there for an escape from the sins of the city or for lessons on Dante, Fallow's chief pastimes. Herman had been dunning the minister for money—at churches where Fallow went to preach, at the sanatorium, it didn't matter, he'd become Fallow's unwanted shadow. "It would be a shame to see this place in ashes," bellowed this force of nature. "I don't run a Jew's marketplace!" was another of the fragments of conversation Camp picked up, when Fallow apparently tried to negotiate a lower payment. Camp had to retain his sober demeanor, but inwardly he smiled, thinking the hostility of this belligerent invader could become key to his own escape.

Tennyson stood at the top of the hill about a half mile from Farringford, gazing over the coastline. The brown cape that covered his shoulders, above his long cloak, flapped in the stinging cold wind. His two staghounds, Don and Duke, were chasing stray sheep. As he listened to the gulls gliding by the edge of the cliffs, he heard the crunch of boot steps.

The sounds of people approaching his solitary perch would normally make the reclusive poet alert for intruding admirers. This time, he expected the sounds. Constable Branagan approached first, and Inspector Williamson, walking almost as briskly as his younger colleague, came next.

"Have you ever," Tennyson said, still peering out at the sea, "felt London so far away, as when you stand right at this spot?"

"Very nice island, Mr. Tennyson," said Branagan, "except that my shoes and trousers are soaked from the dew."

"Dee-you," Tennyson corrected him.

"What?" Branagan asked.

"There's no *Jew* on the grass, Constable," Tennyson said of the pronunciation. "There may be *dew*, but that's quite another thing."

"If you had come to our usual meeting spot near Scotland Yard, it would have saved us some trouble, Mr. Tennyson," Dolly Williamson said. "When I want to stand around outside in the cold, I'll take care of my garden, thank you."

"I'm afraid anywhere in London has become too risky that my friends would find out we've been having conversations," the poet replied. "You do understand that, Inspector? I've been thinking. The descent of man from lower animals, if it is true, helps solve the mystery of man's dual nature. We inherit a great deal from our brute ancestors. The spiritual nature is something else, but the brute nature is there, and remains side by side with the other."

Dolly watched the gulls circle, then gave a slight shrug. "Mr. Tennyson, we've appreciated the information you've given us throughout this ordeal. And we've protected your position. I understand my friend at the War Office performed his role well for his colleagues when he gave you the files of the soldiers you requested, making it appear he simply was charmed by your position as poet laureate."

"When I accepted my honor from the queen," Tennyson said gravely, "I swore my allegiance to God and to England, and that includes the general rule of law and, for better or worse, you gentlemen."

"We have everything we need from you and your companions," Dolly said, impatient to be finished.

"Then why do you still have your damned spies watching Tudor House?"

"We have no such thing," Dolly objected.

"I suppose Robert Browning and the others are simply hallucinating the boat that happens to row by at regular intervals." Tennyson reprimanded his dogs for running too far, then returned to the topic. "I saw it with my own eyes."

"Our detective department hasn't requisitioned the use of a duty boat from the Marine Police for over a year, I believe, when we suspected two rival groups of Fenians were transporting weapons on the river," Dolly said.

"Mr. Tennyson, the message you sent to me last night indicated you had some new information for Inspector Williamson," Branagan broke in.

Tennyson turned away from the cliff and looked right at the men for the first time. "How is Gabriel doing?" Suspecting the answer wasn't good, he went on without waiting. "If you are being honest and really have given up your intelligence gathering, there might be a serious problem. I think you *should* be watching Miss Rossetti carefully again. Very carefully."

"How do you mean?" asked Dolly.

The poet explained that Christina still pursued her inquiries into the London deaths, and he worried for her safety.

"If you believe, as I do, that Mr. Rossetti was responsible, what is your concern, Mr. Tennyson? Miss Rossetti can go in circles if she wishes; no harm will come to anyone."

"The only fault of Miss Rossetti is that she has no fault at all. Intellectually, I accept Gabriel Rossetti's guilt, Inspector. Given all the facts, who wouldn't? But what if Miss Rossetti proves to be right?"

Dolly, annoyance growing in his voice, asked what it was Tennyson was driving at.

"There is a verse by Robert Burns," said the poet, then recited:

> *The trumpets sound, the banners fly*
> *The glittering spears are ranked ready,*
> *The shouts o' war are heard afar,*
> *The battle closes thick and bloody.*

Tennyson rolled the last two lines again on his tongue, and said, "I would give anything to have written that."

"Still, Mr. Tennyson, I don't understand—"

He all but shouted: "Two poets can write about war, but only one writes those lines, because he sees it in a way no one else could."

"You are the poet laureate of all England, Mr. Tennyson, so forgive me if I find it odd to think there are versifiers with greater vision."

"Well! Perhaps it is because I am the laureate that it is absolutely the case. To declare a poet laureate is to put a coronet on a skull. Browning's wife was under consideration to be the first woman given the laureate title, you know, and Browning will never forgive me for it."

"You believe Miss Rossetti sees something more—some more powerful truth—in Dante and in those deaths than all the rest of us. More than you, than me, the other detectives and policemen in my department, the hundred and one newspaper reporters who wrote about it."

Tennyson took a few moments of silence. Then, he said, "If she does, someone else may be hurt or killed. Inspector, tell me, do you really have no doubts at all that you know everything that happened?"

Dolly seemed as though he didn't want to answer, then called for Branagan to prepare to return to the ferry. Tennyson did not try to sway or influence them further, listening to their steps down the path and again watching the gulls, who elegantly swerved just in time to avoid crashing into the cliffside.

Sitting in a seat far back in the half-empty stands was Jeremiah McCord—McCord who went by other names if he was abroad or otherwise motivated to hide, but given McCord was his most common alias this month, McCord it will be. With him was a much younger woman with a dark hat brightened by a large white feather, and a plaid shawl over her silk dress.

McCord watched the races only at intervals, as the freezing, gusty wind—and almost April!—had kept the best horses off the track to save their strength for better weather and bigger stakes. Likewise, McCord's mind was on the chance for much more significant days to come. With his good hand, he impatiently scratched at his beard until he finally caught sight of the man he'd sent for.

The man, who had a scar over his right temple and was dressed like a well-to-do farmer, came to an abrupt stop in front of McCord.

"I promise by the Divine Law of God to do all in my power to free and regenerate Ireland from the yoke of England. So help me God."

McCord, remaining in his seat, waved this away. "You took all the materials from Lombard Street?"

"Aye."

"We will be united again with our compatriots," McCord said with a smile. "Soon enough. Then on to bigger plans."

The Irishman with the scar bowed his head in deference.

"What of the other matter?" McCord asked.

The man shifted his feet nervously. "Sorry, sir, simply can't find that bloke anywhere."

McCord had sent messages to all the hotels Simon Camp had listed. The American private detective had told McCord that he planned to switch rooms every few days. The private detective had also given McCord the aliases he would be using at each hotel.

Urgent news on mutual friend Mr. Alighieri, McCord's messages had read.

It was true. McCord had news that Camp would want to know—according to McCord's informants, Scotland Yard had detained someone in secret, but at the same time Dolly Williamson had begun having real doubts.

The message, though, was just bait. McCord had been corresponding with some associates in America and became convinced Camp was a dangerous man, prone to changing allegiances at the slightest whiff of profit. The Fenians had too many grand operations under way in the name of Irish freedom. Camp, having been in possession of some of the Fenian communications, had to be removed permanently—whether by poison or the point of a dagger.

Except that the man had disappeared.

"Maybe Inspector Dolly convinced the fool to go back home," McCord said after pensively studying the flags flapping in the wind over the opposite stands. "Keep looking for him."

"Should we move ahead with our other plans in the meantime, sir?"

McCord exchanged a heavy glance with his wife at his side.

"Aye," said McCord. "If you can avoid too many people getting hurt, do so."

Christina had been true to her word. She never relented in her attempts to anticipate where the next terrace of Purgatory could materialize in London. She even stopped over at Saint Mary's to inform them with her regrets that she would not be present for a while. During her visit there, she learned that Ethel had run off from the home. *So close to being ready to return to the world, poor soul*, lamented the Anglican sister who told her the sad tidings. Christina thought about Ethel's fears that the distraught new girl, Ruthie, would return to her previous life of desperation, and Christina in turn now feared this heartbreaking fate for Ethel.

Hardly slowing down long enough to sleep, Christina dissected every line and every word of the cantos in which Dante meets the souls purging themselves of the sin of sloth; along the way, she had consulted commentaries on Dante in five languages, even reading her father's intricate notes that Cayley had organized, flooding her with haunting memories of the professore's decline. Her latest excursions in London related to one verse in particular. "*Purgatory*, Canto Eighteen," she had said to Browning as they sat side by side on a crowded omnibus, "verse eighty-eight and forward. Dante feels himself standing there drowsily, until:

> *Taken from me was this drowsiness*
> *Suddenly by a people, that behind*

Our backs already had come round to us
And as, of old, Ismenus and Asopus
Beside them saw at night the rush and throng

"Then the souls come running at astounding speeds. Ismenus and Asopus," she continued, "of course refer to ancient Greek rivers, Dante imagining the flow of crowds at their banks."

So Christina searched out the busiest riverbanks within the city and examined them for any indications that Dante-inspired violence had happened or could still happen. Browning accompanied her to each stop, but she knew he was doing so with increasing reluctance. He thought they were looking for the proverbial needle in the bundle of hay, and she was sure the needle was in their grasp with enough faith and proper application of intellect.

There were usual and unusual interruptions at Tudor House, where she worked on maps of the greater London area. A medium showed up at the door. She came several times a year to Tudor House to determine how much supernatural activity was present, and to listen for signs of Lizzie. Holmes was upstairs at Sibbie's side trying yet another new treatment, Browning was out completing an errand, and Christina was too polite to turn the pushy woman away. As the medium sat at a table, there were some bumping sounds from below the house that seemed to surprise even the ghost-friendly visitor. Perhaps the dormice or another of the animals had dug themselves a hole beneath the foundation, though the noise seemed more deliberate.

"Have you been hearing these spirit noises often, Miss Rossetti?" asked the medium.

"Spirit noises?" came Browning's voice from the next room.

Browning had returned at just this time and, incensed by the presence of the medium, threw the lady out of the house. His face became fiery red. He cried after her, a cry years in the making: "Dung-ball of a human being!"

Another interruption came with the return of Charles Cayley.

"I thought you were in the country, Mr. Cayley," Christina said, her demeanor indifferent. She and Browning were about to cross through the gates on the way to study more locales.

"After our conversation, I realized I could not," Cayley said, swallowing hard. "I could, but I could not. What I mean to say . . . Mr. Browning, could I have a private word with Miss Rossetti?"

"Of course, Mr. Cayley." Browning shook his hand and patted him on the back.

Christina led him to the garden, where the peacocks stared glumly at Cayley.

"William did tell me to come to Tudor House, it's true. *But* that is only because I first asked his permission, just as I asked yours. If he wished me to distract you from something, as you suggest, well, that was his purpose and not mine."

"Very well," Christina said, remaining stone-faced but softening her tone. "I'm afraid I don't have time to spare today for pleasantries, Mr. Cayley. I am truly sorry you had to call off your trip."

"Miss Rossetti, I didn't have to call it off. I wanted very much to go— but with you. I realized, as I prepared my valise, I had no interest in going anywhere without you."

"I . . . don't understand."

"That's just it. Of all the women I know, Miss Rossetti, you *do* understand me. I am perfectly content with my translating. I always have been. But I can be more than content—I can be happy—with you by my side. I think you might feel the same. Are you unwell, Miss Rossetti?"

Christina felt light-headed, rising from the bench and holding herself against it. She could not breathe. She could not think about this *now*.

"Dear Miss Rossetti, I didn't mean to—"

Christina explained that she could not tarry longer—she had urgent things to do.

Browning asked what happened, what Cayley had said that had so upset her. But she would speak only about what they needed to find to help Gabriel.

They reached their fourth riverbank location of the day. Christina examined the area through Browning's opera glasses and studied the nearby bridge, over which a mass of people flowed.

Browning let out a sigh, his impatience finally becoming so great that he could no longer play his assigned part. "My dear Miss Rossetti, we have been going from place to place for days, without a clue or guide, lost in a maze of obscurity."

"Remember, Dante does not understand the true meaning of Purgatory until he does."

"Dante is not in London! I am greatly concerned about your well-being, too, the longer you keep at this. Please, could you put down that pencil so we might speak sensibly about this?"

Christina was sitting on a bench transcribing her observations of the area around the bridge into her notebook as he made his plea. "Mr. Browning, we may speak about it, but I must not lose time. At risk of losing my unlivable politeness, please do not attempt to change my mind by stomping around in the style of an ogre. Do one thing or the other, only do not become ridiculous."

At first stunned into silence, Browning then launched into his argument about the *ridiculous* probability of their finding worthwhile new clues, about how they could be more useful elsewhere, and so on—the fact was, she tried to listen but not for very long. She remained fixed on her purpose, looking for any particulars that could match well with Dante's cantos. She pressed her eyes against the lenses of the pocket-size binoculars.

"Hold your tongue! Look!"

Browning accepted the opera glasses. Weaving through the crowd on the bridge, there was a man running at full speed. In itself it would not have been too peculiar a sight in the rush of London, where the meek were often too afraid to go on sidewalks for fear of being knocked down. But this man was crashing into other people, weaving around them, tripping and jumping right back into a run—as though he could not stop.

Christina called out to Browning to follow. They darted into the crowds, dodging and sliding away from people, trying to get close to the running man.

"Heavens, Miss Rossetti," Browning called, "do you see?"

Christina did. Moving closer, the man's face came into view. It was A. R. Gibson, the eccentric patron of Gabriel and Hughes. Gibson was rumbling in their direction as they struggled to reach him. Soon they found themselves on either side of him, running to keep up with his pace as he rounded onto the sidewalk. He wore his long, shiny coat with the velvet collar.

"Miss Rossetti and Mr. Browning," Gibson said, panting hard as he spoke, "what a gratifying satisfaction to meet you here!"

"Mr. Gibson, we know what's been done to you!" Christina called. "You must stop!"

"But I cannot!" he replied, fear in his voice. His eyes misted with tears. "I hope you do not think me rude."

"Who did this to you?" Browning asked.

Gibson gave a chilling laugh. "Don't you know?"

"Please, Mr. Gibson, you must speak to the police so that they know my brother did not commit the other crimes. You must tell them what has happened to you and how! Let us help you!"

"Why, Miss Rossetti," said the runner, losing so much of his breath that he had to stop speaking, "you do not . . . why, my dear woman, don't you understand . . . and if I stop . . ."

Christina, transfixed, collided with a pedestrian and fell to the ground; Browning tried to stop her fall and tripped and tumbled down with her. By the time they regained their footing, neither could catch up with Gibson, who accelerated to what seemed an impossible speed. Out of breath and strength, they yielded, first Browning, then Christina. They had found the punishment of the Slothful. Now they had lost it. And lost Gibson.

Two young men, their long, flowing coats fluttering in the wind, appeared and kept pace right behind the runaway patron, who turned down another street, out of sight.

"Stop, in the name of the queen!" one of the new pursuers yelled, holding up a glimmering emblem. The other one blew a whistle hanging from his neck.

"Detectives," Browning cried to Christina.

She considered this as she knelt on the ground and fought to catch her breath. "How could they have known?"

Browning contemplated this, his mind turning back to the similarly rapid appearance of Scotland Yarders at the death of Loring, before his face darkened with anger.

A chime rang out in the detectives' corridors. "Wire in!" the telegraph operator called. Dolly burst out of his office, and Branagan ran over from his desk. "It's two of the detective sergeants you assigned the other day to recommence shadowing Miss Rossetti," Branagan said after a quick glance at the transmission. "They were spotted giving chase to a man who appears unable . . ."

"Yes? Yes?" asked Dolly.

"Unable to stop," Branagan finished.

Dolly's eyes widened. "It's the fourth." He ignored questions about the meaning of his comment. "Take me to them, Branagan!"

They hurried into the carriage, and Branagan brought their horses to full speed, heading toward the coordinates contained in the wire. Carriages and omnibuses cluttered their routes, and Dolly, cursing all London, ordered the constable to stop. The detective then unlatched one of the horses and continued on horseback. Branagan rushed to do the same.

Soon both were galloping through the streets, steering around obstacles, human and otherwise.

Branagan pulled his horse next to his superior's. "What did you mean, the fourth?" he called out.

"The next terrace of Purgatory, the fourth of seven—Pride, Envy, Wrath, Sloth . . . The Slothful are made to run around without stopping, until rid of every bit of laziness."

"Another Dante Massacre? Impossible. It can't be, Inspector. We have Rossetti. We have him. If there is another Dante murder, that means he is not the one . . ."

"Not now!" Dolly cried.

They careened through the streets until they reached the commotion of a group of plainclothes detectives and uniformed constables—totaling half a dozen by this point—giving chase to the fleeing man. In just a few minutes after they joined the pursuit, the runaway was twice nearly flattened by conveyances in the street and almost tumbled into a sidewalk excavation. His pursuers, meanwhile, were hindered by the array of obstructions. Gibson was not merely moving rapidly. His pace seemed inhuman.

Shouts and screams flew from every direction. Dolly called out orders to the police officers. Onlookers screamed out pleas and insults at the running man. The man himself cried out that he could not stop. The cluster of horses and men reached the entrance of a railway tunnel. The runner hesitated just long enough that he was surrounded by his pursuers.

Finally, Gibson stopped. His heavy breathing turning into a frosty steam in the air, Gibson whispered, "Forgive me."

A faint smile played on the art patron's lips. It seemed he was about to say more, when his whole body shuddered, his eyes rolled up into the back of his head, and he collapsed onto the street. Dolly and Branagan rushed to his side, as other policemen kept the crowd of observers away.

Dolly caught his breath, wiping away a layer of perspiration.

"He's dead," Dolly said, first to himself, then announcing the same to

Branagan and the others. He examined the man up and down his body before his eyes landed on his boots. "Pull those off. Now! Pull them off now! Carefully, Branagan."

(Around that time, Christina and Browning caught up with the scene, watching from a perimeter of bystanders.)

Branagan followed Dolly's gaze to the deceased man's boots, but they would not budge. Dolly ordered the other men away, then nodded at Branagan.

The constable removed a pocketknife from his coat and sliced the cords that fastened the boots to the man's legs. Slowly removing one of the boots, Dolly peered inside it at a snarl of needles and wires.

The detectives and the scientists they'd brought to Scotland Yard from Oxford and Cambridge huddled around the boots to marvel at the design. They proved to be remarkable and sinister inventions that would be studied by experts for years to come.

An arrangement of razor-sharp needles were positioned in such a way to pierce the flesh deeply as the foot moved down, and provide relief when the foot was raised. They *made* the wearer run. Inside the hollow parts of the boots was a complex series of wires, charged in advance by some kind of battery, poised to deliver a jolt of electricity if the motion of the mechanism stopped for more than a few seconds, a more powerful jolt the longer it stopped—a jolt that proved fatal when Gibson was finally forced to halt his run by the police.

To stop moving meant death.

Repercussions from Gibson's death came swiftly. Many of these, unsurprisingly, concerned Dante Gabriel Rossetti. Dolly was not persuaded that the latest events necessarily vindicated his prisoner, but the authorities were used to Dolly standing aside from popular opinion. The fact remained that Gabriel had been inside a cell when this latest Dante death was perpetrated. Dolly was now as alone in Scotland Yard in his belief in Gabriel's guilt as Christina had been days earlier believing in her brother's innocence. Or had Dolly ever been as convinced as he'd appeared? Truth was, something had not sat well with Dolly since the elation of an arrest subsided, and was further worn down by his irksome interview with Alfred Tennyson.

Christina established an encampment at the police station where Gabriel was still held. Dolly and Branagan, as well as other police officials, tried to persuade her to stay at home to wait. Dolly claimed Gabriel was refusing to eat and that the excitement was not helping him. "When I do decide to leave," she said with steel in her voice to Dolly and Branagan, "it will be with my brother on my arm."

Browning followed Christina to Scotland Yard. He was concerned about her. In addition to the fact that she had hardly been sleeping—a few minutes now and again for the last week—she had seen A. R. Gibson die before her eyes; Browning had looked away at the last moment, but she had not. She appeared emaciated. Perhaps Browning was right that she had been worn down more than ever by the latest turns of events, but Gabriel's imminent release, certainly, had to lighten her spirits.

The intensity of the situation consumed her, and it also gave her that glow, that energy, that tended to take people by surprise. Browning, trying unsuccessfully to coax her to get rest, found himself holding her by the hand, and locked onto her eyes, so serious and bright. There was something heroic about her, like a figure out of a fairy tale wrapped in fire.

Damn Tennyson. Christina was *not* Ba. Browning had not tried to make her so. But she was vibrant and brilliant.

"Miss Rossetti, there is something I must say to you," Browning blurted out.

"Mr. Browning?"

"Look at us—lost adventurers. I wondered, when this all began, if by being by your side, snakelike, stomping around in my ogre fashion, I could be of some use to you, or if *anybody* could be of use to anybody else." Browning started to continue twice before he deflated. His eyes filled with tears and he said, "How do you feel about me, Miss Rossetti?"

"Why, I feel I have known you a hundred years, Mr. Browning."

"My heart, I begin to believe, really is buried in Florence."

"I know it is." She gently withdrew her hand from his.

"I always thought I would want to go back to Florence, but now I don't know. As an old man said to me once of Jerusalem, 'No, I don't want to go there, I can see it in my head.' We outlive some places, people, and things that charmed us in our youth, I daresay. Ba was never very strong, never well, and yet I thought, I truly *believed* love saved her life. All this talk of my fame since my last volumes. You can guess and God knows that the simple truth is she was the poet, and I merely a clever person. My uninterrupted health and strength should have helped me, but look what she made of her mind, despite her limited experiences and her frailness. It is an injustice to all mankind, dear Miss Rossetti, that one does not call you his husband."

Browning rose and looked out the window, where the sky was dark with snow and hail, and the occasional clap of thunder made the glass tremble. He wept into his hands. Christina stood and looked out a different window, then said: "You were fortunate that your Gemma and Beatrice—the woman you had and the woman you needed—were one and the same. Besides, if one's heart *is* to be buried, there is probably no place better than Italy."

English justice moved slowly. In order to review Gabriel's circumstance, there were hearings and meetings between magistrates and commissioners and even, at one point, a conference of officials with the mayor of London.

As days passed, Browning's voice was joined by a chorus of others urging Christina to return home with her mother, or at least to go back to Tudor House, until something definitive had been announced regarding Gabriel's fate. She still insisted that she would leave only with Gabriel. Browning brought meals and books to Christina to sustain her during her vigil, then would go back out to obtain the latest supplies Holmes requested for his care of Sibbie.

Christina examined books of laws and regulations about the rights of prisoners until her eyes were red and heavy. She rested her head when she had to, permitting her eyes to close only when forced by her weakening body.

As Christina sealed herself inside the police offices, the fears of the press and the public of London rose sharply, the realization growing that a murderer remained among them. There were more book-burning parties to incinerate copies of Dante. The booksellers, meanwhile, continued reporting record sales of Dante's *Comedy* and related books, as well as stranger artifacts being manufactured, including Dante calendars and bookends—with a miniature bust of solemn Dante on one bookend, and a bust of a lovely Beatrice on the other.

Unmoored from his expected course in the investigation, Dolly Williamson visited the Gibson home, built by the grandfather of the now-deceased art patron and collector. Liveried servants were wandering around aimlessly, weeping, like a group of ghosts abandoned to the old place. Dolly questioned the domestics and examined Gibson's letters and diaries. Gibson's mother, Annie, had died when he was a child, and not feeling himself loved by his father, the artists who fascinated Gibson became his family—his letters to painters demanded they tell him about their lives, their marriages, their travels. Correspondence from some years earlier also revealed that Gibson forced many of "his" artists to use him as a model in paintings. However much he saw them as family, Gibson also thought himself better and of higher standing than the artists, bargaining with them relentlessly to drive down their prices. He also complained that the subjects he modeled for were not noble enough, and that the practice involved in sitting as a model was too tiresome.

The diaries were just as interesting and rather sad. Gibson had many mistresses—six, by Dolly's count as he explored the entries, in the last four years—including married women, and from what Dolly could gather was father to several illegitimate children that Gibson went to great lengths to avoid.

Back at Scotland Yard, Dolly received his orders from the Home Office to release his prisoner. He sat down one more time with Dante Gabriel Rossetti, who had become gradually more presentable as the opiates ceased to control his body. Not that the painter would respond to Dolly's questions, at least not by saying anything helpful. He gave no indication of understanding why he had been there—not even enough to deny his own guilt, as most imprisoned individuals would whether or not they were actually innocent.

"I cannot. I simply cannot tolerate the chore, however necessary," Dolly said, returning to his office.

"Which chore?" asked Branagan.

"Watching Rossetti go free while we still pine for the truth. Perhaps he is innocent. Perhaps guilty. Is it possible, Branagan, that he is both, or do I begin to lose all my instincts? You do it, please, Branagan. You release him." Dolly was unusually jumpy. He did not have to look far for a distraction. He had received the usual variety of reports from around London that required his oversight.

There were two horses poisoned in a stable; a woman's bloodied clothes and effects found in a stairwell, without any other trace of a woman; then there was a pair of men found loitering outside Clerkenwell Prison.

At the prison wall, Dolly found the constables holding the suspicious characters, who were both Irishmen.

"We're thinking Fenians, trying to plot to climb in and help their friends on the other side get out," one of the constables said. "Good luck trying that. Inspector Williamson?"

Dolly couldn't shake his thoughts about Gabriel and the Dante Massacres. "You empty their pockets and coats? Good. Show me."

"One of them had this in his coat."

The constable dusted the snow off a white ball the size of a large egg.

Dolly examined their other effects and stopped on a card on which was scrawled *16 Lombard*. "This was one of the places where McCord was living," Dolly said.

"Who?" asked the constable.

"Jeremiah McCord. Inspector Thornton believes McCord is one of the new Fenian leaders since we locked up his superiors. Thornton had tracked him to Ironhead Herman, a strongman for some black market opium traders. McCord was attempting to purchase phosphorus from Herman, and I gave authorization to Thornton to allow the transaction . . ." Dolly lost his train of thought. He marched over to where the men were being restrained, holding up the card with the address.

"What was your business with General McCord? Come, come, where is the one-armed incubus?"

The calmer of the two suspects, who had a scar over his right temple, looked right at Dolly. "I promise by the Divine Law of God to do all in my power to free and regenerate Ireland from the yoke of England. So help me God."

Dolly, agitated, received exactly the same answer from the other man.

"Where precisely were these two looking?" he asked one of the constables.

The constable showed Dolly to the place along the wall where the men were first observed loitering. In the meantime, the other policeman accosted the dark-suited Fenian with the ball. "And what were you doing with this ball, Dubliner? Something hidden inside, is there? A map back to the potato lands, I hope?"

"Maybe," replied the Irishman.

"Show me," ordered the constable, tossing the ball to him.

Dolly, who was examining the wall, was on high alert. He steadied his too-large hat. He opened his coat and from his belt removed his ivory white truncheon, swinging the thick baton at his side. Then he was overcome with an unexpected thought. It did not really come to him in words, but rather an emotion, a feeling. If it were put in words, it would have been something like: *I know what happened. I know how the Dante Massacres came about.*

The Fenian studied the little white ball for a moment, then hurled it high into the air, over the wall of the prison.

Dolly spun around toward the man. A sly smirk had formed on the man's face.

The detective's jaw fell open. "That's a signal," Dolly said, then, louder: "They weren't trying to climb over—get back!"

His cry was cut short by a horrendous boom. The prison wall shattered as the fireball of explosions erupted. Where Dolly, the constables, and the Fenians had been standing a moment before, there was nothing but rubble painted in dark blood.

Back at Scotland Yard's police offices, Constable Thomas Branagan filled out the documents required to complete the prisoner's release. When he was finished, Branagan escorted Gabriel to where his sister was waiting for him in the anteroom. Gabriel was polite to everyone at the offices. He told the constable that he needed to speak to his sister alone. Branagan imagined the artist thanking his sister for all her efforts, though this did not prove to be an accurate guess.

Whatever Gabriel might have said to Christina at that moment, in fact, became moot. As he walked over to her little encampment of books and food, he found her fast asleep on a thick blanket that Browning had brought her. She had subsisted without more than two hours' worth of sleep a day for more than a week.

The painter-poet bent his large body down very gingerly over the much slighter figure of his sister, and gave her a soft kiss on her forehead. "Remember me," he whispered. He then turned with vigor and purpose and exited through the door to the street.

Christina stirred herself awake, placing an automatic hand on her forehead where Gabriel had kissed her. In her dreams, her father tossed aside his Dante books, listened to her read her poetry, and gave her a loving kiss on her cheek. She looked around, seeing no one but experiencing a frantic sense that something had happened. *Gabriel*, she thought. She lifted up her weakened body as quickly as she could and stumbled around, looking for any sign of him before rushing outside. There he was: Gabriel. He seemed a phantasm among the ordinary men and women of the city. He stood in the middle of the street under the dark sky.

As they faced each other a stone's throw away, they appeared to be opposites: the slender woman with a severe expression on her thin, strong lips; the wide, muscular bulldoggish man with the sloping gait. As they eyed each other, resemblance grew. The shiny dark brown hair, the projecting nose, and, most of all, the changeable, hypnotic eyes.

She ran over to him. "Come with me," she tried to say, but at the same time he cried to her, "Come with me." His command was not the practical, protective kind that she issued. Gabriel's was a prophetic exhortation—the kind recounted in the Bible that would change the lives of a whole people or nation.

She hardly noticed a carriage that was brought to a stop behind them. Gabriel's paw-like hands led her to the vehicle, and within moments they were seated inside.

Hours before Christina climbed into a carriage with Dante Gabriel Rossetti and before the explosion at Clerkenwell Prison, Browning, reluctant to leave Christina alone at this point, was delivering supplies to Holmes at Tudor House—fresh towels and scented waters to stimulate Sibbie's senses.

Holmes smiled and remained cheerful in Sibbie's presence, feeling that a sentence of death on a doctor's face was as bad as a warrant for execution signed by the governor of a state. Holmes had been speaking to

Sibbie as much as possible, to the point where his voice grew hoarse. He could almost hear his daughter in his ear—Amelia would have teased him, he had no doubt, that if there was a single man who could carry on that many hours of one-sided conversations, it was Dr. Oliver Wendell Holmes.

As the details of Sibbie's previous life were taken in by her dormant brain, the experience could animate the other systems of the body to return to that life. This was Holmes's educated theory, at any rate, and his abiding personal wish. He used the information he'd gleaned from the visits of Sibbie's mother and from Reverend Fallow to speak to her about her childhood; to remind her how her kindness toward the afflicted as a youth was so great that people sought her out as though she could magically heal them; how she read studiously despite not having much formal schooling, and so became an avid student; and how even as her family suffered hardships, she maintained a positive outlook and always believed they could rise above their stations. Holmes silently hoped such positivity about her could influence him, too, to keep believing her recovery was possible.

Finally, signs of real progress. Her eyelids fluttered from time to time. Her hands and feet had begun to twitch. At one point, she stretched her right hand out toward Holmes. This caused a great surge of optimism, which mostly subsided when the movement was not repeated. Holmes reasoned that all these constituted proof this was not a lost cause. (Then again, the history of medicine was to a great extent just a record of self-delusion.)

"Wasn't it all my fault?" Holmes had asked Browning without explanation.

"What do you mean, Holmes?"

"She ran in to try to pull me out when I fell."

"No," Browning replied, "you were trying to save Loring after all."

"Yes, because I thought it was Gabriel stuck in there. I have tried all my theories to help her, Browning, but old theories are like the old men who cling to them, and must take themselves out of the way in favor of the new generation. And if I knew it was Loring inside that trap, a man we thought at the time was our evildoing Cato, would I have taken the same risk?"

"I believe you would have. You dedicated yourself to all of us and our purpose—unlike Tennyson. I should get back to Miss Rossetti."

But then another shining sign of life, not long after Browning departed from Tudor House. Holmes was sitting beside Sibbie, trimming her nails, when she squeezed his fingers. He trembled as if grabbed by a spirit's hand. He asked if she could squeeze his hand once for yes, twice for no. He waited so long he could barely endure it. She squeezed once.

"My dear, do you know who killed Loring? Was there someone other than Gabriel Rossetti involved?"

She squeezed. Yes.

Holmes heard the street door open once again and a voice calling to find out who was home. Reluctantly, Holmes left Sibbie and headed down.

When Holmes was gone, a white-robed figure crept down the second-floor hall, giving the appearance of a wandering ghost. From his belt woven of plant stems hung a small pistol. He had been listening carefully to the doctor-poet's exhortations to the patient, and now he stopped at the open doorway and stared inside the dark room.

Holmes, how d'ye do?" hailed Tennyson, whom Holmes found unwrapping himself from his old ratty coat at the foot of the stairs. He had a walking stick Holmes had not seen before, which Tennyson hung up with great care. From the horrified look on Tennyson's face when he turned to see him, Holmes realized how he must have appeared after his countless hours at Sibbie's bedside. His eyes were red and the skin under his eyes gray, the rest of his face sallow. Holmes explained where the others were.

"And Sibbie?"

"I had begun to think it would be a good plan to get rid of old professors like me. But I have broken down a wall in her. I believe she knows vital information she will be able to share with us."

"Excellent! Shan't we sit for a while, Holmes?"

"We thought you sealed yourself into Farringford like the pharaohs in their pyramids," Holmes said. "Browning believes you ordered the police to follow him and Miss Rossetti. He thinks that it was how they knew where the Slothful would be and also how they were so quickly on the scene at the sanatorium when Loring was killed."

"Pack of lies! Do you notice Browning always believes the worst in me? I'm terribly fond of him, meanwhile," said Tennyson. "And I admire his poetry more than he thinks, though if he got rid of two-thirds, the remaining third would be finer. Do you know in his last work, he makes 'impulse' rhyme with 'dim pulse'? As long as the pronunciation of the English language were forgotten, Browning would be held as the greatest of modern poets. No matter, I've come to speak to you more than to the others. To tell you that you were right."

The laureate found some port and they sat in Gabriel's drawing room, which was almost immediately choked with smoke from Tennyson's pipe.

"There is more about myself in my poem on Ulysses than I like to confess," Tennyson mused. "Ulysses tries to rush fate, like so many of us, in desperation to know where he'll end up after all. He dies—in Dante's conception, at least—for trying to pass over Hell and reach salvation through his own will. My dearest friend at university was Arthur Hallam. A young man who had every right to live a long life, but was taken by disease of the brain not long before I wrote that poem. He died, to our eyes, healthy, and since that day I have done what I have to do to prevent myself from losing hope. 'Ulysses' was written under the sense of loss that all had gone by, but that still life must be fought out to the end. It's hopeful, that poem, more than I am myself. Poetry, I daresay, is a great deal truer than fact. You were right to remind me of that. I could have done more."

"With Gabriel to be released at any time, maybe even as we sit here, there is nothing more for you to do now."

"Come! Do not punish me with my flaws. As far as I know my own temperament, I can stand any sudden thing. But give me an hour to reflect, and I should go here and there, and all will be confused. If a fiery gulf opened in London, I would leap at once into it on horseback like Marcus Curtius in ancient times. But if I had to think about it? No. It is the moral question, not the fear, which would perplex me. Yes, Holmes, I suppose Gabriel must be liberated by the police, but do you really think, in your bones, that the detectives will leave him in peace, unless someone unveils the full truth that only we can find?"

"I suppose I want to believe it for Miss Rossetti's sake, and whatever I learn more from Sibbie may help the cause."

"Sibbie must continue her recovery, and that will take time, won't it?" Tennyson got up, went into Gabriel's library, and returned with Simon Camp's *Dante Murders* booklet, which he placed in front of Holmes. "See what you notice about this. Long before any of this happened, Gabriel was already reading about what transpired in Boston."

"You think Simon Camp's claptrap inspired him?" Holmes asked. "None of this makes sense any longer, including where Camp disappeared to after he so boldly accosted me. What am I supposed to notice?"

"The quality of paper, the ink, and—look at the illustration on the front—even the burning feet of the simonists, which are reversed from the other one."

"What other one, Tennyson? Different from what?"

Tennyson explained that he'd come to realize there was another version of the pamphlet. "The copy Inspector Williamson showed me."

"Showed *you*? He showed me, you mean, on the train. When would Williamson have shown you his copy of this?" Holmes asked with an edge of accusation. "Then Browning was right. You have been secretly talking to the police."

"Dolly Williamson had already been spying on Miss Rossetti, as you know. Yes, I obliged a request from the queen's secretary to join your endeavors and give Dolly information so he could keep the people of London safer, and so the police could stop sneaking around Tudor House—at least he promised to call off his spies, though I had my doubts since that boat was still rowing around here. Never mind that, Holmes. You said Dolly had his version of the pamphlet when you saw him on the train, as well. Do you remember it?"

"How could I remember such minutiae about an old pamphlet he waved in my face?" asked Holmes, though the objection was halfhearted. Litterateurs such as Holmes and Tennyson took in the details of every book they saw without trying. "Perhaps I can recall something of it—perhaps it *was* slightly different in the ways you suggest. What of it?"

"This is a cheap production to begin with. In reprinting a booklet like this, one would avoid even the slightest extra expense. These changes have the markings of a pirated edition. If there was so much demand for more of these, the question is, where did it come from?"

"How do you suggest we find out the answer?"

"Come with me to try, then you can return to Sibbie's bedside to your heart's content."

Tennyson explained he already arranged to rendezvous with a young bookseller whom he had met once before. It was said he performed tasks for operatives of the publishing trade who dealt with the pirating of books and other activities that happened in the shadows.

They found the man outside the British Museum. They heard his cheerful whistling first. "Well, it's a brisk day—brisk!" said the bookseller, whose name was Fergins. In fact, it was a full-fledged snowstorm, one so late in April it had only been matched a dozen or so times in recorded English history. To Holmes, the fellow seemed oddly gregarious for someone who consorted with the most reviled profiteers of the literary world: book pirates. Tennyson handed him his walking stick.

"Oh, then you found it," said the bookseller with delight.

"Where you said it would be," Tennyson replied. "Do you have these hidden all over London?"

Fergins unscrewed the top of the walking stick, then whistled a note of approval. "How I enjoy this method. It reminds me of Don Quixote's famous trial, when Sancho Panza realizes there must be treasure concealed in the cane of a man who inexplicably refuses to let go of it. Enough of me. Are you ready to see our mutual friend in the den?"

Fergins led them through the back of the British Museum into the printed books department. They had to go down a steep steel staircase that seemed to curl around itself. Along the way, their guide spoke with great expertise on the works of both Holmes and Tennyson. All around them were shelves of every shape and size holding books and papers. The place smelled of rotted leather and mold.

"One day everything ever written will be in the British Museum, even newspapers," Tennyson said.

"There: the den," said Fergins, catching his breath and pushing up his white-rimmed spectacles. It was a cage of steel bars, where a man with bright red hair sat at a table bathed in dim light.

Fergins bowed as he exited, while the man with abundant red hair invited them into the cage. It was hard to gauge just how far underground they had gone. It was suffocatingly hot.

"This den is where the transcribers work. I am not one of them, of course, but in return for providing some immeasurably rare books to the museum, I am studying some of theirs for my own purposes. I suppose you know who I am."

Tennyson and Holmes exchanged glances. "We know what you do, but your friend dutifully kept us in the dark about your identity," Tennyson said. He volunteered the names of some of the well-known agents who he'd heard aided the world of literary piracy.

"Frauds, all the ones you name! I am called Whiskey Bill, the most accomplished of them all, practically invented the profession."

"You are all frauds, by the very definition of your work," Tennyson cried out.

"We're not here to debate the finer points of the dictionary," Holmes said.

They heard a sound like splashing, which turned out to be Bill's bare feet soaking in a large bucket beneath the table.

"My toes," the man explained, his eyes dancing under bushy eyebrows, "swell up terribly in the humid air down here. Is it still snowing out there? It's whispered that such a late snow is supernatural punishment for London's vices, the heavens cracking, the proper seasons getting jumbled up into perpetual winter, and so on."

"Mr. . . . Bill," Holmes began uneasily, removing the copy of *The Dante Murders* from his coat, "I believe your friend the bookseller informed you that we needed to know more about this."

"Dante, yes," muttered Whiskey Bill, the excited flush across his cheeks receding. "Tell me, how is your friend Gabriel Rossetti?"

Tennyson demanded to know how he knew anything about Gabriel's involvement in the matter.

"Now, Mr. Tennyson! It's part of our task to know what every literary scribbler is doing, particularly when he's in some kind of trouble. We've heard the police believe Mr. Rossetti has somehow been mixed up in this Dante business, though they were able to prevent the newspapers from printing it until they could be sure. If you must know, I'm quite concerned. Rossetti is something of a friend of mine."

"Indeed?" Tennyson replied with skepticism.

"Who do you think helped him some five or six months back, when he needed to get a manuscript from the grave of his wife? Who indeed, but a man with talents for accomplishing *unusual* literary tasks."

Holmes and Tennyson experienced a newfound interest. Whiskey Bill sensed this and offered a lip-smacking grin before telling them more.

Gabriel—Bill explained—had purchased some rare books about Dante from Fergins's bookstall, and it was Fergins who arranged the first meeting between Gabriel and Whiskey Bill. Gabriel wanted to get back the manuscript of his poems, many of which were based on Dante, that he had impulsively buried with his wife. Bill oversaw the recovery, which required the presence of a medical and a religious observer in case there were any accusations of grave robbing. "I have to beg absolute secrecy to everyone," Gabriel said to Bill at the time, "as the matter ought really not to be talked about." Gabriel described his poems as bound in a rough gray calf cover, to distinguish them from the Bible that someone else put into Lizzie's grave.

"The body was badly decomposed, though we all agreed to keep Rossetti from seeing," recalled Bill, a glimmer in his eyes as he lost himself in the memory. "We started a fire near the grave to disinfect the area. The bound pages were in acceptable condition, considering where they had been for seven years, though a worm had eaten through the middle of them. I even recall one of the poems he wanted most to retrieve was about Dante's life in exile."

Whiskey Bill, somewhat surprising given his slick appearance, recited lines from the poem in question with naked feeling:

> *And rising moon and setting sun*
> *Beheld that Dante's work was done.*

"Rossetti's hands shook as I handed him the manuscript," Bill continued. "His health hasn't been the same since then, from what I understand, as though he had been cursed by the desecration of his wife's resting place, by her spirit or—"

"What is it?" Tennyson demanded, observing the speaker's disoriented expression.

"There was a woman waiting for him at the gates of the cemetery, after we were done with the exhumation. I was finishing arrangements with the sexton to close up the grave, but I could see her from a distance."

"Well? What of it?"

"I'm just recalling, Mr. Tennyson, that she cut a grand figure. Her brilliant hair caught the moonlight, and she held out her hand to Rossetti."

"Are you saying, Mr. Bill, that the spectre of Lizzie Siddal stood at the gates?" Holmes asked.

Whiskey Bill just stared back with a grin, then dried the sweat from his neck with a dirty handkerchief.

Tennyson expelled an *ugh* and seemed ready to get up and leave.

"Mr. Fergins led Mr. Tennyson to believe that you had found some intelligence about the anonymously published Dante booklet," said Holmes. "I'm afraid our time is too short for ghost stories."

"I believe I do have information that will be of use to you gentlemen. But there is the discussion of payment first."

Tennyson erupted, complaining that he already placed the money they agreed upon in the hollow cane as Fergins had directed him. "The bookseller didn't say about owing anything more!"

"I always say," Whiskey Bill replied, "that a bookseller is one-quarter philosopher, one-quarter philanthropist, and two-quarters rogue."

"How much more money are you after?"

"Not *that* sort of payment," said Bill with greedy eyes and a double-gap-toothed grin. "A poem. An original, unpublished poem in the hand of Poet Laureate Tennyson. About a topic of my choice, say . . ."

"A museum? Library?" Holmes tried to help and speed him along.

"A tavern."

Tennyson tried to protest that he needed complete seclusion to write.

"I suppose," the doctor-poet whispered, "Browning would thrive on such a challenge."

Tennyson looked around, blew out a sigh, and grabbed paper and pen the man had waiting for him. When the poet threw the paper back at the blackmailer, Bill read aloud with satisfaction. "'This tavern is their chief resort . . . Gives stouter ale and riper port.' Hear, hear!" he cried.

"It is splendid." Tennyson could not help but admire it himself. "I hope you profit by it. Now, the information?"

"Oh, poetry is a mere drug in the market these days, my friends; there is a glut of it and not enough customers. This I shall just keep for myself." Whiskey Bill nodded, accepting his end of the bargain. "There have been two pirated printings of *The Dante Murders* since its original publication. Supposedly, the author is a former private detective of some kind from America. Here is what is most interesting. One of those printings was ordered privately—I mean, not by one of the usual piratical printers who can find profit in a pebble stuck to a shoe. Highly unusual. Let me see, where did I put it . . . the location these private copies were sent . . ." Bill searched through bundles of papers and books. "They must have had some success selling their copies, I suppose, since I've located a printer who is making new plates for them for *another* pamphlet of the same sort."

Tennyson grabbed Bill's wrist. "A new booklet? What is it?"

"Even as we speak, yes. It's called *In Dante's Shadow, a True Account of the London Purgations by the Author of The Dante Murders*. Here are my notes"—he pulled out a scrap of paper—"both the second pirated printing of the original *Dante Murders* and this new pamphlet have been ordered to be delivered somewhere called the Phillip Sanatorium. I've heard something of it before, a sanctuary of some kind from the sins of the city, no alcohol at all, if you can imagine, but they say that opiates are shipped in by the cartful to placate the residents."

Holmes rose to his feet, feeling the room spinning around him. "The religious observer. Who was it?" he asked. Bill stared back at him, his face a picture of confusion. "The religious observer who came to Highgate to help in the exhumation of Lizzie Rossetti's grave," Holmes continued. "Do you remember the name of the man who was there with you?"

Their informant mulled over the question. "A preacher . . . I think it was Fallows or Fallow. Some name of that sort."

Over at Tudor House, the perpetual sleep that had descended over a young woman finally lifted. Sibbie's blue eyes opened on the darkened room where Holmes had spent so many hours at her side. At almost any other time over the last five and a half weeks, he would have been found there waiting for just such a miracle. But this time, his chair was empty.

She had to take some time to think where she was, what had happened, how she had come to be here in this strange room full of strange objects.

Sibbie rose slowly, gaining balance and strength by the second as her senses gradually returned. Her black hair had grown out considerably, and the back of her hair was matted from so much time in one position. The hair dye had begun to fade around the back of her head, revealing some strands of light brown and others of golden hue.

She moved in a wobbly manner across the room, like a mermaid trying to balance on fins. Very slowly she made her way down the stairs, stumbling a few times as she went, her eyes stung by the light bouncing off the snow and through the windows. She relied on her hands to feel her way. A door from the basement opened and two men appeared, Colt pistols at the ready in case anyone tried to interfere with their mission.

Soon, she was behind the house, in a boat on the Thames, on the first leg of her return.

By the time a carriage brought her to the gates of the Phillip Sanatorium hours later, all her senses had been restored. She climbed down. Her
stride became longer and more powerful as she walked through the gates,
fresh-fallen snow singing beneath her bare feet. As excited shouts spread,
white-robed men and women began to surround her, and Reverend Fallow rushed to her side.

Fallow slowly lowered himself on one knee and bowed his head, and
all the others followed suit in worshipful acknowledgment of their leader,
who had finally returned.

CANTICLE
THREE

DOCUMENT #6:

FROM THE SURVIVING MANUSCRIPT FRAGMENT

OF *IN DANTE'S SHADOW*, BY S. T. CAMP

Isobel Worthington was given the nickname Sibbie in childhood by an aunt whom she loved and with whom she shared a resemblance. From the time of her youth, Sibbie had been recognized as having a rare and soothing influence over the distressed and ill, and an otherworldly effect in inspiring people around her to confess their greatest fears and dreams; there were some who insisted she possessed not merely a bedside manner but near-magical powers of healing. She was visited by spiritualists and mesmerists who observed her, with some concluding she was a veritable prophetess. One supernaturalist tested her with magnetic devices that felt scratchy on her skin, to try to determine the source of her unusual powers.

Her family, more practical, intended her to enter service, and she was considered well suited to be engaged assisting philanthropic men and women who visited charity homes, hospitals, and the like in London. While briefly in service to a well-known philanthropist, she found her employer dead, having poisoned himself, leaving behind a letter professing that he loved Sibbie but could not bear his own disloyalty to his wife and children. (Sibbie had earlier witnessed her father dead from his own hand, too, though in his case without explanation.) In this way she came into the employment of Reverend Fallow, whose career up to the present already has been partially sketched in this booklet, and her power over her subjects was soon perceived by many others around her, including—no, *especially*, the troubled and haunted preacher. He has told the present author that he has known people who would throw themselves from a cliff to be by Miss Worthington's side, a long list that eventually included the reverend himself.

I have included the previous examination of Reverend Fallow's career in an earlier chapter primarily to illuminate the remarkable character of Sibbie Worthington.

While traveling with Reverend Fallow through the Continent on their mission to inspect sanatoria, she accompanied him to visit the mysterious oracle of Dante Alighieri's works, the erratic man known as the Dante Master. This authority on the Florentine bard was struck by how Sibbie shared the spirit of Dante's Beatrice, usually so misunderstood by so-called scholars. Beatrice is believed by many casual readers of the *Divine Comedy* as merely a passive object of Dante's love. In actuality, according to this Dante Master, she is the chief agent of all that transpires in the *Comedy*. It is Beatrice alone who perceives that Dante (and mankind) is caught in spiritual peril, and arranges an unprecedented intervention—she is the most powerful figure in the poem. More than Dante's poetic idol, Virgil; more than the keeper of Purgatory, Cato; or Sordello or Statius or their other guides through the afterlife; or even the once-fearsome Lucifer dwelling listlessly in the pits of Hell. Nor does she allow pity to cloud her judgment and her enactment of divine justice. She is the healer *and* the punisher.

Behold I am, truly I am Beatrice, she announces at the summit of the mountain of Purgatory, as a trembling, sobbing Dante looks on.

The Dante Master instructed the visiting pair, Sibbie and Fallow, in each canticle of the *Comedy*. But those lessons alone were not life altering. It was when the old demagogue gave them his rare copy of exiled Professore G. P. G. Rossetti's treatise on Dante that Sibbie felt overmastered.

"Few have attempted to uncover the true value of the *Divine Comedy*," said the Dante Master. "Fewer still have come so close as the professore."

"What is the truth?" asked Sibbie.

"That we bleed with Dante's words."

She felt a wave of change upon her. The professore's book, to the ordinary eye unreadable and tedious, was a prophetic text predicting the ascendancy of the figure of Beatrice over conventional, failed religions that had become antiquated and irrelevant. Professore Rossetti's pages demonstrated, in fifteen volumes of dizzyingly persuasive terms, that Dante's poem had been meant to initiate a secret sect dedicated to Beatrice and the *Comedy*'s power to save humankind.

"Madness, to some, this *mysterium magnum*," mused the Dante Master on this topic, his lips making a popping sound as though to mock and belittle the doubters. "To others: the truth as yet unsketched by any philosopher."

Sibbie had found meaning and purpose that no reading of the Bible, however passionate, no preacher or spiritualist or magical healer, had ever shown her.

"'Behold I am, truly I am Beatrice,'" Sibbie read aloud from *Purgatory*, as though taking an oath. At the prompting of their mysterious instructor in Italy, she read the words again. *Behold I am, truly I am Beatrice.*

Repeat the words to yourself each day, he told her, seven times a day.

While the visitors were touring the homes and haunts of Dante and related locations, they found themselves at one point caught in a crushing crowd in Rome. Fallow began to panic. He shook, he cried. He felt he was about to burst out of his skin. But Sibbie, turning her ability onto the man who was ostensibly her superior, put her hands on his shoulders, her fingers moving like giant spiders up his neck. Against all logic this calmed him, and suddenly he could breathe.

From that moment on, Fallow was beholden to her. He increasingly served Sibbie's wishes, rather than the other way around, even when to the outside world she still appeared to be laboring as an assistant. He pledged himself to her.

After Sibbie returned to England, she directed the preacher to assist her in finding those who would help her enact the vision and prophecy of Dante. Around this time, as their Phillip Sanatorium began to be organized, the preacher was called to assist in an exhumation of a body in order to retrieve a bundle of poems heavily influenced by Dante—and in doing so became acquainted with the troubled and brilliant Dante Gabriel Rossetti, son of the very scholar whose cult of Dante had mesmerized them. Sibbie, intent on including Mr. Rossetti in her mission, went to find the painter-poet.

Reader, it may be useful to describe further the woman so many, yourselves included, have worshipped or will worship for years to come. She is striking. Her excellent, piercing blue eyes burn through to the soul—examine one of the photographs of her reproduced here, notice those eyes possess a glow with a light when captured by a camera. People who were near her—couldn't help themselves—wished she would look at them, and then wished she might stop. Just as when she looked upon the sacrifice of Brother Morton, she stands strong, long limbed, her hair the color of sunlight. Or, I should correct myself—her hair was so until recently when, under necessity to conceal herself from police attempting to interfere with her mission, she temporarily dyed her hair the dull color of a walnut, and later cut short and as black as ink. But her physical appearance is a modest hint of the inner strength and force that comes out in even the briefest encounter with this woman.

Mr. Rossetti, some say, nearly collapsed upon seeing her at the gates of the Highgate Cemetery after the unearthing of his wife, feeling the stranger's power immediately as sensitive and artistic souls do; soon the brilliant man as well as a number of Sibbie's other new devotees were collected on the grounds of the sanatorium, some moving back and forth between there and London and others residing there, seeming to have vanished from their previous lives in the eyes of outsiders. All the devotees, it is fair to say, needed Dante Alighieri to set their lives on the divine course and, perhaps even more, they needed Sibbie.

I t had been a copper-skied evening in early October 1869. Gabriel could not stop his hands from shaking. The book pirate, Whiskey Bill, and the sexton of the cemetery had finally reached the coffin seven feet under the ground, and were disinterring it by the light of a large fire. Gabriel did not help. He could *not* help. Because of his trembling, but more so because of what he was doing. What vanity had it been, to think that the poems he had interred with his wife were worth disrupting her eternal peace—and his.

But he wanted those poems. He had a right to the product of his own genius, hadn't he?

Gabriel turned to look at the next grave, his father's. He had hazy recollections of the day the old man died. Deprived of his sight, writhing in pain, he had been speaking nonsense. "Where is my mother? She was right next to me a moment ago," the professore moaned at one point.

His mind seemed to grow clear for short periods of time.

"What a consolation it is to have all my children around me! And yet not to be able to see them." Then, to Gabriel: *"Ingegnoso Gabriel.* What mistakes I made. You are like a sheep running amok, full of genius but too lazy and disrespectful to be a Dante!"

Christina and their mother soothed Gabriel and promised him the *professore* did not know what he was saying. Soon, the old man cried out, *"Ah Dio, ajutami tu"*—Oh God, help me—and was gone.

A sheep running amok.

"Here's the *thing.*" The words seeped out of the toothy grin of Whiskey Bill. The redheaded book pirate was holding the manuscript of poems. "Ah, don't touch yet, Rossetti," he said to the eager Gabriel, "we must dry it by the fire and so on."

As the book pirate and a doctor began to treat the worm-eaten manuscript—the pages resurrected from death—with disinfectants, the religious observer—for one was required by their arrangements with the city—walked over to Gabriel, who was preparing himself.

"You're not going to look into the grave, Mr. Rossetti?" asked Reverend Fallow, noticing the intense anticipation of Gabriel's face.

The cool wind blew, and an eddy of sparks flew toward Gabriel and the preacher.

"Yes," Gabriel replied.

"Perhaps I wouldn't, Mr. Rossetti."

"I was assured she would be in fine condition." He hesitated, then asked, "Is she, Reverend? Is she?"

Whiskey Bill read aloud a poem about Dante Alighieri—maybe about Gabriel's father the *professore,* as well—which Gabriel had called "Dantis Tenebræ," from one of the pages he was drying.

> *This is that steep land*
> *Where he that holds his journey stands at gaze*
> *Tow'rd sunset, when the clouds like a new height*

Seem piled to climb. These things I understand:
For here, where day still soothes my lifted face,
On thy bowed head, my father, fell the night.

Fallow's mouth lifted into a pacifying smile. "Of course she is in excellent condition. Her hair continued to grow after death, it seems, and fills the coffin like a bed of roses. But do you not wish to remember her in life, rather than in death?"

"Please understand, Reverend, that I had no intention of disturbing her peace today, I merely . . . I tried so hard to remember my verses exactly as I wrote them, but I couldn't. Even though I wrote them, they were not mine, not anymore. You see, my last volume of verse was hated by some of the bloody critics who say I must choose to be either painter or poet, but these, *these* will set them all right again." Tears welled up in Gabriel's eyes. "I must see her."

He knew. He knew they were all lying about her being in such splendid, lifelike condition. The body down there was not Lizzie anymore. It was a ghoul, a monster who would never again let Gabriel rest.

Murderer.

Reverend Fallow gripped Gabriel's arm as tightly as he could.

"Let go of me! Let me see her!"

"Something else may have pulled you back here," Fallow said with a peculiar air. "Dante. That is what is contained in many of those poems, isn't it? Your visions of Dante Alighieri."

Gabriel thought for a moment that the man could be making fun of him, then, seeing he was entirely serious, nodded. "How do you know?"

"There's much we have uncovered about the power of Dante, which I understand is a birthright in your family. There is someone here to meet you."

Through the gates there walked a woman, her hair bright in the low light of the moonrise. She might have been an amalgam of all the women Gabriel had painted since the golden days of the Pre-Raphaelite

Brotherhood in his search for complete beauty and truth, or perhaps they had all been of her without him ever knowing. He could not decide if this woman before him was a copy or the original.

"Brother Gabriel," she said.

Gabriel turned away from the grave and felt his legs take him toward Sibbie.

Christina felt conflicted as their span of horses carried them onward over rolling hills. Part of her wanted to throw herself from the moving vehicle and plunge into the thickening snow. But she could not bring herself to flee, not now that she was united with her brother. She would not let him out of her sight again. To questions about where they were going, Gabriel gave no response; his lips quivered and eyes widened. He didn't remain completely silent. He spoke with fiery conviction about Dante as their way forward. "Father taught us," he said in a near chant, "for so many years he taught us that very truth, Christina, and we refused, *refused* to listen, but it returns to us."

She pleaded with him to let her bring him to safety where he could recover from his ordeal, and that anything else, everything else, could wait. "*This* cannot *wait*," he said, "for she simply won't allow it. Remember what Dante proclaims: 'This day will never dawn again.'"

One horse's leg became strained, and they had to stop twice for it to be wrapped. The drive went on for hours longer than it would have in better conditions, though she could not keep track of how long they rode along. Christina was tired of talking in circles with Gabriel, tired down to her bones. By the time they neared their destination, she had fallen asleep once again, and Gabriel picked her up, slipping off her boots, and lifted her from the vehicle. When she woke up, they were standing in a circle of people. Her head tipped backward, the first things she saw were several people's bare feet.

She insisted Gabriel let her stand on her own. As she found her balance, a regal woman with the alabaster skin of a classical statue approached them—she hardly recognized this figure as Sibbie, whom she had mostly seen supine and silent in Tudor House until this moment. The quintessential patient. An object, not a subject. Now she wore a white, almost translucent robe. Her hair, glossy black mixed with shades of lighter blond and brown—as if she were a multitude of women—was blowing around in the winter gusts. Fallow was speaking into Sibbie's ear.

Christina's eyes roved, but she tried to fix her expression to hide how her mind was swimming. The residents of Phillip Sanatorium, including Reverend Fallow, all stood in postures of reverence toward Sibbie. The worshipped woman, meanwhile, stroked Gabriel's hair. He bowed his head as if in a church.

"My dear boy," Sibbie said in a hungry whisper, "I've just been learning all that I've missed while I was insensible. What *they* tried to do to you. Are you well enough?"

Gabriel's eyes grew moist and he struggled to speak. Christina was astounded at the woman's effect on her brother—an effect that took an instant hold of him the way she had only seen happen before under two influences, Lizzie Siddal and opium.

"Sister Christina," the woman said, turning to her, the breath behind her words frosting into mist. "We have waited for you for a long time."

"I don't understand," replied Christina, her fatigue swept away by awe.

"You've been welcome here for a long time, my dear. You may not have known that, or perhaps you did without admitting it. Do not fret. I assure you, you are ready."

"Ready for what?"

"Please, my sister does not—" Gabriel tried to break in.

"Base child!" Sibbie turned back to Gabriel with thunder in her voice. "You could not stop yourself and your bottomless urges, and the consequences could have destroyed everything we have made. Oh, folly, when man is asked to serve the ways of God and reminds us he is merely a man!"

Christina thought back to Sibbie throwing herself into the drying shed to pull Holmes from the thick smoke. She was not trying to save Holmes at all—*she was trying to stop Holmes from saving Loring. To stop him from ruining the purgation.*

Gabriel fell to the snow, tears flowing as he begged the woman for forgiveness. Christina continued to try to hide the surge of emotions and fears that filled her, noticing the gathering included not only those wrapped in white robes but also those followers in green garments with swords in their belts.

One of the females robed in white stepped closer to Christina.

Christina gasped with fear and recognition. "Ethel!"

"Here I am called Sister Ethel," said the refugee from Saint Mary's, with a light giggle. With conviction she announced: "I found where I belong."

Christina shook her head, and could only manage to blurt out: "Why?"

"At Saint Mary's, they wanted us to conceal the past, however much we had done wrong and whatever wrongs were done to us. Brother Fallow came to teach us that we cannot run away from those vices, we must expel them, for ourselves and for all those around us."

Christina heard a song before she noticed Ethel and the others were singing. "*Te Deum laudamus.*" Their voices reached her. *We praise thee, O God.*

When she willed herself to find the strength to look back at Sibbie, the leader's hand was outstretched toward her. Christina bowed her head, raised her own hand, and felt the woman's fingers slide onto hers.

O God, the song went on, *in Thee have I trusted—let me never be confounded.*

As the ride went on, the train's speed decreased. Deep, drifting snow swirled out the window as darkness fell. Where there would have normally been glimpses of the spires and towers of London receding, there was a white blur. Holmes and Tennyson heard the conductors speculating whether the next train would be able to run at all. The train passed several depots along the way without stopping because of concerns it could stall in a drift.

Whiskey Bill's information inside his cage at the British Museum had led the two poets to an array of surprising conclusions. If they had pieced everything together correctly, then they had reason to believe Reverend Fallow was at the heart of the deaths—a realization that filled them with more questions than answers, at least not answers to be arrived at in the brief amount of time they had to contemplate them.

After leaving the museum, they had sent messages to be delivered to the police and their friends at Tudor House, and by now they hoped all of them might already be heading toward Walsden. It certainly worried the two travelers to hear that the snow might prevent more trains from going north, but they stayed hopeful that a resolution to all was immi- nent. They couldn't know, of course, that the Rossetti siblings had left well ahead of them with the same destination. If they had known it, if they had known about Sibbie's revival from her sleep, and what was revealed in its aftermath, they would have known to fear for their own safety and certainly for the Rossettis'. What they did know was this: Reverend Fal- low could be holding his next victim somewhere at the Phillip Sanato- rium, and as Holmes pointed out, he would not have been able to forgive himself if delaying even a minute longer than necessary resulted in an- other death.

They made their plans; they would search the grounds of the sanato- rium after they arrived, and if they found traces of a potential victim or a victim-in-waiting—as they guessed they might—then they would shep- herd the captive to safety until the police arrived.

Neither man wished to speak too much about all the things that could still go wrong. Tennyson, as he did in any circumstance when he was not fully comfortable, spoke about himself. He mused on and on about his poems on the Arthurian legends. "By King Arthur I always meant the soul," he explained, "and by the Round Table I meant the passions and capacities of a man. There is no grander subject in the world, don't you agree?"

When Tennyson asked if people agreed with him, he did not pause for the answer.

"Critics wish to make me out as celebrating war, Holmes. By Jove, anyone can see that all my verses about war represent a mood. But the critics are nothing and allow me nothing. For instance, take 'the deep moans round with many voices.' 'The deep' they say I stole from Byron, 'moans' from Horace, 'many voices' is Homer's, and so on . . ."

A sick man talking about himself, a woman talking about her baby, and an author talking about his book never knew when to stop.

Holmes tried to keep up his end of the conversation, knowing there was nothing they could do until they reached the destination that seemed to become impossibly farther away. But distractions of the present took hold. Holmes could not think of King Arthur's quests when he was thinking of Dante's journey on the mountain of Purgatory. The great figures were opposites in some ways. Arthur, said the legends, was consumed by personal tribulations in pursuit of saving the world, while Dante left behind all his personal attachments in order to serve the world, to save humanity from certain doom. As the doctor stared at the dim world framed by the train window, his mind turned to the scene of Dante falling asleep as he moved from the fourth to the fifth terrace of Purgatory— Dante experiences a vision of a beautiful woman, a siren of the sea, who transforms before his eyes into a horrid and foul-smelling witch grasping at him. Dante's dreams constitute a miniature narrative of their own in *Purgatory*, an account of the mystical experience of penitence.

The train chugged along with greater difficulty. Laborers would come and clear the tracks, the train would progress, then more tracks would be cleared. Finally, they reached the station in the quiet hamlet of Walsden. It was all but deserted. They found one coachman who agreed to take them, though he gave them a stern warning about the conditions. The warning was as much about how much the drive would cost them as it was about the conditions themselves. If only the driver knew his desperate riders would have paid a king's ransom.

The snow had piled up in banks. Underneath, the frost was hardening. Holmes thought he could hear the axle grinding beneath them. He was about to shout to the driver, but there was no time. One wheel of the carriage ran up a snowbank, and the entire vehicle separated from the horses and flipped over. Next came a blank space in Holmes's memory—he found himself shivering and sucking in air, his whole body in the snow, the carriage ten feet from him.

"Tennyson!" he called, and repeated it over and over. He found his companion also in the snow back by the carriage. The laureate's leg was trapped under the vehicle. "Help me! Help me with him!" Holmes cried.

The driver stood unscathed, but looked back in a stupor at the poet-doctor's request for assistance. "Did you say Tennyson? Is this the immortal bard of England?"

Tennyson's mouth appeared to unconsciously stir into a smile.

"Help me with him, man!" Holmes demanded again. "He's mortal still, and wounded!"

"The laureate Tennyson! The favorite of the queen's? What have I done?" the driver muttered. "What will they say of me?" Turning to the left, then right, he turned his back on them and ran.

Holmes called after the driver but it was no use. He was gone. Holmes could not lift the vehicle off the poet by himself.

"Nothing to worry about," Holmes said to Tennyson. "Nothing at all." Tennyson drifted out of consciousness. Holmes wanted to shout but knew his cries would be shredded to whimpers by the wind.

Constable Branagan, stuffing Tennyson's letter into his vest pocket, bolted through the halls of Scotland Yard until he found Inspector Thornton, acting superintendent in Dolly's absence, who was in the detectives' billiard room.

"Inspector, I need a posse of men to go north to Walsden," Branagan cried out.

Thornton turned to Branagan and raised one eyebrow at a sharp angle. He took careful aim with his stick and thumped a ball across the table. "I suppose you're aware that the entire department is in awful crisis, Constable."

Branagan let his gaze sneak back to the billiard table.

"This," Thornton said defensively, "helps me cogitate."

"Of course, sir," said Branagan. "But I've received a message about a crucial development in the Dante Massacres."

"From who?"

"There isn't time to explain, sir. It's complicated."

"I'm a little surprised you're not by Inspector Williamson's bedside," Thornton said coolly.

Branagan knew the right response was *Yes, sir*, and to retreat. Instead, he answered, "I'm doing what he would."

Thornton walked to the other side of the table and assessed his position in the game. "Indeed you are. As a matter of fact, Williamson became so engrossed with your bookman murders that he and the Home Office lost sight of the lurking peril of the Fenians, while the rest of us were left to whistle even for our out-of-pocket expenses. I'd expect the commissioner will see to it that your appointment in our division is short-lived, Constable Branagan. An Irishman like you, lending his hand to a Scotsman like Williamson, how will that look to the public where a foreign threat is concerned?"

"My blood is Irish. I am English. My blood is Irish *and* I am English."

"Spare me philosophies. Dolly could be dead by the morning, Constable; I would stick to worrying about that."

"Inspector Williamson will not die—however badly hurt, he will fight through to survive. How will it look, sir, if the newspapermen find out you lost track of McCord after he got his hands on phosphorus by your own secret arrangement with Ironhead Herman?"

Two detectives playing backgammon and a detective sergeant boxing a heavy bag all looked over. Thornton waved their attention away and carefully leaned his billiard stick on the wall.

"You have begun to learn from your time with Dolly."

"He's taught me a thing or two, I believe."

"Very well. I will give you two men and arms, but understand that it will be accompanied by my recommendation to the commissioner that you are transferred away from our department as of tomorrow morning due to a rebellious Irish temperament."

Branagan, with no time to lose by arguing, swallowed down the bitter bargain.

Browning's confusion began at Scotland Yard and soon turned into alarm. After attending to Holmes's requests related to Sibbie's care, then stopping over at his own house to order preparations for the worsening snow, Browning returned to Whitehall, walking the path to the Scotland Yard building. He found Christina's belongings at the police office but no sign of Christina. The place was in chaos. As he tried and failed to locate Inspector Williamson or Constable Branagan, another policeman informed him that there had been an explosion at Clerkenwell Prison when some Fenian agents attempted to break out their allies, and that Dolly had been injured and was being operated on even as they spoke by a team of surgeons. The policeman also said Gabriel Rossetti already had been released to Christina's care.

Had Christina been obliged to leave in such a hurry that she would abandon her things? Browning's confusion grew worse, because at Tudor House, Browning could not find the Rossettis or Holmes, and they were not the only ones absent. Most shocking of all, Sibbie was not in her room.

Pacing the house, he noticed a purple scarf on a hook he was certain belonged to Tennyson.

Had *Tennyson* been back here, or had he left his scarf weeks before and Browning was only noticing it now?

His mind tumbled through the questions. Through the rooms, up and down the floors of the house, onto the roof and back down, on the street and in the garden (*Eeeiu*, the peacocks screeched for him to get away), examining the books that had been most recently consulted on the big table, Browning came no closer to knowing where his companions or Sibbie had scattered in the last hours, and at the same time he was certain something momentous had come to pass, possibly in the twinkling of an eye. He admitted to himself that he was frightened. He noticed something else peculiar. The doors to the cellar were slightly ajar.

He followed the stairs down through labyrinthine halls filled with the surplus of Gabriel's monstrous collections of china, Japanese furniture, and rare musical instruments that had given him a glimmer of purpose after Lizzie died. Led by the light of a candle, Browning found another set of doors where the cellar seemed to end—behind these doors was another staircase leading farther down. *Beneath the cellar?*

He followed these stairs down into a dark, gloomy labyrinth of vaults, recalling William Rossetti's words at the outset of Browning's quest with Christina.

Because of its proximity to the river, the house was actually used for smuggling . . . first of political fugitives, later for supplies and even pirated and forbidden books.

The vaults themselves must have been there for hundreds of years, since the time of the Tudors. The strangest thing among all these relics of long-gone eras was a plate Browning found. It had scraps of meat and cheese on it—not yet rotted.

He heard the faint sound of the dragon door knocker from above.

Never had Browning been so relieved to welcome a messenger, who was waiting at the door and would have given up had Browning taken a few more seconds. Browning unsealed a letter written in Dr. Holmes's hand.

Reverend Fallow is Cato. Get to Phillip Sanatorium. Use care.

He dropped the paper as though struck in the gut.

He rushed over to the train station. Frustrations piled as thick as the snow north of London. The trains already departed from the city (including the one that had carried Holmes and Tennyson) were limping along their routes, and no more trains or hired carriages were going into the snowstorm. Workmen were trying to clear enough snow from the tracks, but after slowing down, the snowfall would start again, or the winds would pick up and move the snow to obstruct the tracks.

Hours passed in which all Browning could do was imagine dire consequences to come from the delays. Finally a conductor came around to announce the next train was being fitted, and soon enough the bell rang out for passengers and Browning boarded. As he walked through the cars, he faced a man he had been looking for hours earlier: Constable Tom Branagan.

"Well, I've begun to be frightened a little by all this bad luck."

"I'm sorry that's what you think of us, Mr. Browning," said Branagan.

He spotted a letter in front of Branagan. The constable could not tuck it into his pocket quickly enough to keep Browning from recognizing Tennyson's hand.

"Our friend Mr. Tennyson has been diverting information to Scotland Yard all along, Constable, as I first suspected at the scene of Gibson's death."

"Could you blame him, Mr. Browning?" Branagan asked. "If we were not at Phillip Sanatorium as quickly as we were when Mr. Loring died, would we have been able to transport Mr. Rossetti to receive medical help in his dangerous opium haze as swiftly as we did? The arrangement between Inspector Williamson and Mr. Tennyson has made sure you were safe. *All* of you. Now we can find Orin Fallow and the answers we've sought."

"Tennyson betrayed our trust. That cannot be justified by any outcome. As for Inspector Williamson, I am sorry for what I heard. I cannot agree with all he's done, but I admit his clasp may be equal to his grasp. How is he faring?"

Branagan gazed down at the floor. "We're waiting. He has the finest doctors around him."

Browning hesitated for a moment before sitting across from the constable.

"I'm guessing," Branagan said, as the train began crawling, "we share the same destination again. The sanatorium. *If* they can clear the tracks enough for us to reach the station. To be perfectly honest, Mr. Browning, we ought to have examined the place closely long ago."

"Why?" asked Browning.

"Months before Reuben Loring died there, Inspector Williamson had received reports of unregulated shipments of opium making their way in that direction."

"Is that something that would normally have been investigated?"

"No, but perhaps it should be. The Home Office debates how much of our time should be taken in tracking opium sold without supervision of the doctors and druggists—opium that is usually in purer forms and more potent. The fact is, asylums and sanatoriums often require larger supplies than are typically available at one time. Scotland Yard usually looks the other way because it's considered useful that certain populations are artificially . . . *dulled*. Phillip Sanatorium was one of those places that seemed harmless to ignore. What is it? What's wrong?"

Browning had fallen into a reverie of thought, his face lighting up as it did in the throes of composing poetry. "Of course . . . ," he rasped.

"There's no reason to hide anything from each other now, Mr. Browning."

"Philip! In Canto Seven of *Purgatory*, Dante enters the region of the late repentant and encounters the shade of Philip III. He's a part of Ante-Purgatory, where shades prepare themselves for the journey up the terraces of the mountain."

"Yes?" Branagan replied, reaching into his bag for Longfellow's translation as Browning continued.

"Follow my thinking, Constable. Philip was not a ruler Dante Alighieri particularly admired; he believed Philip's leadership in war brought infamy to France and that Philip's son brought disgrace. But he places him in Purgatory instead of Hell to redeem him. Reverend Fallow's sanctuary is called Phillip Sanatorium—I suppose when we heard it, we would have assumed the 'Phillip' in the sanatorium's title was named for Jesus's disciple, if we gave the name of the place much thought at all. Not so: it was a reference to Dante all along. And just like Philip III, the people of England, in Fallow's mind, have fallen into disgrace, and Fallow in his demented way offers an entrance to Purgatory to redeem them. There were things the man said that rush back into my head. He called London a 'tossing-and-turning metropolis.'"

"Yes?"

"Why didn't I hear it? Canto Six, *Purgatory*, Dante compares Italy to a 'sick woman who finds no rest upon her downy feather-bed, but by her tossing and turning chases off her pain.'"

Branagan scribbled down Browning's conclusions into a notebook, then turned back to *Purgatory* and copied out notes from it.

The constable then leaned closer. "How do *you* think Mr. Rossetti came to be caught up in this?"

Browning thought about finding Gabriel on the grounds of the sanatorium, and their fear—mistaken, he now realized—that they had been the ones to lead him there. The ten words the messenger had handed him from Holmes remade Browning's understanding of the place and of what may have been happening there. He thought about the turbaned stranger whom Holmes and Tennyson had seen at the church in London before Browning observed him at Phillip Sanatorium. The man's presence conveyed a deep sense of trouble, and he was following someone. But he was not following *them* at all—he was after Fallow, both at the church and at the sanatorium.

"I don't know exactly how Gabriel came to be there," Browning finally answered. "But I suppose you know more about our inquiries than you and Inspector Williamson ever let on. You've been watching us. First through your own spies entering Tudor House, then Tennyson, now the police vessel on the Thames."

"You've confused inferences for facts, Mr. Browning," Branagan replied, realizing he sounded like Dolly. "Inspector Williamson had you and Miss Rossetti shadowed when we were searching for Mr. Rossetti's whereabouts, yes, but no longer. As Inspector Williamson told Mr. Tennyson, we've never sent any boats to Tudor House."

Browning studied him with headstrong skepticism, but found no signs of deception. The train continued to struggle forward for a short time, then halt, nauseating the men. The poet stared at the expanse of white outside the window.

"If that wasn't your boat hounding us after all . . . Green is the color of hope, and appears throughout *Purgatory*. Green . . ." Glimpses of green had been right in front of their eyes: the handkerchief Reverend Fallow had in his pocket; the streamer flapping on the boat that had been lurking behind Tudor House, below Sibbie's room; the garments of some residents of the sanatorium, like the wings and garments of the blond-headed, sword-carrying angels who enforced the rules of Purgatory. Browning searched his memories for the first time they saw the vessel on the Thames. It was after they brought Sibbie to Tudor House. Then came the thumping "spirit noises" when the medium was there. The plate of food in the vaults. "The vessel wasn't there to watch us at all," Browning continued his realization. "They were watching *her*, waiting for *her*. They came in through the underground vaults under Tudor House—the ones that were ages ago used for smuggling—keeping watch on her progress, waiting until Holmes found a way to revive her, so they could take her back. When Fallow visited, he got lost in the house and I had to show him the way out."

He thought about Fallow's face that day at Tudor House, could almost see it before him on the train. The impassioned, calculating eyes locking onto him.

Browning continued: "But Fallow wasn't really lost trying to find a way out—no. He was studying the house for a way *in*, unlatching doors, all for her."

"You're talking about the girl, Fallow's assistant?" Branagan asked, trying to keep up with the rapid flow of conclusions.

"Sibbie Worthington! We thought Fallow was harboring improper affections for her, but if his minions were lurking there, waiting for her, protecting her, it might be the clue to an entirely different story. Constable, what if she wasn't serving the preacher at all, and we were blind to the truth—he was serving her. Whatever has happened there, what if she is the true center of it?"

XXIII

Simon Camp would be roused at odd hours, pulled around by the collar to see some new sight or another he was to chronicle, or to interview someone, or to study a book or documents. The ingenious plans Camp had concocted for escape had so far all remained untested for one particularly inconvenient reason—that class of green-robed fanatics armed with very long, very sharp swords in their belts. He noticed that these guards, oddly enough, all had blond hair. There were usually one and sometimes two armed fiends accompanying him, or guarding a door to his chambers, where he wrote and slept. His activities were mandated and few: mostly, studying Dante or composing his chronicle of the "divine achievements" of his captors, the pages of which were gradually transported to a printer in London. (Camp did not know which, and so hesitated to try to embed any messages asking for help.)

"Do not dwell over the punishments," Fallow advised him of his writing, "they only last until the final judgment."

Camp searched his mind, recalling a verse from *Purgatory* he had just read, in which Dante Alighieri exhorts his poem's readers: *Do not fix your thoughts on the punishments, think of what comes later; at worst it will not reach beyond the great judgment.*

Fallow had transported his entire being, his identity, even his language, into Dante's vision.

There was something comforting in believing that even our faults, especially faults, could be converted into a higher plan. Camp could understand that as well as any man. He considered this only for a flash, cursing his own physical and mental exhaustion.

The latest place Camp was ushered was in a dark and narrow woodshed on the settlement, where one man and one woman, arms and legs tied, had been placed flat on their stomachs. They moaned and cried for mercy; the man pleaded for the Virgin Mary. Camp was less interested in the grotesque suffering of these poor people than in its proximity to the maniacs' central operations.

That piqued his curiosity.

The earlier deaths were meant to be discovered and witnessed. The unseasonable weather at the moment made travel toward London trying. But the masterminds could have waited, so Camp surmised they must have been in a rush to complete their so-called "missions." They were being hunted from all sides and knew it—a distraction Camp could use to his advantage if luck provided him even the slightest opportunity for escape.

Back at the standing desk, Camp was composing his latest enforced chapter to the new sensation pamphlet. He wrote about the despair he had just witnessed of the bound and tied pair—styled after the terrace in Dante's *Purgatory* cleansing humanity's sins of the Avaricious and the Prodigal. As he worked on the chapter, he perked up to hear the agitated voice of the Great Mad Preacher. Since the return of the woman called Sibbie, the minister's demeanor had cracked and curdled. He struggled to maintain the semblance of authority. Camp had not yet spoken to Sibbie— instead he had heard about her from Fallow and the other interview subjects he was given, and had observed her from afar.

That was about to change.

Sibbie swept into the chamber and walked right up to Camp. "This," she said with undisguised contempt, "is the one you're talking about?"

"The work he does will be vital, and he has just the right experience for it," Fallow said, trying to keep pace with her while maintaining a re-spectful distance. "Sibbie, he is the author of that very booklet of Dante phenomena that helped us stir the imaginations of so many, that brought them to Dante in the first place."

Sibbie grabbed the pages on top of Camp's blotter and examined them with a tightly set jaw.

Fallow gave a conspiratorial glance of support to Camp, as though they were allies—which perhaps for this very brief moment they were, more than Camp realized. "Sibbie, we have already begun to put this chronicle in type. When our full story emerges, so will the next epoch for what we are to achieve."

She began to respond, when they were interrupted by an unannounced visitor. Once again it was the imposing Ironhead Herman.

"Well! She is finally back," the swarthy visitor said without pausing for any greetings or trying to quiet his voice. "Just as I heard. Which means my time to collect has come."

"You heard? How?" Fallow inserted himself between Herman and Sibbie. "She's only just returned, Brother Herman. We need some more time to put our affairs and our mission in order, to recruit more men and women and replenish our funds."

"I made certain you were amply supplied with what you needed for your so-called sanatorium, and my patience, and that of the superiors I answer to, is a good deal shorter than you seem to believe."

Camp interrupted. "Say, fellow," he said, turning to Herman, "per-haps you would allow me to ask some questions for the chronicle I'm writing?"

"Enough of that," Fallow snapped at Camp. Then, back to the other man: "A compromise, then, Brother Herman. Circumstances and police interest have strained our resources. A partial amount, perhaps."

"You have one more week," Herman replied.

"We do not need a week," said Sibbie. "Why not give us until sunset?"

Herman fixed his eyes to her. "Very well."

"If you require some assurance from us now, apparently I have something of value right here," Sibbie said.

"Please, Sibbie," Fallow whispered, trying to steer her away before she provoked Herman.

She grabbed a handful of pages from Camp's table and pushed them hard into Herman's chest. "Here. These gentlemen around me apparently believe in the efficacy of a profitable sensation. Payment."

"Say!" Camp cried out, objecting to the treatment of his literary property.

"Sibbie, I beg you!" Fallow exclaimed.

Herman took the pages and tossed them into the air back at Sibbie. He stormed out without another word. Camp, against all logic, felt rather offended at the exchange, both the woman so roughly offering his work and the rogue throwing it around carelessly. Camp was almost relieved when Fallow, groping for his old dominance, ordered him to get down on the ground to collect the papers.

As Camp gathered the sheets of paper, the preacher was trying to delicately reason with the woman who gave him his orders. Camp slowed his chore in order to take in their conversation.

"Ironhead Herman's too dangerous to cross. We must find a way to pay our debt immediately. He'll destroy us."

"Let him try. The debts we tend to are of another kind. He cannot stop what we are doing here. *Nobody* can."

Something in her voice chilled Camp's blood and sent his heart racing. As he crawled around collecting the last of the pages, he saw what he looked for. There were two sword-wielding guards, but neither blocked the door left open by Herman's exit; plus, springing up from his position on his hands and knees could sufficiently surprise them.

At the right moment Camp bolted through the exit. Fallow shouted to the guards to follow, but both of the green-clad men stopped cold when Sibbie ordered that they wait.

"Brothers, I do not want that man Simon Camp to blemish our home again," she said. "He breaks the divine order." She then released them to the chase with the slightest nod of her head.

"We *need* him," Fallow said. "We need Camp."

She shook her head and, with a meaningful grin, replied, "Our needs have changed. Besides, a far more sublime writer is among us."

When she returned to consciousness, Christina suspected almost at once that she had been dosed with opium—not the slight unpleasant aftertaste of it that she, like everyone, had experienced from medicine but a rush of the drug coursing and battling through her body. She now found herself in a poorly lit, cold chamber but felt a source of heat coming from somewhere. Earlier, after being carried by Gabriel onto the grounds of the sanatorium, she had been left dazed and physically sickened by Sibbie's absolute control over the people gathered there—people Christina now realized were Sibbie's followers, Gabriel included, in a settlement of true believers. Reverend Fallow and all the others had been doing the bidding of this mesmerizing woman all along. Christina had been shivering, her teeth chattering as the assembly stood out barefoot in the snow. Fallow began to gently escort Christina out of the cold. They were accompanied by two golden-haired guards in green robes with swords at their sides.

It was just how Dante described the angels guarding the divisions of Purgatory. *I clearly discerned their blond heads, but their faces dazzled my eyes, a faculty conquered by excess.*

As Fallow had led her away, she had been writhing and struggling, reaching out for Gabriel. "Darling, darling, you will be safe here," her brother called out. Fallow brought her into a building where a hot drink awaited her—it tasted bitter but she could not resist the warmth that wrapped itself around her body. Then, the heavy odor struck her. It was familiar. Familiar from the haze that often surrounded Gabriel and

Lizzie, from women and girls she had helped pull from crammed rooms off of narrow alleyways to bring into Saint Mary's. Opium. She began spitting out what she still could. Her vision thickened, and her mind fell into a dreamy, almost peaceful state of blankness.

She came to in the cold chamber with her heart racing. At first she heard voices. A chorus of voices, ten, twenty that became one—her father. The professore.

"You failed, my bantling. You grew to try to control everything around you, but you never could control your dreams. Nor could you stop the coming of Dante against our enemies."

She thought back to the day after the professore died, the night her mother fed all the copies she could find of the professore's Dante treatise into the fire like fresh wood on a long winter night. Christina could see her mother's face. In it mingled horror and relief. Christina, then twenty-three, stood behind her mother and watched the flames curl up around the covers, lick at the pages, ingest the words inside—the words that had simultaneously kept the professore alive and devoured him from the inside.

She'd noticed the stealthy movements of a figure in the next room. It was Gabriel, smuggling out as many copies of their father's book as he could.

She shook away the professore's voice. She felt her eyes closing but struggled hard to keep them open. The worst of her predicament was that she had been separated from Gabriel after swearing to herself she would not let him out of her sight again.

She tried to recite some of her verses to herself to clear her mind.

I planted a hand
And there came up a palm,
I planted a heart
And there came up balm.
I planted a wish,

But there sprang a thorn,
While heaven frowned with thunder
And earth sighed forlorn.

She groped the brick walls and felt her way through a long corridor, then another, toward the warmth. She waited until the poisons in her body lost just a little more of their power. Finally she reached a chamber where there was ample light and heat. She had to blink several times, sure that what she saw before her eyes must have been another illusion of the opium.

Spread across the table was a sumptuous, almost biblical banquet: fruits, nuts, honey, milk, wine. Nothing disappeared when she blinked.

"Darling sister."

She jumped up, startled.

The words came out as a kind of chant.

As she turned around, her eyes landed upon Gabriel's face. Like the food, this was no opium dream. "Oh, my dear Gabriel! Thank heavens!" Because she was so filled with joy and relief at the sight of him—and perhaps because the opium still clouded her vision—it took another moment to realize he was on the other side of two rows of iron bars.

"Gabriel, what is this place? What's happening here?"

The chamber was separated by the bars into two extreme divisions. Her side had light and a small furnace. Gabriel's compartment was dark and cold, except for the heat that escaped from the furnace on her side of the bars. Gabriel sat on the ground in a white robe. His eyes returned again and again to the feast. She noticed what she hadn't observed in the carriage ride, when she had still bathed in the glow of being reunited with her brother: he didn't look well, his usually florid face pale and drawn. The skin around his eyes was much darker than the rest of his face. She recalled something Dolly had told her at the police station. *He's refusing to eat, all the excitement of talking of his release is not good for him, I'd say.*

Christina grabbed a plate of food and tried to push bits through to him. The rows of bars were arranged in such a way that nothing from one side could reach the other.

Gabriel shook his head at her attempts. "This food shall not be for me."

"What did you say?" Christina asked, horrified, barely able to push her voice past a whisper.

"This food," he repeated, "shall not be for me."

It was a line from *Purgatory*—a voice Dante hears on the terrace of the Gluttonous. The penultimate level of Mount Purgatory, where the thirsty and famished shades suffer as they observe delicious food just out of reach.

It was happening again.

Purgatory reborn in 1870.

This time, Gabriel was the so-called shade, the repenting soul. Gabriel would be the one to die.

Her mind was spinning. "You stopped eating days ago. You knew this was coming."

Gabriel turned away.

She could not let him bury himself in silence, to yield to physical weakness and hopelessness—she needed him fighting, and she needed to know more in order to help him. Her body trembling with frustration, Christina had an idea. As the words of Dante's canto flooded her thoughts, she knew all at once how to provoke him to say more. She recited the words spoken by Dante when coming upon a shade in the region of the Gluttonous:

"'O Soul, who seems to desire to talk with me, speak so that I may hear, with your words content you and me.'"

He slowly turned back to her.

"You stopped eating days ago," she repeated.

Gabriel hummed his agreement under his breath. "Of course."

Christina's mind was suddenly sharper, and she thought about where she was when she first made her vow to find Gabriel. Saint Mary's, the woman's penitentiary in Highgate. *Penitentiary*. It was not enough for the women who came there to stop participating in their world of the night, it was not enough to reform themselves. It was a penitentiary—they had to be *penitent*, to demonstrate and display it in order to earn their change.

Christina next thought about Lillian Brenner, the singer impaled with her eyes sewn shut, overheard talking about wine by witnesses who thought her words indicated she was a drunkard. In the second terrace of Purgatory, the shades being cleansed of Envy hear the voice of the Virgin Mary imploring Jesus Christ to turn water into wine at a wedding that had none. Mary's action was the opposite of envy because it ensured happiness in other people. *Brenner's words about wine were part of the design, the experience.* Gibson, running to his death, called out to Christina and Browning, *I hope you do not think me rude.* It was not merely a morbid example of the art patron's usual obtuse eccentricity. When Dante encounters the Slothful on the fourth terrace, now driven to extreme zeal in their movements, they cry out: "We cannot linger, and your pardon I pray, if you take our penance for discourtesy." *Gibson, Brenner, Gabriel, surely Morton and Loring, too, performed their own parts in their deaths.*

"Those were not murders. Morton, Brenner, Gibson, Loring. They knew . . . they all knew what was happening to them. You knew. This is a suicide club."

"Those who know justice are blessed."

"You prepared for this; you stopped eating in order to stage this purgation of the Gluttonous. Why?"

Gabriel pushed himself to his feet. "Sibbie found that each of us possessed a sin that had to be purged more than any other, just as the shades who travel through Dante's Purgatory—just as Dante himself, who knows he is most beset by pride. Me? I always took more than I needed in life—food, wine, women, opium—I loved, yes. I loved excessively. We all saw where it led. It had to come to an end. My child taken away from us, then Lizzie herself gone. Even then, I could not stop, could I? I was greedy still, this time for my art."

"Your art?"

"I had Lizzie's grave torn up to get my precious pages back. A moment of gluttony like no other. Ever since, I was on the path to this. For the first time in history, we have believed in our modern world that we can transgress without consequence and without punishment, as long as not many people see—here, on these sacred grounds, we change that. Sibbie led us to that. To serve as a witness is the first step."

"What do you mean 'a witness'?"

"You're witnessing this next step toward Paradise, this purgation, Christina, just as I witnessed past ones."

"That's why you were at those places? At the deaths of Morton and Brenner. You were there to be a witness, as was Loring—then you were at Loring's. Sibbie, she was there, too, wasn't she?"

Sibbie had been at Loring's death, of course. Before that, there were the unidentified women at Morton's and Brenner's deaths, a blonde and a brunette they had never located: both were Sibbie as she had begun to alter her appearance to avoid any outside interference.

Gabriel's notation on his sketch of the terrace of gluttony, with the faceless shade suffering. *CR—need your help*. He had needed her as witness to this, as planned out by Sibbie. The suffering shade in the drawing was *him*.

"You don't realize all that has happened," Christina said. "She and Fallow have been dosing you with drugs to control all of you."

Gabriel's eyes were glassy. A moment later, he wobbled, then fell back to the ground.

"Gabriel!" Receiving no response, she tried: "Dante!"

His eyes were shut tightly.

Glancing around for some way out, the comforts of her compartment increasingly appeared as a mirage of safety. There was food, light, heat, but no windows, no doors. Running back through the winding corridor she came in, she slammed her body against a locked door made of iron, weakening herself even more. Through the keyhole she cried out.

XXIV

DOCUMENT #7:

FROM THE SURVIVING MANUSCRIPT FRAGMENT

OF *IN DANTE'S SHADOW*, BY S. T. CAMP

The Honorable Mr. Jasper Morton, member of Parliament, had been thunderstruck some months ago to learn, through family documents hidden long before, that he was born before his parents were wed, and that they had traveled out of the country in order to conceal the fact. Here he was: a man who had publicly argued for many decades that he possessed a birthright to the Bristol seat because his father had held it; who had beaten back attempts to add another seat to the House of Commons for Bristol using the same logic, in order to maintain his monopoly on constituents' gratitude and favor. If his father had been sufficient to protect Bristol's interests, he was sufficient. Here he was: a man who stoked the fiercest reactions against the Irish Fenians and with fanfare pushed for expansion of military power into other lands, and he himself was, in a sense, born a foreigner. Now even though Morton continued to stand for election and win his seat, he was lost; everything he had always prided himself on felt like it became mere . . . pride.

His wife badgered him to tell her why he suddenly had such a short temper and prolonged bouts of melancholy. He tried to explain, told her about what he'd discovered in the blasted family papers, but he was an orator, not a speaker; he never managed to express to her what it all really felt like to him.

What Morton felt was immense shame and dishonor. These feelings consumed him, and nothing he did rid himself of them. He began to partake in a clandestine pastime he had only ever heard about, one that took place in the deepest recesses of London midnights, in fireless rooms reached through dark corridors, where in exchange for generous payment, female strangers would whip and beat him with a paddle as he cried. In these perverse, awful, wondrous sessions, the shame would grow and be exorcised at the same time.

Of course, as a politician Morton feared exposure of his peculiar habit, and wore a raggedy black wig and false nose and mustache when he went to the flagellation den. When his wife found the wig and questioned him about it, he merely muttered that he was an "easy target," by which he meant if anyone recognized him, he could end up in the gossip columns, but of course he could not explain to her where he was going, and the exchange left her more confused than before. Mrs. Morton, presuming a constituent must have been harassing or even threatening her husband in order for him to hide in this way, even reported her suspicions to the police.

In the meantime, Sibbie had urged Reverend Fallow to recruit followers for their settlement. They had initiated their mission by printing copies of *The Dante Murders*, humbly authored by the present writer, in order to demonstrate the vitality and power of Dante. (These were pirated copies, it must be noted, losing the present writer his rightful income, *but* I hasten to add, monetary gain must not be considered in relation to a glorious and obligatory spiritual calling.) They also searched out Londoners who already recognized their own sins that had to be purged, even if these citizens did not know how to do so in a true or fulfilling way. Remember the secret den Morton frequented, for example. Sibbie heard of this place where the frequenters actually *longed* for punishment, and began to watch the mixed-up souls who went in and out.

Sibbie called out to Morton as he was about to enter his familiar rendezvous. Sibbie did not crack a paddle onto him like the woman whom he'd come to see, but took hold of him in a different and more satisfying way; she spoke of Dante's revelations—of how the time had come to extract sins from our souls and the collective soul of London. She described how punishment against ourselves was natural, not shameful, even necessary in an age of material comforts, and that the end result would be freedom and—as Virgil put it in stating Dante's quest in *Purgatory*—liberty. Morton was not in control of his own actions or his body, for he belonged to God. For once, Morton felt he was speaking with someone who understood the peace that eluded him, and his entire being was liberated under Sibbie's influence.

Morton began spending time at the Phillip Sanatorium—first occasionally, then frequently, until it seemed he vanished entirely and search parties started looking for him in Bristol. Morton and the other residents of the sanatorium who joined the group did not drink alcohol or use tobacco, though they were given opiates to drink to begin to forget and reject their past mistakes. Fallow had found that the greater the availability of this smuggled opium, the greater the obedience that was inspired.

Fallow would gather their growing number of followers in the large building that had been the machine shop when the property was a mill—now turned into a chapel—preaching of Dante's revolutionary ideas of humanity's purgatorial destiny.

As the settlement's numbers increased, so did its requirements for opium. They had found a supplier in the figure of a man who had been called Hormazd in his own faraway country, but known around London as Ironhead Herman. Through Herman the organizers found Lillian Brenner, an opera prima donna who had come to rely on Herman's steady supply of opium to block out her many anxieties about her future. Fallow had met Herman in the city to make a payment, and Miss Brenner was there in tears, both about needing opium and also about her rival whom she loathed, who was prettier and better than her and who made Brenner positively hate herself.

Fallow, pulling her aside, convinced her to visit the sanatorium, both as an escape from the city and to hear more about a brotherhood and sisterhood that helped clear away all the vices that tormented them, all while granting them the higher purpose of freeing humanity from its burdens. At the same time, Fallow mined his transient congregations of former and present soldiers, and found more members this way, including Reuben Loring, who every night suffered from nightmares of the murder he'd committed years before in a fit of rage against a soldier who had spoken offensively of the natives where they were stationed; from the groups of reformed prostitutes Fallow was invited to address around the city, he found half a dozen warmhearted but sad women.

Among the inhabitants and visitors, not so different from the impressive denizens of Dante's *Purgatory*, were accomplished and highly esteemed engineers, writers, intellectuals, doctors. In Dante's vision of Purgatory, the punishments are not merely carried out, they are memorialized in many artistic forms of images and sounds. So it was at the Phillip Sanatorium where their own artistic genius, Dante Gabriel Rossetti, was sent to be witness and recorder of their purgations—just as Dante Alighieri before him was sent by

Beatrice up the mountain with a similar purpose: to save himself and the world.

Sibbie would hold sessions, sometimes for hours at a time, with her followers, that became a sort of confession. Followers would tell her everything—their stories and sins, the stories and sins of others—without having to be asked. From Gabriel Rossetti's stories, Sibbie learned of A. R. Gibson, who was plagued by inheriting his fortune without ever finding it in himself to exert himself to make his own name. He had no interest in business matters or in the women who harangued him to support children they claimed were his. Gibson would wander art galleries and stare at paintings and scenes of great battles and moments in history, wondering why he could not find his own such moments to live out. Sibbie appeared at one of these galleries in the dead of night, seeming as though she had just stepped out of a painting, or off of a sculpture's pedestal. He met her glittering eyes, which saw right through him.

Gibson would become one of them and, Fallow made sure, would help replenish their precariously thin finances, as had money given by Morton and other followers.

Some who flocked to the Phillip Sanatorium were already devotees of Dante—Rossetti, of course, and Gibson, whom Rossetti had influenced to study Dante through his art and by loaning him Professore Rossetti's visionary treatise—while others knew little about Dante before entering the sanatorium, or had read bits and pieces of the famous Longfellow translation. Fallow taught the words of Dante; Sibbie made all of it come alive.

Some of the members who gathered around Fallow and Sibbie had previously attempted spiritualism, occultism, Millerism, freemasonry, and secret orders of various kinds. But this place, this community erected on the property of the former textile mill, was different. It did not merely spread fear of the world ending, like the

Millerites, it taught that sacrifices—their own sacrifices—would purge a declining world of the sins that were killing them all.

Sibbie anointed a brother or sister of the movement, one by one, to embody a purgatorial terrace to demonstrate to England—and, ultimately, to the larger world—that the time to enter upon a course to Paradise had come. Brother Morton was fitted with the burden of stone that embodied pride; Sister Brenner's visions of envy were sewn into darkness. Witnesses from the movement were sent to each purgation, just as Dante Alighieri on his pilgrimage must pass through each and every terrace. Brother Rossetti and Brother Loring, as well as Sibbie, were among those who watched the remarkable purgations of Brother Morton and Sister Brenner.

Loring was preparing to embody his own chief sin—wrath—when he glimpsed visitors to Phillip Sanatorium he worried would try to stop him. Fallow had already warned him there were inter-lopers searching for him in London. Loring rushed away to enact his punishment earlier than he'd expected, locking himself into the drying shed, where noxious smoke would be released. Loring chanted—*Agnus Dei*—as a demonstration of the peacefulness that finally was overtaking him. Gabriel was witness, once again, and continued the chant as Brother Loring's burdens were released. The mechanism to release the gas had been prepared by two of the residents who were engineers, who also collaborated with a resi-dent shoemaker to invent the boots that Brother Gibson eagerly donned—the boots that would not allow him to stop and give way to his besetting sloth ever again.

Once the seven terraces of Purgatory—Pride, Envy, Wrath, Sloth, Avarice-Prodigality, Gluttony, Lust—are each brought from the page to the life of England, the movement will have transformed humanity. Indeed, with each remarkable death, with the lines of people snaking around the deadhouse in London, with every breathless newspaper column coming closer to understanding, whispers succeeded in recruiting more and more members, until the group's numbers swelled over fifty.

[The next few lines were blotted over with ink and rendered illegible.] Ironhead Herman has just left this room where I am at work writing this. I believe an occasion arises for my escape through an open door, if this paper should fall into your possession before these maniacs [illegible], send the police to find me—I am a close and personal friend of the venerable and august Allan Pinkerton in Chicago and Insp. Adolphus Dolly Williamson in London!—send him for God's sake send anyone for me before it's too late

B ooks. That was the last thing Holmes expected to find as cargo in the overturned carriage while he looked for any tools that could help him free Tennyson. The shipment inside the carriage contained pirated editions of novels, essays, and histories, mostly by British authors but a few American—including Holmes's most popular work, *The Autocrat of the Breakfast Table*, he was rather tickled to find, though not so tickled that his middle name was misspelled by the piratical printers as Wenndell. Booksellers in the villages were less likely to have their inventory inspected by customs officials than those in London, and the scoundrel of a coach driver obviously conspired in their delivery and distribution for extra income.

Holmes stacked a sufficient number of the books beneath the body of the carriage to raise it inch by inch. After several attempts, he was able to slide Tennyson's leg out from underneath. First, Holmes felt like crying and laughing in relief that he had managed to release Tennyson by using, of all things, the fruit of shadowy book peddlers' schemes. They would not be trapped in the snowbank, they would not fall to hypothermia in the middle of a deserted village lane. "Thank goodness Browning made *The*

Ring and the Book as long as he did!" he called out about the thick counterfeit volume that had lifted the vehicle just high enough.

Relief quickly fled. Surveying his surroundings, the snowfall, the blackening sky, Holmes knew in an instant there was no chance any longer for them to reach the sanatorium. They would not be able to get to many places on foot from here even if Tennyson hadn't been injured.

The first thing Tennyson did when he regained his senses was to insist he could walk the two miles in the snow to the sanatorium, in fact he could walk five if need be. Then, when he could barely make it just a few steps, the laureate urged Holmes to go without him to the sanatorium, but of course Holmes would not leave him. They had passed a small inn in a valley on their drive. With Tennyson's arm awkwardly draped over the shorter Holmes's shoulders, they trudged through the snow.

When they reached the isolated inn, marked outside with a large painting of a gold lion, they were completely exhausted from the journey.

"Who would believe I would welcome another lodger, in this storm," the surly German-accented innkeeper said. Holmes, stuck on *welcome* being a very strong word compared to the innkeeper's actual demeanor, did not think much of the wording of a different part of his statement—*another* lodger—until later on.

Once in their rooms, Holmes improvised a bandage for Tennyson's leg and kept it raised.

What bothered Holmes about the turn of events was their lack of knowledge about any developments since leaving London. He hoped that their letters had been received at Scotland Yard and at Tudor House.

As Holmes expected, Tennyson's pain grew much worse as he rested. Sometimes, when the body is in repose, the brain enhances discomfort.

Tennyson made a few nonsensical statements (for instance, "What I admire most in a man is when he does not press upon me any verses of his own"), then told Holmes, in stilted fragments, a story from his childhood.

Tennyson's father collapsed to his death from a combination of alcohol and laudanum, a tincture of opium and morphine. Tennyson, twenty years old, climbed into bed with the body of his father, waiting up all night to see if his ghost would appear.

"That is when I learned," Tennyson murmured drowsily, "poets do not see ghosts."

"Why did you help Scotland Yard, Tennyson? It wasn't just to follow your duty to the queen, was it?"

"I've heard it said it is my verses, Holmes, that made people believe poets were heroes. But we're not, are we? I am called the leader of all poets of our land. If Miss Rossetti or Browning came to harm thinking they were heroes, I wouldn't have forgiven myself. You won't find much in me, after all, Holmes. I have had no life—mine has been one of feelings, not of actions."

Mercifully, the laureate fell asleep while Holmes himself, without realizing it, dozed on the sofa.

Holmes dreamed of Dante, with the hard lines of his nose and chin, the laurel crown that represented his creative triumphs in contrast to his failures as a father, husband, and politician. The sneer on his lips for all that was weak in Holmes and in life, all the vulnerability that Dante had expelled from himself. Dante opened his mouth, but instead of words, discordant noises emerged—noises of death. He reached to shake Holmes's hand, before his grip became a vise from which Holmes could not free himself.

Holmes jumped up from the sofa, his heart in his throat. He was soaked with perspiration. He realized the noises in his dream had intruded into his mind from somewhere in reality. Tennyson still slept soundly and nothing in the room was disturbed. Holmes took a candle and stepped out into the corridor. A coolness swept through him; there was an open window somewhere in the inn, and loose papers flew past him like leaves.

Grabbing one of these, Holmes glanced over it by the glow of the candle. He couldn't believe his eyes. In his hand was a manuscript page about *Dante*—not just about Dante, but about the Purgatory-inspired deaths that had occurred in and around London. Holmes—mystified and mesmerized—followed the trail of pages, collecting them as he went. He read as quickly as he could. With the pages out of order and incomplete, their narratives came in spurts and fragments.

In Dante's Shadow, a True Account of the London Purgations by the Author of The Dante Murders, read the title page he found.

One of the pages told of Sibbie waking from her coma and returning to lead her followers at the Phillip Sanatorium.

Our Sibbie? Holmes thought. *Could it be?* She had warned them the very first afternoon they questioned her about Loring: You cannot understand.

The followers, Holmes pieced together in a combination of his thoughts and what he could read from the assorted pages he gathered, were submitting themselves to be purged of their sins to provide examples for all of England. The murders were not murders at all, Holmes realized; they were by consent of the dead . . . they were suicides.

Then came an incomplete account that alarmed Holmes most of all: that Dante Gabriel Rossetti had returned to be purged of gluttony, with Christina as witness. *They have taken the Rossettis.*

Send the police to find me, was scribbled at the end of one page, *for God's sake send anyone for me before it's too late.*

Only then, scooping up a few more pages, did Holmes notice spots of red on some of them. He searched for the source of the papers. He turned the corner into another corridor, where he was met by strong gusts. An open door led to an open window, the panes rattling in the wind. On the floor were more pages being blown around, and in the corner of the room under the eaves, there was a body slumped over. Holmes approached cautiously, raising his candle.

It was Simon Camp, stripped naked, with the hilt of a long sword protruding from his chest. On his forehead, some of his flesh was cut and bloody. Out the window, Holmes could make out bloodstained footsteps in the snow where the assailant—barefoot, from the looks of it—had fled.

Holmes returned to inspect the body. On Camp's forehead was not merely a random cut as it first had appeared, but a letter.

P had been carved there.

The same letter the angel guarding the gates of Purgatory carves on Dante's brow—representing *peccatum*, or sin awaiting purgation.

When their train reached the station, Browning joined Branagan and the other two policemen in a carriage driven by a Lancashire constable alerted in advance by telegraph to expect them. With the roads barely passable, their journey by carriage was filled with as many stops and starts as the train ride had been. At one point, they passed an overturned carriage in the snow. (Were those books spread out in the snow nearby?) A constable had to shovel away parts of snowbanks at several junctures in order to continue. Once at the gates of the sanatorium, they saw no sign that Holmes and Tennyson had arrived. It was impossible to know for sure; if there had been another carriage there recently, any traces of wheel tracks had been covered by fresh snow. (*Unless*, thought Browning . . . *the overturned carriage?*)

During their train ride, Browning had shared with the eager constable his fears that the next outburst of violence could happen at any moment. "If Sibbie is set on completing the terraces of Purgatory, there are three more beyond the ones we know they have staged: terrace five holds the Avaricious and Prodigal together; terrace six, the Gluttonous; and the final region, terrace seven, represents the cleansing of excessive love, or lust that all souls must undergo."

"Our very presence could prompt the next death," Browning now added as they trudged up the hill to enter the property.

"What do you mean?" Branagan asked.

"I believe that must be what happened with the death of Reuben Loring—their purgation of the Wrathful. Sibbie and Fallow pluck victims from their followers. When they heard we were on the grounds, they did not want to risk being stopped, and they *wanted* us to witness the demonstration."

Browning stopped midstride.

"Mr. Browning?" Branagan said, urging him to come faster. "You look like you've seen a—"

"It's Loring, Constable. I'm just remembering—we were searching for him, and after his death we assumed we inadvertently led the perpetrator to him, at the time, of course, thinking it was Gabriel we led there. But Loring saw us coming. *He* saw us. What if Loring was the one who knew his death had to happen quickly before it could be stopped by our presence?"

"What do you—how does that make any sense?"

It made all the sense in the world. It fit the pieces together perfectly.

Browning thought about the period of Gabriel's life after Lizzie died when the painter-poet would talk about his thoughts of his own death, and thought back to a particular day Browning took a walk with Gabriel and a group of friends above a scenic basin of water. The place was nicknamed the Devil's Punchbowl. Browning had noticed a look on Gabriel's face that day, a glare in his eyes, and suddenly knew that Gabriel was, at that very moment, contemplating jumping into oblivion. The edge was slippery, and there would be no way to save him. Gabriel put his arm into Browning's, and Browning knew why. It was Gabriel's way to choose living. Browning knew the look and the feeling in his friend, because he had experienced the same ones after Ba died. It was the longing that struck the living to know death, to be purified and completed by it.

Browning finally answered Branagan. "Loring—and all of the others— the dying participated in these deaths, Constable. In the *Inferno*, Dante meets souls who fight their fate; in *Purgatory*, the shades embrace it, they want to be seen and known and remembered—'remember me, remember me,' they're constantly pleading—it is their way to salvation. Their *only* way. The victims have been accomplices in this, herded by Fallow, mesmerized by Sibbie."

"Yes!" Branagan seemed to see it all in a flash, and shouted out to the others to hurry.

"Thirteen hundred!"

"What, Browning?"

"Thirteen hundred and 1870!" But he didn't have time to explain.

The former textile mill—the sanatorium so removed from the chaos of the city—the otherworldly utopia: this place now conveyed a menace that Browning and the policemen feared far more than any dark, bloodstained alleyway in London.

S tanding at the rear of the buildings, Ironhead Herman took a big breath. He didn't relish the idea of this place having to disappear, however much trouble it had given him. The Phillip Sanatorium had been a valuable purchaser of their goods. It was here, at this habitat for fanatics, that the young woman and the minister who followed her orders had collected massive amounts of smuggled opium. Herman and his superiors provided so much opium to Sibbie and Fallow's flock that, in conjunction with incidents abroad affecting the trade from India, the overall supply of opium to apothecaries and other dispensaries around London had been periodically reduced.

The drug had changed the reality of people in a way similar to the religions of old. It made the men and women who habitually used it think they were floating through fire, they were dominating the sky, instead of being crushed by the ruthless modern world surrounding them. The need for opium was as fierce as the trade for it.

Herman lifted his walking stick, topped by the grotesque golden beast head, to signal his minions, who swiftly spread out in different directions of the so-called sanatorium. Herman was, by his own assessment, a patient man. But in his way of life, an associate could quickly become a liability. An ally overnight became an example.

Herman's team finished inserting wires into blocks of clay spread out in inconspicuous places around the buildings. He thought about the Fenian fools who had purchased phosphorus from him and built explosives that practically screamed that they did it. As Herman waited, he examined the carved head at the top of his walking stick. It was a representation of the kylin, a mythological beast that would punish the wicked with fire and destruction. The kylin was said to be able to walk on water without causing a ripple. Herman always liked that. No matter how many people were about to perish here tonight, no traces of Herman or the powerful forces he represented would remain. Herman would go on, untouched, unpunished.

XXV

Christina knelt on the ground. She had thoroughly searched the passageway that ended in a locked iron door. She'd even torn apart the platters of food looking for something she might be able to use to free herself from her chamber or to break through to Gabriel's even grimmer compartment. But there was nothing. The only option that was left for her was the one she'd relied upon her whole life when everything around her fell apart, when family peace faltered: to pray.

Pain shot through her from her knees on the hard ground, but she did not stop. She knelt even lower, prayed harder: prayed to God that her brother would not succumb to his starvation and weakness, would find some of his lost strength that had been buried years before with Lizzie; prayed that the family curse that never quite allowed the Rossettis to feel more than exiles in London vanished without taking Gabriel with it; prayed that all the things she had given up in her life to remain devoted to God would now be brought to account.

She prayed to God without questioning his ways. She trusted.

Here, in this dark corner of a forsaken dungeon, she allowed herself to cry—tears flowing that she would never permit to be seen. When she opened her eyes, she stared in amazement at what she saw.

A feather.

A single feather tucked into a crevice in the ground. At first, it was just the novelty that attracted her. When she handled it, she realized something more. This feather's shaft or calamus, the quill that had given voice to so many generations of writers, was so strong and sharp it drew blood from her fingertip.

A massive ball of fire erupted from the boiler house on the far east end of the sanatorium. This was followed by another, two structures down, then a series of explosions on the opposite row of sheds and outbuildings. Flames jumped and crept from structure to structure, as black smoke poured out into the sky.

The bursting flames were a striking contrast with the cover of snow, some of which began to wash away in streams of boiling water.

Fallow charged out from the chapel, his heart dropping into his stomach. "Ironhead Herman," he gasped. "He's waging war on us, Sibbie. We have to get everyone to work together to put it out, get the buckets from the greenhouse! Save what's left!"

Behind him, Sibbie walked at a much more leisurely pace, as if visiting a gallery instead of a raging conflagration. She quietly replied: "No."

He turned to her in a state of profound fear. Fear for his safety, yes. But not only that.

He feared what would become of his mind if all they had built was suddenly taken. Since the tragedy that befell his congregation as a young preacher, and the despair that followed it, the Phillip Sanatorium's bold mission was the first time he felt that thrill in his blood he used to experience at the pulpit. The ability to wield his influence to change people. Sibbie made it possible.

The ecstasies of that thrill had overtaken him upon the first purgatorial sacrifice of Jasper Morton, which he watched from a safe distance behind the crowd of bystanders. He knew everything would change then. How Fallow trembled internally when the three poets, Christina,

Tennyson, and Holmes, came to speak to them in London. He felt a pit of anger form at their attempted incursion. He tried to follow the example of nearby Sibbie's tranquillity, held on to her for strength. They had known investigations would begin, starting after the discovery of Morton's martyrdom and, as a precaution, he and Sibbie had come to London to clear away any traces of connections between themselves and Morton and other members of their group who were cleansing their souls. At Reuben Loring's crowded boardinghouse, they hurriedly ransacked the soldier's papers and books and took all documents that could have linked him to the sanatorium, then brought them in sacks to burn in the church's boiler room. Loring had been studying the cantos of *Purgatory* narrating the terrace chosen for him by Sibbie—the Wrathful. (Fallow had missed Loring's copy of *Purgatory*, kept in a special place separate from the rest of his books.) As the London police began to look for clues into the earlier deaths, Loring and other devotees had begun to flee for the sanatorium.

Now that the flames were spreading over their great sanctuary, across the structures of the former mill, Fallow grabbed Sibbie's arm.

"Have you gone mad?" he declared. "The whole place will be destroyed. There's no way to send for the fire engines to reach us with the road conditions."

She watched the flames chase each other, consuming everything they had worked to build. She tipped her head back, as though being warmed by the morning sun. "Let it come. Let us all enter the final passage. To be cleansed."

"You—" Fallow stopped himself and stared at her. "You had word sent to Herman that you were back."

She did not answer.

"That is how Herman knew to come back, and that is why you told Herman *not* to wait a week for payment, to expect it at sunset when you knew it would not be there. Tomorrow is the thirteenth of April, when Dante is transported to Paradise from the top of Mount Purgatory."

"Not just the thirteenth of April, but Holy Wednesday—just as it was in the calendar of 1300 when Dante ascended. The calendars of 1300 and 1870 are the same. It is all aligned. *All* will be cleansed."

"You expected this. Didn't you? You knew when people cross the opium smugglers Herman represents that he has a reputation for committing arson in their homes and places of business, as warning to others. The seventh terrace, the last purgation, the passage through fire . . . You anticipated this coming all along?"

"I knew you would not have the heart for it," she said cruelly. "You see enemies around us but there are none. Brother Herman was a divine instrument."

"Think about what you are giving up. Through the power of what we have created, there are more and more people—people of all ages, from all parts of society, to bolster our ranks. We can fill England and beyond with our believers."

"When I was taken away, Brother Orin, you became too interested in the feeling of your own control. You surrounded yourself with beauty, you tasted power. The true power in this has always been to reveal the way to the light for all humanity. To reveal the *end*."

Fallow stumbled over himself as he scrambled away.

Browning was shouting to the policemen, "I know how to find the fifth terrace!" just as the first explosions took place. Browning and two of the policemen were knocked over by the force, and the other men held out their arms to shield themselves.

Branagan pulled Browning to his feet. "The fifth terrace?"

Browning, winded, took a moment to find his voice again. In the fifth terrace of Purgatory, he explained, Dante discovers the Avaricious and Prodigal, their wrists and ankles bound. "Dante tells us they are placed facedown because they are not meant to see the sky—not meant to see God."

Branagan called out to the others: "Look for enclosed buildings with no skylights or high windows."

Browning hurried to keep up with the policemen. Narrowing their choices, Constable Branagan used a small battering ram to knock through the door of the woodshed. Branagan turned on the cyclops lamp on his belt to break through the darkness. He and Browning could make out two people, one male and one female, tied up just as Browning predicted.

He recognized the man: the first person they had spoken to when they initially visited the Phillip Sanatorium, the man with the distinctively shaped head, something like an onion. He had been digging or weeding then, but Browning now understood he wasn't doing either. As one of the shades explained to Dante on that terrace of their misdeeds: *We did not lift our eyes on high but set our sight on earthly things*. He was preparing for his coming purgation.

"I think they've lost consciousness," said Branagan. "We need another pair of hands to drag them . . ."

Browning ran back out to call for help. "Over here—"

Another round of explosions. The small structure erupted into flames, consuming the tied-up victims in an instant.

Browning lost sight of Branagan, too.

"Constable," Browning cried out. "Branagan?"

Branagan had leapt away, avoiding the flames by a hair, and dropped into the snow where he rolled to Browning's feet.

A fresh cry reached them: "*Here!*"

Browning spun around at the sound of the voice.

"What was it, Browning?" Branagan asked as Browning helped him to his feet.

"That voice. It's Christina Rossetti."

Christina had heard a click. She had inserted the sharp quill of the feather into the lock of the iron door. Twisting it, turning it, pressing it further, not so roughly that it would snap. Then: *click*. It worked.

What was so peculiar was not the absolutely incredible fact that she had picked the lock and released the bolt with a feather, of all things on earth. What was so peculiar was that Christina had complete confidence it would work—as soon as she held the feather, she knew it would and she knew *why*. She wanted it to be due to a lifetime of devout prayer but knew it wasn't so simple.

The feather, in a sense, had come from Mount Purgatory.

She rushed up a set of crumbling stone stairs, finding no access to the compartment that held Gabriel below. Instead, she found herself outside just as more explosions and fires started. Christina heard voices from somewhere nearby.

"Here! Over here!" she cried.

"Christina?" the voice bellowed—a rousing and wonderful voice vibrating in the air.

Browning was cresting the hill between them when they met.

"Gabriel is trapped. He's in an awful state, Mr. Browning, please help!"

Though there had not been an explosive detonated in the carpenter's shop that held Gabriel, flames from the nearest structure spread to its perimeter.

Browning signaled for Branagan and the other men, who trudged as fast as they could through the deep snow. Christina tried to keep up, but she felt weakened down to her bones from her captivity and the lingering effects of the opiates. She dropped into the snow. Browning looked back at her, but she gestured to him to continue to Gabriel.

Browning and the other men disappeared over the hill. Christina, shivering to the bone, strained to stand up and fell again. A hand came into her view to offer help. It was Sibbie's.

Christina hesitated before accepting.

"I am overjoyed, dear sister, that you were witness to a purification. To your brother's."

"The feather."

"Feather?"

"You left it for me to find. You tested me. You knew I would pray, that I would kneel when I did. You knew I would see it where you placed it."

"The shades of Purgatory each learn that only through prayer does the Divine Will move us forward," Sibbie replied. "Here we learn to live by devotion just as you do. You are one of the pure ones. Oh, I know more about you through Gabriel than you might imagine, Sister Christina. By praying, you found salvation."

"The feather. In one of Dante's dreams during *Purgatory*, a golden-feathered eagle lifts him up and carries him, and when he wakes he has moved closer to the mountaintop."

"What was it you thought about as you looked upon Lillian Brenner's face?"

The deadhouse. Christina had kept her gaze away from the other on-lookers, rushing away in tears and nearly colliding with . . . Flashes of faces returned to her. One of them was Sibbie.

Even with all she now knew about Sibbie, Christina could not stop herself from finding her voice and words persuasive and commanding. She answered without wanting to. "I thought about her eyes, thought that one of them seemed to be *opening*, to burst its wires open, to watch and judge us as we were watching and judging her."

Sibbie rested her other hand on Christina's shoulder. "You have come closer to the mountaintop, too. After so long, we reach the final purgation, that which will save all those who enter it, and all those who learn about what happened here today. Look. Isn't it beautiful, isn't it magnificent? The reflection in the snow and in the sky, as though the whole world is aflame. You've been part of this all along."

"You knew Gabriel would bring me?"

"No. I knew you would come for him."

Christina studied her, her sparkling blue eyes and her unruly hair illuminated by the fiery spectacle surrounding them. She thought of the women over the years—Lizzie especially, though she wasn't the first or last—whom Gabriel believed would bring him into harmony with some order of the spiritual world through their beauty and mystery. This woman awakened similar desires but promised vastly more, an ecstatic absorption into literature, art, life, death, salvation.

"You have continued your father's labors of discovering the way to Beatrice. Had you thought you escaped it? Think of your poetry. Think of the power of 'Goblin Market' over readers that you try so hard to run from."

"That was a fairy tale. I meant nothing profound by it."

"Tales of goblin men appearing to innocents, allegory of sinful consumption. Devotional verses showing the way to God. Don't you see what you've been writing about your whole life? Temptation, weakness, deliverance, your poetry was always about death more than life. You, too, were preparing humanity for what was to come, for what we enact here. Dear sister, they dared expect you to grow up to be a wife, to bring a man ale every night and lace his boots every morning. Instead you have lived your life with trepidation, self-recrimination and doubt, self-sacrifice, penitence, demanding the righteous path for you and for the world around you. Your life has been a purgatory."

Behind them, flames swallowed the structure that held Gabriel. Christina gasped, a tear dropping down her cheek.

"I know you mourn him now," Sibbie said, without any discernible emotion or change in her demeanor. "But remember that our people, Gabriel perhaps most of all, have waited for this day, which has been prophesied to come to all of us. Prophesied by your father's discoveries that Dante would overturn all we think is safe. Think of Gabriel's sad memories and pain: gone like a mist, like trying to pick up water in our hands. The rest of our brothers and sisters are gathered now and you are needed, as well."

"If all who are here today perish, if I perish, who will tell your story in order to convince others?"

"*Because* we perish, dear sister, the story will be told again and again; nothing will be able to stop it. Death—as Dante comprehended—is the only story that nobody can resist. The finale of a writer with your talents and stature will inspire thousands of creators around the world to understand and convey what has happened to us."

Christina threw one more glance at the flaming ruins where she and Gabriel had been imprisoned, then nodded, as if to say, *Take me.*

Sibbie embraced her, her grip warm and generous.

Christina allowed Sibbie to lead her. As they walked—strolled, really, considering the magisterial pace set by Sibbie—Christina studied the destruction. They passed by the crumbling structures of the sanatorium to the grand chapel, ornamented with Gabriel's vivid depictions of the purgatorial deaths.

A group of approximately two dozen white-robed followers huddled together in the middle of the space. Sibbie raised her arms. Her followers trembled and shivered, bowing down to her. At either side, two of the settlement's guardians held out their swords, making clear nobody would leave. Flames ate at the sides of what had once been a massive machine shop, and the ceiling began to crumble down in pieces.

They were there for one last mission. They were there to die.

Sibbie made a sweeping gesture toward Christina. "She has come to us, brothers and sisters, to redeem our world! Removed from pride, from envy, from wrath, sloth, avarice, gluttony. And now, from lust for anything outside of God. Nothing will come between us and our final cleansing! Join with us, Sister Christina!"

Sibbie slipped off her robe, and the followers did the same.

Christina, standing stock-still, studied the naked men and women huddled like sheep in a storm. She saw in their faces the split between fear of Sibbie and fear of their own demises. Then, a burning section of the ceiling crashed down on one of the armed guardians there to enforce Sibbie's will. He was crushed. Christina's eyes darted to the other guardian—his state of mind would be decisive for what she would do next.

Seeing that Christina was not coming any closer, Sibbie's face distorted with betrayal.

"These flames are God's art. Do not try to thwart this," Sibbie said.

"This way to survive," Christina called, her voice ringing out as clear as a bell. "The east path is clear of obstruction, and the police are outside and will help you! You'll save no one by dying today!"

A pillar fell. Christina felt herself pushed out of the way. Ethel had grabbed hold of her a moment before she would have been crushed.

"Ethel, come with me, let me save you!" Christina cried.

Ethel tilted her head and studied her with adoration. "You already have," she whispered. "Remember me, my sister."

The chapel ceiling rained down, layer by layer of Gabriel's vibrant paintings flying through the air, and the walls transformed into flames. The flock of followers was divided between those who would not leave Sibbie and those trying to save themselves by following Christina's directions. The remaining guardian shouted and threatened, pulling his sword, but in the confusion, it was impossible for him to stop those who ran away. The followers who were escaping stampeded. A wall collapsed, smothering two or three of those clinging to Sibbie.

As the others hurried outside at Christina's direction, she turned back to see Sibbie encircled by smoldering ruins. Christina gestured for her to follow. Now it was Sibbie's turn to remain planted in place. Their eyes were fixed on each other for a moment, a moment Christina would remember for many years to come.

Sibbie's mouth formed a word.

Ethel, standing near Sibbie, fell through a hole in the floor as it was incinerated.

A rafter collapsed right in front of Christina, throwing her backward. She scrambled to her feet and rushed out the door. Once outside, she and the others who escaped moved as fast as the snow and debris permitted. The last of the chapel surrendered itself to the flames.

Christina scanned the area until she spotted them.

Browning and a policeman were half carrying Gabriel, whose arms rested around the two other policemen's shoulders.

Reverend Fallow, terror stricken, his wrists in irons, ran alongside Constable Branagan, who gripped his arm.

Christina hurried, and the escapees followed her. When she paused, they paused; when she turned to look back, they did.

XXVI

DOCUMENT #8:
FRAGMENT OF LETTER BY REV. ORIN FALLOW,
DISCOVERED IN HIS JAIL CELL (BELIEVED TO BE
INTENDED FOR THE "DANTE MASTER,"
SO-CALLED, OF ITALY)

[undated]

[no addressee]

It is as it is meant to be. You, who prayerfully taught us devotion to Dante's sacred truth, who overmastered us with his power, would have savored what was accomplished. Not by my doing, I regret to add, for I allowed myself to waver and fall to cowardice, a trait belonging to infernal regions rather than the path to magnificence. As I watched the flames and panic spread with equal rapidity, I found myself back inside that theater, back at the pulpit, surrounded by chaos I could not quell, by riots internal and external. I looked backward, I tumbled. It was she who managed what Dante had dreamed up—laying the true and final path for the rest of the world to redeem humanity.

Many think that Dante was an arrogant man. Arrogant, so it is said, to think that he of all people could record the will of God and point the one true way to salvation. Not a pope or a priest but a mere man. *Not with dogma but poetry. He was exiled, shunned, and ridiculed by many of the so-called great men of his own time.*

Dante's life, in truth, represents humility. He submitted himself to a divine purpose to correct the course of mankind. There were bards who had held a mirror to our human weaknesses before Dante, but none who have ever succeeded in leaving behind the secrets to expelling them.

There were so many times in my life I hid from errors, from my vices, my mistakes. There were times I was confronted, haunted by them. Through dear Sibbie's guidance, I saw firsthand how Dante's words led to a time of purification in ways that the bickering denominations and governments of today fail to do.

Knowledge has never been more available than it is in our nineteenth century; books have become cheaper, and a proliferation of newspapers, magazines, and pamphlets can be found in the homes of the humble laborer. Knowledge *underlies our miseries: knowledge of our family histories, replete with their own vices and errors; knowledge of other people's abilities and gifts that we lack and cannot hope to obtain; knowledge of ever-improving medical advancements that would have saved the life of a beloved child or spouse if only it had existed a few years or months or days prior. Knowledge, too, of how the choices we make in professions, in war, in legislation, in commerce affect other people, other nations. We now know we are the cause of more misery than we ever dreamed, and it is a wonder anyone manages to live with that fact.*

The religions of the world, organized at a time when most of the workings of the world remained obscure, become increasingly obsolete. As such, death, once reassuring, becomes horrifying,

*unanswerable. Deprived of what used to be our spiritual ballasts,
our moral certainties, our peace, we fear darkness, we fear each
other, we fear the foreign and foreigners, we fear the unknown. But
here is Dante. His poem reveals death not as something to make us
afraid but as the very thing that bestows meaning unto us—it is not
a drama of suffering, but a revelation that suffering will save us.
Death is the way—the only way remaining in an age of false
prophets—we come close to the Lord.*

*Was Dante more prophet or poet? I have longed to ask you your
opinions on this proposition, and to learn more of what you foresee
Dante will bring next, and how we might help. Dante foresaw that
Beatrice would guide his life when she was a mere child. I cannot
help but think of Sibbie's work as an unfinished portrait, that those
to whom she has brought Dante will discover what remains to be
painted.*

S ometimes when normal life resumes, despair dissolves inside its
circular routines; sometimes that despair is quieted and interred
underneath the rest, but fortifies and thrives largely unnoticed. Sibbie and
Fallow turned despair into the promise of magnificence, and that was difficult to forget for those who made it out of the former Phillip Sanatorium
alive the day of Lancashire County's worst conflagration in thirty-five
years, on April 12, 1870, when flames were said to be seen miles away as
the fire engines struggled through the snow. When flames were said to
reach the heavens.

Gabriel was one survivor.

Back at Tudor House, he slept. Slept without interruption, not so unlike the time Sibbie had spent a few rooms down. He slept, in fact, more
soundly and completely than he had in years.

When he woke, he did not display the sense of relief that Christina had
anticipated. But no, perhaps she had hoped for it more than anticipated it.

She wanted him to say something like: *Yesterday, I wished to die, but today I do not*. But no. This was Gabriel. Normalcy brought him no comfort. The frequent administration of opium had stopped for long enough that his body did not seem to demand it, and craved it far less frequently—for now. It was impossible to ever say what was caused by the poisons that had been filling his body for years, and what had come from the pure Dantean fervor of his imagination and Sibbie's. Gabriel understood that he had been on a path to death and that he had been given a reprieve. He understood this, but he was sad after it. Christina could not decide whether Gabriel seemed sadder because of what happened, or sad to be removed from his trance. He never quite expressed regret for those dark, dreamy days under the spell of Sibbie's power; when he did speak of it, it was as though he spoke of another man whose experiences fascinated him.

He did ask a question related to those events that sent shivers through Christina's body.

"What do you think it was," he asked, "that she said at the end?"

He meant the word Sibbie's lips seemed to be forming when Christina last looked upon her. Christina knew that most people, in fact perhaps it was not too bold to say *anybody other than her*, would have spent countless hours guessing at the word Sibbie seemed to intone in Christina's last glimpse of her. But not Christina. She threw down a steel door in her mind, willed herself to not pay any attention to it at all, defended herself from falling into any trace of obsession with Sibbie, who was born to absorb obsessions.

What most startled Christina about the question was that she had never told Gabriel she had seen Sibbie move her lips in what seemed to be silent speech. Or had she, and in the hurry and confusion of all that had happened, now forgot that she had? She considered how her parents would address a question such as Gabriel's. Father would expound on its mysteries and meanings, and Mother would ignore it altogether. She chose her mother's technique.

As Gabriel recovered, he spent much of his time tending to his assorted animals. Top, his wombat, died suddenly, and Gabriel held a funeral in the garden with half a dozen artist friends and Christina present. He broke down and cried hysterically over the creature before it was interred beneath his lime tree, so Christina read to the gathering the poem he'd written for the occasion:

My burning soul; neither from owl nor from bat
Can peace be to me now
That I've lost my wombat.

He also painted. Gabriel painted as much as Christina could remember him painting in recent years. This pleased her whenever she thought about it. On the surface, they were typical paintings of Gabriel's, the kind that inspired passion from patrons and many artists, and anger from certain critics who thought them undisciplined and confusing. There were shimmering women in red and gold hues. There were heroic men on the threshold of dangerous actions. The paintings were windows, in other words, to a time and place when life could be redeemed by beauty, rumination, and sacrifice.

She observed small changes in his art—flames and sparks in odd places; death, when depicted, seemed something final and alarming, rather than something awe-inspiring and capable of regeneration. She hesitated to raise any of this with Gabriel, wondering if he even noticed. Perhaps, she thought, it was not his art that had changed; perhaps she had.

"In the past," Gabriel mused in a low voice, indirectly addressing some of his techniques, "my painting tormented me more than I admit. Lately I feel I can paint by a set of rules, which I could teach to any man as systematically as one teaches arithmetic. In painting, dear sister, there is in the less important details something of the craft of a superior carpenter, and the part of a picture that is not mechanical is often trivial enough."

Most surprising, he finally finished *Dante's Dream*, which he had wrestled with for more than fifteen years. It was seven by ten feet, a massive accomplishment both in size and effect. When he unveiled it to his siblings with a twinkle in his eye, Christina stared into the face of the dying Beatrice until she realized she no longer looked like either of the two women who'd modeled for the painting over the years; nor did she look quite like Lizzie, whose likeness Gabriel often painted without realizing it; nor did she resemble Sibbie, the latter of whom had intruded into some of the new paintings. She felt a moment of relief that perhaps in some small way he had been unlatched from the women of his past, but then she wondered if it signaled a search for a new influence yet to be found. The painting was remarkable for its beauty and the fact that it inspired feelings, not thoughts. He seemed so lighthearted about finishing that she didn't think to ask about the face of Beatrice.

"I should not count on a reception from the bloody critics that it deserves," Gabriel said as a kind of warning as he paced the studio back and forth studying the work, growing angry at the idea. "No. This conspiracy to persecute me—well, what remains to be said about it—is widespread and remorseless. Bedevilments thicken."

She assured him that no such conspiracy existed, but he had stopped to stare out the floor-to-ceiling mullioned window to the Thames beyond, where the sail of a lone boat fluttered under heavy storm clouds. Peals of thunder reached the studio.

"Tennyson, that perpetual groan. And Browning! A dandy bloodsucker. Those two sprout a new horn, hoof, tusk, or tail at every step."

"What on earth do you mean? They and Dr. Holmes helped you, Gabriel," Christina said. "They helped me—us."

Lightning flashed around the figure of Gabriel, whose back was facing her, momentarily filling the room with the long shadow of his body. "They wished to discredit me, my dear Christina. No, I am home at last, and never shall I leave it again."

One afternoon, when she arrived at Tudor House, she found Gabriel walking up and down the stairs.

"Did you ever notice," he asked in his velvety voice, "what a *slopperty* walk I have? Just look at it. Look! Like a sailor's. My legs are too far apart."

"You look well," Christina said, the closest she could come to asking him how he felt.

"Without the chloral I fear my old curse will return before long—insomnia."

"Without the chloral, we will have you healthy and content for years to come. As you can tell, I am turning quite into an old nurse."

"By the by, I'm thinking of buying a nice ticker," Gabriel said, miming pulling a watch chain out of his vest and studying the invisible watch, satisfied at the imaginary time on it. "To know the time—sometimes that would help. I have seen one I admired last week. But I don't have the tin. Fifteen pounds . . ."

"I will loan it to you, Gabriel," Christina said.

"Will you? I will pay you back, of course, sooner than you think."

Christina knew he never would. He was overjoyed about the idea of a watch for the next day and a half.

Before they left for a walk that same afternoon, she noticed he had written three words on a piece of paper and pinned it on his wall, as a kind of motto, she supposed.

Frangas non Flectes.

It translated as: *You may break but shall not bend me.* A few weeks later, he'd printed this on Tudor House stationery.

Life continued to pile up its demands on Christina while they had been occupied in such unusual endeavors. She had to oversee various repairs and projects for the house she shared with her mother, brought on by the year's late snowstorms. She had letter after letter, personal and professional, to answer, always copying her response, then periodically burning the bundle.

(Later biographers, after Christina Rossetti took her place among the most celebrated poets of the nineteenth century, would find the first half of

1870 a puzzle in chronicling her life, with so few extant documents and with police records referencing the Rossettis by that point either suppressed or destroyed. Christina, most biographers surmised, probably spent those months holed up at home, suffering from a stretch of feeble health.)

Charles Cayley, who had to be abroad to work on a translation to which he had committed, wrote to Christina that he wished to hear from her as soon as possible about their last, unfinished conversation. She did not know exactly how to reply, so she wrote of the weather, of the death of the Tudor House wombat, of a trip abroad she was planning with her mother and aunts, of her work at Saint Mary's, and some new efforts she had joined to combat cruelty to animals. She also found herself writing a poem to enclose to him:

> *Remember me when I am gone away,*
> *Gone far away into the silent land;*
> *When you can no more hold me by the hand,*
> *Nor I half turn to go yet turning stay.*

That wouldn't do. It went into the flame of the candle and was replaced by:

> *None know the choice I made; I make it still.*
> *None know the choice I made and broke my heart,*
> *Breaking mine idol: I have braced my will*
> *Once, chosen for once my part.*

She did not rush to answer most of her correspondence, a contrast to her usual habits. Instead, she spent her time reviewing her stacks of compositions. She set aside more time to write new poetry and found verses of a variety of sorts—devotional, narrative, elegies—came to her quite easily. She soon surprised her publisher, Alexander Macmillan, at his offices.

"I have a volume of poetry I am ready to publish, if you happen to have interest."

"If! Of course we do, Miss Rossetti," said Macmillan.

"Thank you. It is a volume of nursery rhymes for today. I shall leave you them to see if they suit your needs."

Macmillan called the next morning enthusiastically raving about her poems and began to make plans to put them into print as soon as possible.

"It matters not to you that I am not a parent, and may never be?" Christina asked.

"Why, Miss Rossetti, your children are the very kind who bring the greatest pride—your verse. Keep in mind, as great a poetess as Jean Ingelow herself has never married!"

Early in May, Oliver Wendell Holmes called on her to bid farewell before sailing out of Liverpool. He had arranged his passage to meet his daughter in Belgium on the first vessel that could take him there. He was so full of talk and conversation about museums and libraries he had lately seen, about the Tower of London and Stratford-on-Avon, Christina had a strong feeling that the doctor wanted to discuss anything and everything except what had happened.

"I suppose the wise traveler should never think time away will change him. It will interrupt his routine for a while, but then he will settle down into his former self, and be just what he was before. How small a matter literature is, Miss Rossetti, to the great seething, toiling, struggling, love-making, bread-winning, child-rearing, death-awaiting men and women who fill this huge, palpitating world of ours!"

To her surprise, before they took leave from each other, Holmes did make what seemed a brief reference to the events.

"At night before I sleep, I have been contemplating how liberty is often a heavy burden on a man, Miss Rossetti. It involves that necessity for perpetual choice which is the kind of labor men always dreaded. In common life, I suppose, we shirk it by forming habits that take the place of self-determination. But if a man has a genuine, hearty wish to get rid of his liberty, if he is bent upon becoming a slave to another's doctrine, nothing can stop him."

He added: "Such a time as we had irons ten years' creases out of one's forehead." Then he paused. "Thank heavens it's over." But when he said that, the hand with which he held his teacup shook slightly, and he said the words in a tone of a man who did not believe his assertion.

Despite all Sibbie had done, it still seemed cruel to have to describe for Holmes how the burning building collapsed and exploded around an unmoving (*unmovable* was the better word) Sibbie. Holmes had wanted Sibbie to redeem him for what he thought were his shortcomings. Christina was glad he would soon be reunited with his daughter. At any age, a father's presence brought comfort to a daughter, and Christina was hopeful Amelia's company would be restorative for Holmes.

Browning, always impressing Christina anew with his warmth in his friendships, wrapped Holmes's hand in both of his. "Goodbye, Holmes," he said, "and mind it isn't so long before you come again! There's always a one o'clock meal at my house waiting for you."

Not everyone in their recent coterie seemed in a hurry to pay a call on the Rossettis after Gabriel had settled in again. Tennyson returned to his Farringford estate to heal from the injuries he sustained in the carriage accident in Walsden. Those injuries remained painful for a few weeks although they ultimately proved minor. Still, no trips to London followed. Nor were any invitations extended to the Londoners to come to the Isle of Wight. The laureate walled himself into his burrow, and there wasn't any sign of him at two successive Cosmopolitan Club meetings.

Browning, who called on Tudor House regularly, remained indignant about Tennyson's informing Inspector Williamson of their activities during the search for Gabriel, and the laureate staying away from London and Tudor House in the wake of all that had come to pass only compounded Browning's resentment. He would not speak of Tennyson other than to repeat his position and then gloss it with the comment, "I'm not afraid of him, and he hates me for it. But let him make amends, and I won't mind." On a different occasion he exclaimed: "Tennysonite!"

"Pardon?" Christina asked.

"Tennysonites, Browningites . . . never mind. Thinking back over all that happened, Miss Rossetti, I see that we have been all the time walking over a torrent on a straw. Perhaps life must now be begun anew—all the old cast off and the new one put on."

Christina was content to slip back into her usual seclusion, but before she did she made her own unannounced visit to the Isle of Wight, largely an attempt to encourage Tennyson to mend his friendship with Browning. She hated to think that she, by driving their collective inquiries, caused a rift between friends. She herself easily forgave Tennyson for his breach of their trust. *How could you forgive him, how could you not be full of vinegar and gall for a man who blatantly betrayed you?* Browning had demanded of her.

Farringford had the look of a charmed castle, its windows glowing a soft crimson. As she crossed through the wicket gate, she saw that beneath the sign marked Private were words written in chalk by some local who resented the declaration: *Old Tennyson is a fool.* She hoped the desecration would be removed before he saw it. It only occurred to her when Tennyson greeted her and asked if she had seen the chalk message, that he could have scrubbed it off whenever he'd wanted. Tennyson couldn't stop talking about it. "Whoever wrote it was right. We are all of us fools, if we only knew it! I am the greatest example. We are but the beginning of some better, fuller wisdom."

Speeches like that one, she wished she could tell Browning, was why she had little trouble forgiving Tennyson, who brought her up to his sanctum at the top of the house. They began the way all writers do when visiting each other—by looking at the books the other was reading.

"Poetry, histories, but you'll still not find many novels in my stack, Miss Rossetti. I like novels, I do. What I dislike is ending one and beginning a new one. I should like to have one novel to read in a million volumes, to last me my life."

"I have wondered something, Mr. Tennyson."

"Out with it! You can ask anything at all."

"You say you are the second most shortsighted man in the country. Who is the first most shortsighted man in England?"

"Someone was bound to ask, sooner or later. I have to admit it was Charles Napier," Tennyson said with a frown. "He died some years ago, which I suppose means I *am* the most shortsighted. Ugh. But that did not bring you all the way from the city."

"No. It's Browning."

She should have guessed that Tennyson would prove just as intransigent as Browning, shielding himself from her entreaties in his capacious pipe smoke. It was not that Tennyson wouldn't talk about the recent events. Though when he spoke of them, he did so somewhat circuitously, as though reflected by a wall of mirrors. Tennyson revealed that he had kept some of the pages written by Simon Camp that Holmes had recovered at the Golden Lion Inn in Walsden; Holmes still had some of the others, he believed. He removed these documents folded inside a book, handling them as if they were the Holy Grail, as he told Christina a story.

The story he told was about a friend of Tennyson's who found a poem by the previous poet laureate, Wordsworth, which had never before been published. The poem recorded all the details of a revolting crime. Tennyson's friend, thinking a man of genius such as Wordsworth should never be associated with such an unworthy subject, condemned the papers to the flames before they could see daylight. "It was the kindest thing he could have done," Tennyson exclaimed, concluding the anecdote.

"Mr. Tennyson, you know Mr. Browning has been in a great battle for many years. He is far lonelier than he admits. He needs his friends."

"Dante's great innovation," Tennyson said, hearing her but giving no indication of listening, "was to dare envision poets and literati—Virgil and

Homer, Statius and Sordello—to take part together in affairs of life and death, danger and destiny. After all, what else is poetry?"

She knew at the moment she would not be able to build a bridge between Tennysonites and Browningites.

He picked up some leaves of sage from a dish and rubbed them into his teeth. "That is the best thing in the world to take away the stain of tobacco."

Rising to his feet, he walked slowly to the hearth. He dropped Simon Camp's pages on the fire before Christina could think whether she ought to protest, or whether that was exactly where she wanted them to end up.

"I believe that everything which happens to us we remember no matter what we do. It is all stored up somewhere," he continued dreamily, "to come forth again upon occasion, though it may seem to be forgotten—we shall even remember these ashes forming from these pages."

Christina, without thinking why, recited from one of her poems:

And dreaming through the twilight
That doth not rise nor set,
Haply I may remember,
And haply may forget.

"Say, that's lovely," said Tennyson. "Are those my verses?"

Back in London, Browning remained set on finding every answer to every question. He tried much harder than Christina to interview Gabriel about what happened at the so-called sanatorium, though he was not successful drawing out information. The more you asked Gabriel, the less you received.

Police estimated that eleven of Sibbie's followers, including Ethel and the two followers who were "purged" as Avaricious and Prodigal, perished in the fire. The remains of most of them, including those of Sibbie herself, were never recovered from the smoldering pile of ruins.

Browning and Christina visited Scotland Yard to give their final accounts of the incidents in question for the official police records.

Dolly Williamson greeted them as if old friends. His arm remained in a sling, and he walked tenderly on his left leg. Browning asked after Constable Branagan.

"Home Office transferred him before I returned, I'm afraid," said Dolly. "The lad served me gallantly, and do not doubt I shall watch his career with interest."

"Is it true, Inspector, what the newspapers said of you?" asked Christina. "That you had a vision of the solution to the Dante case before you were injured."

"Something of the kind, Miss Rossetti," Dolly said. "As I stood at Clerkenwell, investigating the report of loiterers, I was thinking of these Fenian warriors before me. Second by second, my mind began to drink in the truth. They weren't frightened of being captured. In fact, punishment was part of their duty, their desire. Then a sickening feeling came over me. Could it be? Could the same have happened in our Dante deaths, that those punished were parties to their fates from the beginning? Before I could say a word to anyone about it, I was thrown clear across the street and laid out cold as a December in Moravia. Saved, as it turns out, only by Dante."

Christina and Browning exchanged confused glances.

Dolly went on: "In my consternation over the obstacles we had encountered, earlier that day I had decided to continue my reading of Dante where I left off, in *Paradise*. A shard of stone pierced me, you see." Dolly brought over the third volume of Longfellow's translation, split almost in half by a gray stone fragment in the center of it. "If I had not been carrying this book in my coat, *that* would have come to rest right in my heart. At least the prison explosion led us to break up the ring of revolutionaries who plotted it, and thwart their future plans. McCord, their mastermind, fled to Dublin, where we have men on his trail. Tell me, are we more afraid of what comes from outside of us, like the Fenians and whatever other foreign danger lurks next, or do we fear most what comes from inside? We relish punishing others, while we are terrified to punish ourselves—terrified, perhaps, because our creativity in tormenting ourselves knows no bounds. But listen to me, I sound like the literary fellow among the three of us. Let us turn back to the subject of your accounts. Mind if I take notes for my reports?"

"Inspector, when you are finished with our interviews, would it be possible for us to have a turn to speak directly with that beastly Reverend Fallow?" Browning asked.

The request caught Christina as much off guard as it did Dolly. She and Browning had not discussed the idea of speaking with Fallow. She was not certain she ever again wanted to see the preacher.

Browning continued. "You see, Inspector, the first suicides wore the clothes of civilians, I suppose as a kind of bridge between everyday life and the new purgatory they believed they were creating. I've been puzzled why in their final 'terraces' they wore the robes of the sanatorium—perhaps it was a gesture to the moral mountaintop narrowing and the witnesses and observers becoming one."

Dolly's reply took them both by surprise.

"Certainly you may ask Fallow about that or anything else you wish. But you would have to find him first, Mr. Browning," he said.

"Simply escort us to his cell," said Browning.

Dolly shook his head, and chewed on a sprig of grass. He explained there were no charges sufficient to indefinitely hold Fallow, and he had been allowed to leave.

Browning worked himself into a frenzy over the idea and listed all the things Fallow had done in the creation of the sanatorium's morbid and deadly mission. Christina tried to placate him.

Dolly waited until they were both quiet before explaining.

"As you know, indeed, as you revealed to Constable Branagan, Mr. Browning, the deaths were not murders after all, but suicides. Of course, the fire killed others, but there is evidence that was the result of arson by culprits outside their strange settlement of believers. Then there is the murder by stabbing of that American pest, Mr. Camp, which we are continuing to investigate, however bereft of clues."

Browning was far from satisfied. "There was someone talked about in the pages written by Camp. Someone they called the Dante Master in Italy. Couldn't you find him, and see what he knew? There must be some way to see to it that Fallow doesn't get away with this."

"We could conjure up charges, Mr. Browning, but nothing that would pass muster at Old Bailey. The most we can prove is that Fallow stoked the darkest imaginations of other people—in that, he was no more guilty than Dante of doing the same and, as it seems we have discovered together, Dante cannot be stopped."

Christina wondered what plagued Browning most, the fading possibility of answering all his questions about the mysterious Dante movement that had changed so many lives—including their own—or the impossibility of finding justice, of ever making amends, for loss and death, for the heart he buried in Florence.

As spring surrendered fully to summer, Christina took another excursion, having a desire to see once more where it had happened. Reaching the property of the sanatorium, she found the heavy gates with "Phillip Sanatorium" still there, but covered in cobwebs and left wide open. Only three of the buildings survived the fire, and the grounds were wild with fresh verdure. A deer loitered near the gates, and ate mulberries out of Christina's hands. She watched the deer run gracefully across the property, not stopping to disturb the other animals, like the ducks that had gathered at the canal, and the cats who went in and out of the ruins, yet somehow seeming the master of it all.

It was beautiful. Standing there long enough, one was left with only a shadowy recollection of the incidents.

A few weeks after her final meeting with Dolly, Christina was walking with William along a busy street in London when she spied Charles Cayley from a distance. His suit, as out of date as the cocked hat and ruffles of Shakespeare, could be spotted ten miles away. In a flash, she thought about the people and activities that filled her life now and in the past—Gabriel, her mother, her poetry, Dante, her father, her lost uncle, her church, her charity. Cayley noticed her and changed direction toward her. She froze.

"Did you arrange for him to be here?" Christina asked her brother.

"Christina," William replied, "who do you mean? What did you see?"

She fell backward, the back of her head landing hard on the sidewalk.

She woke up with her head and neck sore from the fall. William and Cayley were standing over her, looking down with grave concern, along with a man with silver whiskers snapping his fingers. She waited for the wave of embarrassment and self-recrimination to wash over her, but it never came.

". . . quite serious. My sister does not faint," William was saying.

"Look." Cayley gestured toward Christina. "Her eyes. They're open."

"Can you sit up?" asked William, gently placing his hand beneath her head.

"Wait. If you please," Christina said, wanting to stay right where she was. "I feel out of sorts and . . . lazy."

"I should think you are out of sorts, swooning before our eyes," said William. He then must have considered how odd that last word was for his sister, for he exclaimed: "Lazy!"

William consulted more with the silver-whiskered man, who turned out to be a doctor. He assured William there didn't seem to be anything serious to worry about and excused himself from the little spectacle.

Christina examined the sky. You rarely ever stopped to do that in London, there was so much to divide attentions among the buildings, the towers, the people and horses. You never looked heavenward.

"This is not the time, Mr. Cayley," William was arguing.

"I don't care if it isn't," said Cayley. "Miss Rossetti, can't you hear me? I have never been adept at expressing my emotions or speechifying, so forgive me. You take care of so many others, practically of everyone you meet, and you must allow someone to return the favor. Allow *me* to."

"Mr. Cayley?" Christina said.

"Miss Rossetti—" He swallowed hard, for a moment glancing back to William. "I started to say this to you once before, and haven't stopped torturing myself for never finishing. You sent me some verses that I'm sure I didn't fully understand, but they were melancholy and despondent and lovely and made me love you more. You shall never be alone, and you will be all better with me. You will be Mrs. Cayley from now on!"

"It is a suitable match," William admitted.

The sky.

In the London sky she faced something special. The atmospheric conditions caused by the smoke and fog in the air sometimes created a kind of copper vapor unlike anywhere in the world. Christina stared into the unreal heavens and said, "I have thought about what my father believed, that Beatrice was not real, and what you seek to demonstrate, Mr. Cayley, that she was. But she is never real and always unreal in others' eyes. How different Beatrice's legacy might have been had she spoken for *herself*, even the more powerful had she been unhappy instead of happy."

Cayley again looked at William, this time in confusion, then back at Christina, until he had a thought that enthralled him. "How well you know my interests, Miss Rossetti!"

Christina's mind returned to the events in the late winter of 1870, and when she did, it was like tumbling up a flight of stairs—she could not think of any one moment without remembering in rapid succession all of the horrors and tragedies and triumphs. It sometimes occurred to her that with the punishments demonstrated by Sibbie and her followers—the Prideful, the Envious, the Wrathful, the Slothful, the Avaricious and Prodigal, the Gluttonous, and the Lustful—there had never been an attempt made to represent the very first area of Purgatory encountered by Dante: the "Ante-Purgatory." This was the location where humanity's souls resided who were not ready to confront their vices at all. These shades had avoided Hell and its hopeless torments, but were still being prepared for the path over the mountain toward Paradise. Dante provided a poignant depiction of those temporarily trapped near the base of the divine mountain, listening to the beating of the waves as oncoming vessels brought ever more souls. They prayed that, as they waited, the works of the devil would not intrude on them.

Shelter us from our ghostly foe . . .

It was as though she could see them again ranged around her—Dr. Holmes, Tennyson, Browning, even Dolly Williamson, in the search for Gabriel—and in her mind she, too, was listening to the waves as she climbed onward.

"Miss Rossetti," Cayley shouted, in case she lost hearing in her fall. He held out his hand to her. "Dear Miss Rossetti, haven't I loved you since I watched you at your desk in Charlotte Street while I pretended only to do my labors with your father? Take my hand now and be my wife."

She thought about living in Charlotte Street. She would steal into her tiny room to write poetry on the corner of her washstand. It was uncomfortable and awkward writing against that washstand, but it was her corner.

"Haven't you made a decision?" Cayley asked.

"Have you?" William asked.

"Well?" Cayley added eagerly.

A small crowd of impatient and curious pedestrians had formed a semicircle behind Cayley and William around the woman sprawled out on the ground.

"My favorite poet on earth, I cherish . . . ," came a whispered voice. "Please, how I cherish her!" Pushing right through the two hovering men, a young woman leaned over and in the same voice declared, "You're Christina Rossetti. Are you alive?"

Christina's pinned-up hair had come loose in the fall and spread out in a thousand points over the dirt-encrusted ground. Her lips opened into a smile as her eyes floated along the clouds of copper.

INSIDE *THE DANTE CHAMBER*

My novel *The Dante Club* centered on Boston's Dante trailblazers confronting a series of murders in 1865 based on Dante's *Inferno*. While drafting it, I began jotting down ideas for continuing the story. I wanted to progress further along in Dante's vision of the afterlife by moving from *Inferno* to the next canticle of his *Divine Comedy*, *Purgatory*, which happens to be my favorite, maybe because it most closely resembles modern dramatic storytelling. I also wanted to shift most of my focus from American "Danteans" to the fascinating circle of British poets who, contemporaneously, explored and wrestled with the unique poet of Florence.

Knowing I would carry over Oliver Wendell Holmes from the first novel, at a very early stage I decided to recruit Alfred Tennyson (whose poetry is quoted in a pivotal scene of *The Dante Club*), the Rossetti siblings, and Robert Browning, all actual devotees of Dante. I originally expected Browning to become the emotional lead of the novel, but the more I thought about Christina Rossetti, she pushed to the center and drove the story. As in *The Dante Club*, I've aspired to remain as authentic to their real voices and lives as possible, including that of Inspector Adolphus "Dolly" Williamson, whose cases ranged from terrorist conspiracies to the first murder on a train in England, and who years later played an elder statesman role in the pursuit of Jack the Ripper.

Transformations abounded in culture and society when *The Dante Chamber* takes place. Religions had splintered into so many esoteric groups that many Victorians turned away from organized worship and belief systems. Filling this vacuum were movements such as spiritualism, mesmerism, ceremonial magic, and other quasi-religious approaches to life. The "sanatorium" depicted in my novel is both a product of imagination and of research into examples of utopian, apocalyptic, and cultlike collectives of the nineteenth century (including the Millerites, who prophesied specific dates for the cleansing of the world, and may have inspired suicides, and the utopian Brook Farm, whose "Phalanstery," or communal living structure, met a fate that mirrored my novel's Phillip Sanatorium. The spring snowstorms in the novel are based on those recorded in England in 1849, 1876, and 1879). Opiate use, tied to the sanatorium in my story, also became sophisticated and grew into a full-blown trade outside of supervised medical use.

There's an anecdote Lewis Carroll (a.k.a. Charles Dodgson) told that I liked to think of while working on *The Dante Chamber*. He visited Tennyson at Farringford on the Isle of Wight. While they smoked, writes Carroll, their "conversation turned upon murders, and Tennyson told us several horrible stories from his own experience." Tantalizing (Carroll didn't give more details). Tennyson, of course, wouldn't have been talking about the violence he and his companions tackle in my novel—part of the fiction of my historical fiction—but I was intrigued by the many ways this group of figures really did face the dark sides of life. Christina Rossetti, as shown in my novel, worked regularly with aiding prostitutes in desperate situations. Browning held his wife Elizabeth in his arms as she died and was absorbed by it for the rest of his life. Tennyson, in addition to dealing with a pattern of depression in his family, paid close attention to crimes and criminal trends.

(In a twist far into the future, in 2005 Tennyson's great-grandson was found murdered in London, a knife in his neck.)

Then we have the many mysteries of the great and strange and some-times sinister (to paraphrase Henry James) Dante Gabriel Rossetti. As incorporated into *The Dante Chamber*, Gabriel's life included chronic in-somnia, opiate addiction, overdoses, suicidal phases, disappearances, and the exhumation of his wife's body in order to retrieve his poems. At one point, Gabriel, half joking, all macabre, imagines forming "a Mutual Suicide Association, by the regulations whereof any member, being weary of life, may call at any time upon another to cut his throat for him. It is all of course to be done very quietly, without weeping or gnashing of teeth." Like Christina, Gabriel exacerbated the many gaps in our understanding of his life by destroying many of his personal papers, especially those dealing with Lizzie, and leaving instructions to destroy more letters and papers after his death.

The paranoia of their father, Professor Rossetti, lived on in the eldest son. Later in his life, Gabriel, influenced by his heavy use of opiates, imagined Browning was part of a conspiracy (along with Lewis Carroll and others) to write and plot against him. Gabriel cut off his friendship with Browning, and his friendship with Tennyson likewise frayed beyond the point of recovery. The friendship between Browning and Tennyson (to whom Browning really did offer the story that eventually became *The Ring and the Book*) also suffered strains over time, reflected here.

As explored in the novel, Dante Gabriel Rossetti truly was preoccu-pied with Dante, as were all of the Rossetti siblings in their own ways. For the Rossettis, as for so many Victorian-era poets and artists, *Purgatory*, with its emphasis on the ideal but elusive woman, Beatrice, held special appeal. One of Gabriel's paintings of Beatrice, *Dante's Dream*, did in fact take approximately fifteen years to complete. Dante Gabriel Rossetti's tomb even contains a bas-relief of Beatrice and Dante. Christina Rossetti never married (after turning down the proposal of Charles Cayley and also an earlier suitor, at the sight of whom she really did faint in the street). When Tennyson died, Christina Rossetti was abashed at the rumor that she might be chosen the new, first female poet laureate. (She was not offered the position, nor was another rumored candidate, rival poet Jean Ingelow.) When she passed away, her brother William ordered inscribed on her tombstone a quote from Dante:

Volsersi a me con salutevol cenno.

Which can be translated as,

They turned to me with an act of salutation.

This epitaph invites us to imagine Christina taking the place of Dante in the afterlife, gratified to be earning respect from its suffering inhabitants.

The dates of the 1870 calendar were the same as that of 1300, the year Dante claimed he made his journey into the afterlife.

ACKNOWLEDGMENTS

I'm grateful to have been guided through this novel by two irreplaceable and gifted people also instrumental in bringing *The Dante Club* to life: my editor, Ann Godoff, and my agent, Suzanne Gluck. At William Morris, I also thank Andrea Blatt, Raffaella De Angelis, Tracy Fisher, Clio Seraphim, and Elizabeth Sheinkman; at Penguin Press, Casey Denis, Megan Gerrity, Angelina Krahn, Gretchen Achilles, and Claire Vaccaro. The professor who brought me to Dante, Lino Pertile, continues to be patient with my questions and generous in his encouragement. Thanks also for advice from one of my classmates from that original "Purgatory" seminar, Adam Frost, and my go-to expert in forensic science, Mark Benecke. My circle of tireless readers and supporters to thank include Tobey Pearl, Kevin Birmingham, Benjamin Cavell, Gabriella Gage, Joseph Gangemi, and Scott Weinger; Susan, Warren, and Ian Pearl, Marsha and David Helmstadter, and my children, who give me reasons to get out of Purgatory.